SUSAN ELLISON: Fleeing pain and heart-break, she seeks solace away from the strife of an unforgiving world—soon to be bound by conscience to the proud Native Americans of the Dakotas . . . and to a motherless Sioux infant whose father she helped condemn to life in prison.

CLEVE BLACK HORSE: A half-breed rebel in the white man's society, he was convicted of a murder he did not commit. Against the forces of intolerance, he will fight for his freedom—unaware that his future, and his heart, will be unalterably linked to the beautiful woman who wronged him.

A TRIUMPHANT AND UNFORGETTABLE
NOVEL OF LOVE, DUTY, FAITH AND
FAMILY IN THE NEW AMERICAN WEST—
BY AWARD-WINNING AUTHOR
KATHLEEN EAGLE

THIS TIME
FOREVER

KATHLEEN EAGLE

AVON BOOKS ◆ NEW YORK

THIS TIME FOREVER is an original publication of Avon Books. This work has never before appeared in book form. This work is a novel. Any similarity to actual persons or events is purely coincidental.

AVON BOOKS
A division of
The Hearst Corporation
1350 Avenue of the Americas
New York, New York 10019

Copyright © 1992 by Kathleen Eagle
Cover illustration by Fredericka Ribes
Inside cover author photograph by Robert Knutson
Published by arrangement with the author
Library of Congress Catalog Card Number: 92-90554
ISBN: 0-380-76688-4

First Avon Books Printing: November 1992

AVON TRADEMARK REG. U.S. PAT. OFF. AND IN OTHER COUNTRIES, MARCA REGISTRADA, HECHO EN U.S.A.

Printed in the U.S.A.

RA   10   9   8   7   6   5   4   3   2   1

To LaVyrle Spencer, who writes in beauty.

I am truly grateful to the many people who helped lay the groundwork for this novel by sharing their insights and contributing to some aspect of my research. I am especially indebted to my friend, Barbara Livermont; to my friend Ruth Owens, RN; to the staff at the North Dakota State Penitentiary, including Correctional Officer Clayton Marcellais, Counselor Bev Bergson, and Warden Tom Powers.

Author's Note

I have taken a couple of liberties in this story. The annual July 4th rodeo in Mandan is not PRCA sanctioned, and the North Dakota State Penitentiary no longer sponsors the J.C. Stephenson Rodeo.

Prologue

The owl's call stirred Cleve Black Horse toward the brink of awareness. Above the crackling radio static and over the idling hum of the pickup's motor came the haunting, cool night echo. He eased his shoulders up the vinyl backrest.

Somebody must have died.

The thought cracked his sleepy consciousness like a predawn glow. It came from a store of visceral knowledge, which, as was his practice, he was quick to reason away before it had him doing some crazy thing like turning lights on to drive the ghosts away. Only old Indians and kids got spooked by owls. But Cleve clicked off the radio and listened until the call came again. The back of his neck felt prickly. Through the bug-spattered windshield, he saw treetops, etched like ink blots against a sliding wisp of bright clouds. The stringed tone of crickets cheered him. They were the best night singers. Only a half-stoned Indian would keep telling himself that somewhere in those trees, an owl waited, watching.

Don't go out there, Sonny. The gigi *man is out there.*

Cleve rubbed his eyes with the heels of his hands. *Gigi* man. Christ, where had that come from? A few beers and a couple of aspirin for his wounded head, and he had ghosts dancing in his dreams.

He rubbed the back of his neck and took a look around the cab. This wasn't his pickup. This was a late model club cab Silverado with a super deluxe interior and options and trim up the *ozeki*.

It must have been that damn owl that had him thinking like an Indian. He *was* an Indian—he didn't mind saying it—born and raised on Standing Rock Sioux Indian Reservation, which straddled the North and South Dakota state line. But Cleve hadn't been a reservation Indian in years. He didn't talk Indian. He tried not to *think* Indian. But he'd only been back in North Dakota for a few hours, and already he was thinking *gigi* and *ozeki*—words he used as a joke, maybe, when a rodeo buddy called him "Chief" or "Geronimo."

He joked about it more easily now, but still on his own terms. In the old days, it was nothing to joke about. Ever. His name was Black Horse, and his skin was brown, and any redneck cowboy who wanted to make something of it was likely to get his face bashed in. Making it big on the rodeo circuit had changed a few things for Cleve, though. People talked to him differently when he was up there winning. He'd driven some good pickups, stayed in nice places, bought new boots whenever he'd felt like it.

Right now, of course, he wasn't riding so high, and, like it or not, he was driving an Indian pickup. He had to admit the blue Ford he'd left a few miles back below the shoulder of I-94 was a pretty sorry outfit, especially now that it had a blowout and a busted radiator.

So what the hell, his back wasn't bothering him for a change, and his arm would hold out if he taped it up good. He'd take first in saddle bronc and bulls tomorrow and buy himself another pickup, and maybe a nice hat. The one on the seat next to him belonged to a prefab farm building salesman named Arnie Bertram. So did the pickup. Bertram had come along and offered Cleve a ride after he'd slammed the old Ford into the ditch. He'd been lucky. Hitching was still beneath his dignity, and it would have been one hell of a long walk from just this side of Montana clear to Mandan, which was in the southcentral part of the state.

At least he knew where he was. He was back in North Dakota.

But this ride was turning into a big social event with a bunch of duds. Arnie Bertram talked too much. He was the kind of guy who liked to let everybody know he was around. He'd insisted on stopping at every little hole-in-the-wall along the way and telling the locals that he was giving *the* Cleve Black Horse a lift to Mandan for the rodeo. Arnie was a longtime rodeo fan, so he remembered the name. Most people didn't. Actually, it had been ten years since Cleve's position in the standings meant anything to anyone but him.

So now they'd stopped at a hole-in-the-ground next to the highway. Cleve chuckled to himself. *Two* holes in the ground. A two-holer with porch lights and signs. MEN and WOMEN.

It was a no-moon night. The pickup windows were down, and Cleve was feeling the chill. He couldn't complain too much about the delay, since he remembered that he was the one who had asked Arnie to pull over. Jeez, how long ago was that? He'd gone into the can first, and Arnie had followed along a few minutes later with that hitchhiker, Ray Smith. They'd picked Smith up along the highway after they'd left that first beer joint.

If those two were still in there, Cleve figured he must have dozed off just for a minute. He reached under the steering wheel and shut the engine off. The smell of the exhaust was making him sick. He felt as though he'd been kicked in the head by a bull. Thinking about the spider web crack his head had left in the windshield of his pickup, he realized he probably had a concussion, which had to be the cause of his problem. The fuzz was on his brain instead of his tongue, so it wasn't the beer. Cleve was a cowboy. He could hold his beer.

Cleve stared at the sign that said MEN. *Come on, for Chrissake*. They may have been doing something weird in there, in which case he wished they'd just hurry it

up. He didn't care what other people did in the john as
long as they weren't bothering him, but he wanted to
get to Mandan sometime tonight. Tomorrow—or today,
whichever it was—was the Fourth of July, and Cleve
had two events going in one show. Probably rip his
arm all to hell, but he'd been in worse shape and come
through okay.

You can do it, Sonny. You're a cowboy.

The ultimate endorsement for an Indian kid was
always, "You're a cowboy." It meant you didn't balk
or complain or cry or ask too many questions. The old
man, his grandfather, had heaped that expectation on
him before he was out of plastic pants, and he'd been
a cowboy ever since. The old man should have lived to
see how Cleve had stuck it out. Thirty-seven years was
a long time to keep dusting your ass off and climbing
back into the saddle.

And however long he'd been sitting out there was too
long for two guys to be taking a leak. Cleve wasn't
anxious to go back inside, but he didn't want to spend
the rest of the night at some damn rest stop, either. If
his head hadn't been ripe for busting open, he'd have
taken his gear out and started walking. Hell, if he'd had
a few more beers, he wouldn't think twice about taking
the pickup and leaving those two to set up housekeeping
in the john.

There was a phone booth here. Maybe he'd call somebody.

Who would he call? He didn't have any phone numbers. Most people he knew didn't have phones. The old
lady never had one, never would. He'd offered to pay the
deposit and hookup fee, which was a considerable chunk
of change, but she'd told him to save his money. The
phone company would just be taking it out once people
started coming over and running up her bill. That was
why he hadn't been in touch with her in God knew
how long. You couldn't call somebody who lived in
a godforsaken sinkhole and didn't have a phone. He
hoped she hadn't gone and died on him in the meantime.

She hadn't, though. Cleve set his jaw as he watched the men's room door. No chance. The tribe would have tracked him down if his grandmother had died. Indians always made damn sure everybody was there for a funeral. She was still okay.

Hooo. Hoo—oo—ooo.

Somebody must have died.

The hell. Cleve flung the pickup door open, hopped past the running board, and slammed it shut again. He wanted to give that damn owl a scare more than anything, but he figured he'd let the two jerks in the john know he was coming. And then he was leaving, with or without them.

He squinted against the shock of bright light and started to announce his presence. Then he saw the man on the floor. His first thought was that Arnie looked like an overgrown kid curled up under the sink with his back to the door. Then he saw the wine-red puddle on the gray floor. Nearby lay a black leather billfold.

Jesus Christ!

Cleve pushed against the metal door on the toilet stall. The water ran noisily inside a faulty tank, but of course, the stall was empty. It was the only hiding place in the room. The hitchhiker was gone, and poor old Arnie had gotten himself beaten up and rolled.

"Arnie?" Cleve knelt beside him and pulled the short, stocky man over by his shoulder. Arnie's head flopped back like the lid on a cigar box and presented Cleve with a fresh dribble of blood and a fish-eyed stare. His throat had been cut.

Only the owl gave an answer.

Part I

An eagle I considered myself.
But the owl is hooting,
And the night
I fear.

—LAKOTA SONG

Chapter 1

Susan Ellison had worked overtime the night before she was called for jury duty. It wasn't easy to switch gears from treating a child for smoke inhalation and third-degree burns to answering the prosecutor's questions about where she'd taken her nurse's training. The child's pain was still immediate. Susan could still see the little girl writhing against the stark white sheet and hear her screaming whenever anyone touched her. She heard the prosecutor's questions, too, but even as she answered them she had a sense that she wasn't really the character she was playing in this bare, yellow box of a courtroom. She was the nurse tending the child who persisted in her head.

Martin Ness was trying too hard to put Susan at ease. She wished he'd just make up his mind about her. She assumed his questions were designed to help him decide whether she was perceptive enough to see things the State's way in a murder case, but he propped himself against the jury box rail as though they were just two people visiting over the backyard fence, while he asked about her move from Minneapolis to Mandan, how she liked North Dakota, and what ties she had here. Under other circumstances, Susan might have found him pleasant. But she was tired, and not interested in chatting. If she had to serve, so be it, but she didn't see what her religious affiliations had to do with anything.

Ness was more skilled than defense attorney Carter Felch. While Ness approached each juror with the easy smile of a good car salesman, Felch stood at attention and read from a legal pad in a grating tone of voice. He asked her whether she read the local newspapers. Sometimes, she said. She knew what he was looking for, and she was feeling perverse. She told him she preferred the *Minneapolis Tribune* for real news.

"Would you say that the murder of Arnold Bertram was real news, Ms. Ellison?"

Felch's lips twitched as he waited for her answer.

"I read about the murder," Susan informed him.

"Do you have an opinion as to who did it?"

"I hadn't given it much thought. The name of the man who was arrested didn't mean anything to me, and obviously he hasn't been tried yet."

Felch made a note on his pad. "Has the media coverage led you to draw any conclusions about the murder?"

"Only that a man was killed at a rest stop." She hadn't thought about the possibility of ending up on the jury when she'd read about the crime a couple of months ago. She had been on the list for twenty-one months, long enough to forget to worry about being called. At the end of two years, she would have been off the hook with the selection of a new jury pool. Deep in the pit of her stomach, she had queasy feelings about taking part in a murder trial.

"Has anyone close to you ever been victimized by a homicide, Miss . . . *Ms*. Ellison? Do you prefer Ms?"

Susan stared at Felch's stiff-lipped smile. He was about her age, and he was talking down to her. If she'd felt more energetic, she would have laughed.

"Ms. is fine, and no, I've never really known anyone who was murdered."

"As a nurse, you must have treated patients who were victims of violent crimes."

"Yes."

"And how did you feel about that?"

If she told him she was outraged, and she always felt like killing the bastard who'd caused the pain, she knew she could get out of this. But she didn't like the idea of being dismissed by *Mr.* Felch.

Susan answered quietly. "The same way I feel about patients who are victims of illness. I want to help them if I can."

"Ms. Ellison is acceptable to the defense, Your Honor."

Court convened at 9:00, and at 8:50 the following morning Susan parked her gray Honda sedan beneath the yellowing leaves of a tall cottonwood which shaded the corner of the parking lot. Not too early—she didn't want to sit around waiting for the proceedings to get started—but never late. She worked at a hospital in Bismarck, but she lived just across the Missouri River in the smaller town of Mandan. Her apartment was only a few blocks away, but she'd brought her car so that she could run some errands at lunchtime. It was probably silly to lock it with the police station and the courthouse so close by, but she did. In the cities—which to everyone in this part of the country meant Minneapolis and St. Paul—Susan had learned to be cautious.

The sound of her high heels clicking against the pavement made Susan straighten her shoulders and lift her chin a little higher. She sounded official. She *felt* official. She'd had a good night's sleep after working out in her aerobics class. It had felt good to move around after sitting through the jury selection process, which had taken the better part of the day. Thirteen names had been chosen, because the judge wanted one alternate in this case. After her exercise class, she'd called her supervisor on the three-to-eleven shift to say that she had been selected for the jury, and the judge had said it would be hard to guess how long the trial would take. Susan's friend, Callie, had gotten the word and called her later.

"I'll bet it's going to be fascinating, listening to all the grisly details," Callie said. "What's the killer look like? I've heard he's supposed to be pretty good-looking."

"I'm not supposed to talk about it. Besides, I didn't notice." It wasn't exactly true, but it was the easiest way to answer. Pointing out that the man couldn't be called a killer at this point might provoke more comments that Susan wasn't allowed to discuss now that she was a juror.

"I know. I was on a jury once. You don't want to look at them at first. Kind of awkward, under the circumstances. Listen, enjoy it. It's like time off, and how many murder trials do we get around here, you know? Not too many."

"No, not too many."

Susan could see Callie attending a hanging a hundred years ago. A murder in this state was, indeed, big news. A trial could bump the pictures of local children raking leaves from the front page. In the three years since she'd moved from Minnesota's twin cities to North Dakota's more bucolic version, Susan had had to adjust to Bismarck-Mandan's largely unsophisticated character. She'd decided that sophistication was relative, and that the more rural area had everything she needed. The people were friendly, and she felt safe. Most importantly, she was needed.

Susan was an achiever, a woman people could count on to get the job done. She hadn't asked for this new responsibility, but she'd been chosen for it. She touched her lapel to reassure herself that she'd remembered the blue-and-yellow juror's badge. She was an official of the court. She would have hated being excused once they'd gotten her in there and asked her all those personal questions. Having been entrusted with the job, she would take it seriously. She would decide, or *help* to decide, whether that man—the dark, silent figure who'd sat at the counsel table, all but ignored—was a murderer.

She thought of him as she entered the big brick building. During the selection process, no one really talked

about him or the details of what he was supposed to have
done. He was present, but he was like a bystander, watching and waiting. People eyed him askance, as though they
were afraid of what he might do if they actually looked at
him. Susan knew that she had behaved no differently from
the rest. It was only after both attorneys had claimed to be
satisfied with the jury that Susan had stolen a good look
at him.

He didn't look scared. He should have been, Susan
thought. In his shoes she would have been terrified,
but he didn't even seem to be uncomfortable. He sat
there doodling on a yellow pad and nursing a glass
of ice water. At the announcement that the jury was
complete, he dropped the pencil on the pad and raised
the glass, glancing over the rim and directly at Susan as
he drank. There was no hesitation. He'd singled her out,
and he was telling her she was in this with him now. He
knew the truth, and before this was over, she would be
expected to know it, too. It was a challenge.

The jury had been sworn in before court had adjourned
the day before. They'd been told not to discuss the case
with anyone, not even each other, and to assemble in the
jury room before nine in the morning. Susan was one of
the last to arrive. She didn't know any of the others, and
she was not one to make the initial overtures.

The attorneys and the defendant were already seated at
the counsel tables when the jury was led down the aisle
to the jury box. Susan was seated in the center of the
five-chair front row. Good spot, she thought. She could
blend in with the other twelve, but she had a good view
of the witness chair, the counsel tables and the bench.

"All rise."

The black-robed judge's entrance claimed everyone's
attention. The bailiff proclaimed that the Morton County
South Central Judicial District Court was in session with
Judge William Carmichael presiding. Old and wise,
Susan thought. Each attorney had a side to represent,
but she could look to Judge Carmichael for model objec-
tivity. An overhead light shone down on him as he bent

his balding head and adjusted his horn-rimmed glasses to peruse some papers.

"The State of North Dakota *versus* Cleveland W. Black Horse."

Susan looked at the defendant again. She was going to have to look at him openly and often, and she might as well get used to it. She was part of the State of North Dakota. She had no apologies to make. He was charged with first degree murder, and she couldn't worry about whether her staring at him might embarrass him. He knew the truth about what had happened, and she might be able to see it in his eyes.

The whole state, six hundred thousand people, *versus* one man. Already Susan didn't like the odds. But as she listened to the prosecutor, making dramatic use of his deep, commanding voice as he read the grand jury's indictment, she told herself she would get used to the odds, too. If this one man were, indeed, a murderer, then it was he who threatened and offended the six hundred thousand.

" . . . did deliberately and with premeditation and malice aforethought commit an act of homicide upon one Arnold Clifford Bertram, contrary to the laws of North Dakota and the peace of this State."

The grand jury had indicted him, Susan thought. She had actually read little about the case. She seldom saw the 6:00 news on television because she was usually working then. But the man had been indicted on a first degree murder charge, and there must have been good reason.

" . . . discovered in the men's bathroom at a rest stop on I-94, only about forty miles west of us, ladies and gentlemen, with a stab wound the nature of which only a cold-blooded killer could inflict upon a fellow human being."

Susan had seen every kind of stab wound the prosecutor could describe. She had been a triage nurse in the emergency room at Metro Med Center in Minneapolis before she took the position at Bismarck's Med Center

One, where the emergency room was blessedly quieter. There were farm accidents, highway accidents, household accidents, and victims of violence—yes, all that— but the numbers were smaller. She never had stretchers lined up in the hallways anymore. And she saw fewer gunshot wounds and stab wounds "the nature of which only a cold-blooded killer could inflict upon a fellow human being." Susan figured she might be the one juror the prosecutor couldn't shock with talk of gore.

" . . . then stole the victim's pickup and fled. A senseless crime, perpetrated in a drunken rage. The State will prove, beyond any reasonable doubt, that Cleveland Black Horse took advantage of Arnold Bertram's trust, his generosity in offering a ride to a stranger—something not many of us are willing to do these days—and then took Mr. Bertram's property and his life."

The defendant didn't appear to be listening to Prosecutor Ness's opening statement, but he wasn't doodling this time. With shoulders squared and only his eyes downcast, he sat motionless and stared at the table in front of him. Susan wondered what he was thinking. Was he remembering the events as the prosecutor recounted them? Or was the very idea that someone had done this thing as repugnant to him as it was to everyone else in the courtroom?

Callie had been right. Cleveland Black Horse was a handsome man. Susan guessed that he was not a full-blooded Sioux, for his skin and his hair were not dark enough. But there was no mistaking the dominance of his Indian features: the chiseled structure of his face, the hooded eyes, and the aquiline nose. Susan didn't know much about Indians, other than the fact that when they came into ER their blood ran the same color as anybody else's. Generally, they didn't complain much about the pain that was part of bleeding.

She didn't know much about rodeo cowboys, either, but she knew that to be the defendant's profession. He was dressed in the same navy suit, white shirt, and

striped tie he'd worn the day before, a suit he probably would not have chosen for himself if he could see
himself in a full-length mirror. Susan thought of the
Minneapolis businessmen who had worn Urban Cowboy
clothes years ago. Cleveland Black Horse in a navy blue
suit and striped tie was the flip side of that coin. She
watched him shove two fingers inside his collar, trying
to make space for his Adam's apple.

Black Horse turned to watch his attorney gather some
papers and move toward the jurors without offering his
client so much as a reassuring glance. Felch stood stiffly
near the jury box rail and launched his opening statement
in a voice that followed the prosecutor's like a piccolo
echoing a tuba. He said that the prosecution had a flimsy
case against his client, based on circumstantial evidence,
and that Cleveland Black Horse, who was well-known
among the rodeo fans of North Dakota, must be pre-
sumed innocent until the State could prove him guilty
of this crime. He asked the jurors not to make up their
minds about the case until they had heard both sides.

The prosecution's first witness was Daryl Anders, a
dispatcher at the Mandan Law Enforcement Center. Martin Ness produced his first exhibit, the center's logbook,
and handed it to the judge. The book was entered into
evidence by the clerk.

"Were you on duty between 11:00 P.M. on July third
and 7:00 A.M. July fourth?"

"Yes, sir, I was."

"And did you receive a report that a body was discovered at a rest stop on I-94 in this county?"

"Yes, I did."

"Who placed the call?"

"The caller didn't give me his name. He just said he'd
found a dead man in the john."

"What time did you receive the call?"

Anders referred to the logbook. "It was 1:42 A.M."

"The caller reported that he'd found a dead man at the
rest stop, and then he hung up," Ness summarized.

"That's right."

"What did you do after you took the call?"

"Well, I told Sergeant Kramer about it—he was on duty with me that night—and then I called the Highway Patrol."

"Thank you. Your witness, Mr. Felch."

Felch took up his yellow legal pad and approached the witness. "What exactly did the caller report, Mr. Anders? That he *saw* a body?"

"That there *was* a body." Anders punched a finger in the air as though it helped him get each word right. "He said, 'There's a dead man at a rest stop about forty miles west of Mandan. It's awful,' he says. 'Blood all over the floor of the john.' "

"That was it?"

"That was all he said. Then he hung up."

"You say *he*. It sounded like a man's voice?"

"Oh, yeah, it was a man's voice."

"No further questions."

Ness called the patrolman who'd arrived on the scene at 2:15 A.M., followed by the county sheriff at 2:35, who had investigated and taken photographs.

"On your way to the rest stop, were you in radio contact with the Highway Patrol, Sheriff?"

"Yes, I was. Patrolman Richard Bateman encountered an abandoned vehicle at about 2:00 A.M. and picked up the driver, who was proceeding east along the highway on foot. He was advised to detain the driver. I passed the patrol car and the pickup. They were in the eastbound lane, and I was westbound. Meanwhile Patrolman Todd Seizer reported discovering the body." The sheriff nodded toward the row of uniformed witnesses. "Like he just testified."

"Exactly what did you find at the rest stop, Sheriff?"

"The victim, Arnold Bertram, was lying there under the sink in a pool of blood. His throat had been cut."

"With a knife?"

"We never found the weapon. Searched up and down the highway, but we never found it."

"What else did you find in the men's room?"

"His billfold was lying there, too. You can see it all in the pictures, just what we found."

Ness took another folder from the box containing his physical evidence. "Your Honor, I submit the Sheriff's Department photographs."

Felch slid his chair back, speaking as he stood. "Objection, Your Honor, on the grounds that these photographs are likely to be inordinately inflammatory. The defense does not deny that a man was brutally murdered."

The judge asked that the jury be taken to the jury room while counsel approached the bench. "Help yourself to coffee," the bailiff said, nodding toward the tall urn as he closed the door. Nobody moved toward the pot. Instead, the jurors eyed one another.

"We can't say anything about what's going on, huh?"

Susan turned to the smiling young man with red hair. She supposed she ought to start thinking of herself and these people as a team. She smiled back. "No, but that doesn't mean we can't talk. I'm Susan Ellison."

"Dale Larsen." He stuck his hands in his back pockets and cocked his hip. "So why do you think they sent us out?"

"I guess they don't want us to hear what they have to say about those pictures."

"They're deciding whether we can see them," said Margaret Whalen, who was, Susan recalled from the jury interviews, a retired teacher. She was probably the oldest person on the jury. "I've been on a jury before."

"They sure as hell *better* let us see them," Wayne Tidball, the pawnshop owner, put in. "We need to see just what happened."

Susan shook her head as she reached for a Styrofoam cup. "We'll see a corpse. I don't think those pictures can tell us what happened."

The bailiff appeared at the door, and Susan let the cup fall back on the stack. "You can come back in now."

"That was quick," somebody muttered as they filed through the door.

"How much you wanna bet we don't get to see the pictures?"

There were fourteen eight-by-ten color photographs. The glossy finish enhanced the corpse's glassy stare and made the pool of blood shine like dark red wine. The carotid arteries had been severed, along with the windpipe. This was no pocket knife job, Susan realized. The murderer had practically cut the man's head off. As the photographs were passed down the row she heard gasps and clucks of the tongue. She told herself not to look at the defendant just now, but when the last photograph came into her hands, the need to look became compelling. Her fair mind said *no, Susan, don't* as she raised her chin slowly, then stole a glance.

He was expecting it. He stared right back at her, his eyes smoldering defiantly. There was no apology in them, nor was there denial. Susan didn't ask herself why he watched her and not the others at this moment, because there was another question that burned too deeply. She glanced at the photograph, then back at Cleveland Black Horse.

Are you the man who did this?

Figure it out. That's what you're here for.

The photographs were handed to the clerk, and Ness continued to question the sheriff.

"What did you find in the billfold?"

"Driver's license, credit cards, family pictures."

"No money?"

"No money."

"And what did you find *on* the billfold?"

"Bertram's fingerprints. Some smeared prints that weren't readable, but there was one good thumbprint that wasn't Bertram's."

"Have you identified the thumbprint?"

"Yes, sir." The sheriff slid a satisfied look in the direction of the defense counsel table. "It belongs to Cleveland Black Horse."

"One more question, Sheriff. Was the victim wearing any jewelry?"

"There was a nice big turquoise and silver buckle on his belt. You could see it in the pictures."

"No rings, no watch, no bolo tie?"

"No, just the belt buckle."

The fingerprint report was admitted as evidence. Then the medical examiner testified that Arnold Bertram's throat had been cut and that there was a high level of alcohol in his blood.

"Shouldn't have been driving," one of the jurors behind Susan muttered. Susan had to restrain herself from turning around to see if the woman was serious.

Three witnesses from the Buckhorn Bar were sworn in and questioned. All three identified Cleveland Black Horse in court and Arnold Bertram from a photograph, and said that they had come into the bar together that night. The bartender, a man with a lean face and raccoon eyes, was the third witness.

"Tell the jury what you remember about the two men, Mr. Leingang."

"The Indian asked if I had a pay phone, so I told him where that was, and I guess he made a call."

"The Indian," Ness repeated. "You mean the defendant, Cleveland Black Horse?"

"Yeah, him. The guy I just identified. Anyway, the other guy, Bertram, bought all the beer. Three rounds, as I recall."

"Was there anything notable about the way Mr. Bertram was dressed?"

"Yeah, he was all decked out." Leingang made a circle with his thumb and forefinger beneath his own jowly chin. "Big turquoise bolo tie. He wore one o' them chunky gold rings on his left hand and a fancy watch, the kind with the gold and silver watch band."

"A Rolex watch?"

"I don't know much about watches, but you see those gold and silver watch bands once in a while."

"The expensive-looking kind?" Ness persisted as he searched through his box of evidence.

"Looked like a nice one to me. Showy, you know."

"Could this be the bolo tie?" Ness held up a flashy string tie, studded with silver and turquoise.

"Yeah. I really admired that. I'm sure it's the one."

The prosecutor dropped the bolo tie back in the box and came up with another exhibit. "Would this be the ring?"

"Sure looks like it."

More exhibits were entered into evidence.

"Mr. Leingang, did you observe an argument between Mr. Bertram and Mr. Black Horse?"

"I was down at the other end of the bar, so I didn't hear what they were talking about, but I saw the Indian—Black Horse, there—grab Bertram's wrist and kind of slam it down against the bar. So I got nervous and moved on back down the bar in case there was trouble. You know, you get them Indians in there drinking, and you never know . . ."

"What happened then, Mr. Leingang?"

"Well, Black Horse let go, but he said he wanted a ride to Mandan. 'You got it, Cleve,' Bertram said. Then Bertram ordered another round."

"And Bertram paid for the drinks?"

"Yeah, he kinda made a production of it. You could see he had a wad of bills in his billfold. He asked me could I change a hundred dollar bill, and I told him that might leave me short on change. Then he found a ten."

"What time did they leave?"

"Geez, I wouldn't know for sure. It wasn't real late, though."

Ness returned to his table and set the box down carefully, as though he had a great deal of regard for the remaining contents. Felch had not questioned many of the witnesses, but he took a stab at the bartender.

"Mr. Leingang, did you hear any actual arguing between Mr. Bertram and Mr. Black Horse?"

"Well, I saw Black Horse grab—"

"I asked whether you *heard* an argument. Did they raise their voices? Did they exchange words?"

"I didn't hear what they said."

"Then they didn't raise their voices."

"No."

"What made you think they were arguing?"

Leingang shrugged. "Because of the way Black Horse held Bertram by the wrist."

"Was Bertram reaching for something?"

"I didn't see nothing . . . except maybe a little change on the bar."

"One more question. When they left your establishment, did either of the men seem intoxicated to you?"

"Not really, no." Leingang straightened in his chair and glanced at the judge. "I'd've stopped serving 'em if I thought they wouldn't be safe on the road."

By the time court recessed for lunch, Susan had forgotten about her errands. She went home, turned on the public radio station for the afternoon classics, and made herself a tuna sandwich. She sat on a tall stool at the island counter that separated her tiny kitchen from the living room and imagined the Buckhorn Bar on I-94.

She'd never been there, but she knew what it was like. She had seen the dark colors through dim light and heard the country music. She imagined the two men sitting at the bar, drinking beer together. Even as they talked, one of them might well have been thinking of how he would kill the other and take his money. Or maybe he hadn't thought of it yet. Maybe he needed a few more drinks. Maybe he hadn't thought of it at all; maybe one thing led to another: the drinking, the deserted rest stop, the knife, the money, maybe a struggle. What were the chances, as the two men sat there drinking together, that fate was about to plunge them into a nightmare that *both* men would have said could only happen to other people in other places?

Susan glanced at her bookcase. Not a murder mystery on the shelf. She didn't like this business. She'd rather be at the hospital where she knew exactly what she was doing. The doctors would make the decisions, and she would follow their orders quickly, efficiently and compassionately. Maybe she hadn't handled other aspects of her life very well, but she was an excellent nurse. She knew how to respond when someone was hurting physically. She was not trained for this courtroom thing, and she'd begun to worry in advance, just as she always did, about doing the right thing.

After the recess, Ness called the owner of an off-sale liquor store that was located about twenty miles east of the Buckhorn Bar. Terry Mund identified the victim from a photograph and testified that Bertram had purchased a twelve-pack of beer before 10:00 P.M. He closed at 10:00. While he was making change for a hundred dollar bill—he distinctly remembered the hundred—he had glanced out the window and noticed a passenger waiting in the pickup. He couldn't make out the face, but there was only one passenger.

"Were you watching the pickup the whole time it was parked in front of your store, Mr. Mund?" Felch asked in his cross-examination.

"Well, no. The guy—Bertram there, the one in the picture—he asked to use the toilet, and I told him where it was, and then I got ready to lock up. I didn't hardly notice when he left."

"Someone else could have gotten in and out of the pickup when you weren't looking, then?"

"Yeah, I 'spoze."

"Where is your rest room located, Mr. Mund?"

"Back in the storeroom."

Felch looked disappointed. "No further questions."

The State called Patrolman Richard Bateman.

"What did you do when you saw the pickup parked on the shoulder of the highway?" Ness asked.

"I pulled up behind it and looked for a driver. When I saw that it was abandoned, I called in the license plate numbers. While I'm waiting for the check, the call comes in about the reported homicide, and I'm only about ten miles from the scene. And I've got this abandoned pickup with the motor still warm, and the keys are in the ignition." Eager to tell his story, young Bateman braced his elbows on the cushioned arm rests of the witness chair and leaned forward. "Seizer is on his way to the rest stop already, and the sheriff's been called, so I secure the abandoned vehicle and go looking for the driver, figuring he might be walking."

"And you found him?"

"Yes, sir. I found him about three-quarters of a mile east of where the pickup was parked."

"Can you identify the man?"

"That's him, right there." Bateman pointed his finger. "Cleveland Black Horse. He was carrying a saddle and a duffel bag when I caught up to him."

"So what did you do?"

"I flashed my lights, got on the horn and told him to stop, drop his gear, and put his hands up over his head."

"Did he comply?"

"Not right away. He seemed kinda dazed. Just turned around and squinted into the light. I got out of the car and drew my service revolver, and then he tossed his stuff on the ground. I searched him down; didn't find nothing on him. Then I asked him if he'd left that pickup back there. He came back with, 'Which one?' I told him not to get smart with me, so then he straightened out and started answering my questions. He said he'd been driving the blue Silverado. He said he ran out of gas, and he admitted it wasn't his pickup."

"Did you ask him about Bertram?"

"I didn't know much about the murder at that point, and I didn't want to jump the gun on anything, so I just said I was waiting on a license plate check. Then Black Horse said the owner of the pickup was at a rest stop about ten miles back and that he'd been murdered. I told him I was holding him for questioning, and I read him his rights."

"What condition was Mr. Black Horse in? Was he drunk?"

"I could sure smell the beer on him, but I didn't catch him driving or even sitting in the pickup, so I just cuffed him and put him in the car."

"Cuffed him?"

"Put handcuffs on him," Bateman clarified.

"What did you observe about Mr. Black Horse's clothing?"

"He was wearing a long-sleeved shirt and blue jeans. I didn't notice right off—I have to say, it was dark out there—but when we booked him, I noticed stains on his sleeves and his pants."

"And were you not also the officer who searched the Bertram pickup? The blue club cab Silverado?"

"Yes, sir, I was."

"And what did you find?"

"Seven unopened cans of beer . . ."

"Inside the glove compartment, Officer Bateman?"

Officer Bateman turned to the jury as though he'd been called upon to deliver a great punch line. "Besides the pickup registration, a turquoise and silver bolo tie." He paused and looked back at Ness, who was waiting for more. "And a ring," Bateman added. "A big gold ring."

"Are these the items?"

Bateman took the two pieces of jewelry in his hands. "Yes, sir. I tagged them myself."

"Did you find a watch?"

"No, sir. No watch."

"As the arresting officer, you would have accounted for Mr. Black Horse's personal effects, would you not?"

"Yes, sir."

"Did he have any money?"

"There was sixty-four dollars in his billfold."

"Did you dust the pickup for fingerprints?"

"Yes, sir."

"And what did you find?"

"We identified Bertram's and Black Horse's prints. Nothing else we could match up with anything."

"Was there anything else?"

"Empty beer cans. Bertram's prints were on three of the cans, and Black Horse's prints were on all five."

"Your witness, Mr. Felch."

Felch glanced at his client before he stood to cross-examine the witness. It was a disgusted, I-told-you-so look, the kind a child might get from a parent who was more embarrassed by the consequences than the crime. Susan knew then that Cleveland Black Horse's own attorney thought he was guilty.

"Officer Bateman, did you find a watch anywhere on Cleveland Black Horse's person or in his bag?"

"No. We never found the watch."

"And you never found the murder weapon, did you?"

"No, sir, we didn't."

"One more question, Officer Bateman. Did my client try to run or resist arrest in any way?"

"No, sir, he didn't."

The State's expert witnesses testified last. The autopsy report placed the time of Arnold Bertram's death at between 12:30 and 1:30 A.M. on July 4. Finally, Ness exhibited the blue chambray shirt and jeans Black Horse had been wearing when he was arrested. A forensic chemist identified the stains as blood, type B on the pants, types O and B on the shirt. The defendant's blood type was O, and the victim's was B. Felch had no questions for the chemist.

"Your Honor . . ." Ness scanned the jury during a dramatic pause. "The State rests its case."

"I want to caution the jury to avoid all media reports and any discussion of the matters we are considering here." The judge rapped his gavel. "Court stands recessed until nine o'clock tomorrow morning, at which time the defense will present its case."

Chapter 2

When the defense called Cleveland W. Black Horse first thing the following morning, Margaret Whalen leaned over to Susan and whispered, "He must be the only witness they have. Otherwise, I think they would save him for last." Susan nodded absently as she watched the defendant approach the witness chair. He glanced at someone behind her, then briefly at her. There wasn't that cool defiance in his eyes now, and she wondered what he was thinking. Was he worried about keeping his story straight? If she were planning to lie, her face would be hot. It bothered her that he kept singling her out, and she wondered if she looked gullible.

She was open to hearing the truth, she told herself. The challenge was still there. It didn't matter what the defendant thought of her. He hadn't been allowed to ask her any questions, and she couldn't ask him any. She could only watch and listen and try to figure out what was going on inside this man who wore the same navy blue polyester suit, same white shirt, same striped tie. The boxy cut of his jacket was all wrong for his long torso, and he was too long-legged and lanky for his shapeless slacks. Only his worn but polished black cowboy boots were made to fit him.

He eyed the embossed gold letters on the cover of the

dog-eared Bible for a moment, then laid his hand over them and swore to tell the truth. His hand was big and brown, and even at a distance Susan saw that the skin of his knuckles was weathered dry. He took the stand as though he were lowering himself over the top of a bucking chute, fully prepared for a rocky ride. You wouldn't have to read the papers to know this man was a cowboy, Susan thought. Even in that awful suit, you could tell. She remembered the last rodeo she'd attended with her ex-boyfriend, Mel. They'd had a good view of the bucking chutes, and she'd thought those guys looked as though they were easing down into pots of boiling water. And then, one by one, the pots would boil over. Mentally, Susan changed the defendant into the right clothes—his own clothes. She thought it was only fair.

"State your name and address for the record, please," Defense Attorney Felch instructed.

"Cleve Black Horse."

"*Full* name."

"Cleveland W. Black Horse."

"What does the *W* stand for, Mr. Black Horse?"

He cleared his throat. "Wade."

"Current address?"

"Rapid City, South Dakota."

"*Mailing* address?"

The defendant gave his attorney a long, hooded look. "General Delivery, I guess. I have a post office box in Little Eagle, South Dakota, but I'm on the road a lot."

"What is your occupation, Mr. Black Horse?"

"I'm a professional rodeo cowboy."

"What are your events?"

"Saddle bronc. Bulls."

"Bull riding?" Felch said it as though he wanted to make sure he was saying a foreign term with the proper inflection.

"That's right."

"How long have you been doing this?"

"Most of my life. Professionally, fifteen years."

"That's a long time," Felch commented offhandedly as he took a file folder off the top of a short stack on the corner of the defense counsel's table. "I have here an article photocopied from *Rodeo Sports News*." Felch handed the pages to the defendant. "Are you *this* Cleve Black Horse?"

He looked at the pages quickly, then handed them back, as though they were a source of embarrassment. "Yeah. That's me. That picture's twelve years old, though."

"Tell the jury what this article is about, Mr. Black Horse."

"I won the All-Around buckle at the National Finals that year." Black Horse showed no emotion and no inclination to tell the story.

"Is that a rodeo championship?"

Prosecutor Ness rose from his chair and leaned across the counsel table toward the bench. "Prosecution objects, Your Honor. We fail to see what this has to do with the murder of Arnold Bertram."

"I'll show relevancy in just a moment, Your Honor."

"Proceed, but get to the point, Mr. Felch," the judge ordered.

Felch turned back to the witness. "What kind of award is this All-Around Cowboy buckle?"

"It's for winning the most money in a year's time in two or more events."

"This is an award of the Professional Rodeo Cowboys' Association, is it not?"

"The PRCA, yes."

"A national championship, as it were." The defendant nodded. Susan wondered whether this was genuine modesty, which she had not seen in too many men, or something else. *"Is* this a national championship, Mr. Black Horse? You'll have to speak up."

"Yes."

"It would be like 'cowboy of the year,' would it not?"

"I suppose you could put it that way."

Felch smiled. "May we see the award, Mr. Black Horse? It's a belt buckle, is it not? I would assume . . ."

"I'm not . . . I don't wear it."

Ness rose from his chair and tried again. "Your Honor, this is ridiculous."

Judge Carmichael raised a warning hand. "Get to the point, Mr. Felch."

"Yes, Your Honor. In other words, Mr. Black Horse, you are a famous athlete, isn't that true?"

"I guess people who follow rodeo might know who I am."

"Your modesty befits the image of your profession, Mr. Black Horse. Clearly, you are no drifter. In fact, you were traveling the rodeo circuit on July third, were you not?"

"I was coming here to Mandan."

"Were you planning to ride in our annual July Fourth event?"

"Yes, I was."

"And what happened to interrupt your journey to Mandan on July third?"

Black Horse cleared his throat again and started to speak to his attorney. "Well, I . . ." At Felch's signal, he shifted his attention to the jury. "I was headed east on I–94 out of Montana, probably ten miles this side of the state line, you know, before you hit the badlands, and I blew a tire. My pickup went off the road and hit the ditch. I took out a mile marker post and knocked a hole in the radiator." He imitated the motion of the pickup with a gesture.

"Were you hurt?"

Black Horse brushed his dark hair aside and touched the scar. "Hit my head on the windshield."

"Did you try to flag someone down?"

"No."

"What did you do?"

"Got my gear out of the back and started walking."

"You weren't going to walk all the way to Mandan?"

He shrugged and glanced at the jury. "I was going to get there, one way or another. Figured somebody might stop and offer a ride."

"Who stopped for you, Mr. Black Horse?"

"Guy in a blue club cab pulled over and asked me if I needed a lift." He glanced at the sheriff's deputy, who'd been posted near the defense cousel table, then back to Felch. "Arnie Bertram. The guy who got killed."

"You're saying that the victim, Arnold Bertram, stopped and offered you a ride."

"Yeah."

"Were you previously acquainted with Mr. Bertram?"

"Never met him before."

"But you accepted the ride."

"Sure. He said he was headed for Mandan, too, so I figured I'd lucked out."

"What about your pickup?"

"What about it? The radiator was shot. Tire was shot. It wasn't going nowhere."

"Did Mr. Bertram plan to drive directly to Mandan?"

"He said he was going to the rodeo, too. Said he was a longtime fan." There was a flicker of satisfaction in Black Horse's dark eyes. "He even remembered who I was when I told him my name."

"So he was a fan of yours?"

"Well, he recognized me, anyway."

Felch paced from the witness stand to the jury box and back again. "Whose idea was it to stop at the Buckhorn Bar?"

"Bertram's."

"Did he discuss it with you?"

"No. He said he wanted a beer, and he figured I'd want to call a tow truck, so we stopped. The sign said 'Buck Beer.' I didn't know it was called the Buckhorn."

"What did you do there?"

"I asked to use the phone. I called a place in Dickinson, but they said they were pretty busy, so I told them to forget it. Then I went back to the bar, and we had a couple of beers."

"You and Arnold Bertram?"

"That's right."

"Who paid for the drinks?"

"He did."

"And, as most of us do when we sit at the bar and have a beer, you visited. Got acquainted. I wonder—" Felch tried to dramatize his wondering with a theatrical gesture, but it came off as something he'd rehearsed. "What did the two of you have to talk about?"

"Rodeo. He wanted to know who I knew, where I'd been lately, stuff like that."

"Did you tell him?"

"Some."

"Did the two of you at any point have a disagreement?"

Black Horse shook his head and dismissed the notion with a wave of his hand. "It wasn't what the bartender thought. It really wasn't a disagreement. When I told him the garage didn't want to go after my pickup, he said he'd take care of it, and he started to pick up a quarter off the bar. I stopped him."

"How did you stop him?"

"I just grabbed his wrist. Told him to leave it where it was."

"The quarter or the pickup?"

"I meant the pickup. *My* pickup."

"Wasn't he just trying to be helpful?"

"Yeah, but I figured enough was enough. You know, he was driving, buying the drinks, playing it all up big. I told him I just wanted to get to Mandan. So he said okay. End of discussion."

"There was no argument, then?"

"No argument. We had a couple of beers, Arnie flashed his money around, and then we left."

"What do you mean, 'flashed his money around?' "

"He had a fat wad of bills, and he made sure everybody in the bar knew it."

"Do you have any idea how much money Mr. Bertram was carrying?"

"No."

"What time did you leave the Buckhorn Bar?"

"I'd say it was a little after nine."

"What did you do then?"

Black Horse shifted in his chair. "We pulled out on the Interstate, and Arnie took off this turquoise bolo tie he was wearing, handed it to me and asked me to put it in the glove compartment. Said it was choking him. When I had the glove compartment open, he handed me his billfold—said he was tired of sitting on it—so I tossed that in, too. Then he laughed and told me to throw his ring in with the rest. He had a hell of a time getting it off his finger."

"Did he say why he didn't want to wear the ring?"

"No. I figured it was his wedding ring. He wore it on his left hand, and he'd mentioned he had a wife."

"Why would a man want to hide his wedding ring?"

"Objection," Ness put in offhandedly. "Counsel is asking the witness for a conjecture."

"Sustained. The witness has already testified that Mr. Bertram offered no reason for the action, Mr. Felch. Continue."

The color rose quickly in Felch's cheeks, but he went on without much pause. "So you put the bolo tie, the ring and the billfold in the glove compartment of the pickup at Mr. Bertram's request?"

"That's right."

"And that's how your thumbprint came to be on Mr. Bertram's billfold?"

"I guess so."

"Then what happened?"

"We got about twenty miles down the road, and Arnie picked up another rider."

"A hitchhiker?"

"I don't know if he was thumbing or not. I'd kinda dozed off when Arnie pulled over. He backed up a ways and offered this guy a ride, so I opened the door, got out and let the guy sit in the middle."

"Who was the man?"

"He said his name was Ray Smith."

"Did Mr. Bertram know him?"

"Didn't act like he did."

"And you didn't know him."

"Never seen him before."

"Describe him for us."

The defendant turned to the jury. He seemed to be making an attempt to address them all, but he finally settled on Susan, as was becoming his habit. She wasn't going to let it bother her anymore. She decided he probably wanted to tell a person rather than a committee, and she happened to be in the middle. He had her undivided attention.

"He was a white guy, skinny, probably about five foot ten or so, maybe late thirties. Hard to tell about his hair. He wore a stocking cap and one of those long, canvas vests, the kind hunters wear. And I think he was wearing jeans and some kind of boots. It was almost dark, and I was really trying to ignore this guy because he smelled like he hadn't had a bath all summer, but I remember his eyes kinda bugged out at you when he talked."

"Where did Ray Smith say he was going?"

Black Horse looked up at Felch again. "He didn't seem to care. He said Mandan was fine with him."

"Did he say where he was from?"

"South Dakota, he said. Arnie asked him if he was going to the rodeo, too, and he said he might take it in. Talked about looking for a job. I stayed out of the conversation except when Arnie asked if I thought he should turn the air conditioning back on, and I said I'd rather have the window down. Then Arnie asked us if we wanted a beer. I didn't say anything, but I really didn't want to stop again. Smith didn't say, either. Arnie said he wanted to pick some up, so he pulled off at this off-sale place and asked me to hand him his billfold out of the glove compartment. He made a remark about being all out of small bills and hoping this place had change."

"Again, you had Mr. Bertram's billfold in your hand at his request," Felch pointed out.

"That's right."

"So Bertram went into the store, and now you were stuck in the pickup with Ray Smith?"

"No, not for . . ."

The side door opened, and the defendant's attention strayed as an old Indian woman was ushered into the room. A younger man accompanied her, treating her deferentially as he found seats for both of them. Black Horse's expression clouded as he watched. Then he glared at his attorney.

"You were *not* stuck with Smith, then?" Felch prompted.

For the first time since the trial had begun, Black Horse's eyes truly sparked. Felch took half a step backward as the defendant gripped the rail of the witness box and muttered, "I told you to leave her out of this. She's old. She—"

Felch glanced over his shoulder, then pointedly back at his client. "Answer the question, Mr. Black Horse. Were you left in the pickup with—"

Black Horse spoke through clenched teeth. "I told you not to bring her here, Felch."

"This is an open courtroom. Your grandmother—"

"Do you need time to confer with your client, Mr. Felch?" the judge demanded icily.

The courtroom was quiet as jurors and spectators glanced left and right, as if disclaiming any responsibility for the awkward moment.

"No," Felch said quietly. "Nothing has changed, Mr. Black Horse. I have nothing to say about who comes into the courtroom. Please answer the question. Did Ray Smith stay with—"

"No!" The defendant glanced back at the jury box, then settled back and lowered his voice. "No. Smith got out of the pickup after Arnie had gone into the store. Said he had to take a—" Clearly the old woman's presence added a new source of discomfort for the defendant. Before she'd walked in, only his collar and tie had seemed to chafe him. "Well, he said he had to relieve himself. I thought he was going inside, but he didn't. He went around back."

"Around back?"

"Behind the building."

"And you stayed in the pickup?"

"About that time I was thinking of taking off."

"But you stayed in the pickup and waited for the other two to come back?"

"Yeah, that's right. I waited."

"So if the proprietor of the store, Mr. Mund, happened to look out the window, he would have seen only one person sitting in the pickup?"

"He would have seen just me. Arnie came out with a twelve-pack of beer, and then Smith popped out from behind the corner of the building and hopped in on the driver's side and slid over. Arnie got in after him and we took off again."

"So Mr. Bertram opened the door, not Smith?"

"That's right."

"And you opened the door the first time Smith got into the pickup, is that correct?"

Black Horse thought for a moment. "Yeah. I let him in when we stopped to pick him up."

"To your knowledge, then, Smith did not put his hand on either door of that pickup."

"Not that I saw."

Felch nodded. "So you were off again, headed west?"

"That's right."

"And how far did you get this time?"

"Maybe another thirty miles. Arnie was taking it pretty slow."

"What was going on among the three of you during this part of the ride?"

Black Horse told his story to his attorney. His eyes strayed neither to the back of the courtroom nor to the jury box as he spoke of handing Arnie a beer out of the carton, then taking one for himself. Smith had declined.

"Did you find that surprising?" Felch wondered.

"I didn't 'find' it anything. Smith didn't say much. I wasn't saying much. Arnie was putting away the beer and talking a blue streak."

"About what?"

"About some guy who said he was gonna sue him for not putting some building up straight, and about how they ran the same stock at the Mandan rodeo every year and used the same clowns, who told the same jokes. Smith laughed and kept Arnie going on that topic, but I wasn't interested."

"So you had another beer?"

"I guess I must have had two, from the way they counted up the empties. I know I handed Arnie a couple more. He was humming along pretty good."

"Did that bother you?"

"I just wanted to get to Mandan. I thought about. offering to drive, but he was doing okay." Black Horse shrugged. "Long as he could keep it on the road, I figured we'd get there sooner or later."

"Whose idea was it to stop at the rest stop?"

"Mine."

"What was the problem?"

"We were drinking beer." His tone said that the problem should have been obvious, but Felch waited for him to elaborate. Black Horse lowered his voice, avoiding eye contact with anyone. "I needed to use the john."

"So Mr. Bertram stopped the pickup and you went into the men's room. Did all three of you go inside?"

"I went in, and they waited in the pickup."

"Bertram and Smith?"

"Right. But when I came out, they went in."

"Together?"

"Yeah. Arnie made some comment about the power of suggestion. So, anyway, he'd left the pickup running, and the radio was playing. I got in and I don't know if I passed out or fell asleep."

"How long did you sleep?"

"I didn't have a watch. I figure it might have been 11:00 or so when we stopped. It might have been 1:00

when I woke up. Maybe later. But I didn't know that then. My head was pounding, and I didn't see anybody around. I waited a few minutes. Then I went back in the men's john to see what the holdup was."

"The pickup was still running?"

"It was running when I woke up. I shut it off."

"What did you find in the men's room, Mr. Black Horse?"

He lifted his chin and stared at the wall at the back of the room. "Arnie was lying on his side with his back to the door, kinda like he was sleeping. But there was blood. I rolled him over, and I saw . . . that he was dead. That must have been how I got the blood on my clothes." His hands came up off the arms of the chair, as though they'd been called to testify, and he looked down at them, slowly turning palms up. "I had it all over my hands, I know, and I washed it off."

"Did you look around for Smith?"

"Yeah, I looked around. Checked the toilet. But I didn't expect to find anybody. Arnie's billfold was lying there on the floor. I don't know why there weren't any other fingerprints on it because somebody must have dropped it there after they took the money. Anyway, Arnie was dead, and Smith was gone."

"What did you do?"

"I went outside to the phone booth and tried to call the police, but I couldn't get the damn phone to work. The quarter kept dropping through. Then I saw a set of headlights coming, so I ran out to the highway. It was a semi. I tried to wave him down, but he went on by."

"Then what did you do?"

"I got in the pickup and took off. I figured I'd pull off at the first sign of a phone or a town, but—" He looked directly at Susan again. She restrained herself from nodding to encourage him to continue as she waited for the next word. "The damn pickup ran out of gas."

"So you walked."

"That's right."

"And you did intend to report the murder?" Felch

waited several seconds. "Mr. Black Horse? You did intend to report the incident to the police, did you not?"

"Yeah." Black Horse looked down at his hands again. "I was gonna report it."

"But what happened?"

"They arrested me for it."

"Do you know who killed Arnold Bertram, Mr. Black Horse?"

"It must have been Ray Smith." The defendant turned to the jury, as if he were presenting his own case and one statement should suffice. "All I know for sure is, it wasn't me."

"You did not murder Arnold Bertram and take the money from his billfold?"

"No, I didn't."

"No further questions."

"We'll need a lunch break before Mr. Ness cross-examines the witness." Judge Carmichael's gavel punctuated his announcement. "Court stands in recess until one o'clock this afternoon."

Chapter 3

The swivel stool squeaked as Susan swung her knees away from the island counter dividing her kitchen niche from the small living room. Beyond the glass patio door the arm of a lone aluminum frame lawn chair glinted in the autumn sun. The wind chime suspended above it was still. Susan felt a twinge of guilt at staying inside on such a day in North Dakota, where the natives had taught her to begin anticipating winter in mid-August. By late September, every good day was expected to be the last one of the season. As long as she was home for lunch, she should have been sitting outside in the only chair her second-story balcony would accommodate.

Susan missed Minnesota's trees and lakes, but, other than the relentless wind, North Dakota's winters were no worse than what she was accustomed to. North Dakota's wind was the kicker, but she'd decided it was tolerable. Once she had learned to ignore the hard winter forecasts in September, she'd decided she could trade the trees for the beauty of the open spaces, which gave her a sense of freedom. Not that she needed much space for herself, but she liked the idea that it was there when she wanted it. She liked knowing that she couldn't really get herself boxed in because there was so much space here, with no barriers to the free-wheeling wind.

She glanced at the anniversary clock she kept on the bookshelf. It was her grandmother's clock, and one of the few things she'd brought with her when she'd moved. Everything else, including the "starter" furniture her parents had helped her buy, went into a friend's garage sale after she'd finally left Mel. Leaving him had turned out to be a simple matter of making the decision to walk away from something that was not working—probably never had worked, not even in the beginning—and selling the furniture, most of which was hers. Since there'd been no marriage, there were no legal complications. Mel had insisted that marriage was a technicality.

He'd expected her to change her mind. He'd called her once in a while, even after she'd moved, just to tell her that everything was great with him, but he wouldn't mind getting together with her for dinner or a weekend, just for old times' sake. She'd missed him at first, and when he called, he'd always make her laugh. He was good at that—which was why, for Susan's sake, neither dinner nor a weekend was a good idea. The world was full of funny people. Serious people, caring people . . . *other* people. She didn't miss Mel much anymore.

Grandmother's clock was two minutes slow. Susan had to get back to the courthouse soon. Ness would be on next. She wondered what he would do to Black Horse's story, which sounded plausible at this point. It had yet to stand up under cross-examination, but she saw no reason why it couldn't have happened the way he had told it. He'd only had sixty-four dollars when they'd arrested him. Surely he wouldn't have gone to the trouble of killing a man for sixty-four dollars. She wondered what had happened to the watch Bertram had been wearing. And Ray Smith, who had appeared and disappeared into the night. What happened to him? The police had checked it out, hadn't they? No Ray Smith. But how do you find a man named Ray Smith, who only one man claims was there and gone that night?

She wanted to believe Black Horse, and that probably wasn't a good sign. She found herself thinking about him, wondering how it felt to be in his shoes. *Boots.* Black cowboy boots, polished up for his day in court. She'd thought about the victim, too, being grabbed from behind, maybe while he was washing his hands in the sink. Had there been a mirror? Had he looked up and seen the face of his killer? The jurors had been advised not to visit the scene of the crime, and they weren't permitted to question witnesses themselves. They were to listen and observe. Susan had done that. Sooner or later she would be locked in that little room with eleven others, and so far she didn't think anybody had proven much beyond the fact that Bertram had been murdered. His fate had been decided, and Cleveland Black Horse's hung in the balance. Bertram was a stack of glossy eight-by-tens, while Black Horse was a man. She'd seen the life in his eyes.

She was supposed to be impartial. Wanting to believe people was still a weakness of hers, even though she thought she'd taught herself to doubt more readily than she used to. She used to doubt Mel sometimes, but then he had always come up with an explanation. It was always just the kind she wanted to hear.

So what were you doing at Marion Andrews's?

She needed help with her plumbing. Her dishwasher was leaking all over the place.

She needed your help? Why would she ask you?

She said she was going to have to hire a plumber. I told her I could fix it for her. She paid me twenty dollars, and I can use the money. Besides, she lives right above us, and I didn't want all that water leaking in down here. She *paid* me, Susan. I wasn't just being *nice*, for Chrissake!

No, he wasn't just being nice. That much was true. He was innocent until proven guilty, and the burden of proof was on Susan. She wasn't much of a detective. Susan wished she could tell herself that she'd at least had the good sense to refuse to marry Mel Dockter, that she hadn't really *wanted* to marry him, hadn't actually waited around for five years before she'd finally realized that he was never going to change. And if she'd stayed with him, neither would she. She would have continued to support him and mother him and accept his lies, whether she believed them or not, until she hated both him and herself. In the end, she hadn't left hating him. She'd left still wishing things could be different.

She believed people too easily, she told herself, as she washed the corners of her tuna salad sandwich down the garbage disposal. She had to toughen up. Get real. Be objective about this trial. Listen to both sides and weigh the evidence. She knew how a guilty person behaved. She'd lived with one for five years. They were guilty if they spent half their waking hours trying to cover their tracks, but no matter how smooth they were, sooner or later they tipped their hand. Sooner or later something was sure to slip that couldn't be covered.

One slip might have been Black Horse's reaction to the appearance of his grandmother. She was ancient dignity personified. He didn't want her in the courtroom. What kind of a slip was that?

Martin Ness put aside his notes when the judge resumed the proceedings. He slipped his wire-rimmed glasses into their case and set them aside, too. He stood slowly, tapped his fingers against the top of the counsel table a couple of times as if he were gearing up, then straightened suddenly and laid his forefinger against his lips as he eyed the defendant, who sat in the witness chair.

Cleveland Black Horse stared back.

"You are still under oath, Mr. Black Horse," the judge said. Cleve registered the reminder. He didn't think a response was required, and his attention was on Ness, who seemed to be sizing him up. This courtroom was Ness's arena. Cleve was the cowboy on the ground here, and Felch was out of his league in Ness's territory. Cleve told himself to keep a cool head and stay away from the bull's horns.

Ness moved around the counsel table and claimed center stage. "I remember when you were the national All-Around Cowboy, too, Mr. Black Horse. That was big news around here, even though you're technically a South Dakotan. Little Eagle is just across the state line, isn't it?"

Was that a question? Cleve glanced at Felch, who'd coached him to answer only when a question was actually posed, but Felch was still watching Ness.

Ness went on. "You were a local hero here for a while, Mr. Black Horse. You'd gone from the Badlands Circuit to the PRCA—the big time—and we all admired you for that. And then you became the All-Around Champion Cowboy." He paused, and his brow furrowed. "How long ago did you say that was?"

"Twelve years."

"Twelve years." Ness shook his head. "The time does go by. Have you placed in the national standings since then?"

"Twice. Third and eighth in saddle bronc."

"How long has it been since the last time you placed? A few years?"

"Ten years."

"Ten years." Ness nodded, playing it as though they were old friends getting reacquainted. "And how are you doing now?"

"I'm making a living." Cleve wondered what had happened to Ness's claim that his career had nothing to do with the murder. That had made more sense than this casual chat they seemed to be having.

"Full time? Is rodeo your whole livelihood?"

"In the last few years, I've hired on as a ranch hand for a month or two at a time in the winter."

"To make ends meet?"

"Yeah. With rodeo, you win or you don't eat." Or pay your medical bills, and Cleve still owed a few on the last torn ligaments in his left ankle, which had mended only half-assed. But if Ness was looking for some hard luck story, for whatever reason, he was sniffing around the wrong tree.

"Aren't you winning anymore?"

"I win some."

"Win some, lose some, huh?" Ness offered an easy smile. "My business is like that, too. What would you say is your yearly income from rodeo these days?"

What was this guy, a tax auditor? Cleve glanced toward the back of the courtroom, where his grandmother sat. She had the grace not to cause him more humiliation by looking in his direction, even if she couldn't have seen him very well at this distance. He shifted in his chair. "I do all right."

"This year?"

"It wasn't real good this year." He turned his attention briefly to the sheriff's deputy in the front row, who was watching his every move. "It was a short season."

"How were you doing before the arrest cut your season short?"

"I was doing okay," Cleve said firmly. It could have been a damn good season if he'd drawn the right stock and had any luck at all with the judges.

"What was your income from rodeo last year?"

"Objection." Felch rose from his chair halfway. "Mr. Black Horse's income has nothing to do with this—"

"Your Honor, Mr. Felch questioned the defendant about his success in the sport of rodeo, a sport in which success is measured by the amount of money a participant wins. The People wish to show that a need for money may well have been a motive—"

Money? That was only part of it. Cleve measured his success in independence. He'd never seen his father, but he'd heard about him. "Damn good cowboy," his mother had said. "No-good cowboy," was his grandmother's term. Whichever it was, he'd sure as hell had his freedom. As far as his mother went . . . well, that about summed it up. She went as far as she pleased and left him with his grandparents.

The old man had hung on to a little herd of range cows after most of his land had been covered with backwater from the Oahe Dam. Success was a white man's word, Cleve thought. His grandfather hadn't talked about succeeding. He'd talked about hanging on for another winter. Cleve had sworn with every shovelful of dry dirt he'd thrown on the old man's casket that he wouldn't break his back over a few black baldy cows and a shrinking patch of allotted land. There was no freedom for Indians anymore, but there were still a few cowboys left. They followed the rodeo circuit.

"Objection overruled. Continue, Mr. Ness."

"Last year's income, Mr. Black Horse?"

"I don't know. Maybe eight, ten thousand dollars."

"Before expenses?"

"My bookkeeping isn't the greatest, but, yeah. Before expenses."

"Do you have any dependents besides yourself?"

"I, uh . . ." He glanced at his grandmother again. He'd taken pretty good care of her when the money was there. At least, he'd tried. She wouldn't leave that damn shack out in the country. *Isn't that right, woman? You had your chance.* "I usually to try to . . ." His glance ricocheted off the wall and back to his own hands. Out loud, with her sitting there, he couldn't make the claim. "No, not really. I look after myself."

"Do you ever have any problem coming up with entry fees?"

"No." He looked squarely at Ness. The bull wasn't going to get him on that one. "I had my entry fees for Mandan covered. They were already paid."

"Do you have credit cards, Mr. Black Horse?"

"No."

"You had sixty-four dollars for gas, food, lodging and, uh . . ." Ness shoved his hands in his pockets and gazed at the ceiling as he selected words, ostensibly for the benefit of delicate ears. " . . . any entertainment you might decide to indulge in over the holiday. Is that all the money you had?"

"That's all I had." Cleve dismissed the amount with a wave of his hand. "It was all I needed. I planned on sleeping in the pickup, and I was riding the next day."

"The pickup? Whose pickup had you planned to sleep in?"

"Mine."

"But you left that along the side of the road." Ness pivoted toward the witness stand. "Weren't you worried about your pickup, Mr. Black Horse?"

"Worrying doesn't fix a busted radiator."

"No, but garage mechanics do. You say you called a garage. Why wouldn't they tow your truck?"

"They wanted a credit card number, which you've already established I haven't got."

"You had sixty-four dollars. *If* you had called a garage, it seems unlikely that they would leave you stranded like that. If nothing else, they would have had the pickup for security." Ness turned his charm on the jury, moving closer to the box as though he were asking the questions in behalf of their suspicions. "Now tell us, Mr. Black Horse. Did you actually place that call, or were you—"

"I placed the call," Cleve said evenly. "It cost me seventy cents cash, because I don't have a telephone credit card either. And when I told them my name was Black Horse—" Jesus, these people were good at acting like their own bigotry was news to them. "They probably figured the pickup had cardboard windows and the bumper was tied up with baling twine." Stay cool, he told himself. Ness hiked a taunting eyebrow, and Cleve turned the urge to plant his fist in the man's face into a gesture of mock surprise. "I don't know, maybe they hadn't read any back issues of *Rodeo Sports News* lately. All I know is they weren't interested in my pickup."

"And the name of the garage was . . ."

"I don't know. Someplace in Dickinson."

"No idea who it was you talked to when you made that call?"

"Look, I've been over this a hundred times with Felch, and he called every place in Dickinson—at least, he says he did—and nobody remembers talking to me, so . . ." Cleve noticed the horrified look on his attorney's face, and he realized he wasn't going to do himself any favors by pushing Felch. Even if the guy wasn't busting his butt to win, he shouldn't give him cause to want to throw the match. He settled back in the witness chair and tried to hold his tone in check. "But I did try to get a tow truck to go out there, just for the hell of it. Just to make Arnie happy."

"I see." Ness turned to digest the comment pointedly for the jury's benefit. "Just to satisfy Arnold Bertram, a man you hardly knew. Were you anxious to get to Mandan that night, Mr. Black Horse? Were you in a hurry?"

"I was hoping to get there before midnight. Without my pickup, I was going to have to find a place to stay."

"Did you try to hurry Mr. Bertram along?"

"No."

"Prod him? Suggest that the two of you get back on the road?"

"No."

"Why not?"

"It was his outfit. I was just hitching a ride."

"No disagreements, then?"

"Well, except when he wanted to take care of everything for me by calling a garage."

"Oh, that's right. You didn't want him to run interference for you with the garage, even though it might have meant the difference between salvaging your pickup or ending up having to junk it. Is that right?"

Hanging on, or walking away. The ultimate choices. Cleve refused to hang on to what was useless. He walked away from anything he didn't need, and he didn't need a pile of junk that couldn't move him any farther down the road. He didn't need Arnie Bertram to speak up for him, either. The jerk who'd answered his call to the garage had asked for a major credit card number or a Triple A membership, and Cleve had been pretty damn polite about telling him to go to hell. He could have said worse, but he wasn't steamed enough. Not until Arnie had snatched a quarter from the change on the bar and promised to take care of it himself. Cleve had grabbed his arm and told Arnie to forget it.

"It was none of his business," Cleve said.

"He'd made you his business, hadn't he, by picking you up? But by this time you figured you had access to another pickup. Arnold Bertram's. Isn't it true that you were no longer worried about your own pickup because—"

Cleve leaned forward in his seat. "That's really crazy. What kind of a fool would kill a guy for his pickup and then head on into town to compete in—"

"I'm asking the questions here, Mr. Black Horse. *You* say you intended to enter the rodeo."

"My entry fee was paid up."

"But you win a few and you lose . . . maybe more than a few these days. What I'm asking is whether you didn't realize at some point, while you were out drinking with Arnold Bertram, that there was the potential here for a sure thing?"

"No."

"You did say he was flashing money around, didn't you?"

"Yes, but I don't know how mu—"

"And he was wearing some nice jewelry, driving an expensive pickup. Isn't that true?"

"I didn't want his—"

"You *did* notice those things, didn't you, Mr. Black Horse?"

"Not because I—"

"Yes or no, Mr. Black Horse?"

"Objection!"

"Overruled. The witness will answer the question."

"Yeah. Sure. I noticed."

Ness gave the jury members a moment to make their mental notes while he appeared to formulate his next question. The slow walk back to the jury box railing was clearly part of Ness's staging. Cleve watched the jury watch Ness. They were with him, all but the woman in the front row, the one with the long brown hair. She glanced from Ness to Cleve. She was waiting for more from him, not Ness. Some kind of an explanation. He'd noticed the jewelry. He'd noticed the money. Who wouldn't? He'd noticed her sympathy for him, too. At least, it looked like sympathy. Her eyes were almost too big for her face, and they seemed to glitter with some kind of anxiety. Not fear. It was more like she wanted to make sure she didn't miss anything, like she was trying really hard to get inside his head. The rest of them just sat there dull-eyed, letting Ness carry them along.

"Now, let's talk about this hitchhiker, this Ray Smith," Ness decided. "You say you were asleep when Bertram pulled over to pick this man up?"

"That's right."

"But you woke up, you looked up, and there was this man wearing a stocking cap and a hunting vest, is that right? Just standing next to the window."

"That's right." Cleve had been dozing when the pickup slowed down and veered off the highway. The headlights were on, and the last of the sunset was seeping into the hills, as he remembered. Arnie was shifting into reverse and backing along the shoulder of the road, and Cleve had asked what was going on. He'd turned, looked out the side window, and he remembered thinking the leering face outside looked like a turkey buzzard's. He'd rolled the window down so Arnie could do his line and offer the guy a lift.

"Pretty spooky fellow, was he?" Ness asked.

"Yeah." He'd been a little groggy, but he'd opened the door and crawled out to let the buzzard in. He wasn't going to be sitting between those two—one who couldn't quit talking and the other one who smelled like something that fed on road kill—all the way to Mandan.

"You described him as somebody we might imagine stepping right off the screen in one of those drive-in horror movies."

"He just looked like a bum to me."

"A hitchhiker, like yourself."

Cleve showed no emotion. "Yeah. We were both in the same boat."

"And we could presume, if we chose to, that this hitchhiker could have been carrying a knife of some sort inside that vest. They have a lot of pockets, don't they?"

"I don't know. I never owned one."

"But the vest was a good touch, because we can imagine a hunting knife somewhere inside, can't we, Mr. Black Horse?"

"I can't say what he was carrying inside his vest."

"And the stocking cap is good, too, even though it was the middle of summer. You know, it gives a very sinister feel to the story because lately we've been seeing so many of these—"

"Objection, Your Honor."

"Sustained. Save the commentary for your summation, Mr. Ness."

"My question is, would *you* have stopped to pick up a man like this out there on the highway, Mr. Black Horse? Especially late at night?"

"No."

"Neither would I. But you're telling us that Arnold Bertram did."

"Yes, I am. He did."

"And then the three of you went on down the highway, stopped for beer, and this *character*, this Ray Smith, got out of the pickup and went behind the building to relieve himself, is that true?"

"I don't know what he did behind the store. That's what he said he was going to do."

"His exact words were—"

"He said he had to take a leak."

"But there were toilet facilities inside. Mr. Mund, the proprietor, testified that Mr. Bertram used the bathroom there. *Inside* the store."

"Smith didn't go inside the store. He went around back."

"And Mr. Mund saw only one passenger in Arnold Bertram's pickup. You admit that must have been you."

"Yeah. I stayed in the pickup the whole time we were there."

Ness put his hands in his pockets and paced. "Let's see now, you testified that Mr. Bertram asked you to put his bolo tie and his billfold into the glove compartment, and his ring was sort of an afterthought, but when he stopped at Mund's store, you handed him his billfold back. What about his watch? Was he wearing his watch?"

"Yes. I remember him checking his watch later when I asked him to stop at the rest stop."

"That's right, *you* asked for that stop, didn't you?"

"Yes."

"And he checked his watch? Did he make any comment about the time?"

"No. He just looked at his watch and pulled off at the approach."

"You testified that you needed to use the toilet because you'd been drinking a lot of beer. Why didn't you just ask him to pull over on the side of the road?"

"Because—" He wanted to laugh. Damned if you do, damned if you don't. "I generally use a toilet if there's one handy."

"Oh, come on, Mr. Black Horse, guys out drinking beer, they don't usually wait until they get to a rest area before they—"

"I saw the sign." This wasn't casually discussed in a room full of people—white people, women he didn't know. Not in Cleve's world, not by a man who was sober, anyway. He tried to block the courtroom out of his head and spell out the essentials, the way he remembered them, just for Ness. "I wanted to use the toilet. I wanted to take some aspirin. I wanted to get some air."

"Oh, now we have two new reasons for stopping. This is the first mention of aspirin. Were you carrying aspirin, Mr. Black Horse?"

"One of those little tins. I usually carry one in my pocket."

"Nagging rodeo injuries," Ness said, drizzling a glaze of sympathy over his sarcasm. "I can imagine you'd have your aches and pains."

The smiling sonuvabitch imagined him a liar. Talk to the jury, Felch had said. Tell them your side. "I hit my head on the windshield when my pickup went into the ditch. I had a headache that wouldn't quit. And I can't take aspirin with beer."

"Is that why you needed air?"

"Smith smelled like last week's garbage. I thought I was going to puke if I didn't get away from him for a minute."

"Funny Mr. Bertram was able to tolerate it." Ness eyed the jury as he reminded them of the victim, who could once see and smell and feel pain as much as Cleve could. "So you chose to stop at a rest stop, and you went in alone?"

"That's right."

"Why did the other two men wait for you to come out before they went in?"

"I don't know."

"Did you think it was odd?"

"I didn't think about it." That was a lie. He thought it was a damn nuisance.

"Why not? Because of your headache?"

"Because it's none of my business what other people do in the john."

"So you just went to sleep."

"I guess. I don't know—the beer, the aspirin I took, the headache. I don't know what happened to me. I leaned back on that seat, and I was out like a light."

"Strange that you managed to wake up within just a couple of hours if you had all that going on. Do you know what a blackout is, Mr. Black Horse?"

"A blackout?" The word made Cleve feel clammy all of a sudden. *Jesus. A blackout?*

"An alcohol-induced blackout, Mr. Black Horse. Have you ever been so drunk that when you sobered up you couldn't remember exactly what you'd done for some—"

Ness waved his hand. "Some period of time? You just lost that period entirely?"

"I don't have blackouts."

"You've *never* had a blackout?"

"Not since . . ."

"Since when, Mr. Black Horse?"

Not since 'Nam. "Not since I was nineteen, maybe twenty years old."

"Then you *have* experienced blackouts?"

"Once or twice, yeah, but that was a long time ago." He'd fallen asleep, he told himself. Passed out, maybe. He wasn't going to let this guy play with his brain. He'd once tried to take on a whole bar full of Vietnamese civilians, or so he'd been told the next day. He couldn't remember a thing about that incident, but this wasn't like that. "Look, I fell asleep in the pickup; I woke up in the pickup. I didn't have any blood on me or anything. Except on my sleeve, from where I cut my head."

"There was blood on your clothes when you were arrested."

"Yeah, but not when I woke up. I told you how I must've gotten his blood on me." Cleve gripped the arm of the chair and told himself again to stay calm. "I didn't have that much to drink that night. I just fell asleep."

Ness nodded, as though weighing the possibility. "Then you woke up. You went back inside, according to your testimony, and you found Arnold Bertram. Now, you say that you rolled the body over, is that correct?"

"That's right."

"How did the victim look?"

"How did he look?"

"Yes, Mr. Black Horse. You rolled the body over, so you had a dead man in your arms. How did he look?"

Cleve laced his fingers together as he took a deep breath and released it slowly. He hadn't known Arnie Bertram before the third of July, but since then he'd thought about him a lot. Ness was right. Not too many people would stop and offer a guy a ride these days. Maybe Arnie liked to pick up guys. Maybe he just wanted to help out, like he did with the pickup. He was a salesman, and he spent a lot of time on the road. Maybe he just wanted somebody to talk to. Arnie had been quite a talker until somebody sliced his throat.

"Do you remember how he looked, Mr. Black Horse?"

How could he not remember? "White. Waxy. Starey-eyed, but kind of surprised. There was blood everywhere."

"How did you feel?"

That part was hazy. He'd felt like he'd walked into the wrong room. Then he'd felt like he wanted to run. How was he supposed to feel? "Sick. Scared."

"Did you get sick? Actually vomit?"

"No."

"Why not? You said Ray Smith's body odor nearly had you vomiting."

"I've seen dead men before."

"Where?"

"Vietnam."

"What branch of the service were you in, Mr. Black Horse?"

Cleve was relieved by the change of subject. "Army."

"What outfit?"

"Special Forces."

"Trained for guerrilla warfare, right? With . . . all that that entails."

The relief didn't last long. Ness was on another roll, but finally Felch was on his feet, managing a scowl. "Ob-jec-tion, Your Honor. This man is not on trial for serving his country in time of war."

"The question is not meant to impugn the defendant's military service, Your Honor, but to establish his skills." Ness turned to the jury. "The victim's throat was deftly sliced by someone who knew how to kill a man quickly and efficiently."

"Put your question to the witness, Mr. Ness, but let's have fewer theatrics."

"Specifically, Mr. Black Horse, did the Army train you in the most efficient methods a man might use to kill—"

"Yes. I was trained as a soldier for killing." The prosecutor was using everything Cleve had ever done as evidence against him. Cleve felt cornered, and he surveyed the courtroom, looking for some kind of backup. "I'll bet there are other men in this room who maybe—"

"That's neither here nor there, Mr. Black Horse. You were the one who was there that night with Arnold Bertram."

"But I didn't kill him."

"You say you tried to use the phone, and your quarter kept slipping through. Did you try to dial the operator?"

"I didn't dial anything."

"Why not?"

"The damn thing wouldn't take my money."

"Are you aware that you don't need money to make an emergency call?"

"I, uh . . ." Cleve had to stop and think. Was he aware—*that night*, was he aware? He closed his eyes, and he could see the pay phone, the dark trees, and the light above the sign that said MEN. Bertram was dead. There was nothing anyone could do for him except close his eyes for him, maybe cover him with some kind of blanket, get him off the floor and out of the john. He remembered thinking about body bags and helicopters as he headed for the phone. Was he aware that he didn't need change for an emergency call?

Cleve expelled a long breath. "There are all kinds of pay phones."

"The one you used permits emergency calls without money, does it not?"

"I don't know." *Tell it again. Maybe they'll get the picture.* "All I know is, I put the quarter in, and it fell through. I tried again; same thing. This guy was dead, you know? This wasn't any rice paddy. This was North

Dakota, and here I'd just gone into the john and found a man with his throat cut. I probably wasn't thinking too straight. Here comes this semi, somebody who could help. I run out there, hollering and waving, and he goes on by. I'm thinking, Jesus, there's a dead guy in there, and there's another guy running around here somewhere with a knife. The keys are in the pickup, so I jump in and take off."

"Before you ran out of gas, did the thought cross your mind that you could just keep on going?"

Ness made it sound like such an orderly thing—thoughts marching across his mind. They hadn't marched; they'd exploded. His brain had become a minefield, and the way the memory stood out against this dead-ass court-room made him laugh. "Yeah. Yeah, it did. I thought about ditching the pickup when I got to Mandan, because I figured, hell, I've been with this guy all night, and people have seen us together, and who knows where this Ray Smith took off to."

"What Ray Smith, Mr. Black Horse?"

"The one nobody believes exists." Recognizing that fact scared him. He needed to take cover, to protect himself. "So, yeah, I thought about running, because my name's Black Horse. That means . . ." He glanced at the sheriff's deputy, then at his own attorney. "That means I thought about it because I didn't like the idea of being questioned by white cops and white lawyers in front of a—" Finally, Cleve turned to the jury. All white. All waiting for him to say it. Accuse them, as he was accused. But the law didn't put you in jail for convicting the wrong man. They had to see that he was the wrong man, and if he blasted them now . . .

The other faces sent him back to the one he'd come to regard as the pretty one in the front row. He spoke to her. "I wasn't running. I was looking for help, and I ran out of gas."

"If you were looking for help, why did you take your personal belongings out of Arnold Bertram's pickup before you abandoned it?" Ness demanded.

Cleve turned back to him, surprised by the question. "I took my saddle."

"Mr. Black Horse, you just described how agitated you were by the discovery of a body in the men's room. You said that you were so distraught that you were unable to place a phone call properly, and that you ran out to the highway to try to waylay a semi. If you weren't running, why did you clear all that was yours out of Arnold Bertram's pickup?"

"I took my *saddle*."

"A man who has abandoned his own pickup with hardly a second thought, who has just rolled another man's body—" He gestured with his own rolling flourish. "I used the term *rolled* advisedly, since all of his money was taken from his billfold, along with the watch, stripped from his lifeless wrist."

"I did not take his money."

"You took his pickup, and while you were tooling down the highway trying to decide whether to report the cold-blooded murder of the man who had given you a ride, you ran out of gas. Do you mean to sit there and tell us, Mr. Black Horse, with all this going on you actually thought to collect a saddle and a duffel bag?"

"I didn't think." Cleve studied his hands and said quietly, "I just don't ever leave my saddle."

"Because it would have incriminated you, Mr. Black Horse? Isn't that the reason? Is your name on the saddle somewhere?"

"My name's carved—" Cleve glanced at Felch, whose bland expression offered no support. "I don't walk off and leave my saddle bronc saddle, no matter—"

"You walked off and left your pickup, Mr. Black Horse."

"The pickup wouldn't run." Each word slid between clenched teeth.

"No, but you did. No more questions."

"Re-direct, Mr. Felch."

Felch gathered his wits and stuttered as he came to his feet. "I, uh . . . have, uh . . ." He moved to the front of the counsel table and cleared his throat to meet the challenge. "Yes, Your Honor. I do. Mr. Black Horse, let me ask you about your military record. How old were you when you enlisted?"

Cleve stared straight ahead. "Eighteen."

"And how long did you serve in the Army?"

"Four years."

"And were you not decorated repeatedly for valor?" Cleve shifted his attention slowly to Felch as though the question made no sense. "Mr. Black Horse, were you not the recipient of a Bronze Star, a Purple Heart . . . Mr. Black Horse?"

"Yeah. They gave me some medals for . . . doing what I did over there, yeah." He glanced past Felch and directed his answer to Prosecutor Ness. "That was different. That was war."

"I'm sure the *jury* understands that, Mr. Black Horse. And the saddle. That's a vital tool of your trade, is it not? You took it along with you even though you were in a highly agitated state and probably didn't need to be weighed down with anything—"

"Weighed down?" Cleve glowered at his attorney. "Whose side are you on? Sure, I left two pickups behind that night. But I don't walk away and leave my saddle."

Felch turned his back on his client and tossed his papers on the counsel table. "No more questions, Your Honor."

Chapter 4

Summations were delivered the following morning. Susan hoped that the attorneys' final remarks would offer some guiding light, illuminating the pathway toward certainty. Absolute innocence. Positive guilt. By this time one or the other should have been clear. So it was in the movies. This trial wasn't what she'd expected a trial to be. There were too many unanswered questions, and all that the attorneys had offered were stories. The police had a story. The defendant had another story. The most elusive story was the victim's, and Susan would have paid the devil at this point to have heard from Arnold Bertram.

"It is most regrettable that Ray Smith has not been located," Carter Felch lamented, standing rigidly near the railing in front of the jury box. Like a Christmas nutcracker, he moved nothing but his mouth. "If we could put Ray Smith on the stand, your task as a jury would be greatly simplified. But the man was apparently a drifter, and, like a drifter, he disappeared without a trace. So we can't ask him what happened when he went into the men's room with Arnold Bertram on the night of July third. We can't ask Arnold Bertram. We can only ask Cleveland Black Horse, and even *he* can't tell you what happened in the men's room that night, because he wasn't there. The other two men went inside *after* Cleveland Black Horse came out.

"And Cleveland Black Horse had had quite a night. He'd had a tire blow out on his pickup, hit his head on the windshield when the pickup hit the ditch, and he'd had a few beers. That and a couple of aspirin, and yes, he'd gone to sleep. When he woke up, Arnold Bertram was dead, and the drifter who called himself Ray Smith was gone.

"Do we believe him? What's not to believe? We have no murder weapon, no eyewitness to the murder. All we have is Cleveland Black Horse, a man who was just trying to get to the rodeo to do what he does best, ride broncs. Ladies and gentlemen, this man has been a national champion. The best there is. Sure, it's a young man's sport, but Mr. Black Horse can't be faulted for pursuing the career he loves, even if the joints ache more than they used to and the bones are a bit more brittle. No, he doesn't win as consistently as he once did, but the prosecution would have you reason that because of that Cleveland Black Horse killed a man and took his pickup and his money.

"And speaking of money—" Felch planted his hands on his hips. "Where is it?" He challenged the jury, as if maybe they ought to be looking under their chairs. "Three people testified that Arnold Bertram was flashing money around. Sixty-four dollars? Is that the kind of money he was flashing? That's all Cleveland Black Horse had when he was arrested. Sixty-four dollars. No fancy watch, either. The defendant was not in possession of the watch, possibly a Rolex, but a watch that we know Arnold Bertram was wearing earlier that night. On the other hand, the turquoise and silver bolo tie and gold ring Bertram was also seen wearing that night were still in the glove compartment of the pickup, right where Bertram asked Cleveland Black Horse to put them. Now I ask you—if my client stole the money and the watch, then managed to hide them so well that the police have not discovered them, why didn't he take the rest of Bertram's jewelry?

"I submit to you that there is more than a reasonable doubt here. Sure, Cleveland Black Horse *could* have murdered Arnold Bertram. He was there, he admits that. He's big enough, strong enough. He's even had some specialized training in the Army and in Vietnam, where he served his country with high honors. So he probably *could* have done it. But *did* Cleveland Black Horse kill Arnold Bertram?" He let a moment pass, then shook his head. "I doubt it. I seriously doubt it, ladies and gentlemen. The pieces just don't add up. And that's why . . ." Felch glanced at the defendant, who sat back in his chair with his arms folded over his chest as though he were appraising Felch's performance. Felch glanced away, and his voice dropped as he finished hurriedly. "I think you doubt it, too."

There was a shuffling of feet, and at least one sinus passage was cleared as the courtroom waited for the prosecutor to rise and deliver his summation. Martin Ness flexed his back and took one last look at the few notes he'd jotted down on the pad in front of him. Then he left the pad behind. Ness rounded the corner of his table and claimed his space, filling it with his commanding presence. Even as he reheated the old evidence at the beginning of his summary, the audience sat up and leaned in, their faces following his brightness like blossoms following the sun. He used the floor the way an artist uses his entire canvas, gesturing toward the empty witness chair, the defense counsel table and the spectators, who represented "the citizens of this state." He distanced himself from the jury, then approached them, befriended them, became one of them.

The performance was so good it made Susan feel queasy. Ness reminded her of a slick politician, the way he worked the jury with his eyes. She found herself trying not to respond, just on principle. Every time he looked her way, it was as though he were saying, "Are you in yet?"

Surely Martin Ness was a mind reader. He braced his hands against the railing directly in front of Susan and addressed the whole group, but he kept coming back to her.

"No, ladies and gentlemen, we can't offer you an eyewitness's testimony. Arnold Bertram is dead, and it's safe to assume that the only other person in the room when he was murdered was the killer. So if you insist upon doubting until we can produce someone who can say 'I saw him do it,' then this case is likely to go unsolved, the murderer unpunished. Unrestrained. Free to choose another victim and commit this crime again.

"In behalf of the people of this state, I'm asking you to look at what we *do* have. We have witnesses who saw the defendant with Mr. Bertram within an hour of his murder. No one else was seen with them. We have Cleveland Black Horse's fingerprints on the billfold, and no money in it. We have a stolen pickup with two pieces of jewelry in the glove compartment—jewelry the victim was wearing only a couple of hours before.

"What is the defense's reply? A man wearing a stocking cap and a hunter's vest in the middle of the summer." Ness postured, a twinkle in his eye. "Yeah. He must have done it. A man nobody else saw. A man nobody else has ever *heard* of. That's it." He shrugged. "That's it! Cleveland Black Horse was asleep. He saw no evil, heard no evil. He found the body, but he couldn't get the phone to work, so he spoke no evil. He just took the pickup and headed on down the road.

"Do you believe that? Or does the story sound as lame to you as it does to me?" As he spoke, Ness ventured closer to the defense table. "This man *used* to be a big name in rodeo, but he isn't anymore. And he isn't making much of a living at it these days. Now, I'm not interested in what's happened to him in the last ten years or how he's fallen on harder times. But I think we need to recognize the fact that on July third he effectively junked his own pickup. It wasn't worth it to him to try to get it fixed. We need to acknowledge that he was low on cash and that his chances of finishing in the money at the rodeo here in Mandan were no better than anybody else's. He's a has-been in the business, pure and simple. He was on his way to do what counsel says he does best, namely ride broncs, and he was busy tying one on before he got there. He says he doesn't know whether he passed out or fell asleep, but he says he didn't black out. He says he didn't have *that* much to drink that night, and he ought to know the difference. He says he's had blackouts before. So he knew what he was doing that night," Ness said, nodding as if he were satisfied that the point was made. "He knew just what he was doing.

"Look at the facts, ladies and gentlemen. One incontrovertible fact is that Arnold Bertram was brutally murdered on July third of this year. If somebody broke into your house, and you caught a man running away from the scene with your car and your family heirlooms, you'd know he was the one who broke in, wouldn't you? Even if you hadn't actually seen him break the door down, there'd be little room for doubt And there's little room for doubt in this case. Review the evidence. How could any reasonable man or woman doubt that it was Cleveland Black Horse who cut Arnold Bertram's throat, murdering him in cold blood?"

Ness's summation turned all eyes on the defendant. Black Horse shot a defiant glare at Ness, but avoided looking at anyone else. So did Felch. He was already filing papers in his briefcase, which sat on the floor next to his chair. When the judge spoke, Felch sat up and folded his hands on the table as though harking to his master's voice.

The judge charged the jury with the responsibility of weighing the facts of the case and reaching a verdict. He explained that in order to find the defendant guilty of the charge of murder in the first degree, they must be convinced of his guilt beyond a reasonable doubt, which meant being reasonably certain that Cleveland W. Black Horse killed Arnold Bertram. They must be convinced that he knew what he was doing, that he intended to do murder, that he committed the act maliciously. He reminded them that the law did not permit capital punishment in North Dakota, and in the event of a guilty verdict, it would be his job as judge to determine a sentence.

"Your job is to discuss the case among yourselves, comparing your views, bringing all twelve individual perspectives to bear. All of you have heard the testimony and viewed the evidence. You were selected because those of us who are involved in this case, including the State, represented by Mr. Ness, and the defendant, represented by Mr. Felch, believe you to be capable of reaching a verdict without prejudice, without fear or sympathy. The fairest, soundest judgment the human mind can make—that's what we're asking you for.

"Each of you should enter that jury room with a willingness to listen to the others and to speak your mind. You're not expected to be legal experts or detectives. You are twelve people bringing your common sense and experience to bear. Your verdict should represent the consensus of a group of honest, fair-minded, intelligent people. Your verdict, guilty or not guilty, must be unanimous.

"And now the name of the alternate juror will be drawn."

Susan watched the clerk draw the name, feeling stunned by the chance that her name might be drawn. It was a raffle she suddenly realized she didn't want to win. She'd come too far with this now.

"Louise Burnett."

"Louise Burnett is excused with the court's thanks," Judge Carmichael announced. The woman sitting behind Susan scooted past the knees of the other jurors and left the box. The judge spoke to the twelve who were left. "Unless a verdict is delivered before noon, which is only an hour and a half away, we'll bring your meal to you. Your first order of business is to select a foreman, who will deliver your verdict to the court. And now the bailiff will escort the jury to the deliberation room."

Susan was third in line as the jury filed out of the box. She made her way between the two counsel tables without looking at Cleveland Black Horse. He wasn't looking at her, either. She would have felt it if he were. It was a long walk down the center aisle toward the back of the simply appointed courtroom.

Behind the double doors was a small hallway made up of doors rather than walls. The bailiff opened one, and the twelve filed slowly into a small, windowless room furnished with a long table and twelve padded chairs.

"This here's the deliberation room. You got everything you need here, pencils and paper, coffee, on the other side there, toilets. You call me when you're ready or if there's something else you need. The double door'll be closed, but I'll be handy, so just give a holler."

The bailiff left, and the jurors glanced at one another while first one door, then a pair of doors closed them in together.

Mandan was a small town, and some of the jurors were acquainted before the trial. In the past several days, most of them had exchanged amenities and come to know each other's names. They were not friends. But the judge had charged them as one body, and they took their chairs as though they were accustomed to sharing a table together. Ruben Kurtz, an elderly wheat farmer, sat at one end, and Wayne Tidball, the pawnshop owner, took the other end. The women outnumbered them, but the senior men sat at the heads of the table. The local people didn't give the arrangement a thought; it was the way things were done.

Susan thought about it. It wasn't that she cared where she sat; it was just that she noticed and thought about it. Her "city ways" were showing again. Minneapolis was Midwest, too, but the Old World had lost its hold in the cities. There were times when she felt uncomfortable being a woman in Mandan. It was a man's town. She tried to dismiss the notion as she took a chair beside Western-dudded Tammy Berg with the shag hairdo. Margaret Whalen, the retired teacher, sat down on the other side. They all looked at each other around the table.

"Who wants to be foreman?"

Wayne Tidball wanted to get things moving.

"Why don't you do it, Wayne?"

Kurtz wanted to see the right man get the job.

The two heads of the table had spoken. Susan was about to suggest Margaret Whalen, since she had jury experience, but she took too much time to think about it. The ball was already rolling.

"Yeah, you'd be a good one, Wayne." Lorraine Wheatly, a neat and attractive elementary school teacher, added her support. "I move we cast a unanimous ballot for Wayne." She punctuated her suggestion with an uneasy little laugh.

"If that's the way you all want it, I guess I can read the verdict when we come up with one," Tidball said, assuming the role along with the longest pencil from the canister on the table. "Shouldn't take too long to do that."

"That Ness is something, isn't he?" Dale Larsen said as he took hold of the table's edge for balance and tipped his chair back.

"I hear he's gonna run for Congress or something."

"Well, he's sure got the makings."

Tidball ignored the small talk and bounced the eraser end of the pencil on the table as though he had a gavel of his own. "The sooner we get down to cases, the sooner we get done here."

"Now I think we should start by taking a poll to see how everybody stands."

"Should we use ballots?" Margaret asked. She wanted everyone to remember that she'd done this before.

Tidball shrugged. "I don't know why we'd need to. We've gotta talk this over, so we might as well just say it right up front, what we think."

The vote was taken. After the first couple of "guilties," the word was uttered with comfortable, automatic regularity. Only Margaret Whalen, Tammy Berg and

Susan voted "not guilty." Susan had churned the matter around in her mind for days, and it almost surprised her to hear herself say the words. When had the decision been made, finally? She'd been telling herself to keep an open mind, and now there it was. She was not convinced that Cleveland Black Horse had killed Arnold Bertram. Maybe she didn't completely believe his story—she wasn't going to be gullible enough to take him totally at his word—but there was room for doubt on the other side, too. Not just a little room. A *lot* of room. Reasonable doubt. Therefore, he was not guilty.

Tidball cleared his throat. "Okay, so most of us think he did it. Maybe we need to hear from you three women. Why aren't you convinced?"

"Not enough evidence," Tammy Berg said.

"Actually, I'm not sure," Margaret said. "If you believe the story about the other hitchhiker . . ."

Dale Larsen was quick to dismiss the elderly woman's reasoning. He let the front of his chair drop back to the floor. "Nobody saw this guy. They stopped two places, and it was Black Horse and Bertram. This other guy is just something Black Horse made up to save his ass."

"How do you know that?"

"Huh?" Dale glanced from Margaret to Susan, who'd questioned him.

"How do you know there was no Ray Smith?"

"Too convenient," Dale tossed off with a shrug. "The way he supposedly just disappeared."

Rolf Schwap joined in. "Hey, I-94 is a looooong highway." Schwap adjusted the bill of his green and yellow John Deere cap that seemed to be nailed to his head. "How many hitchhikers do you see out there, except maybe at the Fargo or Bismarck exits? And at that time of night? Not likely."

"They got his fingerprints on the billfold," said Tidball. He reminded Susan of Ness. He was used to having the final word. "I'd say that's pretty solid evidence."

"He explained that," Susan said quietly. "And I believe it was one thumbprint."

"Some explanation." Larsen laughed. "Bertram just hands the guy his billfold because he's tired of sitting on it."

"I don't like to sit on mine when I'm driving, either," Ruben admitted, rapping his gnarled knuckles lightly against the table. "Throws my spine off kilter, and that's a fact."

"Yeah, but you're carrying a lot of cash, and you've got this stranger in the car?" Larsen proposed. "You're not gonna just hand it over to him."

Susan tried to draw the others in by appealing with eye contact, much the way Ness had done. "Black Horse is apparently pretty well-known. Sort of a celebrity. If Arnold Bertram was a rodeo buff, maybe he felt as though he knew him."

"Black Horse should've hung it up a long time ago," Schwap said.

"He's not winning anymore."

"That isn't quite true, you guys." Tammy Berg's objection surprised the group enough to draw their attention. She played with one pearlized snap on her cuff, unsnapping it, then lining it up and snapping it again. "I saw him take first in saddle bronc out in Miles City last year. He sure gave 'em hell on that ride."

Tidball's eyes narrowed. "Maybe you should have told them that when they were picking the jury."

"They didn't ask. Besides, that's not why I voted 'not guilty.' It just seems like they oughta have more proof against him, that's all."

"So if he wasn't a cowboy, you'd still say he wasn't guilty?" Larsen grinned and slapped his hand on the table. "Come on, Tammy. You know you can't resist a cowboy."

"He's an Indian, hey. I don't go with Indians no matter how good they can ride." Tammy lifted her chin and flicked her scraggly blond hair back from her shoulder. "Well, you know what they're like when they're drinking."

"Do you think he was drunk?" Tidball asked.

Tammy shrugged. "I wasn't talking about *him*, especially. I'm just saying *most* of them. And I'm just saying, it's got nothing to do with him being a rodeo cowboy because I wouldn't go—"

"But do you think he was drunk?"

Tammy lifted her shoulder close to one ear as she eyed the pencil can. "I don't know. The guy who picked him up said he didn't seem to be too bad off."

"Yeah, but that was later," Larsen chimed in. "What about when they stopped at the rest stop?"

"I had one working for me once." Ruben settled back in his chair.

"Cowboy?"

"No, Indian. Hell of a worker, he was, but come payday he couldn't wait to get into town. Drank up every penny."

"It's a shame when they do that."

"And they wonder why—"

Susan's face was getting hot. She'd heard this kind of talk before, even at the hospital, and she didn't like it. Not that she could claim any Indian friends, but she had black friends back home, back in the cities. There were virtually no blacks in Mandan or Bismarck, which had seemed strange to her when she'd first moved. At a time like this, when she felt like a foreigner, Minneapolis was home.

"Look," Susan said. "I don't think we can assume this man was drunk. The highway patrolman didn't suggest that he was, and that isn't the issue, anyway. The question is—"

Nobody was listening.

"He had to be sober enough to do a job on Bertram."

"Do you think he was the one made that anonymous phone call about the body being in the men's john?"

"Why would he?"

"Could have been anybody made that call. Somebody passing through, maybe."

"He knew what he was doing with that knife for sure."

"We don't even know it was a knife!" Susan felt as though she were trying to carry water in a sieve. "And what about the weapon? If Black Horse did it, what did he do with the knife? And the watch? *And* the money? There had to be more money."

"Why?" Tidball demanded. He'd let the others pile on more suspicion until Susan tried to counter. Then he stepped in, leaning across the table toward her. "Maybe he *thought* there was more. Maybe he got mad when he found out there wasn't, and maybe, *that's* why he killed him."

"Sixty-four dollars is sixty-four dollars when you're broke," Ruben Kurtz pointed out.

"And a pickup that's running."

"He walked away from his own pickup without a second thought."

"Typical. You drive down to the reservation, toward Fort Yates, you'll see four or five vehicles along the highway, just left to rust. They walk away and leave 'em. They don't care."

The men had made up their minds. The women, Susan thought, sat like mice. She appealed to them again. "It doesn't make any sense that he'd kill a man and steal his pickup. Obviously, he was bound to get caught with it."

The other women remained silent.

"Obviously he did," Tidball said for them.

"So what do you think he had in mind?" Larsen asked Susan.

"I'm not sure. Maybe just what he said. Reporting it as soon as he got to a phone." She offered an open-handed gesture. "He admitted that he thought about trying to run so he wouldn't have to answer any questions, but he knew it was pointless. I think he was scared. Anybody would be. And maybe a little confused. It just doesn't make sense that he would—"

"You remember those pictures, Susan?" Tidball was taking the fatherly approach now. "Somebody butchered that man. Slit his throat, clean as a whistle. A thing like that isn't sensible. But it happened, and *somebody* did it. Everything I've heard in this case points to Black Horse. Black Horse did it."

"I don't think so. I think—"

"I think I need a cigarette." Tammy snatched hers off the table. "Can we take a break?"

They drained the sixteen-cup coffee urn. Linda Jessep, who had yet to contribute to the discussion, busied herself making a fresh pot. Tammy Berg, Ruben Kurtz and Dale Larsen tried to stay clear of Yvonne Krause with their cigarettes. They claimed a corner of the jury room, while Yvonne took her coffee back into the deliberation room. Susan followed, having looked at the coffee and decided against it. She smiled at Yvonne, whose return smile was faint, noncommittal. *I'm comfortable where I am.* One toilet flushed loudly, then another. We're in this together, Susan thought. Like it or not. Twelve of us, this close, for as long as it takes.

"Nothing was said about a struggle," Susan mused. Yvonne studied her coffee. "If Black Horse . . . if the murderer took the wallet first and got angry because there wasn't much money, you'd think he would have had a hard time cutting Bertram's throat without a struggle." No response. "Wouldn't you?"

"It probably didn't happen that way."

I'm not changing my vote.

Nice try. Susan wondered if "as long as it takes" meant hours or days. She was still willing to listen to the others' opinions. She *thought* she was. Black Horse's story had some holes in it, and she was willing to have them pointed out to her. That was why there were twelve of them. Twelve viewpoints.

The trouble was, she didn't think much of some of these people. She wasn't even very pleased with herself. Tidball had taken over too readily, and she'd just sat there watching him do it. She'd imagined herself objecting to his being foreman, but imagining was as far as it went. She didn't want to do it herself, and Margaret Whalen was a lame choice. She'd hoped someone else would step in, but imagining and hoping had taken too much time, while Tidball had slid into the job the way he'd slid into that chair at the head of the table. She didn't like him. Whenever she made a point she thought was important, he brushed it aside. And he wasn't using reason or logic. It was pure attitude. Worse, everybody else was falling right into line with him.

She looked up, and there he was, sipping coffee and staring at her. He lowered the cup and affected a smile. "No coffee for you?"

"I had mine this morning."

"I guess we're all anxious to have this over with, right? Get back to the real world."

"I wouldn't want to rush and do a shoddy job here."

" 'Course not. We have to be fair. You can't expect everybody to agree right off. You're a nurse, right?"

"That's right."

"The softhearted type."

"I don't think I'm a *type* at all, Mr. Tidball."

"It's okay. You're playing devil's advocate, and that's okay. We've gotta have a little of that to make the system work."

"I'm not *playing* anything. I just don't . . ."

Tidball wasn't interested anymore. He gestured to a couple of people who were standing in the doorway. Time to gather the flock for another round of talks. They came promptly when he called, snuffing out their cigarettes, bringing their coffee. On their behalf, he said he'd spoken with the bailiff about ordering an assortment of deli sandwiches and soft drinks. Everyone approved. He said he'd told the bailiff they weren't too far from making a decision. Most of them agreed, and the rest kept silent.

On the second polling, Margaret Whalen changed her vote to guilty.

The debate continued. Other than Tidball, Larsen and Susan, there were those who said little, and those who said nothing. Ruben Kurtz put in a comment now and then, apparently to keep himself awake. Margaret Whalen nodded occasionally, but she'd been neutralized. Tammy Berg played with the lid on her cigarette box. Once in a while Gail Bender, a store clerk, would quietly agree with a point Susan made, but Tidball and Larsen had no trouble shooting her down. Susan felt boxed in. Nothing she said made any difference.

Rolf Schwap tucked a dip of chew in his cheek, worked it a little, and spat into his empty coffee cup. He spoke like a man with a mouth full of novocaine. "The fingerprint tells the whole story. Next best thing to being caught red-handed."

"I agree that the thumbprint on the wallet—the bill-fold—is incriminating. That looks bad, *but*—" Susan shook her head and sighed. She was tired of repeating herself. "A billfold isn't a murder weapon. And if he stole from the billfold, where is the damn money? Bertram bought beer—what? a twelve-pack? At the very least, there should have been ninety dollars change from that hundred dollar bill."

"Black Horse ditched it, along with the watch," Tidball theorized.

"Why would he ditch all but sixty-four dollars?"

"It looks less suspicious. It looks like he had *some* money, but not what he would have gotten from Bertram."

"And why haven't they found the money? And the watch? *And* the weapon?"

"Ten miles is a lot of territory to cover. Money blows away." He tossed his pencil on the table. Everybody watched it roll. "Watch is buried somewhere."

"But why not the ring and the bolo tie?" Susan asked patiently.

"Makes a better story." Tidball smiled humorlessly. "You fell for it, didn't you?" Sitting tall, he stretched his back. "So, see? It makes a better story."

"But there's no real proof . . ."

"There's plenty of proof."

"Hard proof."

"It doesn't make sense," Susan insisted. "He was entered in that rodeo."

It was Larsen's turn. "Black Horse might be a cowboy, but he's still an Indian. Everybody knows what they're like when they get to drinking. Sense goes out the window."

"What are you like when you're drinking, Mr. Larsen?"

"You wanna go out tonight? I'll show you."

Susan told herself she'd opened the door for that one, and she could have bitten her tongue. She shook her head and glanced away from Larsen's grinning face. "The point is that people aren't very sensible when they're drunk, no matter what race they are. There's no evidence that Black Horse was drunk."

"He admits he was drinking. That's all it takes."

"Oh, for Pete's sake, *that's all it takes*," she mimicked. "The fact that the man is an Indian has nothing to do with this, and you guys had better get that through your heads."

"Well, it might have something to do with his behavior."

"Maybe his motive."

They were beginning to echo each other. Susan didn't know how to counter the racial comments. They were too outrageous to be debated.

"Motive? Hell, I was married to an Indian." Linda Jessep's voice surprised everyone. It was as though a new face had appeared on the scene. "When he was drinking, his motive for living was to keep on drinking."

"Are you divorced now?" Susan asked. New voice, same old tune, she thought. "Maybe *that's* something you should have mentioned when they were picking the jury."

"They didn't ask me that. Besides, one jackass does not a whole tribe make." Linda folded her arms tightly beneath her breasts and glared at Susan. "I'm not prejudiced. Some of my best friends are Indians."

"Well, I can't say that I know any Indians. And I can't say for sure that Black Horse didn't kill Arnold Bertram.

I just don't think there's any real proof that he did."

A knock at the door caught everyone off guard. Gail Bender hopped out of her chair as though this might be her chance to flee. It was only lunch.

It was a relief to talk about white bread and wheat bread and who preferred regular pop over diet. It didn't matter that the animation over ham sandwiches was exaggerated. Lunch was a welcome time-out. The tension in the room eased. Susan needed a breather, but she hung back longer than the others and settled for one of the last sandwiches. She reached for wheat bread without checking the filling. She looked around for the napkins that were being passed from hand to hand, and she saw the faces of her fellow jurors. They were all smiling as they peeled the plastic wrap away from their sandwiches. Time out for friendliness. Whether it was sincere or not, let it be, she told herself. Maybe after they ate, things would be different.

But things were not different. After two more pollings, Tammy Berg voted *guilty* and asked that they break for a smoke. The bailiff brought word from the judge. Was the jury close to a verdict? Tidball returned a note, glancing up at Susan as he wrote it.

She returned a level stare. "What's your answer?"

"Eleven to one. I'd say that's pretty close."

"Yeah. And I'm about ready for supper," Schwap said.

A few minutes later, the bailiff brought another note. Tidball read it to himself first, then announced, "The judge thinks we ought to call it a day. Start fresh in the morning. After all, it is a big decision we're making here, whether to put this guy away or let him walk the streets again."

"That's not our decision," Susan reminded him. Her objections to anything Tidball had to say were coming automatically now. "All we have to decide is whether he's—"

"Guilty or innocent."

"Guilty or *not* guilty."

"Yeah, right. Same damn thing. You know, little lady, this is costing me money. Every day I'm not in my shop costs me money."

"Best job I've had in four months," Larsen said. "I don't mind coming back tomorrow."

"Well, we got no choice. Let's go home and catch some reruns on TV and just put this out of our minds for a few hours." Tidball turned to Susan. "Except you. I'd say you've got some thinking to do. You know, there's eleven of us who think he's guilty. So what are you looking at, Susan? Be honest. His big brown eyes?"

Susan was steaming. When she got this angry, she was afraid if she said much more, the tears would come. She hated that. "I'm looking at reasonable doubt," she said, managing an even tone.

"Reasonable? You're just giving Black Horse another night in limbo, *little lady*."

Chapter 5

Cleve had been stuck in a cell shaped like a sliver of pie for eighty nights and seventy-nine days. He had passed the first eight hours of his stay in the isolation cell down the hall. He'd told them he wasn't drunk, and they'd said they could see that, but he'd had alcohol on his breath, and rules were rules. Rules required him to spend eight hours on a raised slab with a mattress covered in green plastic and a matching pillow, a wool blanket, and a stainless steel toilet. A video camera, which he thought of as the roving eye, was mounted out of his reach. The deputy had offered a sweet-ass smile when she'd assured him that the camera wouldn't pick up anything when he used the toilet. Nothing but the sound.

The deputy had been Violet. He didn't care for Violet. She thought she was cute, but she wore too much eye makeup, and she was a piss-poor cook. So was Eddie, who was usually on from seven to three. The only deputy who could cook worth a damn was Myra. Myra's brown uniform was a little tight on her, but as a human being, she was okay. She made him laugh, and sometimes she slipped him a candy bar or a pack of cigarettes. When he got out of this mess, he thought he'd ask her out. She wasn't bad looking—wore her hair soft and long, the way he liked—and she and her old man had split the sheets, although the papers weren't signed yet.

She'd told him a lot about herself. Probably more than she realized. She would find an excuse once in a while to come into the dayroom, or he would come up with an excuse to call her, just to see another face. Her regular shift was three to seven, so she was responsible for supper. Thank God. She knew how to make meat and potatoes without cooking the life out of them. It was Myra who locked him down at night, too, and she liked his jokes about her coming to tuck him in. Cleve knew what she needed. She had looked after him in that way some women had of just being nice. He figured on returning the favor by giving her what she needed in that way he knew he had. The way most women liked. Nice and easy.

Cleve flopped over on his side. Jesus, it was a mistake to think about stuff like that now. He had no timepiece in the cell and no window, but he knew it was early morning, because that was when he got the horniest. He was rested and dreamy, and his mind was full of women.

So was the jury. Only four men were huddled up somewhere with those eight women. He wondered how that worked. Had they been arguing over this thing yesterday until it was too late to reconvene court? Come nine A.M. would he be looking at those twelve white faces again? He remembered the way they'd all looked at him as if they were getting ready to spit when they'd passed those photographs around. They should've seen Bertram in the flesh, with his head dangling off what was left of his neck and his blood running all over hell. They would have gotten a bellyful then.

Nobody should have to die that way, Cleve told himself. Maybe he should've said that to the jury, but he knew he couldn't have pulled it off as dramatically as Ness did. Ness had only seen the pictures, but he managed to sound like someone who had actually looked into Arnie's lifeless eyes and touched his blood. How was a guy supposed to describe that moment to a bunch of people who hadn't been there? For all the effort Cleve had put into cultivating protective calluses, he still hated the sight of spilling blood. It made him feel cold and numb, and he always had to look away.

In a moment like that he was an easy target. There had been guys in his outfit back in 'Nam who'd talk about kills and how the guy looked when he went down, what bullets could do to the human body. Cleve always made sure his kill was dead, and then he refused to think about it or talk about it. After 'Nam, he'd refused to go hunting. No more going for kills. Some guys got after him about not spurring hard enough. Some guys liked to tear the wings off flies, too. Guys like Eugene . . .

"You fight like a woman!"

Eugene was big enough to take on anybody in the high school. Cleve was younger and smaller, but he wasn't going to let the fat pig steal from him without a fight. He watched Eugene circle slowly, wagging his fingers in a come-on gesture. Cleve glanced over his shoulder and caught a glimpse of his grandfather's grin. It was enough of a distraction to allow his cousin to take another clear shot at his face. Cleve could feel the membranes bursting in his nose and the warm blood filling his nostrils. He had to open his mouth to breathe. Eugene became a watery blur. Cleve told himself he wasn't crying. His eyes were just watering.

"Now leave my stuff alone!" Eugene shouted.

"I didn't take your damn stuff, you nigger! That's my rope."

"Yours is busted."

Eugene turned to walk away. Cleve launched himself like a deer fly after a horse's rump. Rage and blood tasted the same in his mouth. He tried to get a hold on Eugene's stringy hair, but Eugene reached back and flicked Cleve off his shoulders. It was the fall that knocked the wind out of him, but Eugene laughed, and took credit for it.

"That's for calling me a nigger. I'm a full-blood. You're the nigger."

It was the worst of insults, and it had nothing to do with being black. Cleve wouldn't even run across many blacks until he joined the Army. He'd lost both the fight and the rope his grandfather had just bought him, so the insult went unanswered. His face burned with shame as he looked to his grandfather for some kind of support. The old man wasn't smiling anymore.

"Get up off the ground, Sonny."

Cleve was expected to fight his own battles. When he lost, Grandpa cleaned him up and drove him to the clinic.

He'd learned to stand up for himself. He didn't like the way this legal business worked. You had to let someone else do your fighting for you, and Felch was no fighter. Maybe the jury was battling over him now. Four men and eight women. They wouldn't convict him, not over a thumbprint. That was all there was. One lousy thumbprint on a billfold. He hadn't been charged with theft.

Felch had wanted him to cop a plea, but he'd refused. This place was bad enough. It was newer and cleaner than the little jail he'd spent four days in down in South Dakota for breaking up a bar. That had been a long time ago. He'd spent the night in jail a couple of other times— once in Fort Yates, once in Baker, Montana—but he didn't know too many cowboys who hadn't slept off a drunk behind bars once or twice. Felch had warned him that the only way to make sure he didn't get life was to plea bargain. "You're crazy," Cleve had said, which Felch hadn't taken kindly. It wasn't Felch's ass; it was Cleve's. And the state pen would kill him.

Felch had been a mistake. *If you cannot afford an attorney, the court will appoint one for you.* Sixty-four dollars wouldn't buy an hour's worth of legal advice, and Cleve had figured a lawyer was a lawyer. He'd sure been wrong about that. Felch acted like he'd had a poker up his ass most of the time, for one thing. Like

he was doing a guy a big favor to come over to the jail
and talk with him a few times. Hell, none of this was
Cleve's idea. Felch said he couldn't get the bond reduced
because of the "serious nature" of the crime. Cleve didn't
think Felch had tried very hard.

The other thing about Felch was that he thought Cleve
was guilty. He'd never said it in so many words, but
then he was a white man. White people could *say*
anything, but it took a while to figure out what they
actually *meant*.

Once Cleve had made it clear that he wasn't pleading
guilty to anything no matter what Felch said, Felch had
proposed a dog-and-pony-show defense. He'd told Cleve
to come up with a list of "respectable" witnesses who
knew him well and could tell the jury what an honest
citizen he was. Cleve knew damn well what "respectable" meant, and it rubbed him the wrong way, but he
gave it some thought. He knew some cowboys, but the
only "respectable" one he could think of had died two
years ago. He knew one rodeo clown who was a deacon
in some church, but he was laid up in the hospital with
a fractured skull. He'd lost touch with the guys he'd
known in the Army, and even if he could have tracked
them down, he didn't want to drag them into this.

He didn't want to drag *anybody* else into this. How
about "female friends," Felch had suggested in that tippy-
toe way he had of saying things. Sure, Cleve knew some
women. Some better than others, but he wasn't going to
tell the whole goddam state which ones he knew best. He
wasn't the kind of man who went around talking about
the women he slept with, and he wasn't going to ask
any woman to talk up for him, either.

Especially not his grandma. Watching her walk into
that courtroom, hobbling the way she did these days,
he'd felt as though the murder weapon had finally been
found and plunged straightaway into his gut. Felch had
wanted to put her on the stand so he and Ness could
poke pins in her the way they'd done to him. He knew
what they would have asked. Why had she, instead of

her daughter, raised Cleveland Black Horse? What kind of a grandson was he? Had he caused her much trouble? Had he looked after her once he'd become a man? Once he'd become a big rodeo cowboy?

Sparing her all that was the least he could do for her, but Felch hadn't even allowed him that—not totally. She'd had to sit there and listen to them call him a murderer. He hoped to God she wouldn't be there today. She was a proud old woman. For all that he'd taken from her and all the grief he'd given in return, he hadn't touched her pride. Not yet.

Without warning, the ceiling lights illuminated the room, and the door to the cell opened. Cleve took refuge under the crook of his arm and gave his eyes time to adjust. In another moment he tossed the blanket back and swung his legs off the cot. The wake-up calls around here were about as subtle as a bucket of cold water, but because he was considered to be such a dangerous man, his accommodations were private.

There was no line for the shower. He stood under the hot water for a full five minutes, letting it pound on his back. This was the best part of the day in this joint. He wouldn't mind spending the whole day right there, being caressed by warm water.

Or by the woman in the front row of the jury. She was pretty in a pale, fragile sort of way, and she always dressed up, like she had something important to do. Her name was Susan, and she believed him. He was as sure of her as he was of his own name. If there were an empty chair next to hers someplace and he walked up, she wouldn't try to tell him that place was taken. And she wouldn't scoot away to avoid touching shoulders with him. She had listened to him the same way she'd listened to the cops and the lawyers, with the same willingness to hear him.

Her eyes were bright blue and clear, like the carnival glass candy dish Grandma had always kept on the shelf by her bed. Once he'd held it up to the sunlight to see if her teeth were really in there, waiting to bite him if he touched that dish. All he'd seen was a pattern of blue sun catchers winking at him from inside the glass, just like those eyes in the first row of the jury box. Susan's eyes.

There wasn't any point in telling his story to anyone else on the jury. Their eyes were flat and distant. Four men and eight women. He usually did better than that with women, but not this time. It wasn't male and female this time. It was red and white, and one of their kind, a white one, was dead. You talk, we listen, wasn't that the way it was? Only one of them was listening. Cleve had been an Indian before he was ever a cowboy. He was back where he started. They wanted to talk to him or for him, but they didn't like to listen. But Felch had said the decision had to be unanimous. If they didn't all agree, it might be a hung jury. All he needed on his side was one, and he thought maybe he had that.

Cleve climbed out of the shower and dressed in his orange coveralls and scuffs. The pancakes were served with Violet's usual flourish. The tray clattered on the table, and she stood there, hip-shot and arms akimbo, with that dare-you-to-try-me look only half veiled under lashes she'd stuck on a little crooked that morning.

"Is that enough syrup for you?"

Cleve used the plastic spoon to lift the top pancake and have a look. "Plenty."

"I see somebody did up your shirt yesterday."

"Myra. I didn't ask. She offered."

"How nice. Guess today's a big day for you."

"Looks like it."

"I sure wouldn't want to be on a jury." She swung her hip the other way. "Of course, I wouldn't want to be where you are, either."

"I have a dream, Violet." He looked up from his pancakes and smiled slowly. "About you."

"What do you mean, a dream about me?"

He knew how to get this one going. She was a tease, and she had big buck fantasies that started out with the notion that a man like him had no business even thinking about her. She suspected that he tried to stop himself, but since he couldn't, she thought she'd just square her shoulders and give him something to fuel the fires of his imagination. He knew she didn't doubt that he wanted a white woman, and that she wondered how white her skin would look if she put it next to his. He'd been around long enough to have run across her type more than once. They all thought they were one of a kind. He was tempted to tell her that even after eighty-one days he wasn't desperate enough to play out her fantasies, but he resisted with an abrupt laugh.

"About once a week, same dream. It's beautiful." He sat up straight, turning more fully toward her. "I dream that you're locked up in here, and every day, three times a day, you have to eat my cooking."

"If you don't like it, you don't have to eat it."

"I know." He shrugged and went back to the pancakes. "But I've gone hungry before, and I don't like the feeling."

"Eddie'll be in to pick up the tray. However it goes, you'll be out of my hair soon."

"Actually, I've never been in your hair, Violet. Never even been curious—" Violet vacated the room in a huff, and the electronic locking system hummed in her wake. "—about what it would feel like."

Eddie brought Cleve's clothes in just before nine and told him to dress and be ready. He was ready, but the morning dragged on, and no word came. Cleve stretched out on the cot and smoked a couple of cigarettes. He only had three more. Maybe tomorrow he could go out and buy another pack. If they wouldn't let him go, maybe he'd try it anyway. Maybe somewhere between the courtroom and the correction center, somewhere along that long corridor that crossed the street, connecting the two buildings, he could convince them he was sick, and they'd take off the cuffs. And then he'd run.

Sometimes the urge to run got so strong it made him feel itchy inside his skin. It was the feeling he'd had the night of the murder. Like 'Nam all over again. Like he was hot and cold, both at once, and there were tentacles growing out of the damn trees. That night the walls of that roadside can had closed in. He'd had to get out or be trapped with death inside that little box.

Outside the men's room, it had been quiet. Dark and still. Even the crickets had gone under cover. But not the owl. In the trees that surrounded the picnic tables—inky shadows, all—the night wind rustled the leaves, and the owl's voice answered.

You? You?

Hell, no, not me.

Then *Who? Who?*

Shit, they're not getting *me*.

There was one time when he knew he had run. One time when he'd failed to hold his ground, but, hell, they'd *all* run that day. The whole damn army had run. The U.S. Army. The army that never lost a war. But the VC poured in behind them, just like Violet's syrup soaking into every pore of those heavy pancakes. He didn't like running anymore than he liked eating the pancakes on his plate this morning or the Asian mud the enemy had pushed his face in that morning so many years ago.

You can't run, Sonny. There's no place to go. You have to learn to fight your own battles, stand your ground.

He was glad the old man hadn't been there to see it. He remembered that little jungle road they'd called a highway and the tail-turning they'd called an orderly withdrawal. "Nobody likes running," the sergeant had said, "but nobody wants to get shot, either."

Was he running away that night? From what? The blood? The call of the owl?

The U.S. Army never ran. They *evacuated*. They had full gas tanks.

Cleve heaved himself off the cot and jammed his cigarette into the black plastic ashtray. He hated going into that courtroom, but he hated sitting here more. He turned on the TV to get some noise in the room, then turned it off again. It had to be almost noon. He drank cold water from the faucet in the sink, which was next to the toilet, which was next to the cot. He felt like a caged animal. Some woman he'd been with for a while had coaxed him into a pet store once, and he remembered the feeling he'd gotten when he'd seen those puppies in their cages, one stacked on top of the other. He couldn't breathe. Couldn't expand his chest. He'd told her he'd wait for her outside, and he'd gotten the hell out of there.

As soon as they let him out, he was going to find a pet store and buy one of those pups. He'd take it out to the country, to his grandma's place, and let it run free.

He'd have to get a job first, before he could liberate any puppies.

He stuck his face down close to the sink and rubbed cold water over it. When he stood up, the water ran down his neck and into his shirt.

Jesus, why did they have to spend so much time talking about how broke he was? It had probably been a year since he'd sent that old woman anything, and he was ashamed to look her in the face. Sure, there'd been times when the money had been better, but when Ness had called him a has-been, Cleve had almost blown the whole thing by leaping over the table and breaking the man's neck. Asking him about using the john instead of just pissing by the road, talking about his sixty-four dollars and his declining income—hell, they'd stripped him down in front of those women and sized up his balls for major surgery.

Maybe Susan believed his story out of pity.

Just so she believed it. Otherwise he was going to be one sorry puppy.

"You've got a visitor, Black Horse," Violet, the morning deputy told him.

"Is it my lawyer?"

No answer. Violet loved to cut him off. Cleve hated talking through that intercom, but he wouldn't mind talking to someone who could take his mind off the waiting. He'd had a couple of visits from local cowboys since he'd been arrested, and they'd told him they thought he was getting a tough break. Then they'd talked rodeo.

Cleve could always tell that someone else was on the floor when Violet came through the door with that deputy sheriff look on her face. She couldn't resist giving him her smart little smile when she clapped the cuffs on his wrists.

"If court reconvenes, I'll have to cut you short."

Cleve laughed. "You might be able to cut me off when I'm talking, lady, but there's no way you could cut me short."

She scowled as if she couldn't imagine what her prisoner would have to laugh about. Cleve was still chuckling to himself when he pulled the chair up to the window in the visiting booth and sat down. He stopped laughing when he looked into his grandmother's wizened face.

Her eyes were vacant. No shame, no disappointment, no anger—nothing. She just stared at him. Her face reminded him of neglected tack, mottled and weathered to the point that no amount of saddle soap could restore any of its former suppleness.

"Why did you come?" he asked quietly.

"Mr. Felch told me it might help you for me to be there."

He shook his head and sighed. Might have helped him with the jury, Felch meant. Seeing her there hadn't done *him* one damn bit of good. "I mean, why did you have to come here, Grandma? To the jail?"

"I caught a ride up with the ambulance. I told that driver he better not forget to pick me up, either."

Cleve had to laugh. She wasn't going to the hospital, but no matter what the government regulations, no Indian ambulance driver would deny the demand of a woman like her. By virtue of her long life, she was one of the grandmas. Her head was covered with a filmy dark blue scarf, knotted under her chin, and she wore a blue sweater over a black dress, just like all the grandmas.

"Who was the driver?" Cleve asked. Not that it really mattered, but it was a safe question.

"Marvin Tusk."

"He won't forget." Cleve heard somebody moving around in the office across the hall, and he suddenly felt pressed for time. "I'm sorry I haven't gotten home much lately."

"Your mother got so she never came back, either."

"It's not the same, Grandma. There aren't that many rodeos up here." He glanced away and cleared his throat. "I was coming to see you. After the Fourth, I was gonna drive down that way."

"Your pickup was broke down," she reminded him.

"Well, I was gonna buy another pickup after . . ." It felt like a lie, so he couldn't finish it.

"Your mother was ashamed to come back after she finally got that white bum to marry her."

The white bum was not the same man as the no-good cowboy. In Grandma's house, neither man had a name. "I'm not ashamed to come back." That was no lie, but it sounded pretty lame.

"She came back," the old woman recalled. Cleve knew what came next. "In a box. Her big white man didn't even come with her that time."

"I remember." He heard more footsteps, and he stiffened for a moment and listened, but they went the other way. "Grandma, I didn't do what they say I did." She nodded once. "You believe me, don't you?" She nodded a second time, and he released the breath he hadn't known he was holding. "Good. I don't know about that jury. I don't think they believe me."

"You think they'll keep you in jail?"

"If they say I'm guilty, they'll send me to prison."

"For how long?"

"Till I'm as old as you." He looked up and smiled so she'd know he was teasing. She liked to be teased.

"You should have stayed home, Sonny."

"There was nothing for me to do there, Grandma. They took the land a long time ago."

"I stayed," she said stubbornly. "Your grandfather stayed."

"Yeah, well, maybe I didn't belong. I'm not a full-blood. I'm not a rancher, either. I've got other fish to fry."

She glanced behind him, where there was nothing but two feet of space and yellow wall. "You belong here?"

"No." Cleve rolled his eyes and rocked back in his chair. "Christ."

"Then where?"

"In a bucking chute," he spat.

"You're all broke up, Sonny. I know how many times you've been laid up. You're gonna get killed one of these days." She lifted her chin. "You get out of here and come home."

"Don't go to the courthouse anymore, Grandma. Okay?" He waited for her assent, but she just held her chin up in the air and stared at him. "I'll come home as soon as I can," he promised softly. "Just don't go back to the courthouse."

The judge had met with the jury just before lunch for a pep talk. He didn't envy them their task, he assured them, but they were twelve honest, intelligent people, and he didn't doubt their ability to reach a verdict in this case. The jury system was the best judicial process there was, and it was up to them to see that justice was served. Their neighbors and fellow citizens were depending on them. Like all jury trials, this one cost time and taxpayers' money, but the money would have been well spent when this jury reached its verdict.

"Now, ladies and gentlemen, I charge you to go back to the deliberation room with every intention of reaching a consensus in this case. It isn't easy. It's *never* easy. But it has to be done."

Susan knew what was coming when the door was closed behind them. She took her seat, heard the sighs, tried to ignore the mutterings, and braced herself for another onslaught. She'd tried to win some of them over—the few like Tammy and Margaret, whom she knew to be capable of changing their minds. But realizing the uselessness of that effort had left her with no strategy but to refuse to give in. She began to see herself as the holdout, the one who wouldn't listen. Couldn't listen. The issue was no longer Black Horse's guilt or reasonable doubt of same. It was Susan's stubbornness. It was her need to be right, even though eleven people insisted that she was wrong. She couldn't walk away from this situation on the premise that they could think what they would. Somehow, they had to reach a decision on this. She had to keep reminding herself and trying to tell the others that what *this* amounted to was a man's life.

They came at her like harpies, pecking at her from all sides.

"What about Arnold Bertram's life?"

"Are you going to let his killer go free because you're afraid to make a tough decision?"

"Eleven of us saw through Black Horse's bullshit. Even if you can't see it, Susan, why don't you just take our word for it? *Consensus*, the judge said."

"Let's take another vote."

"You ready for another vote, Susan?"

It didn't matter whether she was ready. They voted anyway. Eleven guilties. One not guilty.

"How can you be so sure?" Susan demanded. She turned to Tidball. "I wish you'd enlighten me. I really want to know what you're basing this on."

"The evidence."

"What evidence? Name one solid piece of—"

"The blood," Larsen put in. "The pickup, the stuff in the glove compartment—everything adds up."

"It doesn't add up to anything but a maybe." Susan clenched her fists and tried to hold on as she pounded her points softly on the table. "I think you want to blame this man just because there's no one else to blame, and I don't think there's enough reason—"

"You don't think," Tidball said, sounding like a parent. "That's the problem. You feel sorry for the guy, plain and simple. He's a loser, and you feel sorry for him."

"He's an Indian."

"And you feel sorry for him," Tidball repeated.

"I do not feel—"

"I say we take another vote. You ready for another vote, Susan?"

Eleven guilties. One not guilty.

Susan dropped her face in her hands and kneaded her forehead with her fingertips. She remembered the defendant's claim that his head had been pounding that night, and the police report attested to the crack in his windshield. She felt it, too. She didn't feel sorry for him and this was *not* a sympathetic headache. It was pure frustration.

Her father had said she was too softhearted, and she ought to know a loser when she saw one. Mel Dockter was a loser in a charming package, he'd said. Her mother just said she was being stupid, letting some guy use her because she couldn't admit to being wrong about him. A hundred people could tell her what kind of a man Mel was, and Susan would go on insisting she knew better. But she was wrong about Mel, and she had admitted it. It had hurt so badly that she'd moved away, and every day now she questioned herself in all aspects but one; she was a good nurse.

Now she wondered why it hurt the way it did. Was it because she didn't want to leave Mel, or because she hadn't been right?

"Let's try again."

"Good Lord, how long is this going to go on?" Susan pleaded.

"Long as it takes, I guess. What do you say, Susan?"

Eleven against one. Can they be right? Am I wrong about this, too?

"What's it going to be, Susan?"

Reasonable doubt. What was reasonable? Who was reasonable? Had Susan ever been reasonable? She looked at Tidball, sitting there at the head of the table. He didn't look anything like her father, but she felt as though she were in her father's presence. *You always have to learn the hard way, don't you, Susan? You're too stubborn for your own good.*

"What do you say now, Susan?"

"It's wrong," she insisted, her throat burning with frustration and the tears she knew would follow. Her feeling of powerlessness became nausea. "Nobody proved anything in there."

"It's tough, but it's not wrong. Eleven votes. We just need one more, and we can go home. What do you say?"

"You heard—"

"You're the one who's wrong. You can't change eleven people's minds without a damn good—"

"All right!" Her whole face burned now, and the tears streamed freely down her cheeks. "All right, I'll say it. Guilty!" she shouted, and her voice cracked. "The man is guilty." She closed her eyes and saw his face, and she knew this wasn't right. "Somebody has to be, and it must be him."

"The verdict's in."

Cleve let the news sink in. His grandmother had left, and he'd gone back to his cell to wait. He looked up at Myra, who was standing in the doorway. She didn't know any more than he did, but there was feeling in her eyes, and it prickled him.

"What are you looking at?"

"Nothing. I'm just . . . hoping it goes well for you."

"You don't think I did it?"

"No. I don't think so."

"Whatever the jury's got to say might change things." He reached for his jacket.

"If you didn't do it, you're not guilty. Remember that." She stood there stiffly, obviously feeling awkward with the role of cheerleader. "And remember, there are appeals. I mean, you know, if . . . well, just keep that in mind. Your lawyer can always appeal."

"It's not over 'til it's over, huh?" She gave a little smile and nodded. "It ends today," Cleve said. "I've had enough of this shit."

"I hope you're not talking about my cooking."

He knew she held the handcuffs behind her hip. When she shifted from one foot to the other, she gave him an apologetic look, and he smiled and offered up his wrists. "Where do you want them? Front or back?"

She said nothing, but snapped the cuffs on him carefully, as though she were adding a decorative touch to his outfit.

"Your cooking's fine, Myra. I might even be back for supper."

"I hope not."

He'd walked the corridor many times, but it had never seemed this long. His escorts usually commiserated about their hours and laughed when he cracked a joke about his, but today they were as stoic as two undertakers. In the anteroom just off the courtroom they stopped to remove the handcuffs.

"You ready for this, cowboy?"

Cleve took a deep breath and let it out slowly. He'd had coffee and cigarettes for lunch, and his head was spinning. "I've been ready for eighty-one days."

"Good luck."

He didn't notice which one had said it, but it sounded sincere, which surprised Cleve and even lifted his spirits a little. The tall deputy led the way, and Cleve kept his eyes on the back of the man's head. Then he saw Ness and Felch, and neither of them looked too relaxed. Of course, neither of them knew anything yet. Cleve figured Felch was hoping he hadn't embarrassed himself, and Ness was jockeying for position to run for some office. When Cleve took his seat, Felch didn't say a word.

"All rise."

The judge's pace was brisk. He took his seat, glanced

at the defendant, and ordered, "Bring the jury into the courtroom."

Cleve stared at his hands while they filed by. He waited until they were all in the jury box, all seated, telling himself to keep waiting, keep guessing. If he looked at them, he'd know, and he was afraid to know.

"Ladies and gentlemen of the jury, have you reached a verdict?"

"We have, Your Honor."

They had. Cleve lifted his head, and his eyes disobeyed him, straying not to the judge, but to the twelve who knew. The old farmer, the young teacher, the pawnshop owner. No expression. No hint. The cowgirl was looking down, picking at her ragged cuticles. The older lady's soft, hollow cheeks looked whiter than usual.

"Is the verdict unanimous?"

"Yes, it is, Your Honor," the pawnbroker declared.

Cleve looked toward the center of the front row, then. Unanimous meant they'd all agreed, and he knew he'd see it in her eyes. Her bloodshot, teary blue eyes. She'd been crying.

Jesus Christ.

"The defendant will rise and face the jury, and the clerk will record the verdict."

Cleve felt the presence of the two deputies as they moved in closer behind him. They didn't have to bother. He stood, but he didn't have the heart to run. He wasn't facing *them*. Not all twelve. He was facing the sweet-faced woman in the front row. The one who had *listened*.

"Ladies and gentlemen of the jury, how do you find the defendant? Guilty or not guilty of the charge of murder in the first degree?"

"We find the defendant guilty, Your Honor."

The buzzing in the courtroom spiraled around Cleve's head like an electric saw. The woman glanced away, and a tear fell on her maroon blouse, spotting it darker between her breasts.

"Does the defense wish the jury polled?"

Felch uttered the beginning of a refusal, but Cleve

grabbed his arm. "Does that mean each one has to say it to my face?"

"Yes."

"Then, yeah, I want them polled."

The roll was called. The first voices were female. They spoke the word softly, but they spoke it without hesitation. Susan was third, and once he'd heard her say it, hoarse and regretful though it came, he ignored the rest. Maybe she'd believed him, but she had gone their way. She looked him straight in the eye and told him she had.

"Mr. Black Horse, have you anything to say before I pass sentence?"

Cleve spoke to the judge. "What's there to say? You guys just made a big mistake, but I don't suppose anybody but me is gonna lose any sleep over it." Then he turned, and the deputies jumped to attention until they realized what he was looking for. They moved aside just enough to let him see that the old woman wasn't there.

He'd made his mistakes, too, and one of them was never sparing her his first thought. She always came later. He knew damn well that over the years, she'd lost plenty of sleep over him. Then he noticed the large sign mounted above the place where she'd sat. It said, "Liberty lies in the hearts of men. When it dies, no court can save it."

He turned toward the front of the courtroom again mumbling to no one in particular, "I'm glad they didn't forget to pick her up."

"Cleveland W. Black Horse, you have been found guilty of murder in the first degree. It is a grave crime, one which deprives a family of its breadwinner and the community of one of its valued members. You are a threat to the people of this state. Therefore, you must be incarcerated to ensure our peace and safety. I sentence you to be imprisoned in the North Dakota State Penitentiary for a term of life plus thirty years. The time you have spent in the Combined Law Enforcement Center in Mandan will be counted as part of that term."

"You can try to appeal," Felch muttered.

The voice seemed distant, like everything else around him. Cleve felt a hand on his shoulder and knew it belonged to one of the deputies. They wanted to get him out of there so everyone else could go home. He glanced at Felch and saw that the look in his eyes held no promise, nor any real interest.

When it dies, no court can save it.

Part II

I could draw you hence, were you on a distant
  island;
Though you were on the other hemisphere.
I speak to your naked heart.

—OJIBWA SONG

Chapter 6

Vera Bone Necklace stuck the tape down on the baby's diaper while she watched her three-year-old rip the cover from an old issue of *Boys' Life.* A nurse passed the doorway of the small waiting room at the end of the surgical floor, pausing only to raise an eyebrow at the child and offer Vera a tight-lipped smile. Then she moved on, her crepe soles squeaking against the tile as she turned a corner somewhere down the hall.

"Don't do that, son," Vera said, but there was no threat in her tone, and the child dropped the cover on the floor and tore off the first page. "Ehhhh. Behave, now. That nurse will come back and see what you've done to her book. Then she'll be mad."

The boy gave his mother a wide-eyed, testing stare. She might have been tired, but she wasn't really angry, and she would stand between him and any white woman who might get mad at him. He tore another page, just to hear the sound it made. His mother gave in with a disgusted grunt, and when he looked at her again, she clucked to him, a signal that he should be ashamed to cause any more trouble. He left half the page intact and laid the magazine aside.

Vera counted on her husband, Tommy, to be out of her reach whenever there was trouble, and he was running true to form. She had left the four older children with her neighbor and brought only the two youngest with her to the hospital. Tommy had her car, too, so she'd caught a ride with Clifford Crow, the policeman who'd brought word of the accident. Vera didn't have a phone. Her sister, Darcy, had run her phone bill up once too often, so she'd had it taken out. Darcy was in real trouble this time, though. Vera could feel it. The doctor hadn't said as much, but she could tell he didn't expect Darcy to make it through the surgery.

To boot, Darcy was at least six months pregnant, although nobody knew it but Vera. Darcy had been on the rodeo circuit, barrel racing well into October, and she didn't want anybody telling her when she ought to quit. Vera wondered why Darcy had bothered to tell her. She knew Vera wouldn't think much of her racing around like that while she was carrying a baby, but the people who knew Darcy best didn't waste much breath trying to tell her what to do.

"I want a gum," the child on the floor announced.

Vera turned the pale orange paper over and held it up. "See the turkey, Mikey? Just like in Uncle's shelter belt." The boy reached for the pamphlet.

"Have a Low Cholesterol Holiday" meant nothing to him, and the line drawing of a Thanksgiving bird held his attention only briefly. "I want a gum."

"I don't have a gum. After a while I'll get you a pop."

"I want a gum."

"Just wait, now. Auntie's hurt. We have to wait."

Vera smoothed Mikey's thick black hair back from his low forehead. She'd have to cut it soon. It was almost down in his eyes. Vera sat the baby up and he started rooting around between her ample breasts. She glanced left and right before stuffing little Jordie's head under her sweatshirt. He latched on quickly, and she smiled as she adjusted the big white shirt over his shoulder and pulled her purple parka close around her own for a little shelter. Jordie was almost eighteen months old, and she'd decided to wean him soon. She would miss this sensuous sucking of a small, hungry mouth, and she had also decided that Jordie would be the last one for sure. She had enough children. She couldn't take care of any more.

She'd told Darcy that. Darcy didn't want to be pregnant, and Vera had told her that she wasn't raising any more babies. She wasn't going to feel bad about telling her that, either, no matter what happened. Vera never said much about the wild crowd Darcy ran with or the way she liked to party, but she had told her to go to a prenatal clinic. She'd given Darcy a pamphlet about the risks that smoking could harm an unborn child, but Darcy had left it lying on the kitchen counter. Abortion was never considered, nor was marriage, nor giving the baby up for adoption. Vera didn't suggest any of those as options. They might be somebody else's options, but not theirs. Even pamphlets could be unrealistic about what an Indian woman did, and what she just didn't do.

The trouble was, Darcy never said anything about what she planned to do with a kid. She just went right on the way she always had, trailering that white horse of hers from rodeo to rodeo and doing as she pleased with the money she was winning. She started buying her jeans a little bigger and wearing overblouses. She figured she'd have the kid in the off-season. Darcy never took anything seriously. She always left that up to Vera.

Clifford Crow had said that a bridge piling was the only thing that kept Darcy's pickup from tumbling into the river. She'd been unconscious when they'd pulled her from the wreckage. Other than that, he hadn't said much. At this point, it didn't matter why she was drunk in the middle of the day, or why she was headed for Mandan at a suicidal speed. Darcy always did what she wanted, and she never needed a reason for doing it.

The elevator bell rang. Vera sat up quickly, deftly disengaging the baby from her breast and sitting him on her hip as she stood up. He scowled at her and blinked back at the sudden brightness, but he didn't fuss. She heard the doors open and close. She watched the doorway, thinking the news might come now, and she wanted to be ready. She'd been waiting a long time, but she was used to waiting. She was used to tending children while she waited for long hours at the Indian Health Clinic or the Tribal Offices or the Bureau of Indian Affairs building. Applications, decisions, services and life's necessities—she signed up and stood in line, usually with a couple of kids in tow. She always knew when it was her turn because someone wearing a name tag and keeping some kind of list would actually look at her, the way the three people who'd just gotten off the elevator were doing now.

A man in green and a man and a woman in white. They were all medical people, and they had all the answers. Vera's heart raced as she followed them with her eyes. Either they didn't want to tell her, or they wanted it to be a dramatic moment. Where was her worthless brother, anyway? Devron should have been there. Tommy should have been there. She knew what was coming now, and she didn't want to hear it from these medical people. She held the baby close.

"We lost her, Mrs. Bone Necklace," the man in green said. It sounded to Vera as though he were speaking in a big, empty room. "There was a great deal of internal damage—kidney, spleen, bowel. And, of course, the uterus . . ."

"The baby's holding his own," the man in white said. He wore a name tag, but Vera was suddenly more nearsighted than usual, and she couldn't make out what it said. "He's small, but he's a fighter. I can tell right now, he's going to fight hard to live."

"Darcy's baby?" Vera realized that while she'd been waiting, the last thing she'd been expecting was the birth of a baby.

"Little boy. Two pounds, thirteen ounces. I'm Dr. Weeks." He extended his hand, and when Vera took it, he laid his other hand atop hers. She was not comfortable with the gesture. "I'm the neonatal specialist. Do you have more family coming?"

"No."

Dr. Weeks cleared his throat as Vera pulled her hand away. "You remember Miss Ellison from the emergency room, don't you?"

Vera glanced at Susan and tried to remember. There had been so much confusion, so many questions, so many people. All she remembered was her sister's battered face, slashed and swollen beyond the point where anyone but Vera could recognize her. But Vera would always know Darcy. It was Vera who'd seen to the damage after Darcy had been kicked in the chin by a horse or bashed in the nose by a girlfriend. Darcy would either laugh it off or cuss everyone out.

But not this time. Vera looked at the two men, then the woman again. "She's dead?" She'd expected it, but it didn't seem real, standing there in that clean and quiet place and looking up at those three distant people.

"I'm very sorry, Mrs. Bone Necklace," the doctor wearing the green suit said. "With multiple internal injuries, the pregnancy just made it more complicated. It's a miracle that the baby's alive."

Vera's own baby squirmed to get down. She shifted him around to her other hip. "It's way too soon."

Susan glanced from the child in the woman's arms to the one who was dragging his mother's big blue denim bag into the creamy vinyl seat of a waiting room chair. He wore Wranglers—Susan hadn't realized they made them that small—with red patches on the knees, and he'd lost one tennis shoe. He looked up at Susan as if to determine whether she was a tattletale before he started digging around in the bag. Usually an accident brought a family out in force, Susan thought, but here was just one sister with two little kids to worry about.

"Do you have friends here in town?" Susan asked. "Perhaps I could call—"

"No." Vera's expression was as flat as her tone. "Do I have to sign more papers? How soon can I get her home?"

"We have a day care center here at the hospital where they can look after your boys while you—"

Vera shook her head at Dr. Weeks's suggestion. "They'd put up a fight. What about Darcy's baby?"

"He's in our neonatal unit, but he's very—"

"I want to see him. Then I'll sign all your papers. I know you've got papers."

"I'll take you to see the baby," Susan offered. She smiled at the little boy in the chair, who was still searching through the denim bag. "What's your name?"

"I want a gum," the boy said.

"Mikey," his mother supplied.

"Can you find your shoe, Mikey?" Susan extended her hand to the boy. "I know where we can get some gum."

Mikey shoved the bag aside and scooted down from the chair. He wanted to know, too.

Susan stayed with the children while Carla Simpson, a nurse in obstetrics, took Vera to see the baby. Mikey was satisfied with a stick of cinnamon gum, but Jordie whimpered when his mother disappeared behind two big doors. Carla came back with stuffed bears, compliments of the hospital, for both children. That and a cracker subdued the baby.

Darcy Walker had been in labor when she was brought into ER, but she'd never regained consciousness. Susan had gone up to surgery and watched the tiny child's Caesarian birth. He was no bigger than the surgeon's hand and too frail to squall, too weak to breathe on his own. His mother was dead, and soon he might be, too. It made Susan hurt inside just to see it all happen, as though an egg had been smashed, but somehow the bird inside, a fragile wisp of a thing, still struggled. Susan smiled at the fat-cheeked baby who sat in her lap. Black hair, black eyes, tawny skin. A beautiful, healthy child.

An Indian child. Every Indian face Susan saw these days reminded her of Cleveland Black Horse. Guilt rose up in her, and she pushed it back. The trial was over. Cleveland Black Horse had nothing to do with these children. Susan was not responsible for him. She was responsible to her patients, one of whom had been Darcy Walker, and now she was doing what she could for Darcy's family.

Vera's boys latched on to their mother like magnets when she returned to the waiting area. Susan had already overextended her supper break, but Vera was visibly shaken now, even though her stoic demeanor still supported her. She sat on the sofa beside Susan and took Jordie into her lap.

"He can't live very long, can he?" Vera asked dismally. "His skin looks like tissue paper."

"He's critical, but if he can survive the first couple of days, he might make it."

"Will he be normal?"

"I don't know." Susan knew this was the time for reassurance, but she sensed this woman's greater need for honesty. She had no answers, but she could offer honesty. "I'm not sure I know what normal is."

"Darcy was normal, I guess. She liked to have fun. She loved horses. She'd take her time with them, bring them along until she could get them to do anything." Her sense of Darcy was suddenly immediate and overpowering. "She was my little sister. Just twenty-three last summer."

"I know. I'm sorry."

"I only had one sister."

"She was very pretty."

Her face was battered, her body broken, and she'd left a child. Another baby. Vera looked around her, feeling desperate. "I've already got six kids, and there's nobody else that can take him."

Susan wanted to touch the woman's hand, but touching never came easily to her. She cast about for some suggestion, some hope. "Would the father be . . ."

"Darcy was kind of wild, if you know what I mean."
She shook her head quickly. "He's so little. The doctor
said if she wasn't pregnant, she might have lived."

"No, he didn't say that. He said that she was very
badly injured, and that it was even more complicated
because she was pregnant."

"Well, she shouldn't have gotten pregnant in the first
place, and she shouldn't have been so . . . so reckless.
She shouldn't have died." Vera laid her cheek against the
top of Jordie's head. Her voice quavered. "She shouldn't
be dead."

"I know. You're going to miss her." *Oh, God, I want
to say something, do something . . .* "Usually they ask a
minister or a—"

"I told them no. I don't know anybody here, and I've
got to call somebody for a ride. My other kids—"

Susan was about to offer to drive the seventy-two
miles herself when she was paged to report to the emergency room. It would have been an empty offer, since
she was on duty, and she knew there was no one to fill
in for her. It was unusual for her to forget, even for a
moment, that she was on duty. But this woman needed
a friend. Susan went to the nurse's station down the hall
and came back with paper and pencil.

"Here's my address and phone number, Mrs. Bone
Necklace. If there's anything I can do, you know,
please . . . the baby will probably be here for a while, and
you must be his closest relative, so I know you'll be—"

"I don't know." Vera stared at the cracker in her
baby's hands and shook her head again in a gesture
of futility. "I don't know what I'll be doing, except . . .
I'll be burying my sister."

"That won't be an easy thing to do." The paper gave
Susan the excuse she needed to touch Vera's hand. It
made her feel warm. "He's in good hands here. Such a
tiny little fellow. I'll check in on him, too, and we'll keep
in touch. Okay?" Vera nodded. Her tears were gathering
now, and Susan hated to leave her. "Do you have a name
for him?" she asked gently.

"I haven't thought . . ."

"It's okay." Tentatively, she touched the woman's sleeve. "We'll take care of him. You have enough to think about right now." Vera nodded again as she squeezed her eyes shut. "I have to go." Susan hated her own hand for drawing back. She hated whatever there was inside her that kept her from being the demonstrative sympathizer she wanted to be at times like this. She called it professional distance, but she wanted to put it aside just this time. She laced her fingers together and backed away reluctantly. It wouldn't happen the way she wanted it to, but she'd offered what she could.

"What's your name again?"

"Susan." Vera's asking felt like a compliment, and she hurried to add more. "Susan Ellison. I wrote it on the paper for you. I'm on three to eleven, and otherwise I'm usually home. Really, if I can help at all . . ."

Vera's nod was slight but sure.

Beyond Vera's sight, Susan hurried to get downstairs where she was supposed to be. The emergency room staff was gearing up for another patient. Busy day, she thought. When her shift was over, she would check on the baby.

Amy Jundt nearly bowled Susan over as she wheeled the crash cart into the first bay. "Heads up, Susan. They're bringing somebody in from the pen. Stab wound." Amy parked the cart. Susan's double take made her laugh. "Lock up the good silver."

"Never mind the silver," Dr. Conlin, the new intern, put in. "Keep an eye on the drug cabinet."

Susan steeled herself as she had on two other occasions since the trial two months before. Each time an inmate was brought in, she fully expected it to be Cleveland Black Horse. It didn't matter that there were hundreds of other prisoners or that the first two had been false alarms. She couldn't drive the notion from her head that sooner or later they were going to bring him to the hospital for something. She heard the siren, saw the lights flash as the

ambulance pulled into the garage, and she pulled her
professional cocoon tightly around her as she stood
waiting. *Do your job*, she told herself. *A patient is a
patient*.

The ambulance doors swung open, and the paramedics
slid the stretcher out, lowering the wheels as it came.
Susan felt a little jolt in her stomach when she saw
his face. His pallor held a strangely yellowish hue. He
turned his head and saw her, too, and his eyes reminded
her of two black holes, drained and empty. For a moment
the commotion around them faded, and there was only a
silent mutual acknowledgment.

It's you.

Then the stretcher rolled and the commotion resumed
as a photographer followed the patient in. His handcuffs clanked when he tried to block the photographer's
efforts to get a shot of him. One of the paramedics
tried to shoulder the newsman away, but he was persistent. Susan stepped back and lost sight of Cleve's
face.

"This the guy that started it?" the newsman asked as
he trotted alongside the stretcher, still trying to maneuver
for a clear shot.

"This is the guy who's bleeding. How'd you get in
here, Reilly?"

"It's Black Horse, right?"

"You're in the way, Reilly," the paramedic said.

"What happened, Black Horse? You wanna give me
a statement? I'll print your side of—"

A security guard intervened. "Talk to the warden,
Reilly."

"I wanna hear from this guy. You think there's maybe
a powder keg out there at the pen just waiting . . ."

Reilly's questions receded into the garage as a second guard blocked his entry into the hallway. Susan
moved quickly, but she felt numb as she approached
the soles of two bare feet, which loomed ahead of her
like cutouts in a dream. Leg irons. Two armed guards
for one injured, barefoot man. Apparently he'd been

rated a high security risk. Susan gripped the rail on the stretcher and became part of the team. She saw the blanket, the safety straps, the khaki shirt, but she avoided his face.

The blood pressure cuff was in place, and the vital signs were reported as the whole unit moved like a millipede into the first ER bay. *Just do the job*, Susan told herself. On orders, she would start an IV in the brown arm with the blood-smeared hand. She was ready with the swab, the butterfly, the glucose and water. *A patient is a patient.*

"What happened here?" Dr. Conlin demanded.

"Some kind of scuffle in the shower," the slighter of the two security guards reported. The beefy one had assumed a post at the foot of the stretcher. "This guy got it in the thigh with a shiv. 'Course nobody knows how it got started or who did the stabbing."

"Not even you?" Conlin muttered to his patient as he started snipping at the bandage high on Black Horse's thigh. The khaki shirt was all he was wearing.

Cleve said nothing. His head was swimming, but he figured he might stay conscious if he concentrated on the fact that he couldn't trust anybody around him, least of all the one familiar face. He wanted her to know it, too, and he stared at her until she looked him in the eye again.

If it hadn't been for his eyes, she would have said it couldn't be him. His face was thinner, and his hair was cropped short around his ears. The quick flash of hatred in his eyes connected with the bare wires of her guilt, and there was no mistaking who he was. She had the urge to apologize to him despite the number of times she'd told herself that he was the one who was guilty, not her. But she swallowed the words on the doctor's order for an IV. She reached for Cleve's left arm, which was tethered to the right, but he jerked them both away.

"These handcuffs are kind of a hindrance," Susan said to the guard who stood behind her.

"That's what they're meant to be—for him. Can you work around them?"

"I suppose." She wanted him to acknowledge the fact that she'd tried, but he just glared at her when she laid her hand on his arm again. "Please hold still. This will only take a second. We just want to help you," she told him, hoping she sounded reassuring.

"You and every other uniform I run into these days," Cleve snapped. "Never seen so goddam many helpful people."

"Shut up," the security guard ordered. "You do what you're told."

"Then get this bitch away from me."

Susan wanted to disappear into the white curtain that had been pulled around them by one of the staff, but she took a firm hold on his arm and swabbed the crease on the inside of his elbow.

The guard at the foot of the stretcher folded his arms over his chest. "That kind of talk'll land you back in the hole, Black Horse. Haven't you learned?"

Cleve ignored the cool feeling spreading over his arm as he eyed the guard's holstered sidearm.

"Hasn't had time to learn much," the short guard said. "Right out of orientation he headed straight for disciplinary segregation. Can't get along with people. You don't get your choice of the staff here, Black Horse."

"I don't need all this conversation, gentlemen." Conlin nodded to Susan. "And this man needs blood."

"Don't waste the good stuff on him, Doc." The big guard chuckled as he returned Cleve's hot stare. "Bad man like you oughta get what he's got coming, Black Horse. Bad blood."

"Fuck off," Cleve muttered and turned away. He connected with Susan again, and for a moment she saw something different in his eyes—a fleeting question or a second thought about her trustworthiness, maybe. "You, too," he told her as he bent his arm, rattling his own chains and shutting the door on her access to his bloodstream. "Go stick your needles someplace else."

"We can hold you down, and I can stick it in your neck or your foot. You've got lots of veins, but I'd just as soon use one in your arm."

He shot her a black glance and turned away, but he straightened his arm again. Susan swabbed again. "Can you make a fist, please?" she asked quietly.

The directive almost amused him, and he didn't want to be amused. "Easy. Where do you want it?"

"Just make a fist."

He complied, and the blue veins puffed up insolently on the soft side of his arm.

"The blood's all been tested," she said as she slipped the steel point just under his skin. It was Conlin's job to explain what was going on, but the intern could just as well have been working on a cadaver. Too often, it seemed to her, the Indian patients were treated as though they didn't speak English. Black Horse's face was turned away, either from her or from what she was doing to him, but she continued to speak to him softly. "It's as safe as you'll find anywhere. The technician will take a sample and cross match yours while we get the IV started. Nobody's going to hurt you. We're all here to—"

His eyes flashed at her again. "You think you're talking to a kid, lady?" She didn't flinch. She didn't back off. He sighed and lifted his chin. His mouth was dry. Worse, he felt like he was going to puke right there in front of her. Bad enough he had to let her poke holes in him. "Just get the job done, okay?"

"Okay."

Truce. Maybe a little trust, she thought. But no explanations. He spoke English perfectly well, and he wasn't interested. She knew damn well it wasn't the IV she wanted to explain. Did she expect him to understand? To commend her? To give her some kind of blessing before he went back to his cell?

I had no choice. It was eleven to one, and the judge said things like duty and consensus, and I hope you really did it, because if you didn't . . .

Go in peace. You did the right thing.

But when was I right? Was I right when I gave in, or before that?

It doesn't matter anymore.

But it does to me because I need to be . . .

"Right?"

Susan looked up quickly and found him scowling at her. "I'm sorry. What did you say?"

"I said you're probably just as anxious to be out of here as I am. You got enough tape on that?"

Susan saw that she was pulling more adhesive tape off the roll, and she'd already taped the butterfly and its tube to his arm several times. Adhesive tape looked pretty flimsy next to those handcuffs. "Yes, I need to be—" She tried to avoid his eyes, but it was impossible. It was the same dark-eyed, mind reading look that had haunted her all these weeks. "—sure."

"You seem pretty sure." He accused her with his eyes. "Must be nice."

Amy Jundt appeared at Susan's elbow with a pint of whole blood. "I can ask them to get somebody to relieve you, Susan," she said quietly.

"No." She owed him this. Not because of the trial, she told herself quickly. She owed him what she owed any patient. "No, there's no need to do that."

"But isn't he the guy that—"

"Let's get this hooked up, Amy. The man needs blood."

"Nothing to worry about, folks," the big guard said. "This boy's not causing anybody any more trouble today. We've got him covered."

Cleve was past caring. He'd been riding on anger, but he was feeling so queasy that the anger was slipping. He felt as though he'd just killed the bottle and was ready to slide under. The baby-faced doctor had shot something into his leg, and he could feel him tugging around down there. He remembered the grin on Dietz's face, and then the shock of pain in his own thigh. He was learning the hard way. *Left you your balls, Black Horse. You might still need 'em.*

Christ, this pimple-faced kid in a white coat was dinking around too close to the same spot. Cleve wasn't even sure what he was wearing at this point. He tried to lift his head to see, but it felt like a sack of cement.

"The doctor is taking some stitches in your thigh. How are you feeling, Mr. Black Horse?"

"Rocky." She had a nice voice, he thought. Kind of like a mother's voice.

"You've lost some blood."

That must have been the kid playing doctor. Cleve ignored him. White doctors never seemed to tell you anything you didn't already know. Cleve had made a lifetime project of bleeding or breaking something on a regular basis, so he figured he was the expert here.

He looked up at the overhead light and saw the plastic bag dangling from a hook. Its long red tail stung his arm. He wondered who'd bled for him. They didn't pay for blood in this state. He knew; he'd tried selling his once. For all the bleeding he'd done, none of it had ever gone into a plastic bag.

"Are you still with us, Mr. Black Horse?"

She slid into his fuzzy field of vision. He'd lost track of what they were doing to him, but she was keeping herself busy. Pretty voice. Pretty woman.

She stood over him now. Just stood there, and she looked like maybe she was sorry. If he hadn't felt so spacy, he would have shown her his disgust. He would have turned away. But right now there was some comfort for him in the soft-eyed way she watched over him.

"Whose blood is this?" His tongue felt thick.

"I don't know," she said.

"Yours?"

"Could be."

"You give blood?"

"Sometimes."

"Figures." His head was swimming, and he knew he was talking stupid, but at least he was still talking. He didn't want to pass out now. He didn't trust any of these people. "What type?"

"I'm O positive."

"That's the good kind." Jesus, was he drunk? Sounded like he was trying out a pretty lame line. *What's your blood type?* Were they injecting him with Jim Beam? He felt like laughing. He saw an ugly, bearded face at the foot of the stretcher. "O positive is the good stuff, Gross. Comes from this nice lady here. Not some sorry sonuvabitch like . . ." He tried to find her again. She was easier on his eyes than the guard was. " 'Cept this nice lady helped put me inside."

"Don't . . . don't talk about that now."

"I thought you . . . you'd be . . ."

Susan watched him drift off. She felt sick, but she knew her strong ER constitution would carry her through. Chances are he's guilty, she thought. He wants to spread the guilt around, and you're a prime candidate.

Her self-talk didn't do much for that sick feeling, but she kept it going. She was a nurse above all else, she reminded herself. She was always able to do her job. There was never anything personal between Susan and her patient, and she had to keep it that way. Guilty or not, that was his problem. His blood pressure was her problem.

"Just about finished," Conlin announced. He turned to the nearest guard. "I want to keep an an eye on him for a couple of hours before you take him back to the prison infirmary."

"We'll be keeping an eye on him, too."

Susan wouldn't. Her job was done once he left ER. As she stepped back from the stretcher, which was on the move again, she noticed his bare feet. Too little time to get him dressed, but plenty of time to clap him into those leg restraints. Of course, it was for her protection, too. *The State of North Dakota versus Cleveland W. Black Horse.*

The leg irons rattled when Susan pulled the blanket down and tucked it around Cleve's feet.

Chapter 7

Amy Jundt glanced at the clock above the hospital information desk as she hurried past. She was glad Darlene
was busy at her post with a group of elderly women,
because she didn't want to take the time to chat. Amy
was worried about Susan, who'd probably be late for
her shift again if somebody didn't pop in on her up in
neonatal and give her a nudge. Tardiness was becoming
a dangerous habit with Susan. Even though it was never
more than a few minutes past three when she reported,
their supervisor, Marsha Ricks, always let the whole
Emergency staff know when she was watching somebody's habits. She made a point of turning her wrist
slowly and studying her watch as the nurse who was
sliding from grace walked through the door. Ricks was a
nitpicker. Amy had seen Susan get three such warnings,
and she hated to see a reprimand go into Susan's file over
the little Indian preemie she'd taken such a shine to.

Not that he wasn't a cute little guy, in the same way
newborn gerbils were sort of cute. But Susan had always
been such a paragon of professional virtues. She kept
to herself a lot, but Amy liked her. Susan was easy to
work with, and Amy wanted her to stay around. She had
the feeling that if Ricks decided to put the pressure on,
Susan might go elsewhere. In two years, Susan hadn't
developed any close ties that Amy knew about, and she

was too good a nurse to put up with the hassle if Ricks decided to get on her case.

Ricks had been on Amy's case for years, but Amy ignored her. Amy had friends in high places. Like a brother-in-law, to be exact. Griped the hell out of Ricks. Amy smiled as she pressed the elevator "up" button and watched the numbers above the door flash in reverse. Neonatal was as high as she was going today.

Susan sat beside the incubator, talking softly to the tiny child as he slept. He was too small to suckle enough to get all the nourishment he needed or to breathe on his own, but he took what the tubes brought him and made it work for him. He hadn't gained weight, but he hadn't lost much, either, and he was staying alive. It was a steep and rocky uphill climb for one so small. Susan called him Sam, after another little boy whom she'd watched fight the same battle in a different hospital. Since the first Sam had survived, Susan hoped the name would bring this child strength. Vera had approved, and Samuel Walker had become a vital statistic on the state's registry.

Sam Number One had enjoyed a distinct advantage. He'd had parents. His mother and father had wanted him desperately, and their constant vigil had been a beautiful thing to watch. Sam Number Two had his Aunt Vera, who worried about her own children every time she left them to look in on Darcy's baby. Susan sympathized with her. She told Vera to stay home and stay in touch; Sam was in good hands.

Susan could touch him only through sterile gloves. He couldn't be taken from the incubator, but Susan was there every day to help tend him and to talk to him through the plastic walls. Dr. Weeks had welcomed her volunteer efforts to provide sensory stimulation to help the infant survive, but he'd warned her about becoming too personally involved. She'd heard the doctor out, told herself to keep his good advice in mind, and continued her visits. Sam was short on family, and so was Susan.

"How's he doing?"

Susan turned, startled. She hadn't heard Amy come in. "Hangin' in there," she said. "Am I late again?" She glanced at the wall clock. Time seemed to slip by like river water when she spent it with Sam. She had to keep reminding herself that she had another schedule.

"Not yet. The ER Ogre is plotting to come down on you with both feet if you don't mend your ways pretty quick, though. What time do you generally get here?"

"Lunchtime. I usually get some lunch in the cafeteria, and then I just like to look in on him." Satisfied with the casual sound of her answer, Susan lost herself in the plastic bubble again. "He's cute, isn't he?"

"That's not really the first thought that comes to mind, but I guess he could grow on you if you were looking in on him." Amy pulled a chair up next to Susan's and sat down. It took some rubbernecking to get Susan to glance her way. "For several hours each day. You're getting too close, you know."

Susan shrugged. "His aunt has six kids, and she's really all he's got. I've got a lot of time on my hands. You know what the research shows about how much babies need to be touched and held, and a preemie in an isolette needs—"

"Needs to bond. It works both ways, you know."

"I can handle it."

"As soon as he's strong enough, they'll send him down to Fort Yates to the Indian hospital. That's if he lives."

"He'll live. Just look at him." A smile softened Susan's slender face. "Watch his little mouth move. He'll be sucking on a bottle pretty soon."

"And you'll be up here feeding him."

"Won't that be wonderful? When I can . . . when he can be taken out and fed? He's really a miracle baby to have survived what he did."

"He's not out of the woods yet, and when he is . . . How much do you really want to handle?"

"I just want to see him get stronger."

"We all want that, but you've always seemed like the model of professionalism. You do your job well, but you keep an emotional distance."

"Sometimes you have to give a little more, just to be sure you still can."

They watched the sleeping baby together. His mother-lessness sent silent distress signals, but only Amy steeled herself and turned her face aside. "Does this have anything to do with that man getting sent to prison, Susan?"

"What do you mean?"

"Just that you were on the jury, and now he's in the pen. He's an Indian; so's the baby. I don't know. It just seems—"

"This baby didn't kill anyone."

"Did that man?" Susan looked surprised. She glanced at the clock and folded her arms tightly around her middle, as though for protection. Amy didn't really want an answer now. "You should have asked to be relieved when they brought him into ER, Susan. That was risky, for you to be around him like that."

"They had him shackled, hand and foot." Her voice was hollow, her eyes darkly haunted. "I don't think there was much danger of his attacking me."

"Maybe not, but you didn't need to see—"

"Besides, he'd lost so much blood, he could hardly lift a finger."

"That wasn't what I saw." Amy laid her hand on Susan's arm. "And it wasn't your fault that he got hurt, Susan."

"I know that. He was just another patient."

"Like this baby's just another patient?"

Susan fought to ignore Amy's hand. Her instinct was to move, stand, turn away. She thought about Cleveland Black Horse. "I don't know whether he really killed that man, Amy. He said he didn't, and his story seemed plausible. They never found the weapon or the—" Somebody else ought to know this, she told herself. It wasn't a confession, exactly. She'd tried to put it behind her, tried not to talk about it, but that just made her think about it more. "There were too many unanswered questions as far as I was concerned, but the rest of the jury . . . well, I guess I let them convince me to . . ."

"I'll bet anyone who's ever been on a jury like that goes through the same thing you're going through. You didn't need to be in ER when that man came in. That's what's skewed your perspective."

"That's ridiculous." She wasn't *anyone*, and it didn't matter who else had been through it. Friendly as Amy's face was, Susan saw no glimmer of empathy in it. She glanced away. "Anyway, Cleveland Black Horse has nothing to do with this baby." Sam's hair would be just as dark and thick, but his eyes would be smaller, and he might never be able to carry his slight shoulders as squarely. "He really doesn't look like a murderer, does he?"

Amy smiled at the child, who lay unnaturally still. He lacked even a good startle reflex. "Hardly. But he does look like a prisoner."

"All right, all right." Susan scowled. "I meant Black Horse."

"I don't know what a murderer is supposed to look like, but I will say that guy looked pretty angry."

"Wouldn't you be angry if somebody stabbed you in the leg while you were taking a shower?" Amy raised a teasing eyebrow. "Seriously," Susan insisted.

"If I were in prison for murdering somebody, I guess I'd expect—"

Susan waved Amy's expectations away. "There's a lot of prejudice around here. Sometimes it's subtle, sometimes blatant as hell."

"Against Indians?"

"You should have heard the way some of the people on that jury talked. The men were just plain pigheaded, and the women went along with them, I think out of habit. Or maybe it was just easier that way. The path of least resistance."

"Maybe. But you said they convinced you."

"I said I *let* them—" She shook her head and jammed her hair behind her ear with a flick of her fingers. "Oh, the hell with it. It's done now. I'm only one person, right?"

"Right."

Susan nodded toward the isolette. "That's Sam, too. Just one little person."

"Let's go to work, Susan."

Sam took his first bottle from Susan's hand. As the weeks passed, she was there often to take him from the isolette and hold him, feed him, and change him. On the pages of a purse-sized calendar she charted his growth gram by gram and centimeter by centimeter. She wrote nothing down while she was on the floor, but she held the numbers in her head until she got to a private place—her car or the women's bathroom—and there she made notes. Once when she'd strayed into the children's department at Dayton's, she'd thumbed through the pages of a baby book. She caught herself reading Sam's entries on the empty lines, and she put the book back quickly, glancing around like a would-be shoplifter.

Dreams were one thing, foolishness another. When it became public, it looked foolish. Her calendar would look foolish to the people she worked with. Worse, it might look serious. Amy might ask her for reasons, and Callie would question her plans. Susan had neither.

At least, not until Sam was transferred to the Indian Health Service Hospital seventy miles away. Susan wasn't there to see him go. The government had paid his bills in Bismarck until he no longer required intensive care. The order came down, and the ambulance was there to take him to Fort Yates. Susan had known it was coming, but she hadn't prepared herself for the rock-bottom loneliness she felt when she approached the big window and saw a strange child in Sam's isolette.

Two days later, she saw the classified ad headed "Nurses Needed." Four days after that, she drove to Fort Yates for an interview.

* * *

Vera Bone Necklace squinted as she peered through a multicolored row of T-shirts that flapped in the crisp February breeze. A gray car slowed near the edge of her barren front yard. Nice car. Pretty new. No dents. Didn't belong to anyone she knew. Dismissing it, she lined up two more shoulders and pinned them to the plastic line.

Vera got a look at the woman in the gray car as she ducked between the legs of a pair of jeans to reach for the laundry basket. It was that Susan Ellison, getting out of the car right there in front of Vera's place. That white nurse from Bismarck. What could she want here?

Vera snatched up the basket and shoved it inside the back door while the mutts, Elvis and Bigfoot, raced around front trying to see which one could yowl the loudest. The neighbor's dogs joined in, but for once they stayed in their own yard. Vera followed her dogs along the pathway between the side of the house and her husband's two junk cars. The yard was full of junk. A bicycle with two flat tires, a dead car battery, a piece of deer carcass that one of the mutts had stolen. Vera wanted to go inside and close the door, but the nurse was looking at her and smiling as though she maybe didn't notice anything else.

"Hi, Vera! I had to ask for directions twice, and the second boy I asked said he was your nephew. How are you?"

"Good." She offered her hand and thought it was nice that Susan removed her glove for the handshake. She wondered which of her brother's boys had been so unusually cooperative.

Susan shoved her hands in the pockets of her trim blue coat. The big, black, flop-eared bitch growled, but the yellow male cranked his tail in a wild circle and wagged his whole back end. It struck Susan that the tail was wagging the dog, and she laughed. Then she said, "I came down to see Sam, and I ended up getting a job at the hospital."

"Here?"

Susan nodded. "I've always wanted to work in a rural

clinic. This is a nice little hospital, and they offered housing and really good benefits, so I thought, this is my chance." Vera didn't seem to notice how cold it was. They'd visited a couple of times in the sitting room down from Newborn Intensive Care and had coffee together the day they'd named Sam. But Vera seemed to be staring right through her, as though she'd forgotten who Susan was. "You're the only person I know in Fort Yates, though. I just thought I'd—" She glanced down at her toes, which looked silly in a flimsy pair of pumps on a day like this. The unsodded yard was hard-frozen, cracked and brown. "—stop by."

Vera cocked her chin toward the front door. "The little ones are asleep inside."

"Oh. I wouldn't want to . . ."

"But you can come in." Vera waved her hand and hissed, and the dogs slunk away from the steps. She led the way. There was no storm door. "You drink coffee?"

"If it's no trouble."

The baby had fallen asleep in a playpen in the corner of the room. Vera had picked up the deck of cards the children had scattered earlier, and she'd scrubbed spilled milk and puppy pee from the linoleum. The room smelled of Pine-Sol and fried macaroni, which she'd cooked for dinner. She directed Susan toward the kitchen table, where she'd set a box of groceries she'd collected at the commodity warehouse that morning. A dairy surplus meant extra cheese this month. "It's kind of a mess," she mumbled as she moved the box.

"Oh, well, you should see mine."

Vera knew exactly what she'd see. Little glass figurines, pictures of flowers and girls in pink dresses, clean walls and thick carpets and everything in just two colors. "You can tell I've got a house full of kids."

Susan hung her coat over the bright yellow vinyl backrest of a kitchen chair and smiled. "Yes. They really do fill a house, too, don't they?"

Vera decided the coffee in the percolator was still

good. She took two mugs from the cupboard. "You got any cats? I'll bet you've got a cat."

"I had one in Minneapolis, but I gave her to my mother."

"Dogs?"

"No. No dogs."

"We've got puppies out back. Kids keep bringing them in, and they make a mess. I don't like to have dogs in the house."

"I don't blame you." Susan made a point of not looking around, but she noted that the house was clean, if sparely decorated. It wasn't fair to pop in on somebody without calling, but Vera had no phone. "Sam's doing well, don't you think?"

"You use sugar?" Vera opened the refrigerator and stuck her head in. "I've got milk, too," she called out from behind the door. "Real milk, not powdered."

"Black is fine." Susan accepted the steaming cup with a nod and a whispered "Thanks." It tasted like ashes. Susan smiled. "He's gained two ounces since I last saw him."

Vera sat across the table, set her coffee down and ignored it. "He's almost three months old, and he still looks kind of pitiful, like he was just born yesterday."

"It's been an uphill climb for him."

"He's retarded, isn't he."

It came more as a statement than a question, but Susan suspected that Vera had been told very little and had asked few questions. "He's developing slowly."

"But he's going to be retarded. You can just tell." Vera shook her head slowly while she examined the slicks that floated over her coffee. "Darcy didn't take care of herself. She kept right on acting like she always did. Crazy and wild."

"It's hard to tell how much damage that accident caused, how much damage her drinking might have caused, or whether—"

"I knew it." Vera slapped the table. "I read a pamphlet about it. Alcohol syndrome something."

"Fetal Alcohol Syndrome. I don't know if he has that, Vera. Neither do the doctors. Sam was so small at birth and suffered so much trauma from the accident, it's hard to predict what kind of development we can expect. But we know he's going to need special care."

Who's we? Vera thought, but she decided to ask, "What kind?"

"Well, he'll need therapy, for one thing. Infant stimulation, where they kind of have to show his muscles what to do to make his arms and legs work. He's going to be slow to crawl, slow to walk."

"Slow to think." Vera slid her palm along the edge of the table and let the anger bubble up again. "That damn Darcy." It surprised her to hear the words, even though she'd thought them many times. Darcy was young and pretty and had everything going for her, but she didn't appreciate any of it. It was like she'd just up and checked out, flipping everybody off as she went. And Vera was doing her damnedest not to hate her for it. She looked at Susan. "I shouldn't say that, should I? She's dead. She was my only sister, and she's dead. I should be glad for that baby. Glad to have something left of her." She gripped the chrome edge of the table. "I *am* glad."

"I'd like to help you take care of him," Susan offered quietly.

"Is that why you took a job down here?"

"It's probably part of the reason. I think he knows me. I think he recognizes my voice, and I think . . ." Vera looked surprised. *Don't push*, Susan told herself. *You'll scare her off.* "It's a good job, and it's a new challenge. That's the main reason I came."

"You've never had a baby?"

"No." Vera still looked puzzled. "I've never been married, either."

"Never wanted to get married?" Susan glanced away, and Vera chuckled. "Sometimes I wonder why I ever did. But the kids are worth it, you know? It's just that they suck up all your time and energy, till you've got nothing left for yourself. Another baby, geez . . . They've asked me if I'm going to take him."

Susan didn't want to know what Vera had said. "He's better off where he is right now."

"I know. They said his digestive system isn't developed enough yet." Vera knew she shouldn't have been relieved when they'd said that, but she was. She wanted them to keep him for a while. She wanted them to tell her that it was the best thing.

"And they've got him on a heart monitor." Vera was staring into her coffee again, which made it easier for Susan to say her piece. "I want to help, Vera. I want to do as much as . . . as you'll let me do."

"I'm scared to bring him home, you want to know the truth. This time of year, we've got ear infections and colds, one after another." *Jesus, Mary, another baby.*

"When he's ready—" Susan folded her hands tightly in her lap and prayed this be no offense. "I could take him."

"You mean, like, foster care?"

"I mean—" *Please, don't say no, don't say no, don't say no.* "I would really like to be Sam's mother."

"Darcy was—"

"I know." Susan raised both palms. "His real mother. I wouldn't forget that. But I'm a nurse. I could . . ." *I could really botch this if I don't back off.* "It's something to think about, Vera. There's time. For now, if you'd just let me help you with him . . ."

Vera thought for a moment and smiled. "Looks like little Sammy's got his own private nurse."

Chapter 8

❧❧❧❧❧   ❧❧❧❧❧

The faraway whistle wooed Cleve away from a good sleep. *Long train comin' at you, loverboy. Turn over and get yourself primed.*

Sweet, sweet sound, starting soft and slow, coming on steady. The bedsprings squeaked as he shifted to his side and slid his hand into his shorts. He could see her pushing through the mist, banking a curve and hugging the river as she came to him. Again she whistled.

Coming closer, darlin'. Gonna take you away with me.

He pressed the side of his face into the pillow and dreamed of riding her, fast and free all the way to the end of the line. His heart tried to tag its rate to her rhythm as he lay there letting her build up his steam. Chug chug. Chug chug. Chugchug chugchug chugchug. She roared over him, pumping him hard and filling his head with her wild cries. *Ride on, baby, ride on.* God, she was good. She didn't care if the whole cell house heard her. The hell with them. She was his. His own Midnight Special, shining her everlovin' light on his worst nighttime needs.

Cleve released a long, slow, unsteady breath and reached for his cigarettes. Good sex called for a good smoke. He wondered if he'd ever be able to look at a train again without getting a hard-on. Chances were he'd never see one again except through a chain link fence, anyway, so the old Soo Line was probably safe. Good old Susie.

Susan.

Shit. Where had that come from? Any bitch but that one, he told the fantasy maker in his head. Talk about chain link fences—Nurse Susan had helped forge his. She might be a turn-on if he decided to resort to mental masochism.

He lit his cigarette and went back to trains. Trains made good lovers. They covered up their tracks, along with a guy's heavy breathing and his occasional groan. Maybe he wasn't fooling anybody, probably nobody gave a damn how he got off. He'd been in this hellhole for over a year, which was long enough to know the meaning of every sound that came down the tier in the dark of night. He'd learned to listen for the kind that might be a threat and let the rest drift past. Except the trains. He lost himself on a train whistle's wail.

He thought about another time and another Cleve, so young and green and hungry for the high life that he'd walk twenty miles or better just to enter up in some backyard jackpot rodeo. Walking was good for him, his grandmother used to say. After his grandfather died she used to let him start up the old blue Ford once in a while, but no way in hell would she let him drive it out of the yard. So Cleve usually ended up walking as far as Little Eagle, and if he couldn't find a ride there, he kept walking.

He drew deeply on his cigarette and imagined the gravel skittering beneath his boots, the clay ruts carved in the roller coaster road to town, and the sun warming his face. He could hear the crow and the meadow lark. Then along came the freight train, bursting onto the scene between two buttes and sailing past him the way a jackrabbit might pass up a toad.

Cleve took another slow drag and blew the kind of cloud that train would leave behind. He liked the way the big cars made the tall grass bow down as they flew by. Freight car, freight car, cattle car, cattle car, coal coal coal coal, freight again. Green and white for Burlington Northern, brown and white for Soo Line. He remembered running along with it, fast and free, and imagining a long gray trail of smoke in his wake. He loved that long, low whistle. *Look out, up ahead. Train coming through.*

He couldn't keep up, but his spirit tagged along even when he slowed to a chest-puffing jog. Back in those green spring days he'd dreamed of cutting a wide swath, just the way the train did. He was going to cup his hands around his mouth and shout it out. *Look out, up ahead. Big man coming through.*

Yessir, he was a train lover. Sexy Soo. He chuckled. That was him. Sexy Sioux.

Sue.

Susan.

Sexy, hell. Think about trains.

He thought about how he and Billy Bad Heart used to walk the tracks when they were kids. Whenever the train came, they'd wait 'til the last second, wait for the whistle and the terrible look in the engineer's eyes before they dove for that sea of grass and rolled over and over, exactly the way they'd seen it done in movies. Cleve would squat down on his heels, plant his knees in the grass and peer through the quick succession of wheels to make sure Billy was on the other side. They'd make their boasts, but they never really knew who'd waited longer to make the jump. If either of them had a penny or a nickel, it had been left on the tracks to be flattened by those clack clack clacking wheels. Having that coin in your pocket was like carrying a piece of the train, a measure of its power and speed.

Once they'd jumped into a boxcar on a train that was pulling away from the McLaughlin stockyard. It was dark inside and reeked of fresh cow dung, but they'd found a dry spot in the corner of the car, where they'd braced themselves when the car lurched forward. They inhaled dust and smoke to fuel their bravado, looked each other in the eye and swore to ride to the end of the line. Then they peered through the slats and watched the little South Dakota town slide away.

The landmarks flashed by in Cleve's memory. Ranches owned by white cattlemen who ran their stock on Indian land. Gravel roads that led to Indian towns, where the owners of those pastures lived in dirt-floored log houses or three-room shacks built by the government as payment for land it had taken for its dams. A billboard advertising the world's best steak at a local restaurant made the boys wish they'd eaten before setting out for the end of the line. Years later, when Cleve had become a connoisseur of T-bones, he'd gone back for the steak he'd hungered for as a boy, and he had found the ad's claim to be true. A steak like that would have kept him home that day.

By the time they'd sped past Rattlesnake Butte, which rose over the rippling prairie grass like a coastal promontory, they'd begun to feel homesick. Mobridge, at the southern border of the reservation, was the end of the line for them. It had been a long hike home. Cleve smiled as he remembered the look on his grandma's face. She'd betrayed a little bright-eyed pleasure before she'd lit into him for being gone all day and most of the night. Damn, she was mad! She reminded him of a gimpy mule when she ran, and she'd almost caught him that time.

Cleve stubbed his cigarette out in the ashtray on the nightstand and turned his face to the wall. Thinking about home was almost as stupid as thinking about women. *Think about trains.* What he thought was that, if he had another chance, he'd let that train take him as far as it went, and then he'd hop the next one. Beyond that chain link fence, one road led to another, and another. Inside it, he'd found the end of the line.

He dozed a little, but couldn't get back to sleep. Finally he gave up. He was on the kitchen crew, which meant he had to get up earlier than everyone else. But it put him on the second tier of the cell house, which was one hell of an improvement over the fourth tier, where all new "fish" started out. The East Cell House was close to ninety years old, one of the few warehouse-style cell blocks still in use. It was a four-tiered human zoo. The top tier was always hot, no matter what the season. The cigarette smoke and institutional stench gathered up there like a thick cloud of refinery waste.

Straighten up your act, they'd told him, and you'll move down and eventually into one of the newer units. But Cleve had spent most of his first year on the fourth tier, except when he was in The Hole—Disciplinary Segregation—for fighting, missing count, verbally abusing his least favorite officer. Once he drew a stint for getting drunk with Whitey John, who'd lived in the next cell, the "house next door." Whitey had paid dearly in cigarettes to have a pint of Everclear smuggled in on a delivery truck, and he was a good neighbor. He liked rodeo. After lights out they'd quietly passed the bottle between them until Cleve managed to forget why he'd always made a point to stay away from Everclear. The regular three A.M. count was their undoing.

Cleve brushed his teeth and washed his face in cold water. He'd disciplined himself to quit wishing for morning showers and to forget that somewhere in this world toilets came equipped with seats. It was that kind of remembering that got him into trouble. The little things ate at him, like sitting behind bars and waiting for "the man" to come by and count you in with a population of convicts, or like watching him go through the drawers in your nightstand, examining your state-issued underwear. Cleve tried to tell himself it was no worse than being in the army. You followed rules, stuck to the schedule and didn't bother anybody who didn't bother you.

Joe Dietz had bothered him, and the next time Dietz had made a move, Cleve had felt obliged to return the favor. Not with a homemade shank in the leg, which was Dietz's style, but with a paralyzing ball-buster and a broken nose, done with a quick knee and a deft hand. Cleve had enjoyed watching the sneer vanish from Dietz's face like a comic double take. He'd recalled that expression often during his fifteen-day stay in the hole, which struck him as a small price to pay for so much satisfaction. Later he'd learned that the incident had earned him a measure of respect from the other inmates. Respect was fine if it meant being left alone by all the jerks in this place.

Cleve didn't mind working in the kitchen. It was better than the laundry, where he'd started out when they'd finally given him a job. As a troublemaker he'd drawn a lot of time as an unemployable "lay-in," which meant hanging out in his six by nine foot cell and going out of his mind with boredom. It also meant earning no money for commissary purchases or for hiring a decent lawyer to get him out of there.

He wasn't getting rich at a dollar sixty-five a day, but he'd gotten a friend to claim his pickup and sell it for him. Three hundred dollars was a start. The only other thing he had of any value was his saddle, and he wasn't selling that. He was also learning to be thrifty. Except for two pair of jeans, purchased at the commissary, he wore state-issued clothes. He bought cigarettes, but he decided he could do without a radio or a TV or even an electric fan, all of which could be purchased through the commissary with pay earned inside and stored up in an inmate's account. Use of the library and the gym were free, and Cleve used both regularly. He'd also decided to apply for a chance to take some college classes.

In the kitchen John "Baker Man" Kohler ran a clean operation. Everybody scrubbed up and wore a hair net around the food, and nobody moved from one task to another without cleaning up after himself. Weekly menus were posted, and Kohler's recipes were followed to the letter. It was prison policy to see that inmates ate well. The food wasn't half bad. In fact, the Baker Man's bread was as good as anybody's mother's.

"Hey, Bro."

Cleve didn't turn around, but he mumbled a greeting to Grease McKay while he dried his hands. He didn't want to be anybody's "bro," least of all a sleazy slick like

Grease's, but Indians behind bars were pretty clannish, and Cleve didn't want to be accused of being an apple, either. Red on the outside and white on the inside could get you trouble from all sides. He took a butcher's apron from its hook and slipped it over his khaki shirt. He'd adjusted to the idea of wearing an apron, but the hair net still felt like a damn spider's web.

Grease sidled up to Cleve and whispered, "Got an extra smoke?"

"Christ, Grease, why don't you get your own?" Inmates were prohibited from borrowing, loaning, or giving each other anything. Selling any property had to be done through prison authorities. But Grease was a compulsive moocher. Cleve wondered why they didn't put him in treatment for it; they had therapy for everything else. Moochers Anonymous. Why not? He took another apron down and handed it to Grease, along with a cigarette.

"I will. I'm a little short this week, but I'll pay you back, Bro." Grinning, Grease jerked his chin in the direction of the group that was gathering around the door to the chef's glass-walled cubicle, which served as an office. "See the new fish? What do you think a pitiful-looking white boy like that would have to do to get himself in here?"

Cleve gave the boy a cursory glance. Red hair and freckles, for God's sake. Skinny as a fence post. Must've been some hard-assed judge who'd put a kid like that inside. Grease was still grinning. "Why don't you ask him?"

Grease cackled. "Somebody might see me talking to him. Ruin my rep."

"As what? Big Indian?"

"As a man, Bro. Look at him." He laid a hand on Cleve's shoulder. "What do you wanna bet he likes little boys? Probably why he's here."

Cleve pulled away and headed for the coffee urn. "Why don't you borrow some dish·soap from the Baker Man and wash your hair, Grease?"

"Whatsa matter with my hair? I wash it."

"Yeah, well, stay away from my coffee." He filled a cup and made a pretense of checking it out before he sipped. "Can't stand greasy coffee. What are we cooking, Baker?"

The chef joined Cleve at the coffeepot. He liked this cowboy, even though he'd been hell on wheels after he first came in. After fourteen years on the job, Kohler had learned to get along pretty well with murderers and thieves. Some of them, anyway.

"French toast. You're gonna slice bread, Black Horse. You and the new kid over there. Dawson's his name."

"You gonna trust me with a knife again?" Cleve followed Kohler to his glass box and watched the key slide into the lock. Possession of keys separated the good guys from the bad guys. "That's two days in a row."

"It went so good yesterday, thought I'd try it again." Kohler handed him a knife, and Cleve signed for it. "Inch and a half slices. Don't skimp. Nobody likes a skinny piece of French toast."

Jimmy Dawson approached Cleve cautiously. His palms were sweaty, and his spit was clogging up his throat. He knew who Cleve was. He read the newspapers. He'd also seen a lot of prison movies, and Cleve looked as though he could've played a leading role. He was an Indian. Probably had himself an Indian gang that lifted weights together and preyed on white guys who got themselves into this place for being sick and stupid. Jimmy hung back until Cleve turned from the bread board and scowled at him.

"Okay, Dawson, the knife's checked out to me, so it looks like you take the bread over and soak it in that stuff." Cleve pointed to a stainless steel bowl full of the Baker Man's specially seasoned egg batter. "You do this right, you never know what kinda challenge might come along next."

Jimmy offered a tentative smile. That was a joke. The muscle-bound murderer wearing a hair net had made sort of a good-natured joke. Geez. "You been, uh . . . working in the kitchen long?"

"A while."

"You've had other assignments? What's the best one?"

Cleve grunted and pushed a stack of sliced bread across the board with the blade of the knife. "Sleeping." He shrugged and added, "Depends on your talents."

"What did you do?" With a cool glance, Cleve warned him to watch it. Jimmy swallowed quickly. "For a living, I mean. Before you came here." He knew the answer, but he wasn't sure if it was okay to talk about it, and he wanted some hint.

"I made French toast."

"You don't strike me as a cook," Jimmy said, smiling tentatively.

"If I strike you, kid, you'll know you got too nosy."

"Sorry."

The kid had a lot to learn, and he was obviously scared shitless. It wasn't fair to put a wimp inside. Cleve wasn't about to wet-nurse one, either, but he couldn't stand watching the way the kid's hand trembled every time he reached for a piece of bread, as though he expected to lose a finger any minute.

"I was a rodeo cowboy."

Jimmy's milky, freckled face brightened. "Oh, yeah, I can see you doing something like that. Bulls?"

"Bulls and broncs. You wanna move this along here?"

"Sure." Jimmy popped several slices into the bowl at once. "You like working in the kitchen?"

"Beats cleaning toilets."

"Yeah, but everybody has to do that. Nobody's going to do it for you." He looked up to confide, "I just got out of orientation."

"No shit."

"Yeah. You know, some of it doesn't look so bad. After a while you can get music lessons, take college classes, even take up a hobby. Like leather tooling. Ever done any leather tooling?"

"Nope." He had, but it was easier to deny it.

"You could make your own saddle or something."

"I got a saddle."

"Well, you could make something else. I did some leather tooling when I was in high school."

"You don't look old enough to be out of high school."

"I'm almost twenty."

"Jesus." Cleve shook his head and reached for another loaf of crusty bread. "Not even old enough to drink yet."

"I don't drink, anyway. I went through treatment when I was in ninth grade." Jimmy figured a show of trust might put the leader of the Indian gang on his side. "So how long have you really been here?"

"Too long."

"I'm in for three years." Jimmy took a deep breath and quietly confided, "I don't think I can take three years."

The kid wanted to cry on his shoulder, and Cleve didn't want to hear any more. Damn kitchen was heating up. He wiped the side of his face on his shirt sleeve. "Think of it this way. In three years, you can get your two-year degree while you're making leather belts for your whole family."

"Nobody in my family would wear any belt I made them."

"Then sell the damn belts." Was he supposed to feel sorry for somebody who only had to do three years? "How much more bread you need, Grease?"

"Just keep it coming, Black Horse. Looks good. Looks tasty." Kohler was everywhere at once, sticking his nose over each man's shoulder to make sure the meal was prepared to his satisfaction. A security officer watched over the inmates, too, but his interest was not in the cooking details. "Get the syrup out, Richardson," Kohler ordered another crew member. "Short line's coming in thirty seconds."

"Are we in the short line or main line?" Jimmy asked Cleve. "They told me, but I forgot."

"We're not in any line, fish. We get what's left."

Work in the kitchen took up most of the morning. At 11:15 all areas were cleared, and inmates returned to their cells. Cleve hated the loud metallic slam the automatic locking system made when it shut. At least four times a day, every day. Slam! Locked into that box and counted, the way he used to have to count the old man's cows. But then he'd been on horseback, and there was a clear blue sky over his head and grass rippling across the hills as far as the eye could see.

He lit a cigarette and cussed himself out for letting the thought of a horse between his thighs creep into his head. Last summer he'd been in Disciplinary Segregation during the annual prison rodeo. He'd told himself he didn't want to ride anyway. Not behind a scroll of barbed wire that was put there to contain him instead of the livestock. This year he was going to ride. It was four months away, but he could already taste the arena dust.

The guard's heels clicked along the metal tier as he approached, counting his prisoners. Cleve sat on his bed, elbows planted on his knees, and blew a stream of smoke as "the man" walked by, counting aloud. Cleve wasn't a man. He was a goddam number. He wore it with his picture on the ID card clipped to his left shirt pocket. Number 15359. Rodeo cowboys wore numbers. Basketball players wore numbers. Soldiers wore dog tags with numbers. Cleve had been all those things. Number 15359 was different. It was a number that disgraced a man's name. He wondered if anybody in his family would wear a belt he'd made in the prison hobby shop.

After the count cleared, the staccato lock-popping sounded down the line. Back to work. Dinner was served to the main line, followed by exercise class. The weather was pretty good for March, and Cleve was bursting to get outside. Fully one-fourth of the inmates were Indians, and every one of them had cut his teeth on reservation-style run-and-gun basketball. For an hour and a half, it didn't matter where they were. They had two hoops, a ball and an asphalt court that could have been the best part of any BIA school yard.

Jimmy Dawson had been assigned to the volleyball game that was going on next to the court, and Cleve tried to ignore the fact that the fish was taking a lot of heat for being pretty damned useless to his team. That kid was going have to start looking out for himself, or else getting walloped in the gut with a volleyball was going to be the least of his worries. But it wasn't Cleve's problem.

Cleve whirled at the shriek of Coach Bremmer's whistle.

"Traveling! Ball goes to white."

Panting heavily, Cleve scowled into the sun. "Traveling, my ass!"

"Traveling, you *wish*," one of his teammates razzed.

Cleve fired the ball at a spot two feet in front of the prison recreation director, and it bounced into Bremmer's hands. "Give it a rest, Black Horse. Substitution," he called to the sidelines, and Whitey John trotted out to the court for the red shirt team. Cleve backed off, wiping his face on his sleeve. The breeze felt cool in his damp hair. Considering how short-winded he'd gotten, he knew the last thing he needed was a cigarette, but he lit one anyway.

"They kick you out, too?"

"What?" Cleve turned toward the voice and found Jimmy Dawson smiling up at him. Kid shouldn't smile, he thought. Made him look like a girl. "You mean the game? Coach needs glasses. We're taking up a collection."

"A collection? I thought we weren't supposed to have any money."

"We're gonna use commissary tickets. Get him some Coke bottles." Cleve laughed. "You take everything too seriously, kid."

"Well, I'm . . . a fish out of water, you might say."

"That's funny. That's a real hoot. You keep it light, you'll be okay."

"Did you keep it light when you first came here?"

"No." Cleve spat a stream of smoke. "Hell, no, I wanted to kill anybody that crossed me."

"I remember reading about you." Jimmy waited for another warning, but Cleve was watching the basketball game. "You pleaded not guilty."

"So?"

"So, I was just thinking . . . you probably didn't do it."

He wasn't going to get mad. Jace Red Hawk had just gotten a half-court swish, and Cleve enjoyed watching his team increase their lead. "I'll give you one free piece of advice, kid. Don't ask anybody what he's in for. Even if you know, you don't ask about it, and you don't go around telling people what you're in for. You just do your time."

"My biggest mistake was pleading not guilty. The first time I pled guilty, but I was still under age, so they put me in treatment. But the second time—"

"I don't want to hear about either time." He hoped an icy stare would make his point. "Got that?"

"I have to go to treatment here. Everybody will know."

Cleve dragged smoke into his lungs and shrugged. "A lot of guys go to AA."

"It's not alcohol treatment."

Jesus Christ. Grease was right. Cleve turned away, letting the breeze carry a trail of smoke from his lips. This kid, who looked like a choirboy, had Cleve pegged all wrong. He was no damn social worker. He didn't want to hear any of it, didn't want to imagine this timid, sickly-looking boy shoving his hand in some little kid's pants. Cleve wasn't interested in anybody else's problems, or why they did the stupid things they did, or what kind of miserable childhoods they'd had.

"I don't give free advice very often, kid," Cleve said quietly.

"I'm not telling you what I did. Like you said, I'm not gonna talk about it to anybody."

"You get an A on lesson one."

"Do you know Joe Dietz?"

Cleve sighed. He watched Whitey John miss a lay-up, then turned to Jimmy Dawson again. "Now for lesson two. Stay clear of Dietz."

"Somebody said you beat him up once."

"Don't believe everything you hear."

"How do I stay away from him? Every time I look around, there he is. He, uh . . . I think he knows what I did, and he said something to me about—"

Cleve's glare finally shut Jimmy up. He didn't want to hear about Dietz's suggestion anymore than he wanted to hear about Dawson's crime. The name of the game was self-preservation.

"I was too generous with that first mark I gave you. You're right, fish, you're all out of water. This is no nice little stock dam. This is a cesspool, and you'll either learn to swim in it, or you'll go under." The kid was giving him big, scared eyes, but Cleve wasn't buying. He wasn't pouring his blood into any plastic bag. "And I ain't no lifeguard, fish, so get off my leg."

Jimmy Dawson turned to walk away. His shirt was at least two sizes too big for him. The boy must've had a coathanger for shoulders.

"Hey, kid. You stay away from Dietz."

Chapter 9

Mikey and Jordie Bone Necklace both wanted their soup in the same Flintstones bowl. It was the only bowl in the house with cartoons on it. Susan had checked. She thought about breaking the thing and giving each one half, but it was plastic. Thanks to the schedule she'd set for herself, she was as cranky as the two boys. They were supposed to be sick, which was why Vera hadn't taken them to Head Start and Day Care, and part of the reason Susan had agreed to babysit. The other reason was that Vera had Sam.

Susan set two brown melamine bowls of chicken noodle soup on the table. Mikey complained immediately. "I don't want it in that bowl, I said."

"Want my bow!" Jordie was almost three, and he was king of the house because he was Vera's baby.

"Just get up to the table, Mikey. Jordie, get up in your chair. Next time I come, I'll bring another bowl with pictures on it, okay?"

"The one with Dino is mine." Mikey crawled into a yellow kitchen chair and situated himself on the two round sofa pillows Susan had put there for him, but Jordie hung back. "Jordie takes everything," Mikey grumbled as he picked up his spoon.

Susan couldn't argue with that. Spoiling Jordie seemed

to be one of Vera's few pleasures, but Susan'd kept her opinion to herself. She pulled Jordie's trayless high chair up to the table. Among other things, Mikey had been required to give up his chair when Jordie got big enough to use it. "Get up here, Jordie," Susan ordered. "You've got to eat your soup so you can get better."

"No!" Jordie's scowl turned to an impish grin, and his black eyes twinkled. He wanted to be chased.

"He's not sick," Mikey grumbled between spoonfuls. "He's just making off sick. *I'm* sick."

Again, Mikey had assessed the situation with a child's uncluttered insight. He had an ear infection, and Jordie just had a runny nose, but Jordie always got whatever Mikey had. "Your mom will be home soon, guys. Then we'll take your temperatures and see who's still sick. Come on, Jordie."

"No soup!"

"Fine." Jordie reached up to the table for a cracker, and Susan scooped him up and plunked him in the high chair. "But whatever you eat, you're going to sit at the table with it." He rocked back on the fulcrum of his butt when she pushed the chair up to the table, and he lurched forward as she parked it. The soup under his nose caught his interest.

Mikey sat up attentively. "Sammy's awake. Hear him?"

Susan listened for a moment, then smiled. Sam rarely cried when he awoke from a nap. His call was like a monotone song that he sang not so much for attention as for his own entertainment. Susan followed the sound down the short hallway to Vera's darkened bedroom. He was sitting up in the crib.

"What a big boy," Susan cooed as he smiled and raised his arms to her. He was actually small for sixteen months, but in view of his struggle to survive, he was, indeed, a big boy. He could scoot on his belly and sit up on his own, which were major accomplishments for one whom some of the experts expected to be no more active than cut cauliflower.

Susan picked Sam up and hugged him, and he rewarded her with a delighted squeal. She'd worked long hours to bring him this far, but he had worked, too. No one knew the extent to which the baby's brain had been damaged, but neither could any expert predict a limit to his progress. Susan firmly believed that Sam possessed a will, not only to live, but to grow.

"Have you missed me, Sam? Hmm?" She took a disposable diaper from the box on the floor and laid the baby on the bed to change him. He needed a dry jumpsuit, too. "I had to meet with some people this morning, and I have to go to work at three, but we'll do our aerobics together, okay? We'll get your legs working."

Sam had been in the hospital for most of his first year. Respiratory problems and an underdeveloped digestive system had made it impossible to care for him at home. Susan had worked the three to eleven shift at Fort Yates Indian Hospital and spent much of the rest of her day in the nursery with Sam. She'd begun taking him out when the weather was nice, taking him home on her days off, and Vera had made it clear to the staff that she was grateful for the help. She told social worker Melinda Jefferson that she just couldn't handle another baby right now, and that Susan was her friend.

The arrangement had worked well for a while. At Vera's request, Social Services had given Susan temporary custody of Sam. Susan's profession suited Sam's needs ideally. She worked with an infant stimulation therapist to help Sam learn to use his muscles, a process that didn't come naturally to Sam the way it did to most babies. But when Susan had applied for permanent custody of Sam, bureaucratic red tape became a huge worm with no head and no tail.

"Want some lunch?" Susan asked her smiling boy as she leaned close to his face. His eyes were bright and brown, but abnormally small, and his cheeks weren't fat the way Jordie's had been at Sam's age. But he looked a little like his impish cousin. He grabbed a handful of her hair and gave it a tug. "So strong! My goodness, a little Samson I've got here." She scooped him off the bed and promised, "Lunch with the big boys. How's that?"

Sam's diet was still limited to soymilk, but he was thriving on it now. It had been several weeks since he'd last been in the hospital with diarrhea, which was life-threatening in his case. It probably wasn't good for him to live in close quarters with ear infections and runny noses, but the judge dismissed that argument when she'd brought it up to him. "I don't care how 'special' he is; that's something he'll have to get used to. Being around kids is good for him. He belongs with his aunt."

Vera wanted Sam to stay with Susan. She'd said as much in writing. But Judge Isaac Dunn of the Standing Rock Sioux Tribal Court had warned that Susan was getting too close to the baby, and that Sam was going to get attached to her, too. He said that if Vera didn't accept her responsibility as Sam's aunt, he would place Sam in a home of his choosing. The tribe was officially opposed to the adoption of Indian children by non-Indian parents.

Susan heard the front door open. She grabbed Sam's blue blanket and hurried out of the bedroom, hoping Vera's husband hadn't popped in unexpectedly. He was supposed to be out of town with some country and western band he knocked around with. Susan was relieved to hear Jordie greet his mother with his usual shriek of excitement. In the next breath he was whining to get his way.

"I don't have any cookies," Vera was saying when Susan brought Sam into the kitchen. "I suppose this one's been bad, huh? He gets like this when he's sick."

"Who, Jordie? He was okay. I don't think there's much wrong with him, Vera. It's Mikey—"

"I got an A on that math test I told you about." Vera turned her attention from Susan to Mikey, who was standing by the back door with Elvis, the yellow mutt. "I told you I don't want that dog in here. Shht!" She shooed him away from the puddle of soup on the floor beside Jordie's chair. "Get away, now. Put him out."

"See?" Susan shifted Sam to her left hip and snatched a rag off the counter. "And you thought you were too old to go back to school."

"I think I'll take up bookkeeping next semester." As if they'd got this routine down pat, Vera took the rag, wiped up the spill and handed it back to Susan, who rinsed it in the sink. All the while, they talked. "I had it when I was in high school, but I didn't finish it. That's when I got pregnant and quit."

"When did you get married?"

"A year later. After basketball season was over. Tommy made All-State. Graduated from high school and everything."

"Well, now you've got your GED, and you're on your way."

Vera had been on her way before she'd met Susan, but Susan thought she'd been a key goading factor. Once she'd overheard Vera telling Tommy that she'd signed up for classes, and he came back with, "What the hell for?" A job. "Shee-it. What job? They'll never give you a job that'll pay as good as ADC."

When Vera had completed her high school equivalency, Susan had brought over a cake to celebrate, and Vera's kids had demolished it in one sitting. Tommy was off somewhere with his band. Tommy had been unemployed so long he wasn't even counted in the unemployment statistics, and Susan wondered why Vera let him come around. Vera was the breadwinner. The more children she had, the more aid she collected. It would have been easy to take on the seventh child and collect another payment. Susan worried about that, and for months she'd expected Vera to tell her she'd decided to keep Sam.

But Vera had taken one step, then another. Susan had actually had little to do with Vera's choices. But as long as Susan had Sam, Vera stayed on course. She'd been awarded a Basic Education Grant. She'd put Jordie in Day Care. She'd registered for classes at the local Indian community college. Darcy's baby hadn't changed

Vera's dreams, and she had no intention of going back on them.

"It's pretty interesting." Vera cleaned Jordie's face and hands with an old washcloth. "I always thought school was boring. Same old stuff every year. And I never thought I was smart enough to take classes at the community college, but I'm doing pretty good." She sounded surprised. "I want to see if I can get an office job, maybe."

"It's hard when the kids are sick. It's hard . . ." Vera eyed the baby in Susan's arms.

"It's hard with Sam. I know." Susan knew that Vera tried to keep her distance from Sam. She didn't even like to pick him up. When Susan came over on her days off, one of the older girls, Bobbi or Crystal, usually handed Sam over to her. She was the one who knew what Sam needed. The bond was there.

"I went to see Judge Dunn this morning," Susan said as she fixed Sam's bottle with one hand. "He won't change his mind about the adoption."

Vera took some cold macaroni from the refrigerator and gave it the sniff test. She held it out to Susan in an offer to share, but Susan shook her head. "I had soup."

Vera opened a drawer and untangled a fork from a jumble of assorted utensils. "If you hadn't asked to adopt him, they probably would have let you keep him temporarily. You know, they wouldn't have thought you were trying to over on him or something."

Susan chuckled at Vera's use of the local expression "over on him" as she took Sam and his bottle to the table. He grunted eagerly as he took the nipple in his mouth and sucked. She hadn't consciously taken over. Sam had come along, and she was there; that was all. Now they belonged to each other. "I want it to be legal," she said. "I don't want somebody coming out of the woodwork and taking him. The judge even said he was going to talk to your brother, Devron."

Vera waved the notion away with her fork. "Devron'll

never take him. Devron's wife divorced him years ago. What would he do with a baby?"

"I don't know, but Judge Dunn says the Tribal Court has full control over Sam's custody in the absence of a natural parent. And he says he'd never let a white woman adopt an Indian child."

Vera dropped her fork in the bowl. "Eeez! That old man! If he could see the way you do those exercises with Sam, and the way you—" She shook her head and scooped up another forkful of cold pasta. "What does he think is wrong with it?"

"He doesn't think it's right to take an Indian child away from his people."

"Maybe not, but you said you'd raise him here."

"Once the adoption was final, the judge says he'd have no way to enforce that." She watched Sam suckle. His eyes were closed, and his little mouth was working over that nipple the way any hungry baby would. "Nobody planned it," she said absently. "I was working at the hospital, and you had all you could handle. I just started looking after him."

"Sam thinks you're his mother."

"I think he's my baby." It seemed like the time for some words of wisdom, but she had none of her own. " 'Nothing is good or bad, but thinking makes it so.' "

"We just got done with that in English. Shakespeare, right?"

"Mom." Jordie tugged on the hem of Vera's flowered overblouse. "Mom, I want cookies."

"I don't have any cookies," she answered, then continued talking to Susan. "I can't keep Sam and still go to school. I can't count on Tommy to watch kids. Seems like I've always had somebody in diapers, even when I was a girl." Jordie wouldn't go away. A saltine. That was as close as she could come. Jordie dropped it on the floor and walked away. "I'm thinking of having my tubes tied."

"Too bad you didn't have it done right after Jordie was born. It would have been easier."

"Tommy didn't like the idea of his wife getting fixed. Said he might want me to have another kid for him." She sighed and joined Susan at the table. "And I guess I was thinking, if I couldn't, somebody else might."

"Whether you do or not, somebody else might."

"Yeah, but he's married to me." Vera wondered why a pretty woman Susan's age wasn't married. She'd been pretty once, too, she told herself. Pretty enough to get Tommy to really marry her. Maybe Susan hadn't been able to get her man to marry her. So she'd left him and come to the reservation to forget. Maybe that was it. "He likes being a father," Vera said proudly. "He brags about how many kids he's got."

"What part of being a father does he like?"

"Picking out the name." Vera's eyes crinkled at the corners and her eyes sparkled. "Just kidding. He's good with the kids sometimes. He plays with the little ones when he's around." She glanced at Jordie. The boys always reminded her most of Tommy when they were little. "You should hear him sing. His band's playing at the bar in Selfridge this weekend. You oughta go hear them."

"I've got to work this weekend."

Vera's mouth tightened. "You can't take Sam back, then? Not even temporarily?"

"I went to Social Services after I saw the judge. Melinda Jefferson said we might be able to work something out since you're going to school—some kind of temporary foster care. I'll have to find a sitter during my shift from three to eleven." She set the bottle on the table and put Sam to her shoulder. She liked rubbing his back. "It was easier when he was in the hospital. I could just check him out and take him home."

"I'll go with you to see Melinda."

"The judge said I was getting too close. Boy, I've heard that one before. That's what people in Bismarck told me. What's wrong with getting close? That's what Sam needs."

"I just want to be his auntie, you know?" She heard

Sam's pre-upchuck gurgle and went for another rag. Susan caught most of it in the blanket. This was what they called an underdeveloped digestive system. Vera talked as she mopped. "For once I want to be like a regular auntie. I took care of Devron and Darcy, and now Devron's older boys come over here when they're on the outs with their mother. Half the time I think Tommy wants a mother instead of a wife. When do I get to be something to somebody besides their mother?"

"How about a friend?"

"Never had much time for friends."

"Neither have I. Not since I was in school. He needs a bath."

Vera brought two bath towels, and they used one side of the kitchen sink. The soymilk smelled like sour mash.

"Melinda said there might be another avenue we could pursue if we knew who Sam's father was," Susan said as she snapped Sam's clean T-shirt. She decided she'd waited long enough to bring this up.

"What avenue?"

"Obviously this man, whoever he is, has no interest in claiming Sam." She picked Sam up off the counter and cuddled him. He liked to be cuddled. "He must've heard that Darcy had a baby before she died, wouldn't you think? Or maybe read about it? It was in the newspaper."

"Who knows?" Vera put some soap in one of the bowls in the sink and ran some water. She avoided Susan's eyes. "Maybe she . . . she probably didn't tell him."

"You have no idea who Sam's father might be?"

"I don't think it makes any difference."

"It might make a difference, Vera. If we could get him to admit paternity and give me his permission to adopt Sam, our problems would all be solved."

"Or you might just be asking for more problems." Vera sloshed the water around enough to make suds.

"I don't think so. Put yourself in this man's shoes,

Vera. You had a fling with a woman, and you find out she died and left a handicapped baby—*your* baby— who's already got a good home lined up but just needs to make it legal. Wouldn't you be glad to sign the papers?"

"You'd just go up to him and ask him?"

"Of course, I would." But she couldn't imagine what she would say to him. She looked at Sam. "Yes, I would."

Vera dried her hands, tossed the towel back on the counter, then folded her arms beneath her breasts as she turned to face Susan. "You are a crazy woman. You don't know what kind of . . . The best thing is just to leave it alone. Don't go looking for any more—"

"You know, don't you?" Susan stepped closer. "Vera? Darcy told you about Sam's father, didn't she? Of course she did. You were the only one who knew she was pregnant, and you were the one she would have confided in."

"This guy's worse than no good. You're not gonna want to go looking this guy up. No way."

"I will. Just tell me who he is."

"The guy's locked up in the State Pen. For life." The shocked look in Susan's eyes gave Vera some satisfaction. Susan always thought she had all the answers. "Sam's father is a rodeo cowboy named Cleve Black Horse. He's also a murderer." Calling a spade a spade gave her another burst of satisfaction. That big shot cowboy had caused a lot of trouble for a lot of people. Tommy was no prize, but at least he wasn't a criminal. And as for Darcy . . .

Vera shook her head and laughed mirthlessly. "My sister sure could pick 'em."

Chapter 10

It had been a while since Cleve had been summoned to the warden's office, and he wondered what he'd done to merit a "personal interview" this time. A uniformed security guard ushered him through a series of monitored gates. Each automatic slam-lock at his back reminded him that he wasn't going far. Only the good guys had keys. The guard knocked on the warden's door, and it swung open immediately. Warden Everett Steiner had been waiting.

"You can wait outside, Roger," Steiner said to the guard. He glanced down at Cleve's hands. "Let's dispense with the cuffs. Cleve's not as angry as he used to be. Right, Cleve?"

"I'm controlling my temper a little better these days." Cleve lifted his wrists toward the guard's key. "I don't much like The Hole."

"Good. We don't want you to like it, so I guess it still works. Have a seat, Cleve."

Cleve rubbed his wrists and accepted Steiner's invitation. His custody level, which had been reduced from maximum to close, still required that he be handcuffed when they moved him to a less secure area. Even if he served his full sentence, he knew he would never get used to wearing those handcuffs.

Rather than head for his desk, Steiner took a chair across from Cleve, a gesture that let Cleve know he wasn't in for a reprimand. In that case, maybe he could relax a little. Steiner was just a man trying to do a job. It had taken Cleve a while to see it that way. He'd needed to fight somebody, but he'd decided Steiner wasn't the right man. He was too fair-minded. There were a few hard-assed guards who liked to throw their weight around, but the warden made an effort to keep them in line. He wanted inmates to come to believe that the system was fair. He believed in rehabilitation. If you were interested in getting your shit together, Steiner had the program for you. Alcohol abuse, drug abuse, sex abuse—the North Dakota State Penitentiary was an inpatient recovery program. If a guy had a problem, this was his end-of-the-line chance to solve it. *If* a guy had a problem.

The warden planted his elbows on the arms of his chair and stuck his beefy hands together like two forks. He leaned forward, and Cleve expected a revelation. "I want to talk to you a little bit about your future, Cleve."

"My future? Here?" So much for the revelation. "That's sorta like talking to a gelding about his breeding prospects."

Steiner had to smile. Black Horse was smart, and when he wasn't brooding, he had an irresistible wit. "You can't beat it, Cleve. You can't stop those doors from locking you down. Best thing to do is get with the program." He tipped his head to direct Cleve's attention to the corner of the desk. "Cigarette?"

"Thanks." There were only two missing from the pack. Steiner didn't smoke, but he always offered. In his quest for cooperation he never separated an inmate from his coffee or his cigarettes. Cleve helped himself and used the fancy brass desk lighter. "I applied for a new job assignment," he said on the tail of a stream of smoke.

"I know. You requested a transfer to Roughrider Industries, and you've got it. How does the metals shop sound? There's an opening there."

Cleve shrugged. "Long as it pays better than washing dishes."

"You can make it pay if you stay out of trouble. Go by the rules, just the way you did on the rodeo circuit."

"I'm not out to be your champion prisoner, Warden. I'm trying to pay the bills, that's all."

Steiner nodded. "There's an opening in upholstery, too, but Dietz is there. I want to keep you two apart."

"Then let Dietz have the sofas. I'll make license plates."

"And stop signs. Ever take a potshot at a stop sign when you were a kid?"

"Sure." If twenty-five counted as a kid.

"So did I." Steiner had a cocky-jock way of smiling. "Give the cons something to do, we used to say. When you're a kid, you never think it might be you or one of your buddies someday." He shifted in his chair. "Look, Cleve, I don't care what a guy did to get himself in here. My job is to give him a chance to turn his life around."

"What life?"

"The only one you've got. The here and now. We only put on one rodeo a year. A lot of people were disappointed when you couldn't participate last summer. You're not gonna miss out next time around, are you?"

Cleve savored the acrid taste of his smoke while he avoided Steiner's eyes. His gut twisted like a corkscrew whenever he thought about riding behind bars. His thighs ached to slide into the saddle, but he tasted bitter bile. Every sorry sonuvabitch in the joint talked about entering up and making an ass of himself in the big prison rodeo. What a joke this would make out of his All-Around buckle.

"Well, anyway, we're looking forward to watching you ride, Cleve," Steiner said. "But we've got other programs we can offer you, too. We want to see you take advantage of every opportunity we can make—"

Cleve had heard it all before. Given that you're a criminal, and a dangerous one at that, here's how you can make the most of your situation. One thing he'd learned during the past eighteen months was that it was a waste of breath to profess your innocence. Nobody was listening. Everybody who was in the pen figured he'd gotten a raw deal. Life was unfair, and you could hear the ways counted till judgment day inside these walls if you wanted to be the only one listening. Once convicted, a man was guilty as hell until he could find a way to prove himself innocent.

When Steiner left him an opening, Cleve decided to make his day. "I was thinking about taking some courses."

"College?" Steiner smiled as though there was something in it for him. "Sure, I think we can work something out with a job sharing arrangement at the shops so you can get a full forty hours in. Most guys we get here are looking for a GED first, but you've got a high school education and all that army experience. You're a prime candidate for the college program."

"If you're gonna be in prison, you might as well be in school." Cleve chuckled as he reached across the desk for the clean glass ashtray. "Used to think it was the other way around."

Steiner was beaming. "Well, you're definitely going to be a busy man. You might not have as much time for lifting. Might lose some of that muscle you've been building up there."

"I'll find time for that." Cleve stubbed out the cigarette and rubbed the ash around in a circle, thinking he'd leave his mark on Steiner's fine glass. "One thing I've got is time."

"We'd like to see you make use of the alcohol treatment program, too, Cleve."

He shoved the ashtray away. "What for?"

"You know the answer to that. Ninety percent of our inmates are here for a crime they committed while under the influence. That includes you."

"I'm no drunk."

"You've spent time in The Hole for drinking."

"If you were on the inside here and somebody offered you a bottle, would you turn it down?" Cleve asked.

"I don't know. But I'd pay the price if I didn't."

"I paid your price, Warden. And I keep on paying. In piss." He saw himself handing one of the nurses that damned plastic cup, and he smirked. "Whenever they have a slow day down at the infirmary."

"You tested us." Steiner shrugged. "That means we test you more often. Probable cause."

"I think the 'probable cause' is that your so-called correctional officers get a thrill out of watching me take a leak, like they're not just sure how it's done." Steiner was laughing, but Cleve figured if he ever lost it again and took a punch at somebody, it was likely to be when they were checking him inside and out for whatever it was they thought he had.

"They have to make sure it came fresh from you, that's all."

"I got little enough I can call mine, and none of it's private any more." Cleve wanted another cigarette, but not one of Steiner's. Suddenly it felt like selling out to take something from The Man. "But, see, you wouldn't know about that, Warden, which is why gettin' me in here just to sit around and bullshit like one of the guys doesn't quite make it with me. I don't need your treatment program."

"Well, if you change your mind—"

"When do I get transferred to the shops?"

"You can start tomorrow." Cleve nodded and started out of his chair, but Steiner motioned him back down again. "That's not all I brought you in for. You've got no visitor's list, Cleve."

Cleve settled back in the chair. They'd been through this before, too. "I don't want anybody coming in here to see me. That's the one bit of privacy I'm allowed."

"Visitors from the outside help a man to keep things in perspective. You sit behind bars too long without any contact with the outside, you'll start imagining this is all there is. There's nothing beyond these walls."

"What does life plus thirty mean to you, Warden?"

"It sounds pretty grim. I don't deny that. But if you behave yourself, you'll get your sentence reduced for good time served." Cleve knew all about North Dakota's "good time" law, but Steiner figured a lifer like him needed to be reminded that being carried out of there in a body bag wasn't inevitable. He might walk out an old man, but at least there was hope that one day he'd be free again. "You've stopped trying to deck everybody you meet. That's step one."

"Yeah, well, I haven't stopped fighting." His smile lacked humor. "I figure there's gotta be a better way, and I'm looking for the right lawyer."

"I hope you get your chance to appeal. And if you do, I wish you luck with it." He offered Cleve a form. "Meanwhile, I'd like to see a visitors list in your file."

Cleve ignored the paper. "No visitors."

"Look, Cleve, you need to see people. People who aren't cons or guards or wardens. People who—" Steiner slid one edge of the paper between his thumb and forefinger and looked at Cleve as though he had problems to unload. "I might as well tell you, I've had a request from a woman—"

Cleve stiffened. "Jesus Christ, Warden, she's seventy-four years old, and she can barely get around. You think I'm gonna let her come in here and see me like this?"

"This lady's a little younger than that."

"My grandmother . . ." Cleve let the argument dissipate as he tried to figure out what other woman would even remember where to find him.

"She's no grandmother." Steiner tossed the form back on the desk. "It's a little touchy. She tells me she served on the jury that convicted you."

Cleve scowled, his brain buzzing as though he'd downed a straight shot on an empty stomach. "Are you shittin' me?"

Steiner shook his head. "Ordinarily I wouldn't approve a meeting like this, but she's working as a nurse at the hospital in Fort Yates. She brought along a letter

from a social worker down there. Says this Susan
Ellison—the nurse—has an important matter to discuss with you regarding a relative. It may be that your
grandmother—"

"Did she say anything about my grandmother?"

"No. Apparently there's a confidentiality issue here,
and I'm inclined to respect that just because you've
come a long way, and I think it's important for you
to be in touch with your family. The woman's a nurse.
It's probably a health matter. You think you can handle
seeing her?"

Cleve nodded. He stood up slowly, remembering the
last time he'd seen the old lady blinking back at him
through a Plexiglas window. She was sick. Had to be
something complicated, and she must've asked the nurse
to come up and explain it to him, get him to agree to
something, to decide on something. Christ, why him?
Where was Uncle Jake? Had he fallen off the wagon
again, or had he just taken off and left the old lady high
and dry?

And what in hell was that Ellison woman doing in
Fort Yates?

"Do yourself a favor, then," Steiner suggested. "Don't
bring up anything about the trial. Just stick to whatever
this family business is."

"She's here now?"

"Waiting out front." Steiner opened the door and sig-
nalled for the waiting guard as he went on talking.
"I'm not taking any chances on any kind of setup. Not
that I'm accusing anybody of anything, but she'll be
searched, too."

Cleve hated being searched. He knew he'd be pat
searched before they took him to the visitor's room
and strip searched after she left. That was the policy.
The thought of it always made his skin crawl, but he
smiled anyway. He watched the guard reach around to
his back pocket for the handcuffs, and he offered up his
wrists without the usual hot glare. Even as the handcuffs
snapped shut, the thought of pretty little blue-eyed Susan

from the front row letting them pat her down just so she could pay him a visit made him smile.

Susan bent over and swept her hair over the back of her head, combing through it with her fingers as the gum-snapping female officer instructed her to do. The prison atmosphere was so intimidating that she put aside any indignation she might have felt at being ordered to mess up the hair she'd carefully styled and restyled before she'd come. The uniformed guards and the gates with their automatic locks made her forget every instinct but to cooperate, get her business done, and get out of there.

The guard was a wonder. Susan couldn't imagine anybody, man nor woman, crossing this lady. Six feet tall if she was an inch, huge shoulders without any kind of padding, and a bustline to match. Remarkable, too, was the way she snapped her gum and hummed snatches of an Oakridge Boys tune at the same time, while she looked inside Susan's mouth, checked her ears, her shirt collar, and ran her hands all over Susan's upper body.

"Ever been searched before?"

"No." It made her skin crawl, and she didn't feel like chatting with the woman while it was happening.

"Haven't you ever been to the gynecologist?" Susan's stiff silence brought out a chuckle. "See? We're always getting searched. What you've gotta do is think about something else, like what groceries you need to pick up on your way home. Spread your feet apart."

Susan stared hard at the fluorescent light above her head while the woman moved behind her. She felt queasy. It was that gynecologist remark that did it. How far was this going to go? White ceiling, white walls, green linoleum, shadowless light. She couldn't think of anything she needed from the store. The cold, drab room might have passed for clinical, or it might have been cheap and convenient, but the hand that moved over Susan's slacks, between her legs, and over her crotch belonged to neither doctor nor lover. It felt like a violation, even though she submitted to it. They had put her purse and jacket in a locker in the lobby, and she'd walked through a metal detector. That should have been enough. What did they think she was hiding? She took mental inventory of everything she'd put on that morning, wondering which piece might have been against prison rules.

"I don't think this one's had any visitors before. I think you're the first." The voice behind Susan was on its way up. "He's still under close security. That's why we're going through all the preliminaries."

"Are there more?" Susan asked.

"No, that's all." The guard opened the door and directed Susan down the hall. "If this is your first time, I'd better tell you the rules. You've gotta sit one person to a chair. You can't sit in his lap or anything. You get two kisses, hello and goodbye. That's it. If you don't cut 'em short, the visiting room officer'll do it for you."

"I thought there'd be a window to talk through."

At the guard's signal, another door was automatically unlocked, and she ushered Susan into the visiting room. "Nope. This is it. All the comforts."

It was the sofa that surprised Susan most. *Three* sofas. The brown flowered one with the pine frame reminded her of the one in the rec room in her parents' house. She had a crazy, quick fantasy of herself in Cleve Black Horse's lap, the two of them making out on the sofa like teenagers. His handcuffs were getting in his way.

Susan laughed, letting go of some tension, and the guard joined in. "Well, most of the comforts," she amended.

"No, it's not that. It's the idea—" Susan waved it all away—what she thought, what the guard thought— all of it so ridiculous. "There won't be any kissing. I hardly know this man. It's purely . . . business, I guess you'd say."

"Then you want to watch yourself. The room's full of cameras. Think of them as protection. The visiting room officer will keep his distance and let you talk, but if he tells you to sit somewhere, you sit where he tells you.

And if the inmate threatens you in any way, you let us know."

"I will."

When the guard left, it was just Susan and the officer stationed at a desk on a raised platform at the other end of the large room. Between them was an array of tables and chairs.

"I'm here to see—"

"Cleve Black Horse, right? They're bringing him in. Have a seat."

"Where should I sit?"

"Nobody else here. You can sit anywhere you like."

"Thank you."

She chose a small table at the back of the room. He'd probably be more comfortable if they had a piece of furniture between them, and she would, too. She thought of him simply as *he*. She told herself she wasn't afraid of him. Killer or not, he was Sam's father, although Vera was certain he didn't know. She was a little nervous about telling him, and all this security wasn't doing her any good. Just protection.

She was out of her element, and she knew she'd have to make a conscious effort to appear confident. *Assertive*. This was an assertive move on her part, and assertiveness was a good trait. It got results. She took a deep breath and released it slowly, glancing at the clock. It was almost 2:30, and she hadn't eaten anything all day. She was jittery, not scared. No need to be scared. She wasn't part of this. She wasn't in jail. She was on the outer edge of the block, just visiting.

Cleve Black Horse came through the side door. He stood there for a moment, just watching her. There was no sign of recognition, no anger, nothing. He just watched her. She wasn't going to put on an act for him. This was his territory. He'd agreed to see her, and now he was standing there, waiting for her to squirm. She could wait, too. She folded her hands on the table and met his stare until he finally moved toward the table she'd selected.

His face was no longer hollow. It was lean and hard, but not thin. She saw Sam in his face. A little bit, anyway. His wide mouth and square chin. Enough to make her feel soft inside. Her heart thudded in her ears along with the sound of his footsteps, boot heels and pulse beat hammering hard against each other. The closer he got, the stronger and more powerful he looked, but he still moved like a cowboy—lean-hipped, loose-limbed, and cocky. His dark hair looked damp, and he wore a khaki shirt and jeans, but no handcuffs.

He took the seat across from her. That was as far as he was going. The rest was up to her.

"I'm Susan Ellison." She waited for an acknowledgment, but none came. "I guess they told you, but I wasn't sure you'd remember me by name."

"I remembered."

His soft, even tone brought some relief. "How's your leg?"

"Scarred."

"Have you had any trouble with it since—"

"No. It healed up fine."

"I just . . ." The healing was good news. Of the few concerns they could possibly share, his injury seemed the safest footing to venture out on. "It was quite a surprise when they brought you into ER—you know, to see you again."

"I'll bet."

"It was a bad wound. I'm glad—"

"Is this a follow-up call, or what?"

"No." He still didn't seem angry, so she offered a little smile. "No, it's nothing like that. I guess I'm a little nervous. It wasn't easy, getting in to see you, but now here I am, and here you are, and I guess I'm kind of surprised that I actually got this far." She shook her head and cast a glance at the ceiling. "That sounded ridiculous."

"What's wrong with my grandmother?"

"Your grandmother?"

"Is she sick or something?"

"I don't know anything about your grandmother."
Now he looked puzzled.

"Suppose you cut the chatter and tell me what you're
doing here."

The cowardice was what she had to cut. Right now.
"I want to talk to you about . . . your son."

"I don't have a son."

"You didn't know about him, but—"

He was losing patience. He'd just had a shower—
2:15 on the schedule, and if you missed it, you missed
it—dressed, and had himself pat searched, all for this
song and dance? His shirt was sticking to the back of
the chair. "I don't have any kids. If somebody's going
around saying she's had a kid for me, she's lying."

"His mother is dead." Susan took a deep breath and
blurted out the name. "Darcy Walker."

"Darcy?" His eyes widened, then narrowed again.
"Darcy's dead?"

"You didn't know?"

"I don't get much—" He didn't *want* much news
from the outside. He didn't want to know who else
got arrested, who needed money, who died. There was
nothing he could do about any of it. And if she'd been
sent to find out what was going on with him, she'd just
found out all she was going to. He was there, they
weren't starving him, and he didn't have any kids.

Damn. Darcy Walker? "How'd she die?"

"You know, it's very strange. Ironic, really. The same
day you came in with that knife wound—it was a year
ago in November—Darcy had an accident. Her pickup
went off a bridge. She was unconscious when they
brought her in, and she died on the operating table."
She took the blank look on his face for shock. He
moved his hands over the table, groping for something.
"I'm sorry."

"Hell, she was—" He brushed his palm over the table
as though he were sweeping crumbs away. "We were
just friends. She was a barrel racer. Ran into her once
or twice, had a few drinks. If she had a kid—"

"She was pregnant when she had the accident. Six months, maybe a little less. Miraculously, the baby lived." Susan laid her hands on the table opposite his and tried to look him in the eye. "His name is Sam."

"I don't care what his name is, he's not my kid."

"Do you know Darcy's sister, Vera Bone Necklace?" No answer. He was studying his hands. "Vera was the only one who knew about Darcy's pregnancy, and the only one Darcy confided in—about who the father was. She said—"

He looked at her defiantly. "I don't care what she said. The kid's not mine."

"There's . . . no chance?"

"No way."

"You never—"

"Lady, where do you get off? I'm not stupid. I know how you get to be a father, and how you avoid it, okay?" His eyes narrowed, making her feel smaller. "What's your interest in all this?"

"Vera is Sam's closest relative, but I'm—" *Not really his mother. Darcy was his mother.* "I was there when he was born. He was premature, of course. He wasn't expected to live, but he did. He's a special child. He spent months in the hospital, fighting for his life."

"And you were the nurse who was there with him." Cleve's tone was flat.

"Yes, from the very beginning. Vera has six children of her own, and with Sam's special needs, well, she just can't handle it all. She's taking classes at the college."

"Good for her."

"I had temporary custody of Sam, but when I petitioned the Tribal Court for permanent custody, they said that he belonged with Vera."

"Who already has six kids," Cleve recited for her.

"It isn't just that." The man was bored with the whole thing. She was going to tell him how she felt, even though she knew it didn't matter to him. "Sam belongs with me now," she said quietly. "He's my baby."

"Is that why you're working down there now? Because of this kid?"

"I applied for the job after he was moved to the Indian Hospital." She felt as though he was staring right through her. "I'm glad I did. I've met some wonderful people, and I enjoy my work." He didn't care about that, either. She'd never seen such a stony face. "I may not be able to get custody of Sam unless his father is willing to agree to it."

It had seemed impossible to her at first. Cleve Black Horse had begun to fade from her nightmares, and now he was back again. Only it wasn't a dream anymore. Everywhere she turned, he was there. She had to get used to it and work around it. So did he, she decided. He probably had the right to hate her, but not Sam.

"I know I'm asking a very personal question, and I know I have no right to expect an answer. But maybe Sam has the right."

He lifted one corner of his mouth, and Susan half expected his face to crack. "As soon as he gets old enough, let him ask for it, then. How old did you say he was?"

"He's almost seventeen months."

"Is he as attached to you as you are to him?"

"Yes." If he was looking for her softest spot, she was directing him right to it. But she needed an answer. "Look, I'm asking for him. It's very important. Please. Is there any possibility—"

"You've got balls, lady. I'll give you that." But let her beg for the rest.

"I know this is a terrible invasion of your privacy—"

"Privacy?" He chuckled, half amused. "What's that? What did they do to you before you came in here?"

"They . . . searched me."

"Did they check your hair?" He took satisfaction in her shy nod. "Your mouth, your armpits?" Again she nodded, and he felt good. "How about between your legs? Huh? They make you take your clothes off, too?"

"No! No, they didn't. I had all my clothes on. But they did . . . you know, they did search."

He knew. He could see it inside his head, and he wanted to hit somebody. Not her. Maybe the visiting room officer.

"You must've wanted to talk to me pretty bad, to let them do all that." Jesus, she looked like a little girl all of a sudden. Small, scared, embarrassed. He tried hard to feel gratified, but it wasn't working anymore. Something inside him howled that she had it coming, and he started to tell her that, but his voice went soft on him. "They call that a pat search. I got one, too. After you leave here, I get strip searched." He lowered his voice and glanced away. "I don't know anything about privacy anymore."

"I appreciate your willingness to—" The words sounded sterile, even to her. "To see me. The warden told me that you haven't wanted any visitors. I guess I don't blame you if they do that to you every time."

"He said it was something about a relative." He had damn few. He wondered if she knew that. "I figured it was my grandmother."

"I thought it did concern a relative." She gave him a moment, but he offered nothing. She dug in and pressed him. "You never slept with Darcy?" Those X-ray eyes pinned her fast. "I'm sorry. I need a straight answer, and I don't know how else to get it but to keep asking."

"Would you believe me if I said 'no'?"

Don't say it. Please. "I guess you wouldn't have any reason to lie about it, under the circumstances."

"What circumstances? Nobody's blaming me for her death, right?"

"Of course not."

"Nobody's saying she drove off a bridge because I got her pregnant, right?"

"Not that I know—"

"I didn't kill her, so I don't have any reason to lie." He rubbed his hand over the back of his neck. His hair was still wet. "Except that Darcy had a kid, and you wanna say it's mine."

"If you're not his father, then we'll never know who is. You're the only one Darcy named."

He smoothed his dry palm over his moist one. A moment later, his soft answer surprised them both. "I slept with Darcy. Once." He looked up. "One time. Somewhere in Wyoming, I think."

"Would it have been—"

"Late May, early June. Somewhere in there." The look on her face made him cock her half a smile. "You like that, huh? That's what you wanted to hear?" He wasn't going to tell her he wasn't the only one. He didn't know for sure. Darcy was always looking for a good time. "It doesn't prove anything. She never told me anything about a kid, and her sister can say anything she wants now that Darcy's dead."

"I know. But you see, the judge says that in the absence of a natural parent, the Tribal Court has custody of Sam. So I'm looking for a natural parent."

His dark eyes were cold. "One who'll say you can have him."

"That's right."

He let the numbness take him. It was a skill he'd practiced so often he didn't have to think about it. "Tell you what, you seem to be the only one who wants him. Courts don't raise kids."

"You wouldn't want him? I mean, if you knew for sure—"

"I'm doing life plus thirty here." Her fair face colored a little. "Of course, you know that."

"I would be a good mother to him. I *am* a good—"

"So why won't they just give him to you?"

"I'm not an Indian."

"So?"

"So, it's against the tribe's policy to allow non-Indians to adopt Indian children."

"Oh, yeah?" He didn't know much about the tribe's policies. They didn't affect him much anymore. But watching her shift in her chair, uncrossing and crossing her legs, that affected him. The numbness only went so far. "You gotta keep both feet on the floor in here. That's the rule." He kept a straight face, watching her shift around again. He'd almost forgotten how much he enjoyed teasing a woman. Any woman. Even Susan Ellison.

"I understand their concerns, and I'm sure you'd want him to grow up appreciating his heritage, but Sam's needs are—"

Cleve's jaw tightened. "Get this straight: I don't give a damn how this kid grows up. Chances are, he's not mine." She looked surprised. He was damn sick of this heritage thing. The last guy who'd asked him to join the inmates' Native American Culture Club had almost gotten his face bashed in. If the kid *was* his, he was a mixed-blood, and he'd spend the rest of his life trying to figure out what that was supposed to mean.

"I never cared much about dancing Indian or stringing beads. A lot of white people take in Indian foster kids."

"I want to adopt him." She thought of Judge Dunn's first question. "No, I'm not married."

"I remembered that, too."

"And chances are, he *is* yours." How was she going to get through to him? "I didn't know Darcy. Do you think she would have lied to Vera about you?"

"You mean, *under the circumstances?*"

"Well, if she were going to pick a father out of the clear blue—"

"You don't think she'd pick a convicted murderer."

"I don't think so."

"Because you wouldn't?" It was hard to look at her and think about her sitting on that jury. He told himself not to think about it. Looking at her otherwise was pretty nice. Darcy had been nice-looking, too. "I didn't know Darcy very well, either. I always thought of her as a kid from back home. Good little barrel racer. Then she started turning up at parties. We started teasing each other about being from the rez." Old times. Something else he didn't want to think about. Old, dead times. "It's the shits, you know. Her getting killed like that, so young."

"I know."

"But it happens a lot down there." Susan nodded. From the look in her eyes he could almost believe it mattered to her. She had nice eyes. "I want some time to think about all this."

"I understand."

"I get four hours of visiting time a week. I never use any of it." He glanced down at his folded hands. "You wanna come back next week some time?"

"When?"

He had to think because sometimes he lost track. Today was Monday. "It gets pretty crowded in here on weekends."

"I have Mondays off."

"Monday, then. You'll have to talk to the warden because I don't have a visitor's list."

"I'll talk to him on my way out." *While they're strip searching you.* She wanted to apologize for the officers. For the jury. For herself. But what good would it do? "Would you like me to bring a picture of Sam next time?"

"You can't bring anything like that in here." He stood abruptly. "Besides, I don't think I wanna see any pictures. I don't know if I believe any of this."

"But you'll think about it?"

"Yeah, I'll think about it. You'd better get going now. They close up at three." He watched her push her chair back and stand up. She had small breasts, a little waist, a woman's round hips. She was no freight train, but she'd do. He stepped to the side of the table and took a step closer. She didn't back off. She smelled of wildflowers hiding in tall grass.

"Do me one favor."

Susan's mouth went dry. "What's that?"

"Find out how my grandmother's doing. Grace Black Horse. She's from Little Eagle."

"Do you want me to go see her?"

"No. Just ask around."

"Okay. I'll see you next Monday, then."

He must have been crazy. The bitch who put him there. She was smiling at him, and, goddam him, he wanted to smile back. He turned on his heel and stalked up to the desk to get himself out of there. He had to be hard up as hell.

Chapter 11

The day the letter from Bernard Whitestaff came, Cleve splurged on a Coke and a chocolate bar from the commissary. Whitestaff had agreed to take his case, and he'd said money wasn't a big concern. A lawyer who wasn't concerned about getting his money up front was a rarity. Cleve had written a ton of letters, so he figured he was an expert on lawyers. He also knew he didn't want the court to assign him somebody. Whitestaff sounded almost too good to be true, but Cleve had checked him out and discovered that he had a good track record. He'd worked for the American Civil Liberties Union before going into private practice in Minneapolis. In his reply Whitestaff had said he was always interested in the civil liberties of "his" Indian people.

Probably Chippewa. Cleve's first inclination had been to write back and tell Whitestaff that this didn't have anything to do with *Indian people*. He wasn't looking for any treaty loopholes—hell, that kind of stuff never got settled.

You never know about those Chippewas.

That was his grandfather talking. Cleve had to laugh at himself and send off a letter right away, letting Whitestaff know he was glad to have him on his side and looked forward to meeting him personally. He figured he'd never get that old man out of his head, but he resolved to let

Whitestaff handle the case his way, Chippewa or not. At least he was no Carter Felch.

The candy bar hadn't gone down as easy as he'd been dreaming it would. Too sweet after all those months of going without. He'd been accused of becoming a health freak, but what he'd really become was cheap. Cutting corners was a ritual with him lately. He figured if he had to live like a monk, he might as well go all the way. If Whitestaff wasn't interested in the money he'd saved, he'd decided to buy his conscience some relief by having part of his account sent to his grandmother.

There wasn't much time to waste shootin' the bull over supper. Twenty minutes until the buzzer sounded to clear the dining room. If you wanted to talk, you did it with your mouth full. Inmates didn't stand on ceremony. Cleve couldn't resist harassing Grease about what he'd put in the dressing and giving one of the new guys a bad time about the way he slapped the pork into his tray. Closely monitored by a guard, the chow line moved quickly. There was also an officer posted along each wall. The dining room was a good cauldron for brewing trouble.

Inmates were territorial creatures. Tables were not assigned. You staked your claim and defended it, subtly or otherwise. Cleve sat with Whitey, Jace and Jimmy. He wasn't being clannish, but figured he had to sit somewhere. The other guys hadn't been too happy when Jimmy had joined them after he'd transferred from the kitchen to the hobby shop. Still, they didn't question Cleve's judgment that the kid needed a place to sit, no matter what color he was.

Whitey John could put away more food in less time than anybody Cleve knew, but even as he shoveled it down, he liked to talk about it. His food and everyone else's.

"Yeah, Cleve, I can't believe you've got any appetite left after you pigged out on that junk at the commissary."

"You don't wanna get yourself a dunlap like Whitey's," Jace warned. "His roll done lapped way over his belt. Look at it, sittin' in his lap."

"Cleve's never gonna get fat," Jimmy said. Jimmy took every conversation seriously. Unless somebody was actually laughing, Jimmy couldn't spot a joke. "He could probably eat a whole bag of chocolate every day and never gain an ounce."

Jimmy knew all about Cleve's waistline. He was making him a belt in the hobby shop. Cleve wasn't supposed to know about it, but it was hard not to guess when he caught the kid checking out the tag on his jeans down in the shower room. He really didn't want any of this, but he found himself talking to Jimmy the way his grandfather had talked to him.

"You're the one needs to eat, kid. You're gonna blow away pretty soon. Over the fence and out across the prairie."

"Eeez, that's thirty days in The Hole," Whitey said solemnly. "Accidental escape. That's a bad offense."

"Hey, Cleve, I'm gettin' out next month," Jace said. "Now that you're shakin' loose with some of that *maza ska* you've been savin' up, why don't you buy my TV off o' me?"

"I don't need a TV."

"Why? Because you read all those sexy books?"

"Cleve's been reading law books," Jimmy put in. "And legal journals, stuff like that. Now that he's got himself a good lawyer, he's gonna beat this rap."

Whitey stuffed half a roll into his mouth, then talked around it. "I heard about Whitestaff." Word got around fast, Cleve thought. "That's one smart 'skin, you know? He can tell anybody off anytime he wants. You read about him all the time in the *Lakota Times*."

"Since when did you start reading?" Jace asked.

"Since my sister gave me a subscription for Christmas." Whitey popped the other half of the roll in his mouth, looked around the table and scowled. "Hey, I read. Like to keep up with what's goin' on in the world."

"Pine Ridge, South Dakota isn't exactly the world," Jace said. He looked to Cleve for approval. "Thinks he's keeping up on all the news."

Whitey ignored the cut-down. "You really reading law books, Cleve?"

"Some."

"How about sexy books? You read any good, sexy books lately?"

"Some."

Jace laughed. "Forget it, Whitey. The kind he reads don't have any pictures. They don't show tits and ass; they just describe 'em in words."

"Ehn'it?" Whitey's eyes widened. "Library books?" Cleve nodded, smiling. The familiar "rez talk" tickled him as much as the expression on Whitey's face. "I could go for some of that."

"Just finished a book you might like, Whitey. A Western. Took it back to the library yesterday."

"Shee-it, Cleve, he wouldn't have time to finish it. He's only got three more calendars left to do, if he's lucky."

"You couldn't finish a book in three years?"

Jimmy was never going to be anything but a fish. Whitey laughed. "Haven't finished one in twenty-three years. Keep losing my place."

"Better get with the program, then." Everybody loved it when Cleve did Steiner. He had the officious tone down perfectly. "Put your time to good use. Get an education. We'll start you out wherever you left off on the outside."

"They haven't found a third grade teacher yet," Jace said.

Whitey bristled. "Shit, what's the name of that book, Cleve? I'll go check it out." He glared at Jace. "I'll read the whole damn thing, too."

Joe Dietz slid up to the table, unnoticed until his voice pricked the conversation like the point of a needle against a thin-skinned balloon.

"Have they made a squaw out of you yet, fish? They sure haven't had much luck teaching you how to play basketball, so they must have some use for you."

Without looking up Cleve dropped his fork in his tray. "Nobody's had any luck teaching you any manners, Dietz."

"Anytime you say, Black Horse."

"You're not worth spending time in The Hole for." He pushed his chair back and stood slowly, both hands on his tray. "Unless you can't stay clear of my table. I'm real fussy about keeping the dogs outside while I eat."

They faced off, each holding a tray. Cleve assessed Dietz's tense stance, the knife and spoon in the large compartment to the left and the fork handle under his right thumb. The noise around him died suddenly. Out of the corner of his eye he saw a guard closing in.

"You're not too fussy about the smell of fish," Dietz muttered. He shifted his attention toward the guard, then relaxed his shoulders one at a time and took a step back. " 'Course your kind wouldn't be."

Jace started to his feet, but Cleve put a hand on the younger man's shoulder. He felt hot, and a red foam clouded his vision, but he held his body in check and let Dietz pass.

"We can take him in the weight room," Jace whispered.

Cleve turned and saw the excitement in Jace's eyes. "Then they'll shut the weight room down."

"Just for a while. I'd rather break that sucker's arm than lift weights any damn time."

"We'll find a better way." He looked Jace in the eye. The kid had a month left, and he was ready to risk an assault charge. Cleve nodded toward the dish tank. "Let's get moving."

Jimmy followed Cleve through the traffic area, which was the intersection of the corridors that connected the cell blocks with the rest of the prison's facilities. The traffic control officer watched them pass his window. He'd been alerted by the dining room officer. Dietz and Black Horse had been pawing the ground like two thick-necked bulls. Maybe he should give them all what they wanted to see. Maybe he should just say the hell with it all and take one good shot . . .

"Time to clean house, huh?"

Cleve glanced past his shoulder at Jimmy's freckled face. "Looks like that's what Dietz wants."

"No, I mean it's Saturday. Time to clean our houses."

"Oh. Yeah. It's Saturday." Hang on to the routine, he told himself. The routine kept him going. Meals, work, recreation, study. The rest was craziness.

"Dietz wants you to screw up, Cleve. He wants you to go after him."

"If he keeps this up, I'll have to. I've whipped his ass before."

"Yeah, but it didn't stop him. It's a game. He's a lifer, too, and this is how he wants to spend his time."

Cleve tried not to think about what the term *lifer* meant. He couldn't apply it to himself and stay sane. "Jimmy, why don't you put in for pre-South? You've been here long enough, you could qualify. Get yourself out of the old cell house and into a nicer part of town. Away from Dietz."

"I'm not gonna let him bother me."

"Okay, then, just do it because it'd be good for you. A few months in pre-South, and then you check in at Holiday Inn South." He'd taken the orientation tour. The newest unit didn't look half bad. Like being locked away in a motel rather than the stacked cages they were headed for now. "Air conditioning. No bars on your door. You'd like it there."

"You mean 'Suck-Ass Unit'?"

"Who cares what a bunch of hard cases call it? You haven't been charged with any infractions. You'd get right in."

"Are you gonna try for it?" Cleve laughed, and Jimmy bristled as they followed the line toward the fire escape style stairs on the end of the cell block. "You wouldn't, would you. You're no kiss-ass, and neither am I."

"They've only got two slots for guys like me. Hell, you get a bunch of long-term guys in there, nobody else'll ever get in. The waiting list for those two slots is as long as your arm." He looked back over his shoulder at the boy who hung on his every word. "Yeah, I checked on it. I wouldn't mind kicking back in South for a while. Besides, my jacket's full of incident reports. Yours is clean. Go for it, man."

"That would put us on different chow lines and everything. I'm trying to get a job at the shops, like you. I asked for metals."

"Jesus, Jimmy, will you get off my leg once?" Cleve hated it when Jimmy looked at him like a puppy he'd just kicked. Give a little whistle, he'd come running back, wagging his tail. "Listen, you've gotta learn to take care of yourself."

"You going up to the weight room tonight?"

"I don't know. I think I've got a visitor coming."

"Susan?" he whispered. He'd never met her, but he felt privileged to know about her. Cleve had trusted him with her first name, then told him not to mention it to anyone else. "I thought she came on Mondays."

Five Mondays in the last two months. Cleve had thought he would just string her along to see what she'd do. When he wouldn't say much about Darcy's kid, she stopped asking. She came to see him anyway. He knew she had simply buried her motive until the time might come when she'd have a better chance of getting what she wanted from him, but he was willing to play along. He didn't have anything better to do. She had a soft voice and a sweet smell.

Lately the Midnight Special had blue eyes instead of a white headlight. He had a name for her now, and he rode her harder than ever. He wanted to see how long he could make her keep coming.

"Guess her schedule's different now," he told Jimmy as they filed up the cell block steps. "She wrote me a letter." She'd told him to call her if Saturday was a bad time for him, but inmates could only make long distance calls collect, and he'd be damned if he was going to call her collect. So he had to let her come.

He *wanted* her to come. Come whenever he asked her. Come whenever she wanted to. Come just for him. He'd never so much as touched her, but he thought if he did, she'd come some more. Just for him.

God, his head was full of it. Full of *her*, and he told himself it was only because she was his only link to something almost real. Almost normal. Christ, she'd *put* him there, and now he looked forward to seeing her. He put up with all their groping over him just to spend an hour looking at her. Sometimes they didn't talk much, but she seemed to know he just liked having her there, and she'd always stay until he told her it was time to go. When she was gone, he would wish that he had touched her shoulder or her hand, just to see what she would do.

She'd probably back away from him. After she'd just been patted down, it wasn't likely she'd want him to touch her. She'd be as repulsed as he was each time she left, when they made him strip down.

"I'll skip the weight room tonight," Jimmy said when they reached Cleve's tier. Jimmy had another flight to go.

"She won't get here till after seven. I'll go in and spot you for a while."

He hadn't called. Susan took that to mean that he would see her on Saturday. She had some shopping to do anyway, so even if he turned her away, the trip wasn't wasted. She turned just before she reached the railroad crossing at the east edge of town and followed the fork that led to the big brick compound. Without its massive tower and tall fencing, it might have been a school or an old military compound like Fort Abraham Lincoln, a couple of miles to the south. The abandoned army post was now used as an Indian technical training center. Both functioned in a kind of otherworldly isolation—

one next to the airport, the other beside the railroad tracks—yet both were long-standing landmarks in a city not much more than a century old. And both spoke volumes about the history of Indian-white relations and all the connotations of *assimilation*.

The training center, run by the various North Dakota tribes rather than the federal government, was always scrambling for enough money to pay minimal salaries and maintain the old buildings. At the penitentiary, at least a fourth of the inmates were Indians, even though Indians comprised less than five per cent of the state's population. Before Susan had moved to Fort Yates, none of this had concerned her. She hadn't known any Indians except the ones she saw in movies. Now she did. Now she had a son, and that made all the difference.

Foliage shadows played over Susan's car as she followed the tree-lined road that ended in the prison's parking lot. Few places in Bismarck could boast of such well-established trees as the elms and cottonwoods that surrounded the lot, the staff housing, and the entrance to Administration. It was a warm, quiet spring evening, the kind best spent outdoors. Susan locked her car.

After being searched she was escorted to the visiting room, where she discovered that Cleve was right about the Saturday night crowd. The sofas were all occupied, and most of the tables were taken as well. She reported to the visiting room officer, then stood next to the wall wishing that Sam's therapist hadn't changed her schedule and that Vera would stop complaining about how hard it would be to keep Sam once the kids got out of school in a couple of weeks.

God help her, she was standing there in the middle of a room full of prisoners. Convicted murderers and rapists. She was waiting to spend the evening with one of them. She wasn't even sure what she could say to him this time. He hadn't shown any inclination to declare his paternity. Why should he? It surprised her that he was even willing to talk to her. It surprised her that she was *able* to talk to him. He didn't make it easy. But he didn't make it impossible, either.

The room got quiet when an officer warned somebody about "getting too friendly." Susan looked around for the culprit, hoping to find out what "too friendly" meant, but no one looked guilty of anything. People shrugged, went back to their visiting, and the din rose again. A door opened, and Cleve walked in. He saw her right away, and she smiled and waited for him to make a move. This was his territory.

He made a quick assessment. Two open tables. The one closest to Susan was out. Dietz was sitting there bullshitting with somebody ugly enough to be his brother. Susan was glued to the wall, looking a little lost. Too damn crowded on weekends. She seemed glad to see him, maybe because he was a familiar face in the crowd. She had a pretty smile, and without thinking, he let it get to him. He let it make him feel good inside just for a moment, like a guy whose girl had come a long way to see him. He nodded toward the table on his side of the room, and he watched Dietz as she crossed the room.

Don't even look at her, you slimebag.

But he did, and so did his damn brother.

"You were expecting me, weren't you?"

Cleve nodded and led the way by seating himself. He'd seen guys pull chairs out for women, but he'd never done it himself. She had no trouble sitting down, talking all the while, which he knew to be her way of getting comfortable.

"I wasn't sure how to handle it. I know I can't call you except in an emergency, and after I sent the letter, I thought if you tried to call, and I wasn't home—"

"I didn't."

She closed her mouth and looked across the table at him.

"I can't call you, either," he told her.

"I hope this isn't a bad time."

He chuckled. "I canceled all my plans for you. What's up?"

"Well, nothing, really. I just can't come Monday."

"You got a new schedule?" *Or somebody else to see on Monday?*

"No. I still have Sundays and Mondays off, but you said Sunday was the busiest day, and during the week I spend a lot of time at Vera's, trying to help out with Sam." She'd never told him about Sam's physical therapy, and she decided this wasn't the time.

"You look like you've been up all night. Is the kid sick?"

She shook her head. "Not at the moment. He was having a few problems—you know, baby stuff. That's why I didn't come to Bismarck last week. He's better now."

"You need some rest, lady."

He sounded concerned, which surprised her. "Do I look that bad?"

"No." She had dark circles under her eyes and even less color than usual. But she was a woman. "You don't look bad. Just tired."

"I've been trying to get the judge to place Sam back with me, at least temporarily, but he won't budge."

"And you're losing sleep over it."

"I'm okay." She ran her fingers through her hair and stuck it behind her ear. "Your grandmother came into the clinic the other day."

"What for?"

"Her blood sugar was low. Your uncle brought her in."

"Did you see her?"

"No. She came in about one o'clock. I've asked one of the clinic nurses to keep me posted. Greta Silk. She says she knows you."

"You told her you were coming up here?"

"I told her you'd been a patient at Med Center and that you'd been in touch with me, worried about your grandmother. She said to tell you hello."

"I went to school with Greta." Tall and stocky, as he remembered. Hell of a basketball player for a girl.

"Damn, that was a long time ago. So how's the old lady doing? She holding up okay?"

"For a woman her age who's had diabetes as long as she has, she's doing very well, according to Greta. I'd like to meet her."

"Suit yourself. Just don't try telling her she's got a great-grandson she didn't know about." The flash in her eyes made him chuckle. "She'll be up here ripping me up one side and down the other for being a no-good cowboy."

"That might be all the proof I need."

"Yeah, and then you'd have to fight her for him." He waved that notion away quickly. "Nah, I'm kidding. She's too old to raise another kid."

The prospect was something she hadn't worried about until now. Maybe she didn't want to meet her. "What about you? We never talk about you. Have you started taking classes yet?"

"Just started. I'm taking English, psychology and criminal justice." He shook his head, half smiling. "How do you like that? Criminal justice."

"Why did you choose those courses?"

"That's what they're offering."

"Sounds interesting enough."

"No, it doesn't." He wasn't going to sit there and let her talk to him like some kind of counselor. "It sounds like school, and you've been to school."

"I haven't had criminal justice."

"Neither have I." He eyed her casually for a moment. "Why do you come up here to see me, Susan? Why do you want to come to a place like this?"

"Because I know you're Sam's father."

"So what? What good does that do you if *I* don't know I'm his father?"

"You haven't said you're not. You haven't refused to see me, and I know I'm your only visitor."

"So this is charity work?" She glanced behind him, and he wasn't going to put up with that, either. "Is it? Like the kid nobody else wants?"

"No." She hated it when he turned on her this way. She knew whenever he got angry, he was thinking about the trial. Without any discussion, they'd agreed not to air it, even though it was always there, just below the surface of everything. They talked around it. His crime, her judgment, who was guilty and who was innocent were matters to be locked in a box and set aside. The pretense allowed them to go on seeing each other, for whatever reasons each one had. "We've become friends, I think. Isn't it crazy?"

He shrugged and glanced away. "There's a guy in here whose girlfriend turned him in for selling cocaine. She comes to see him every week. He counts the days between visits."

"Is he in treatment?"

"Oh, yeah," he drawled, "they've got him in treatment." He sprawled in his chair and studied her. "See, I can't figure out what kind of friends we are. Every time you come up here, I give you a bad time about something."

Her smile was almost coy. "You're not very good at it. You usually end up joking about something else, so it isn't a really bad time."

"Sure. This is a great way to spend a Saturday night, hanging out in the visiting room at the pen."

"Am I keeping you from something?"

"Working out. I usually lift—" He scowled and shook his head, genuinely puzzled. "I could see it on Mondays. Monday's usually kind of a drag, but Saturday night? You oughta be seeing some guy on Saturday night."

"I am."

She was cute. He had to smile. "You don't want to get involved, right?"

"Right."

"You don't want to rush into anything."

"Right."

"Yeah, well, take a lifetime to think about it. Meanwhile, these cameras are for your protection."

"So they tell me."

"Seriously." He sat up and planted his folded arms on the edge of the table, still studying her eyes. "You're not going out with anyone?"

"I don't have time."

"You saddle yourself with a kid, you'll never have time. And it won't be easy to find a man who wants you *and* the kid. Some other guy's kid." He sat back again, as though to get a different perspective. And give her one. "Not that a lot of guys wouldn't find you attractive. Hell, every guy in this room watched you walk over to the table."

"I didn't . . . mean for them to do that."

"You didn't have to." She had that satisfied look women got when they knew they had a man going. He wanted to see it, then take it away. "What happened, Susan? Did some guy screw you over?" Bingo. He could see it in her eyes. Small victory for his side. But not real satisfying. "Somewhere along the line you got hurt."

"Who hasn't? Hmm? Somewhere along the line?" His sympathy, if that was what it was, pricked her pride. "All I really care about right now is Sam."

"Yeah."

They stared at one another, wanting more said, each wanting it to come from the other.

Susan hurried to fill the silence. "Cleve, I've wondered, you know, you usually read about cases like yours where—" His eyes narrowed, but she ignored the warning. "Aren't you going to appeal?"

"We're not going to talk about that." She glanced away from him, but he waited until he had her attention again. "Okay? I thought we understood that."

"I do," she said, her tone contrite.

"And if you're worried that I might get out sooner or later and try to take this kid from you—"

"No, I'm not. But I do wish . . ." She tossed her hair back and sat up straight. "No, you're right. We can't talk about that. What's done is done. And you can't take Sam from me because I don't have him."

"I've got no use for a kid."

"A child isn't something you use, Cleve."

"Isn't it?"

He could think of a hundred things people used kids for. A hundred things he wanted no part of, including trying to make points with God or whatever it was Susan was doing. She was looking at him as though he'd just fed her something putrid, but he had no retractions to make. She'd brought up the wrong subject. She closed her eyes and took a deep breath. Yeah, she knew it, too.

"I need your help, Cleve. If you could—"

Neither of them had seen Dietz approach.

"Has Black Horse told you about his boyfriend, lady? His little Jimmy?"

Cleve's chair clattered to the floor. He whirled and faced a guard who'd moved faster than he had. Susan stood, dumbfounded by the blur of motion and the quick response of the guards. The insinuation had barely registered with her, but already Dietz was on his way out, and a second officer was about to remove Cleve, who backed away.

"Just give me a minute." He turned to address a third officer, standing on the platform at the head of the room, as though he might have the final say. "*He* came at *me*, hey."

"Let's go, Cleve. There's no infraction yet. Not unless you give us trouble."

With Susan at his back, Cleve stood his ground. "Let me get something straightened out here. Then I'll go back to my house quietly, okay?"

The guard's nod was almost imperceptible, but it gave Cleve leave to turn to Susan. She stood between him and the wall, eyes gaping at him like a double-barreled shotgun. He put his charge to her softly. "You believe him, don't you?" He stepped closer, shutting her off from the rest of the room. "Answer me, Susan. Do you believe what he said?"

"I don't think—"

"Don't think about it. Just answer. Guilty or not guilty."

"It's none of my business."

"You made it your business by coming here and giving me—" He wanted to shake her and wake her up. "I want to know if you believe what he said."

"No. I don't believe it." She wanted to tell him she knew he wasn't a murderer, either, but something inside told her she'd reached the limit. Their fragile relationship could bear no more.

"I've got no use for kids. I mean that."

"I believe you," she assured him.

"A guy could go crazy in a place like this, you know? Sometimes I think I might—"

The unguarded look in his eyes betrayed a vulnerability she'd never seen before. Perhaps no one had, nor ever would again, and in that moment she reached for him without her usual hesitation. She touched his forearm below his rolled sleeve, rubbed the soft underside, traced the bulging veins to his pulsepoint, and slipped her hand into his. His eyes brightened as he tightened his hand and skimmed his thumb back and forth over her knuckles.

"Let's go, Cleve," the guard said.

"I'll come back next week," she whispered. "They'll let me, won't they?"

They'd let him kiss her. Right now, before she left, he was entitled to one kiss.

"Come on. Let's go."

"Wait one goddam minute." Cleve shrugged away from the hand on his shoulder, but he turned and humbled himself beyond his usual capacity. "Please. It's important."

"Thirty seconds."

Cleve turned his back on his shabby world and filled his head with Susan, who had touched him. Still touched him. Still held his hand.

"There's a lawyer in Minneapolis who's agreed to take my case. Indian guy. They say he's good. I'll write to him, tell him about the kid. Sam. And I'll drop you a line with his name and phone number. Maybe he'll have some ideas."

"You'll help me?"

"We'll see what this guy says. Okay? I don't know if there's anything I can do, but we'll see." He could kiss her. God, he wanted to kiss her, just to see what it felt like.

But the hand was on his shoulder again.

"You'd better get some rest, lady." He squeezed her hand, then backed away.

"Will they let me see you next week?" The guard reached for the door, and Susan followed as Cleve was ushered out. "Don't let that man get to you, Cleve, okay? Don't get into any trouble because I'm coming—" The world beyond the visiting room door swallowed him up.

"—back next week. No matter what."

Chapter 12

Dear Susan,

My lawyer's name is Bernard Whitestaff. He's from Minneapolis but will be in Bismarck on June 1 if you want to see him. His phone number is 612-897-3825. I told him what it was about and he said it sounds interesting. But don't get excited. He thinks everything a person tells him sounds interesting. I also told him I don't know if the kid's mine, but I guess he could be.

There's a rodeo out here in July. I can ride this year if I don't do anything like bust Dietz's face before then. Dietz was the guy who made that remark in the visiting room. Him and I don't get along. Anyway I should be able to ride and I thought you might like to come. Maybe my grandmother would like to come too if you could bring her. I want to show her I'm okay so she doesn't have to feel bad about me being here. You would have to go out and see her. She hasn't got a phone. She lives out in the country aways, but if you go to Little Eagle somebody can tell you how to find the place. That's if you want to come. You've got time to think about it.

I used to go to Indian boarding schools when I was a kid but I never used to write letters until I came here. Still don't write many, not to friends anyway. There's not much to tell unless you want to know what I had for breakfast. I pretty much like the classes I'm taking. Work in the metals shop is going ok too. This one kid Jimmy Dawson made a nice horsehair belt for me in the hobby shop. He's latched onto me kind of like a puppy. Not for what Dietz said, but for his own protection I guess. He's pretty wimpy and that's not his only problem. But you can't go kicking puppies around, right? This is no place for young kids no matter what kind of stupid thing they've done.

Gotta go to work now. Think about the rodeo.

Cleve

Susan read the letter four times. His admission that Sam could be his son sounded promising. The invitation to call his lawyer was gracious, but it was the part about his grandmother and the line about the puppies that made Susan smile each time she read it through. Trying to forget about the bars on his door and his inmate number, which was part of the return address on the envelope, Susan imagined Cleve sitting down at a desk and writing to her. She could smell his cigarette smoke on the paper. His bold, unslanted handwriting was neat and even. He penned her neither anger nor sarcasm, and he made an effort to think of good news to tell her. She felt undeserving.

Does the defendant wish the jury polled?

Does that mean each one has to say it to my face?

Yes.

Then, yeah, I want them polled.

How many times had she wished she could do it over, differently this time? She would offer to be foreman before Tidball got in there. She would be more confident and much more persistent. She would use every one of the hundred arguments she'd thought of since the trial. Why hadn't she thought of them at the right time?

She could have held out longer, too. Every time she read about a trial somewhere that went on for months, jury deliberations that lasted weeks on end, she wanted to go back and do it all again. She'd given up so easily.

She'd let all the arguing wear her down. She'd looked him right in the eye and told him she believed him to be guilty of murder, and for a long time she had been able to tell herself there was a better than even chance that he was. She couldn't tell herself that anymore. Seeing him regularly, talking with him, reading his letter—it all tipped the balance in his favor. There was a much better chance she'd sent an innocent man to prison. She wondered why he tolerated her at all.

Maybe she shouldn't see him again.

She studied his signature, touched it with her forefinger.

Maybe she could still get a letter out to him in today's mail.

Dear Cleve,

Thank you for your letter and for referring me to Mr. Whitestaff. I called him right away. He sounds like a very nice man. He made it clear to me that you are his client, and he will be representing your interests in any matter concerning you. He agreed to meet with me to discuss Sam's situation only because you asked him to. I'm having lunch with him on the first, after he meets with you. He said that I will probably need an attorney, too, and that he could recommend two or three who are familiar with tribal laws. His concern for your situation is evident, and if he's as good as you say, I think you've got the right man on your case. I hope he can help you.

I'm anxious to see you ride in the rodeo. Thank you for inviting me. I don't know much about rodeo, but I've heard that you're a wonderful bronc rider. I haven't had a chance to see the South Dakota side of the reservation yet, but I'll plan to drive down there soon and look in on your grandmother if you'll write to her first and introduce me. I won't mention Sam when I see her. I'll leave that up to you. But, of course, I'll be happy to take her to the rodeo.

I enjoyed your letter, as I enjoy our visits. If you get

the urge to write to a friend again, keep me in mind. I may not have much to tell, either, but I'm good about answering letters. Especially from people who love their grandmothers and don't kick puppies around. Take care of yourself. Don't bother about Dietz, who is obviously a jerk and not worth your trouble.

I won't be in Bismarck this Saturday, but I'd like to stop in during visiting hours on the first, which is Monday evening, if that's all right with you. After we've both seen Mr. Whitestaff, we'll have a lot to talk about.

See you soon.
Susan

Cleve kicked off his boots, lit a cigarette, lay back on his bed and read the letter over again. Pretty businesslike, most of it. Thank you for this, thank you for that. Very polite. He wondered what she was doing Saturday night. None of his damn business. Hell, he was just curious. He went back to the part about lunch with Whitestaff.

He wondered where they'd go. Someplace nice. Someplace where the menu wasn't on the wall and you didn't eat off a tray. She'd tell him about the kid, and Whitestaff would very smoothly tell her how wonderful she was for offering the little orphan a home. She'd like that. She'd give him a nice smile for saying that. Maybe she'd give him more than a smile.

Christ, he was thinking like an asshole. Susan wanted the kid, simple enough. He'd set it up between her and Whitestaff himself, just to help her out. He hadn't counted on any lunch, but, hell, it was just a meeting. That was the way classy people had their meetings. She always came to see him looking classy, acting classy. More than once he'd wished he could at least offer her a cup of coffee when she came to see him.

But she wasn't coming Saturday. Did she think she could just come any time—first Monday, then Saturday, now Monday again? He had a schedule, too. No way was she gonna jerk him around like some kind of puppet. She had things to do? Fine. He had things to do. He took a quick, hard drag on his cigarette, looking for a rush.

"Swine on the line."

"Queer on the tier."

Somebody downstairs was standing jiggers, and the word was being passed upstairs that The Man was coming. Cleve wondered what they were up to. The second voice sounded like Jimmy's. If the kid got himself into some kind of shit between now and the end of July, he was on his own. Cleve wasn't about to miss out on the rodeo. Not this year.

She said she'd come. She'd even bring the old lady. Maybe it wasn't such a good idea, getting them together, but it was the only way he wanted his grandmother to see him. Ridin' high.

He reached up, found the ashtray by instinct and crushed the last of his cigarette, still tamping after the ash was dead. He studied the letter. He liked her handwriting. It was fine and feminine, like the small pink flower that was embossed at the bottom of the page. Right below her name. How did she manage to get his palms to sweat with just a letter?

What the hell, he knew damn well how. He was what you called a real captive audience. Anything that smacked of woman gave him a hard-on worthy of Mount Rushmore. That thought conjured up such a crazy image, he laughed until he had to sit up or choke.

"Funny letter?"

Cleve blinked back the tears, and his grin faded. On the other side of the bars stood an officer who wanted in on the joke. "Ever been to Mount Rushmore?" Cleve asked.

"Yeah."

"Big suckers, ain't they?"

Bernard Whitestaff was a large man, but even though he carried more weight than Cleve did, his features seemed finer. His eyes were light brown and piercing, like a cat's, and his lips were thin. He had a radio broadcaster's voice, but he might have been dressed for television. Susan enjoyed his humor along with her chicken-stuffed crepe. They shared mutual interests in Minneapolis, spoke of her background and his, danced around the business at hand until both plates were nearly empty. He ordered dessert. She passed. She stirred cream into her tea, and he dropped the bombshell.

"Cleve says you were on his jury."

"Yes, I was." It was bound to come up. She hoped he wouldn't hold it against her. "What else did he say?"

"About that? What else is there to say? He was found guilty."

"Yes, he was."

"Damnedest thing I ever heard of. You get hooked up with this little preemie after the mother dies in the hospital where you work. Turns out the guy you convicted might be the baby's father."

"I was thinking Cleve might not . . ." Might not tell him? That was stupid. The man was Cleve's lawyer. "We don't talk about the trial. It makes it easier, you know, if we just don't talk about it."

"I spent a lot of time with Cleve today, and we talked about a lot of things. I've studied the evidence against him and the transcripts, and I don't think he got a fair trial." He raised an admonishing forefinger, then lifted his elbow to allow the waitress to put his cheesecake in front of him. "What's more, I don't think he had anything to do with killing Arnold Bertram."

"I don't think he did, either."

"Because you've gotten to know him?"

Susan shook her head. "I was never convinced that he was guilty."

Whitestaff frowned over a small glass pitcher of strawberry sauce he'd poised for pouring. "The verdict has to be unanimous. You voted to convict him."

"I know." Lord, she needed to talk, and Whitestaff was easy to talk to. "It's legal for me to talk about this now, right?"

"It's history now. You can talk about it."

"Good. I've wanted to tell someone about it because it's really bothered me. I hope I never have to serve on a jury again." She paused for a sip of ice water. "I thought the evidence was all circumstantial, and I kept telling them that. There was more than reasonable doubt. At first there were three not guilty votes, then two, then just one. Me. We went round and round for two days. I know that's not a long time, but at the time it seemed like an eternity. I couldn't convince the rest of them. The judge met with us again, told us that we were an intelligent group of people, that we had a duty to reach a consensus. Eleven against one. I gave in. They convinced me that I was being naive about the whole thing."

"Naive?"

"By believing him. It could easily have happened the way Cleve said it did. They never found the murder weapon. Obviously Cleve hadn't taken the man's money. I thought it was quite possible the whole thing happened the way Cleve said it did." She gestured over her tea cup with an open hand. "But a lot of it was a matter of taking his word."

"Which you were willing to do?"

"*Reasonable doubt.* That was one of the terms that I kept coming back to."

"We're big on terms in this business." He ate a forkful of cheesecake, taking time to let it melt in his mouth while he considered. "Why didn't you tell the judge you couldn't agree with the rest of them?"

"Because he said we had to agree. Eventually. We had to reach a consensus, and it had to be—"

"Not if you were convinced the prosecution hadn't proved its case. Even a minority of one has the right to send the message to the judge that she doesn't agree with the rest of the jury and won't change her mind. Just call the bailiff." His catlike eyes narrowed. "Didn't the judge tell you that when he instructed you?"

"No."

"He should have. Of course, they can instruct you any way they want. Nobody wants a hung jury. It's a big expense to the taxpayer. But it happens."

"Then they have another trial?"

"That's right. Start over." He played it cool, as though the conversation were just a way to pass the time while he ate his cheesecake. "What were the issues? What convinced the rest of them he was guilty?"

"They didn't believe there was another hitchhiker."

"Why not?"

She lifted one shoulder. "He was never found."

"Nobody really looked for him, far as I can tell. What else?"

"You want to know the truth? I think it was racial. They all believed Cleve was drunk, and they kept saying—"

"He was never tested for blood alcohol level. How would they know he was drunk?"

"They talked a lot about the beer, how many stops they made, how many cans were found. And he passed out. At least, he thought he did."

"I've gone over the transcript. There was some talk of a blackout, although Ness carefully skirted that issue after he'd planted the idea. He wanted a first degree conviction, which meant proving intent."

"Cleve had had an accident earlier," Susan pointed out. "He'd hit his head."

"A point which Felch neglected to hammer out. I think Cleve had a concussion, and I think he slept through the whole thing."

"So do I."

"He didn't get any medical attention when they locked him up in the drunk tank that morning, either."

"But if they didn't test for alcohol—"

"It's standard procedure, even if they just smelled it on him. He'd been drinking. Doesn't mean he was drunk."

"I think to the jury, just being an Indian meant that he was drunk."

Whitestaff mashed graham cracker crust with the back of his fork, one crumb at a time until he had them all. "Did they say that?"

"They said things like, 'You know how they are when they're drinking.' One said she'd been married to an Indian. Another one said he'd had an Indian man working for him who always got drunk on payday."

He looked up from the plate. "They were *all* talking like that?"

"The ones who talked at all. Several of the women just sat through the whole thing and let the men do most of the deliberating. The women nodded on cue. It was like the dark ages of male supremacy."

"Welcome to redneck country." He smiled. "Where a man doesn't touch 'women's work' and women don't make any big decisions."

"Not everyone here is like that."

"Sounds like Cleve ran up against at least eleven of them. And the twelfth one caved in."

"The judge said—" Susan ran her fingers over the handle of her cup, but she didn't pick it up. "—*consensus* means—"

"I know what it means. You know what an eternity is, Susan? It's life plus thirty." She looked up at him, and he nodded for her. "You've had a hard time with this, haven't you?" She didn't have to answer. "You talk to anybody about it?"

"No. Not really. No one would listen."

"Well, don't. I'm not sure how to fit you in. You're not impartial anymore. You've got an ulterior motive for getting Cleve off."

"I don't see how trying to correct a mistake could be construed as an ulterior motive."

"You can't correct your mistake. What's done is done. You can't ever vote on that verdict again." He pointed, not at her, but at her cup. "You want to adopt a child you think is Cleve's. That's where the ulterior motive comes in."

"That has nothing to do with—"

"It has everything to do with it. Cleve couldn't sign over custody of that child to you, even if he established paternity. Not as long as he's an inmate. So you've got a vested interest in getting him out somehow."

"You mean he couldn't legally—"

Whitestaff shook his head slowly. "Not as long as he's a prisoner."

"I didn't know that."

"I figured you didn't. So you and I know that you didn't start off with an ulterior motive."

"Sam still has nothing to do with this."

"Let's keep it that way. Even if Cleve were willing to claim him and turn him over to you, the tribe might fight it. And they'd probably win. There have been a number of cases on other reservations where the tribe takes custody rather than let non-Indians adopt. Sometimes even over the birth mother's expressed wishes."

"Sam's mother died before he was born, Mr. Whitestaff. I have no other children, and I can give him—"

"The particular circumstances may not be as important as the precedent your adopting him might set." He pushed his empty plate back. "I'm not saying you aren't going to get him, and I'm not even saying you shouldn't. I don't know. What I am saying is that Cleve's my client, and I wouldn't advise him to relinquish his right to a child he's never had a chance to meet. *If* the child is his. He doesn't seem totally convinced."

"I know." Susan sighed. "The child is his. I have no doubt of that."

"If you were the mother, I'd probably take your word for it. But I'd still be advising Cleve."

"I understand that."

"Then I'm going to ask you to put this paternity thing on hold, for everybody's sake. It's Cleve's murder conviction we need to be concerned about. I'm going to get this case thrown out, then get him out on bail. And I don't think they'll retry him on the same charge— maybe not at all. They botched up too many things."

"You mean he'll get off without actually being acquitted?"

"That could easily happen."

Susan glanced out the window. A street light turned from red to green. "I've never told Cleve about the way I changed my vote."

"Do you want to tell him, or shall I?"

"I've wanted to tell him, and I've also dreaded it." The question came quietly. "What will he think of me?"

"What does it matter?"

"We've become friends."

"And you want him to help you get that child."

"But Sam—" She squared her shoulders and looked him in the eye. "I'll tell him myself. If I had known about the option of telling the judge—"

"He would have called you all in and talked to you again, probably. He would have kept you at it a while."

"How long?"

"Depends. You were in a bad spot, Susan. I'll try to explain that to Cleve." She started to speak, but he cut her off. "Listen, maybe it would be better if you went on home and let me tell him the whole thing. I can tell him what happened in the context of how I'm going to handle his case. I don't know him very well yet. I don't know how he'll respond, but maybe it's best that you let him hear it from me. Then give him a few days to put it all in perspective before you see him again."

"I'd be chickening out." She rolled her eyes at the thought. "Again."

"I don't think so. He's going to have a lot of mixed feelings. Maybe the fair thing to do is give him a chance to sort them out before you say whatever it is you want to say to him about it."

"He might not want to hear it."

"He might not. I suppose it depends on what it is." He offered a sympathetic smile as he dropped the blue cloth napkin on the table. "I've decided to stick around for a few extra days. I've read the transcripts, but now I want to go over everything—investigation, evidence, *everything*—with a fine-tooth comb. What you've told me helps."

"How much longer do you think—"

"These things take time. Cleve's not getting out for a while yet."

"This has already taken almost two years out of his life."

"That's true." Again, he smiled. "But it's nothing new. He's not the first Indian to get screwed by the courts." He anticipated an objection, just because he'd heard it so often. "Yeah, I know. It happens to other people, too. Do you know how many crimes *against* Indians go unsolved? Indians get murdered, raped, ripped off, and nobody pays attention. Some white guy gets his throat cut, and they've got an Indian on the scene who's had a few beers—hell, they're not looking for anybody else. They've got their man."

"Cleve's case is a cause for you."

"Cleve's a brother." He tapped his fingers on the table before pushing back from the table. "I'm going to get him off."

Cleve let his chin drop to his chest and held his arms straight out from his shoulders as though they were nailing him up. He submitted quietly these days, assuming the position for a pat search without being told.

He'd been sorely tempted to refuse to see her this time. Whitestaff had tried to feed him a bunch of bullshit about what a tough spot she'd been in, and how she'd been carrying all this guilt. Hell, it was no big secret she'd helped convict him. He knew that; he'd shoved that to the back of his brain a long time ago. She had no excuse for jacking him around. In her letter, she'd said they would have a lot to talk about after she saw Whitestaff. She was right. But she'd sent Whitestaff back instead of coming herself.

"Pretty nice-looking woman you've got waiting to see you, Cleve." The officer stepped back, and Cleve lowered his arms to his sides. "You're clean. Seems kinda silly for them to keep searching her down every time she comes in. You can tell she's no troublemaker."

"What do you know about women, Casey? Don't you know the pretty ones cause the most trouble?"

Casey led the way to the visiting room door. "You worried about her steppin' out on you? She's sure gotten to be pretty regular about visiting."

"I got no reason to worry. She's just somebody to shoot the bull with once in a while, that's all. Somebody different."

"Geez, if that's all it is, maybe you'd like to introduce me to her."

"Maybe you'd like to introduce me to the governor. Drive me up to the capitol and get me into his office for a personal interview." Casey gave him a look, and Cleve laughed. "Why not? It's a fair trade."

"Some of you guys would sell your own grand-mothers."

"Mine's a little old." The automatic lock popped, and the officer opened the door. "Don't think she'd interest you, Casey."

They stepped inside and surveyed the room, which was relatively quiet for a Saturday afternoon. "There she is. Nice smile," Casey said. "You have yourself a good visit, Cleve. What did you say her name was?"

"Sister Mary Margaret." Just seeing her took some of the edge off his anger. She was sitting at the small table off to the side of the room, the one they had silently agreed was theirs, and he knew he'd take the chair across from her, as always. Sometime he wanted to sit next to her on the sofa. But not this time. His defenses were down already. He glanced at Casey. "I'm her favorite charity."

She looked uneasy, and he decided he liked that. He gave her more cause by not returning even a hint of a smile. Greeting her with a wordless nod, he took his chair, folded his hands on the table and stoically sat waiting to see what she was going to do with all the rope she'd given herself.

"Say something, Cleve."

"I think that's rightfully my line." He watched her stare at her hands. Her chin trembled slightly, which he told himself was a nice touch. Nevertheless, her discomfort became his. "I don't have much to say. Whitestaff says he might be able to get me out."

She looked at him with glossy eyes. "That's the important thing. I'm really glad." She paused. "Did he tell you what I told him about the jury deliberations?" Cleve nodded once. "I guess I didn't do my job very well."

He agreed, but for some reason he wasn't anxious to tell her that. "He said he thinks he can show racial prejudice from start to finish." He shook his head. "What I want him to prove is that I didn't do it."

"If he can just get you out of here, that'll be a good start. Maybe they'll find Ray Smith." He stared at her, and she anticipated his questions. "I do believe there was a Ray Smith, and I believe he must have killed Arnold Bertram. I let them convince me that I was wrong, and I—" Still he stared, while her stomach twisted itself into a knot. "Well, you know what I did."

"You said I was guilty. You think I don't remember?"

"But I knew better. I changed my—"

"Maybe you weren't the only one who knew better."

"I knew it was wrong."

Her confession came softly, and he didn't know whether he hurt for her or for himself. "What do you want me to say?"

Her face was full of tears that wouldn't fall. "I wanted to tell you before, but you didn't want us to talk about it."

"Did you?"

She glanced at the ceiling light. "I guess not. Not really."

"It doesn't matter. If you'd stuck to your guns, Whitestaff says they'd have declared a hung jury and gone through the same thing all over again."

"With a different jury."

"Different faces. Same kind of people."

"Nobody ever wants to serve on a jury. It's not an easy—"

He pounded the table with his fist, and his quiet tone hardened. "I don't want to hear about it, Susan. It's done."

"But I've regretted it every day since."

"Whitestaff said the judge didn't instruct you the right way. So you didn't know what else to do. Right?" He waited for her response, but she sat with eyes downcast, like a chastised child. "You changed your vote because you thought you'd be there forever if you didn't. I'd probably have done the same thing." She glanced up gratefully, but he had a reminder for her. "I don't want to be here forever, either."

"I know." *And I know—oh, God—it's my fault.*

"Sometimes I think I'd do anything to get out."

Anything? Here was a new worry, and she embraced it obediently. "Please don't. Then you'd have to live with it."

What was she talking about? What was a little guilt compared to what he was living with now? He wanted her contrition, not her advice, and he smiled. "You seem to be doing okay." He figured he could handle a guilty conscience as well as she. He thought about the past Monday again. "You enjoy your lunch with Whitestaff? He came over here, talking you up. I hope he pleads my case as well as he pleaded yours."

"He thought it would be best if he explained—"

"Best for who?" Cleve's quick laugh was humorless. "It was the old good news-bad news routine. Good news is, she believed you. She voted not guilty. Bad news is, in the end, she changed her vote." He glanced at the door, through which he would soon return to his cell. "Like I said, it doesn't matter."

"But in a way it's all good news because it just shows you didn't get a fair trial. You have the right to a fair trial," she said hopefully.

He stared past her. "You said you were coming to see me Monday night." The reminder of her promise hung in the air quietly for a moment before he looked into her eyes. They were as blue as the sheer cotton blouse she was wearing. "What did you think I'd do if you told me about all this yourself?"

"You've never let me—" Feeble excuse, she told herself, then admitted, "I thought you'd be angry. God knows you have a right to be angry."

"Do I?" Needing distance from her, he tipped his chair back and sprawled his long legs out over its sides. "So what? So what if I get good and pissed at you, Susan? What are you worried about?" He tossed a nod over his shoulder. "These cameras are for your protection."

That wasn't it, and he knew it. "I should never have gone along with the guilty verdict. It didn't feel right, even after I'd heard their arguments over and over until I thought I could see their side. It's never felt right since, and every time I see you—"

"You worry about whether you can still get what you want from me."

His eyes were glazed voids. She had to think for a moment. "Sam?"

"What you came for in the first place, right?"

"Yes. My original intention—"

"So you asked Whitestaff to find a nice way to tell me all this shit, so we could still be . . . friends." He made the word sound insidious.

"I'll find a way to get Sam. You couldn't help me now, even if you wanted to, according to Whitestaff."

"Which is why you told him—"

"I told him about changing my vote before he said anything about the fact that your being in prison makes it impossible for you to help me gain custody of your son."

"*My* son?" His chair's front legs slammed to the floor, but he kept his voice down. "You're taking a lot for granted, as usual."

"I could say the same for you."

"But you won't, will you?" The argument skidded across the table and stopped dead for lack of momentum when he smiled knowingly. "Because you don't want to piss me off."

"No, I don't. That certainly isn't why I came all the way up here to visit."

"What if Whitestaff asks you to help me? Are you going to admit to some judge that you screwed up?"

"If it comes to that, yes."

"If it comes to that." He shook his head, chuckling. "What a friend. Even if I'm not willing to cut any kind of a deal with you over this kid?"

"Sam has nothing to do with this, Cleve. I'm not looking for deals. It would be a relief to be able to tell a judge what happened in that jury room."

"Whitestaff says he needs more grounds than just that, but he seems to know what he's looking for. Seems to think it's there to be found." He studied her eyes, wherein he knew the truth would reveal itself. "You believed me?"

"I saw no reason not to, but since I was the only one, I thought—" She sighed as she let the back of her hand flop against the table. "—that it was hopeless, and that maybe I was wrong. But I've always known it was wrong to change my vote, and I don't know how to apologize for a thing like that."

"Try apologizing for not coming Monday night when you said in your letter you were going to."

"It was more important for you to see Mr. Whitestaff then."

"You don't know what's important to a guy who's stuck in a place like this." He leaned across the table to confide, "You don't wanna be jacked around. You think you're going to be seeing a woman on a certain day at a certain time, and you carry that around in your head all week. Then she doesn't show—"

"I'm sorry, Cleve." She laid her hands lightly atop his. His eyes brightened as she spoke softly. "I'm sorry I'm such a coward. I wish I'd stuck it out."

"I did fine without any visitors." He smiled. "But now you've screwed that up, too." As a test, he turned his palms toward hers. It surprised him when she didn't draw away. Her hands felt cool. He closed his around them slowly. "You'll really come to the rodeo?"

"I'm looking forward to it." She raised her eyebrows hopefully. "I could bring Sam."

"No. No kids. Not here." Maybe the boy was too young to know the difference, but Cleve would know. It didn't matter whose kid he was. "Just you, and maybe my grandmother."

Chapter 13

Cleve blocked out the noon sun with his hand. Above him a hawk wheeled and dipped, then caught a lift on a shaft of warm air and rode it high above the treetops without the slightest flutter of a wing. In that instant Cleve decided about the only thing he'd trade for eight seconds on horseback that afternoon was maybe eight seconds on that bird's wings. From up there he could look down on the walls, the tower, the fence, and the warden, who was pacing up and down the row of portable bucking chutes like the cock of the walk.

It was a clear, calm day, but it was hot, and it was going to get hotter. Spectators were filling up the viewing stands behind the chain link fence. The prison rodeo was a popular event in Bismarck. People could count on seeing some wild rides, since inmates with little to lose tended to be eager risk takers. Few of them had ever done any rodeoing. Some had never been on a horse. This was a chance to show off to their families and maybe come away with a few bucks into the bargain.

Since it was an amateur rodeo, Cleve had declined to compete for money, even though nobody had barred him from it. He would ride exhibition in saddle bronc and bull riding, and the judges would score him, just for his own satisfaction. He'd asked Steiner not to use his name in any of the promotion and not to announce his PRCA experience. Some people would remember. He figured there would be some buzzing in the stands when his chute gate opened. But he wasn't pro-rodeo anymore, not as long as he was a prisoner. His innocence made him feel no less unworthy of the Association right now. He couldn't even bring himself to wear a cowboy hat behind bars, so he'd bought himself a pair of aviator glasses to shade his eyes instead. He adjusted them, then leaned against a steel corral panel and searched the stands while he turned up the cuffs on his new chambray shirt.

They weren't up there yet, and the show was going to start pretty soon. Maybe the old lady backed out at the last minute. Maybe she got sick. The thought of coming to this place probably sickened her. He should have stuck to his original resolve to keep to himself. Seeing Susan, even occasionally, had only intensified his loneliness. Lately he'd been thinking a lot about the reservation, a place he'd gladly left behind years back. It was for damn sure he had no history of homesickness, but lately he'd imagined Susan being there, frequenting the places he remembered, seeing the faces, passing the time.

Sometimes he'd let himself think about it until it made him ache, and then he'd promise himself he'd tell her not to come anymore. Of course, he never followed through. Even the ache was almost sweet. He'd been half tempted to buy himself a radio and turn on the country music, hone a nice edge on those lonesome feelings.

Christ, this place could eat away at a man's self-respect.

And now, here he was, checking out the grandstands like a coyote looking for supper. He should have been trying out saddles. He should have been checking every rivet and strap to see that the loaner rigs were put together right. He wished he had his own. It had been a long time since he'd used somebody else's saddle.

He noticed a slender woman making her way along the bleachers, followed by an older one. He did a little rubbernecking. Not them. Hell, he wished he could stop thinking about those two women and get his head into this poor imitation of his best game.

He wished he could fly.

Susan hurried around the front of her car, dreading what she knew she was going to find. It was her second flat tire in as many weeks. This one was a doozy. She'd lost the whole tread. Peeled away like an orange rind. She should have known the sale price on the tire had been too good to be true. She motioned for the old Indian woman to roll the window down, then shrugged apologetically. "Flat as a pancake, I'm afraid."

"You got a spare?" the woman asked tonelessly.

"Oh, yes, I wouldn't be without a spare on these roads." Highway 6 was paved, but many of its tributaries were not. Susan smiled feebly. Despite Susan's wish to make a good impression on this woman, they had spoken little during the hour and a half they'd been on the road together. Grace Black Horse didn't know it yet, but she was Sam's great-grandmother. The first time they'd met, Susan had driven out to the little three-room house in the country, introduced herself and accepted Grace's offer of coffee. She told Grace that she was a nurse at the clinic and a friend of Cleve's, and Grace indicated that she'd been expecting somebody. The rest of the conversation had been as sparse as it was now.

"You know how to change it?" Grace asked.

"I've managed it before. I'm not the best at it, but I know how." The woman nodded once and turned to stare out the windshield. Susan looked up and down the two-lane rural highway, feeling chagrined. She'd talked Grace into taking this trip, promising that if the sun got too hot for her, or the bleachers got too hard, they would go indoors. Grace just wanted to be sure she had a reliable car, and Susan had sworn up and down that it was. Now it was perched on the shoulder of the road, tipped over a steep, grassy slope on the passenger's side.

Susan started to open Grace's door. "I'll try to hurry so you won't be out in the sun long."

"I'm staying in the car."

"But . . . I don't think that's a good idea."

"It wasn't a good idea to come."

"The car might fall or something." Grace returned a hooded look that said it had better not. "Okay. Would you hand me the keys?"

Grace's kerchiefed head disappeared from the window, then returned. The look on her face hadn't changed, but she handed Susan the keys.

Susan had the spare tire and the tools laid out in the gravel when a pickup pulled over and parked in front of her car. The door slammed. A grinning cowboy rounded the corner of the pickup box, pushing his shirttail into the back of his pants.

"You got some trouble?" He hunkered down next to the tire and determined the problem. "Hoo-wee, that's a flat sucker, ain't it?"

"Yes. Very. It's a new tire, too."

"Tell you what, I got a hydraulic jack with me. Have it fixed in no time." He brushed his hands on his thighs as he stood. "You want to ask Grandma to step out for a minute?"

"I already did. She'd rather not."

The cowboy adjusted the brim of his hat as he surveyed the lay of the land and the position of the car. "Well, I guess she's all right where she is." He produced his jack, jammed it under the bumper. The front end rose as if it were on an elevator. Eyes front, arms folded beneath her bosom, granite-faced Grace rose with it. The cowboy ignored Susan's tools and used his own, spinning off the lug nuts with a flourish. "Headed for Mandan?" he asked without looking up.

"Bismarck."

"Taking Grandma up for some doctoring?"

"We're going to the rodeo."

Now he turned his head and squinted up at Susan. "The one at the Pen?"

"Yes."

"You must really like rodeo."

"Mrs. Black Horse's grandson is riding."

"Black Horse?" Beneath the brim of his straw hat, his brow furrowed. "The guy who killed that salesman a couple of years back? They shouldn't let him compete. Hell, he used to be a pro."

It hadn't occurred to her that the man would know who Cleve was or what he was supposed to have done. She wanted to come to his defense, but she backed away from the scorn she heard in the cowboy's voice and let his judgment go unanswered.

He continued to talk while he pulled the flat tire off and replaced it with the spare. "Name's Randy Weist. You from around here? Don't believe I've seen you before."

"Fort Yates."

"Teacher?"

"Nurse."

"You must be pretty new."

"Not really."

"Interesting work?"

"Yes."

"So what are you gonna be doin' while Grandma goes to the rodeo?" He lowered the car, set his jack aside, then fit the hubcap in place. When he realized he was still waiting for Susan's answer, he cocked one hip and stuck his thumbs into his belt. "You're not really going out there to the Pen, are you?"

"Yes, I am." Susan glanced at the spare tire, now ready to roll, and smiled. "I'm going to the rodeo. We really appreciate your help. It would have taken me much longer, and we don't want to miss Cleve's ride."

"We don't?"

"No, *we* don't." She opened the car door and grabbed her purse off the front seat. She felt Grace's scrutiny, but didn't look up as she dug out her wallet and ducked back out into the sunshine. "Can I pay you for this, Randy?"

"On the house this time, since you're in a hurry. Next time, you can let me buy you a drink. Didn't catch your name."

"I guess I didn't introduce myself." She jammed a five dollar bill into his shirt pocket. "There, we're even. Thanks so much."

Randy stepped aside and returned Susan's wave as she drove around his pickup. She glanced in the rear view mirror as she pulled away, muttering, "There won't be a next time, Mr. Weist." She turned to Grace. "We're not leaving Bismarck tonight without a decent set of tires, Mrs. Black Horse. That I promise you."

"Good." She nodded. "It's good you paid him. Looked like a no-good cowboy to me."

"I have to admit, it was a good thing he came along when he did. We're going to be late as it is, and with my luck we'll run into a speed trap just before we hit Mandan."

"Don't drive too fast. I don't like fast driving."

Cleve helped Jace Red Hawk set his bareback rigging, then watched him hang on wild-eyed until the whistle sounded. Jace scored a "no time."

"Missed him out," the announcer said, which meant that Jace hadn't taken the first jump with his heels positioned over the horse's shoulders. "How do we pay him off, folks? That's right." The applause was scattered. "Now that he's on the ground he can hear you. These boys have made some mistakes, but missing the horse out of the chute ain't a crime in this state. Nice try, number twenty-one. Jace Red Hawk, ladies and gentlemen. Heh-heh. Those are just the last two digits of Jace's number."

Cleve had stopped attending to rodeo announcer chatter a long time ago, but that remark stuck in his craw. Jace clipped a clod of dirt with his boot heel and looked up dejectedly at Cleve, who was sitting atop the empty chute. Cleve offered an approving nod and waved him over. Jace grinned and picked up his pace. People thought every Indian spent his boyhood saddle-breaking ponies on the rez, but Cleve knew that Jace had spent winters in boarding schools and summers with relatives in Minneapolis and LA.

As Jace came through the gate, Cleve hopped down and slapped him on the back. "Nice ride."

"Damn." Jace shook his head. "I missed him out."

"Yeah, but you stuck him. You rode him all the way."

"I did, didn't I?" Cleve nodded and smiled. "You see them up there yet?" Jace asked. The smile disappeared. "Your grandma and your girl?"

"She's not, uh . . ." There was no point in disclaiming her. Among Indians, any woman who'd shown the kind of interest in a man that Susan had offered Cleve was assumed to be his. There wasn't much of this "just friends" stuff. "They're not here. Least, I haven't seen them."

"Lot of people out there. Be hard to tell in a crowd like that."

"How about your brothers?"

"Yeah." Jace beamed. "I seen 'em come in. Look." He dropped a hand on Cleve's shoulder and pointed toward the top of the grandstands. "Second row from the top and—two, three, fourfivesix—seventh from the left, that's Bill. And then Rookie, the fat one. Then Merle."

"Oh, yeah."

"They're staying for the feed afterwards." Jace laughed. "Probably why they came. Rookie never misses a feed. Hey, there's Whitefish. Lookin' a little paler than usual."

Jimmy had been given a nickname, which meant a degree of acceptance. He was still a fish, and he was white. Neither characteristic was much more than tolerable, but Cleve had determined that Jimmy would be tolerated, and he was. He reminded Cleve of a gangly cull that Grandpa had marked for butchering. Cleve had been assigned to hand feed the heifer, then, months later, to shoot her. When the old man came out to the pen and found the soft-eyed heifer still standing, he'd taken the rifle out of Cleve's hands and relegated him to washing dishes and hanging out the laundry for most of the winter. Whenever anybody who came to the house made a joke about the boy doing the work of a *winyan*, a woman, the old man repeated the humiliating story. But Cleve remembered the way that heifer had looked at him when he'd shown up with a rifle instead of a pail of corn. He could have done it if she hadn't been so damned pitiful.

Just like Jimmy.

"What the hell are you wearing tennis shoes for?" Cleve demanded. "Damn bull's gonna break all your toes."

"I don't plan to let him get near my toes. I'll be in and out of there so fast, you guys' heads'll be spinning." He glanced at Cleve's low waist. "See you're wearing your belt."

"Gotta keep my pants up with something." He grinned. "How's it look?"

"Well, I don't know. I'm the one who made it. What do you think, Jace?"

"I think you oughta stick to making belts and stay away from bulls, Whitefish. You're gonna get your skinny ass kicked."

"I think it looks pretty good, too." Jimmy adjusted the bill on his grimy yellow baseball cap and squinted up at the stands. "Have you seen them yet?"

"Who?" Cleve was sorry he'd told anybody.

"You know who. You said Susan was bringing—"

"I've got more to think about than who's up there watching this so-called rodeo. If they can't get here, it's no big deal."

"It's a long drive," Jimmy reminded him. "They'll get here."

Susan hoped the spare tire would hold out for another thirty miles. She checked her watch, then glanced at

Grace, who was watching the speedometer. Weighing her own anxiety against that of the older woman, she eased off on the accelerator and checked for approval from her passenger. Grace settled back in her seat and, for the first time, initiated conversation.

"You've been to this place before to see my boy?"

"Yes, I have." There was quiet fear in the woman's voice. "It's really not so bad."

"He's never let me come. This is the first time."

"I know. He's a proud man."

"That's his whole trouble. He's got too much pride. But maybe not enough where it counts."

Susan wondered where it might count with Grace, and she remembered Cleve's claim that Indian traditions were of little interest to him. "He's kept tabs on you. I think that's one of the reasons he lets me come—you know, because I work at the hospital—so he can find out how you're doing."

"You know him from before?"

Before the trial or before Cleve went to prison? Susan chose the latter so that she could answer simply, "Yes."

"He's got the same idea his mother had. Indian's not good enough for him. He wants a *wasicu*—a white girl." She glanced at Susan. "I'm old. I can say what I think."

"I think you've got the wrong idea."

"I'm not *that* old. I know what's what." Grace sighed and looked back out the window. "He stayed away too long. That's what got him into trouble, just like my girl."

"You mean, his mother?"

"Stayed away too long. Come home in a box. Now they got my boy locked away in a box." She watched the road for a while. "It's not like it used to be, you know. Women used to raise their own kids. Grandma helped out, but the young women, they stuck by their men, and they raised their kids. That's what a woman is for."

Susan wasn't going to question Grace's judgment. Not now, while she was hanging on every word, hoping the woman would reveal more about her grandson.

"People act crazy these days. They drink around and act crazy. Old people aren't safe. Little ones aren't safe." Another silence passed, but there was more to come. Susan had learned to wait. Finally, Grace raised a forefinger in her direction. "One thing I know for sure. My boy wouldn't kill nobody. He acts tough sometimes, but it's all for show. 'Stand up for yourself,' his grandpa used to say. You know, he had a soft heart, that boy. He started riding his grandpa's cows just to show how tough he was. Pretty soon people brought their horses over for him to break, and he'd say, 'Watch me ride this one, Grandpa.' Because when he wouldn't let them buck him off, his grandpa really liked that all over. After his grandpa died, he still kept at it."

"I've never seen him ride, but I understand he's still very good."

"He doesn't know when to quit. When he was younger it was okay, I guess. Young bones mend easy."

"I know it's a rough sport."

"That's the way men like their games. It's always been that way, I guess." There was a smile in Grace's eyes. "So my boy goes for a nurse. For once, maybe he's being smart."

"Really, Mrs. Black Horse, it isn't . . ." How could she tell the woman what it wasn't without telling her what it was? She wasn't altogether sure what it was, herself, so she switched gears as she slowed to navigate a curve. "He's taking college classes now. He probably mentioned that to you in his letters."

"*Letter.*" Grace glanced at Susan to make her point, then looked out the window again. A small stand of badland hills seemed to fly past. "You sure like to drive fast."

"I'm only doing fifty-five. We're already late."

"They shouldn't start so early." What she meant was, they shouldn't start until all the people were there. "He said something about some college. I had to laugh. He never liked school. He was smart, but he didn't like

going to school. And he never liked ranching. Not much
else for a man to do down there unless he wants to work
for the BIA. He could have had our place if he would
have stayed around. 'Course they took most of the land
when they built that dam down there. Flooded the best
land we had. We moved our house to higher ground, and
we stuck it out, but most people picked up and moved
to town." The story was one of Grace's favorites and
worth retelling. "That was a long time ago. A lot of
things changed when they dammed up that river."

"I've heard other people say that, too."

"I used to have a nice garden down on that bottom
land. Nothing wants to grow up on that flat where the
house is now." Grace thought for a moment, then turned
to Susan. "They won't keep him locked up until he dies,
will they? He's half white, you know."

"I don't think that really matters, Mrs. Black Horse.
I think the important thing—"

"He used to play in the dirt while I worked in the
garden. Made little towns out of sticks and mud. Little
rocks. And he'd sing." She hummed, a little reedy and
off-key in the way of old women. " 'Jesus doesn't want
my soul,' he'd sing. I used to take him to church with
me, but I don't know where he got those words."

Susan couldn't say anything. Her throat burned.

"I know he didn't kill that man. In the war, maybe he
killed, but not for money. He wouldn't do that."

"No." Susan cleared her throat. "He wouldn't."

"I didn't think he'd come back from the war. I thought
I'd lose him then. Not this way."

"This new attorney can help him." She took a deep
breath and ventured, "I really believe this Bernard
Whitestaff is going to find a way to get the whole
thing cleared up."

They crossed the river into Mandan, and Grace sat up
and looked around, as though getting her bearings. The
tires whined on a bridge that spanned the railhead, where
coal cars were lined up on several sets of tracks. They
stopped at a traffic light. "I saw my boy when they had

him in jail over here. This Mandan jail." She couldn't
see it from the intersection, but she indicated the general
direction with a jerk of her chin. "They can't keep him
locked up like that. Pretty soon it'll kill him."

Cleve made a clean ride in the Saddle Bronc event.
Not as flashy as he would have liked. He'd drawn a
low-octane horse who started out with a couple of crow
hops, then offered a little half-hearted bucking and delivered Cleve back to the chutes as though they'd just gone
for a ride around the block. Cleve hopped off and landed
on his feet. The judges scored him high, maybe out of
respect, but more likely because it didn't count for anything. The fans cheered in the same vein. Cleve brooded
over a cigarette, glared at the grandstands, which could
have been empty as far as he was concerned, and waited
for his second event.

His bull was a chute fighter. Cleve backed off twice
when the bull tried to jump into the next stall. Jimmy
climbed up the railing, hoping to stick close to his idol.
Each time the bull clambered up on his hind legs, Jimmy
spun away like a shooed fly, but he kept going back, as
close to Cleve's side as he could get.

"Geez, Cleve, I think you oughta ask for a different
bull."

"This is the one I want." Braced on the top rails he
lowered himself gingerly, as though easing the lid from
Pandora's box.

"But he's meaner'n hell."

"That makes us even." Cleve curled his hand around
the braided bull rope and felt the rosin on his glove take
hold. At his nod, the gate swung open.

From the first jump, Cleve knew he'd make the ride.
The brindle cross-breed was a high kicker, his favorite
kind of bucking bull. The cow bell clanked beneath the
bull's belly, and the shapes and colors in the arena
became a swirling blur as he rode the crest of the animal's power. It was just the two of them now. No guard
dared touch him. No rules applied. The bull's hide rolled

between his thighs, but Cleve's balance was perfect. The bullrope was a fulcrum, not a tether, and with his free hand, he was able to touch the sky.

The power was his. Seeming chaos was in his control. He reveled in every punishing jolt, gloried in the bull's wildness. They became one in muscle, motion, and madness, so that the world might shudder and stand in awe. Cleve ignored the whistle. "No time" took on new meaning. This was not an event. It was a reclamation. There was no pain in his arm or his back until after it was over. Only after he had bailed to the ground of his own accord, climbed the fence to safety, and dropped over the other side into the real world, did he feel the strain he'd put his body through.

"That was one hell of a good ride, Bro." Jace was there to clap a congratulatory hand on his back. "What were you tryin' to do? Ride all the buck out of him?"

"Had him goin', didn't I?" Grinning broadly, Cleve stuffed the glove into his back pocket as Whitey John and Jimmy joined them behind the chutes.

"Yeah, you did. 'Til way after the whistle. How long was that, Whitey?"

"Two weeks, ten days," Whitey drawled.

"Almost twenty seconds," Jimmy said. He missed the look of amusement that passed among the other three. "I thought you were *never* getting off. Didn't you hear the whistle?"

"Sure did. Decided to take my time, since I'm not taking any winnings." He punched Jace's shoulder. "That old sonuvabitch gave me a good ride, didn't he?"

"He was sure kickin', and you was kickin' right back."

They laughed, sharing in the exhilaration.

"I've been watching the stands," Jimmy said. "I think they're here."

Cleve jerked his head around toward the crowd and blurted, "Where?" The chutes blocked his view, and when he looked back at his friends, hot embarrassment pricked him. He wanted to take back his unguarded response.

But Jimmy smiled and tugged at Cleve's arm to move him into a better position. He pointed to a spot beside the viewing stand, where two women stood. "Is that them?"

Just between him and Jimmy, Cleve didn't try to suppress his own smile. "Sure is."

"See, I told you."

When it was Jimmy's turn, Cleve, Whitey and Jace leaned over the corral rail jeering and cheering him on. He was pale as milk, but when his friends hollered for him to "Get in there!" he joined the frenzied pack in the chase for "hard money." The bull pawed and snorted, taking his pick of fools to give chase as he taunted them with the money flapping from his horns. Jimmy managed to come up with a few bills and a scrape on his cheek. Next, Whitey came out of the gate with a mighty yelp, atop a recalcitrant "broom tail" in the wild horse race. The winner definitely wasn't Whitey. The horse stopped short halfway across the arena, dipped its head, and sent him flying.

The final announcement bade the rodeo participants' guests to report to the reception area to enjoy the picnic in the prison dining room. Most of them understood that they would pass through security first, but Susan forewarned Grace. Still, the buzzing metal detector shocked some of the placid folds from the woman's leathery face. With no pockets in her dark purple dress, no jewelry, and no buckles, Grace became agitated on the third try through the archway. Impatiently she waved away Susan's whispered suggestion of bra fastenings.

"What would I be wearing one of those things for?"

One of the officers found the warden. Steiner greeted Susan by name and introduced himself to Grace with a reassuring smoothness. "You must be Cleve Black Horse's grandmother. He sure rode like a champion today, didn't he?"

"Yes." Recovering the air of an elder, Grace permitted her hand to be shaken.

"I don't like putting everybody through all this, especially a lady like you, but we do what we have to. Sometimes the littlest thing can end up causing us trouble." He considered Grace's apparel for a moment. "I wonder, do you have any hairpins under your kerchief there?"

"Yes."

Steiner smiled and nodded, glancing at Susan to include her. "They must be the big, old-fashioned kind for long hair?"

Grace stood unmoving with her hands folded around her middle. "Yes."

"We'll have to ask you to take them out, I'm afraid. I know it's a bother, but some of these guys, they could get hold of one of those pins, and you can't tell what they might use it for."

Grace stared him down while she untied the knot under her chin and pulled off the filmy black scarf. Then she began plucking the pins from her silver-gray hair.

"May I help you, Mrs. Black Horse?" Susan offered.

"Put this in my bag," she ordered, handing Susan the scarf. Their purses had been stowed in a locker. "Every time you go to one of these government buildings, it's always something they don't want you to have. You don't know what they're going to take." She shook her head, and a single long braid uncoiled itself from her nape and swung down her back. She offered Steiner a handful of pins. "It's hairpins next."

Steiner laughed. "You're right. It's a crazy world. I'll get you an envelope to put those in. You have beautiful hair, Mrs. Black Horse."

Grace's smile was a bright surprise. "You have nice manners, Mr. Steiner."

Susan breathed a sigh of relief when she and Grace passed security without a pat search. They were taken to the dining room, where families, many with children, waited for the men who were rodeo cowboys for the day.

As the men, all freshly showered, filed through the doors, smiling and searching for familiar faces, Susan glanced at Grace and prepared to be moved by the reunion of a grandmother and the man who'd been more son than grandson. He came into the room, and Susan stood so that he would see them more readily. He hesitated for a moment when he saw them, looking from one to the other as though he were just making certain. Grace used the table for leverage and came to her feet more laboriously than usual, but there was a new girlish animation in her eyes.

The embrace Susan anticipated didn't happen. Cleve nodded her way and said, "Hi," as he jammed his hands into his pockets and presented himself for his grandmother's inspection. He wore jeans and a new yellow shirt. This was the first time since the trial that Susan had seen him in anything but prison khaki. He looked wonderful.

Fully a head and a half shorter than he, Grace pinched and patted his arm and crooned. "Eeee, Son-ny, is that you? You look so different."

"It's me, Grandma. How're you doing? It's good to see you."

"What do they feed you here? Tiger meat? Look at you."

He shrugged. "I've been doing some of those exercises, like that one doctor told me to do. You been feeling okay, Grandma? Taking your insulin like you're supposed to?"

"My legs aren't the best, you know, but I get by."

"Your hair looks nice."

"Ayyy." She brushed the sides back. "They took my pins."

"Security?" He glanced at Susan, and she nodded. "Did they, uh . . ."

Susan shook her head. "The hairpins set off the metal detector." She reassured him with her eyes. *It's all right. There was no search.* "The warden helped us get through without any problem."

Grace poked her grandson's chest a couple of times, and Susan was reminded of the witch in *Hansel and*

Gretel. "But here I thought you'd be looking just skinny and *unsica* in this place. You've got more bulges than that bull you just rode."

"You saw the ride?" He looked up at Susan and smiled. "So what did you think?"

"You were terrific," Susan said quietly. She didn't want to intrude on the reunion, but neither did she want to be left out. Here was tenderness expressed in unexpected ways. She smiled at Cleve. "I couldn't believe how long you stayed up there."

He basked in her admiring gaze, but he gave the characteristic cowboy shrug. "I was having a good time."

"It reminded me of one of those awful carnival rides, only you can't shut it down when the time's up. Is it hard to get off?"

"Nah. You just jump and try to hit the ground running." He didn't expect her to understand what it was like to be on top with things going his way. "Guess I didn't hear the whistle." He glanced around the room, noting that some groups of people were standing around visiting while others were forming a chow line at the steam tables. Jace waved at him from across the room, and he nodded back. "Did you drive straight up from Little Eagle?" he asked, almost absently.

"I got down there a little early."

"She forgot we're on slow time," Grace said, referring to the fact that the reservation straddled the time zone.

"But we got going in plenty of time," Susan added. "Then, right out in the middle of nowhere, I had a stupid flat tire. I know we missed your first ride, and I'm really sorry."

"A *stupid* flat tire?" He chuckled. "Were you smart enough to change it?"

"Smart enough, but not fast enough. Some cowboy stopped to give us a hand. Otherwise, we'd have missed the whole rodeo."

"Cowboy?"

Grace tapped Cleve's chest again and nodded at Susan. "She was a pretty sight, this one, bending over that tire all pink-faced and worried. That cowboy came along looking for strays." Grace tittered behind her hand. "But this *wasicu* girl handled him pretty good."

"Oh, yeah?" He slanted Susan a meaningful look. "You tell him you didn't want to be late for the prison rodeo?"

"That's exactly what I told him. *After* the job was well underway." She smiled. "Well, he had a hydraulic jack."

"You get that tire fixed before you leave town tonight."

"It's shot. I'm taking it back where I got it, because I have a feeling I've got three others just like it."

"You should stay in Fort Yates tonight, Grandma. Stay at Grandma Mary's."

"I thought of that already." Grace patted his arm. "Don't worry. I won't have your girl out on the road all night, taking me home."

"You don't stop calling her that, you're really gonna embarrass her."

They sat down at the table. Susan had learned to think of the table as a private island and to ignore the people who'd claimed the surrounding islands, but Grace folded her arms beneath her bosom and counted the number of uniformed officers who stood guard around the perimeter. "Do they watch you like that all the time?"

Cleve followed the direction of her survey. "Yeah, pretty much. Believe it or not, some guys don't want to be here."

"Everybody I talk to, including myself, says this is not right. You shouldn't be in here."

Cleve laughed. "You been talking to yourself again, Grandma?"

"Eee, this one." She gave his arm a playful push. "You know what I mean."

"Talks To Herself Woman, they'll be calling you."

"Eee, this one."

His amusement didn't quite camouflage the gratitude in his eyes. "I know what you mean, Grandma."

The distant past sat side by side with the present in Grace's aged mind, and she moved easily from one to the other. "They put my grandfather in an army prison for a while," she related. "They said he was a hostile renegade. He used to tell us kids about it, and he never wanted my mother to let them take us away to school. Me and Grandma Mary, we cried the first time and hung on to Mama's skirts. 'We'll be good,' we were saying." She squinted at Cleve. "Do they let you go outside sometimes?"

"Every day. We play basketball a lot. They give you a job to do, and they let you go to school." He put his hand on her shoulder. "Imagine me, volunteering for school." She giggled, and his hand slid away. "It's not so bad if I keep myself busy."

They sat quietly, letting the kitchen clinking and the din of surrounding voices fill the silence.

"You never killed that man, Sonny."

Cleve leaned forward, bracing his hands on his knees. "I've got a different lawyer, Grandma. An Indian guy from Minnesota."

"Chippewa?"

"Probably. I didn't ask him. I think he's a half-breed, like me. Anyway, he's good. He's going to find a way to get me out of here."

"A Chippewa lawyer?"

"Yeah. Grandma, I don't care if he's Chippewa, Crow or red Chinese, if he can just get me out of here."

"I thought lawyers were supposed to be smart guys."

He shook his head, chuckling. "You want something to eat? You sit tight while we get you some food." With a look he asked Susan to go with him, and they both pushed their chairs back. "You want coffee, Grandma?"

"Yes. And sugar."

"No sugar." He turned to Susan as they made their way among the small tables. "She isn't supposed to have sugar, is she?"

"Probably not. I think she's testing you."

"She didn't give you any trouble, did she? On the way up?"

"No, not at all. I didn't think she was going to talk to me much, but after we had the flat tire, she loosened up a little."

"She can be pretty bossy sometimes. But she seems to be doing okay, doesn't she?" He glanced back at his grandmother, who sat rigidly with her hands in her lap. "She looks good."

Susan nodded and claimed a place at the end of the line. "I'm sure you've put her mind at ease by letting her see you."

"She's told that story about her grandfather a hundred times. Indians going to jail is old news."

"What have you heard from Mr. Whitestaff?"

"He thinks he's put a pretty good case together."

"He took a deposition from me."

"He says the police investigation began and ended with me. They didn't really try to find Smith. There was evidence of other fingerprints, blood stains that didn't match up—a bunch of stuff that the police didn't do anything with, and Felch just let it go." Talk of the trial still bothered Susan. Cleve leaned closer, as if the lawyer might be lurking nearby. "Wonder what tribe Felch is, huh? Probably some ancient enemy of the Sioux."

"Like the Chippewa?"

"And the Crow." He glanced his grandmother's way and chuckled. "People joke around about it now, but with the old people, you get the feeling they remember stuff that you know damn well happened before their time."

They reached the serving counter, and Cleve grinned at the man who stood behind the servers, engrossed in his supervising. "Hey, Baker Man, I want you to meet somebody. This is my friend, Susan Ellison." He handed Susan a tray and took two for himself. "John Kohler. I used to work for him in the kitchen."

Kohler took a step closer, nodded and muttered, "Howdy do, ma'am," which amused Susan. The big man seemed shy, and she wondered whether he was an employee or an inmate. She decided not to ask.

"I need two meals, one for my grandmother."

"You sure gave that ol' bull proper hell, Cleve."

"Yeah, nice going, Cleve," came the rejoinder from someone ahead of them in line.

"You had a nice ride, too, Al. Take second?"

"Third. Dobe got first, and Wiley took second."

"I wasn't paying a lot of attention to scores, I guess. Just enjoying the show." He held up his trays for hamburgers and told Susan, "I was watching for you guys. After a while, I figured you weren't coming."

She followed suit. Back in the kitchen, more burgers were sizzling on the grill, and the aroma made her hungry. "I'm glad you asked me to bring her."

"You're getting along okay? You like her? I mean, she can be kinda testy, and some people don't like to put up with it." Grease McKay was on hand to add baked beans to the tray. Cleve spared him a nod and moved on to the salad bar. "I didn't like to put up with it when I was growing up, but I didn't have sense enough to remember she was old enough to be my grandmother."

"I like her."

Once they'd moved beyond the bottleneck at the salad bar, they had some breathing room at the coffee urn. Cleve handed Susan the cups, one at a time, and she listened while she filled them. "You know how, when you really want something to happen, sometimes you make promises?" He cast a glance upward. "Like, to The Man Upstairs?" Susan smiled and nodded, and he knew he'd never tell this to anyone else. "I really wanna get out of here. I keep thinking about all the things I've done that maybe I should have been arrested for. Like the way I've treated her. So that's one of my promises—to do better by her. She raised me, even though I wasn't her son. Kinda like—" His fingers lingered over hers as the last full cup changed hands. "—you and Sam, maybe."

The look in his eyes left Susan a little short of breath.

"If you could keep tabs on her for me until I get out, let me know if she's sick, or if you think she needs anything."

"She needs your letters."

"Okay." He took the cup, and still he held her gaze. "I'll write to her. But she doesn't have too many relations left, and the ones she has are about as bad as I am."

"You're not bad."

"Well . . . thoughtless, then. I just thought if you—"

"Even if she likes me, Cleve, she *loves* you. I can't replace you. But I'll do what I can."

He set the cup in its compartment on the tray. He knew she would, and that was the part that made him uncomfortable. She thought she owed him. She also thought it best to pacify him, just in case it became possible for him to return the favor. He had to take what he could get, but he didn't like the way everybody's motives were stacking up to be so complicated.

"Would you rather have something besides coffee?" he asked as they headed for the table. "I can get you some tea."

"This is fine."

"You're about to find out what prison food is like. Just what you've always wondered, right?"

"I've thought about it lately. Among other things."

"Well, forget about 'other things.' This is the highlight of the day." He set both trays on the table and touched Grace on the shoulder. She was nodding off. "Does this look okay for you, Grandma?"

"I can't eat this much." She eyed Susan, then smiled. "False teeth, you know."

"They look natural." Susan sat down, putting Cleve in the middle. "I never would have guessed."

Cleve winked at the old woman, whose eyes twinkled back at him as she giggled.

Once the rodeo cowboys left the dining hall, they became prisoners again. After they were searched down, they returned to their cells for lockup and count. The clanking of boot heels against metal stairs echoed through the cellhouse. The big event was over, the visitors had left, and the "big empty" was all that was left. Cleve found Jimmy lying on his bunk with his face to the wall. He had moved in next door to Cleve after his transfer to the shops had gone through. He'd had no guests, so he'd skipped the festivities.

Cleve slapped the bars on his way by. "Nice goin' today, kid."

"Thanks."

Cleve stepped into the space he called his own and leaned against the wall separating his cell from Jimmy's. "Wanna do some lifting later?"

"No."

Jimmy never turned down any offer Cleve made, which was kind of sickening sometimes. When Cleve was feeling mean, he was tempted to jerk the kid around a little, just to see that whipped puppy look on his face. But right now, he was feeling generous enough to ask, "Something wrong?"

"Ran into Dietz a while ago when I wasn't looking."

Cleve lit a cigarette and nodded to the officer who was strolling the tier and taking the count. He really didn't want to hear about Dietz, and if he didn't say anything else, he wouldn't have to. He shot a stream of smoke toward the top of the bars. "So?"

"So nothing. He, uh . . . he's got this thing about me, you know?"

"Just stay away from him."

"I try."

Try sounded like a feeble word. A futile word, coming from a kid like Jimmy. Sooner or later, Dietz was likely to get what he wanted from him. Cleve had made a habit of minding his own business, and this kind of thing was only his business when somebody tried to mess with *him*. He hadn't fancied himself anybody's savior since he was eight years old and he'd hit one of his mother's boyfriends over the head with a soup ladle, trying to make him stop pulling her hair. The sonuvabitch had laughed while his mother took a switch to him, teaching him once and for all that if two people were determined to screw each other, the best thing to do was stay out of the way.

"What if you get out?"

It surprised Cleve to hear Jimmy's voice right next to the wall. He hadn't heard him move off the bunk.

"I mean, I hope you do. It'd be great if you did. But then—"

"You've gotta learn to stand up for yourself, Jim. You can't depend on anyone else. Nobody else can take care of your problems for you."

"I know." A silence passed. Then Jimmy spoke quietly. "I'm doing real good in my treatment group. They've gotten me to talk about stuff I never thought I'd tell anyone. About things that happened when I was younger."

Cleve didn't like the idea of telling a bunch of people some pitiful story about your family and how poor they were and how everybody beat up on everybody else. He didn't see what good it could do. What was done was done.

"Can I tell you something, Cleve?"

"No."

Cleve dragged heavily on his cigarette. He hoped it was sinking in this time. No true confessions. He wasn't making any; he wasn't hearing any. The officer passed by again and mounted the steps to the tier above them. There was water running overhead, and a couple of cells down, somebody was taking a leak. Somebody pretty tall.

"Would *you* tell *me* something, then?" Jimmy whispered.

"About what?"

"Are you in love with Susan?"

"Christ, Jimmy. Where did you get—"

"She's beautiful."

"I've hardly touched her. How could I be in love with her?"

"Easy."

"You're so full of shit, Jimmy. I don't know where you come up with some of these ideas of yours."

"You should have seen yourself today, the way you were watching the stands, looking for her."

"I hadn't seen my grandmother in two years, for Chrissake."

"You should have seen the way your face lit up like a kid at Christmas. You know damn well you're in love with her."

"If I am, it's only in my head."

"I don't think so."

"And the head's connected directly to the dick, kid."

"By way of the heart."

"Give me a break, will you? She's the only woman I've been able to see in two years."

"She's the only person on your visitor's list."

"Yeah, well, she wouldn't be there either, except . . ." Except what? When had he last cussed out her whole ancestry for spawning the woman who'd condemned him to rot in this godforsaken place? When had he last counted the ways he could get back at her, starting with the kid she wanted so bad? The only thing he'd been counting lately was the days until the next time she said she was coming. He told himself it was an indulgence until Whitestaff came up with something better for him to look forward to.

"Except what?"

"Except I like her looks."

"I don't blame you. When I get out of here, I hope I can find me a girl."

"There's a lot of them out there." Cleve stuck his cigarette in the corner of his mouth and began unbuttoning his shirt. He'd bought two civilian shirts and worn them both in the same day. He folded the yellow one, put it in one of his two drawers and took out a white T-shirt.

"But they don't go for me the way they go for guys like you. Even if one ever does, sooner or later I'd have to tell her—"

"You don't have to tell her anything. You get yourself straightened out in that group of yours, and then you let sleeping dogs lie."

"But you've gotta be honest with a girl about stuff like that, Cleve. Otherwise, it'll never work."

"What won't work? It works just like electricity, kid. You get yourself plugged into the right socket, and the lights come on, the music plays, and you're in heaven." The locks popped open. Cleve put his cigarette out and pulled the T-shirt over his head. Then he grabbed his towel and stepped out on the tier. Jimmy was waiting. Cleve smiled and flipped the towel over his shoulder. "You get an urge to spill your guts, find yourself a gray-haired bartender who's heard so much he's forgotten it all."

Jimmy laughed. "I gave up drinking."

"Bartenders make better coffee than girlfriends do."

"I'll bet Susan makes good coffee."

"Think so?" Cleve laid a hand on Jimmy's shoulder and turned him toward the steps. They were going to the weight room. "I'll make it a point to find out one of these days and let you know."

Part III

Now this is the day,
Our child,
Into the daylight
You will go out standing.

—ZUNI SONG

Chapter 14

A mistrial. Cleve turned the word over in his mind as he separated his property from the state's. *Mistrial* was a loaded word. He wasn't even sure he understood what it meant. It sounded almost like *mistake*. He'd told them they had the wrong man a long time ago, but it didn't sound as though that was the mistake they were acknowledging.

Mistrial. They hadn't done it right. So now what? Would they go back and try again? All he knew was that Bernie had arranged for his bond to be paid, and he was getting out today. It felt a little like being discharged from the army. One day you thought you'd never get out; the next day the orders came through, and everything was moving so fast it made your head spin.

"Better move it, Black Horse. Your ride's coming at noon, and we've got a lot to do to process you out." The officer's tone lacked enthusiasm for what Cleve considered to be damn good news.

"I'd like to step out to the basketball court for just a minute."

"You haven't got time for that."

"It'll only take a minute."

"Sixty seconds, max. The warden's expecting you, too, and he's a busy man."

The officer followed Cleve through the door to the exercise yard. Concrete walkways and slabs were brightened by the morning sun. Cleve put on his dark glasses and strolled past a raucous volleyball match. He was walking tall as he headed for the basketball court. He dropped his duffel bag on the ground in time to catch Whitey John's pass, then turned and shot the ball for two. Whitey whistled his approval as the ball slid through the net into Jace's waiting hands. Cleve held his hands up in a T, and Coach Bremmer allowed a time out.

Grinning, Cleve offered Jace a handshake. "Look me up when you get out."

"Yeah. Next month, I hope. I was all set last month, but it didn't work out." Squinting into the sun, Jace grinned like an adolescent prankster. "Too many infractions. Hey, what's the first thing you're gonna do when you walk outta here?"

"Tough call, huh, Cleve?" Whitey clapped a hand on his shoulder. "You gonna get drunk or get laid first?"

Cleve shoved his hand in his pocket and came up with a book of commissary tickets and a few tokens for the prison vending machines. "Doubt if I can buy either with these."

"Might be good for something over in the women's section," Jace said. "Whitey claims to know a whore over there."

Cleve laughed and shoved the tickets back. They were nontransferable, but Whitey got the tokens in Cleve's handshake. "You guys have a Coke on me," he muttered. "And stay out of trouble, okay?"

"Right," Whitey promised.

"Don't let Grease take over the team, now. He doesn't know basketball from pocket pool."

"No shit. I'm captain now." Whitey made a serious face. "Don't you come back here, Cleve. You don't belong here."

"Who does?" besides Dietz and a whole crew of bad asses just like him, he amended silently, and he sought Jimmy's attention with a glance toward the back of the little group. "You gonna shake my hand, kid?"

Jimmy watched his own feet step forward. Reluctantly, he stuck out his hand.

Cleve took it, resisting the nagging temptation to squeeze the boy's shoulder, or maybe just ruffle his red hair. Jimmy needed to start thinking of himself as a man. "You'll be out soon."

"Another two years."

"You'll get some of that time shaved off. Just don't take any shit off anybody, okay?"

"I won't." He looked up, making a valiant effort to smile. "I wanna know if Susan makes good coffee."

"Don't be giving me any of your crazy ideas." He gave Jimmy's slight hand a squeeze, hoping to communicate a little encouragement. "You hang tough, okay?" Jimmy nodded and let his arm flop against his side. "All you guys. Hang in there."

Cleve tried to clear the gritty feeling out of his throat as he headed across the gym. Now he remembered why he'd always avoided goodbyes. The whole damn melodrama made him feel soft inside. He wished he could walk straight through the building and out the door, clean and simple. But Steiner was waiting.

Cleve took the chair across the desk from the warden, who was lining papers up, edge to edge, making sure the release procedure had been followed step by step. He signed the first paper, then extended a passbook across the desk. "You've got one thousand thirty-six dollars in your account. It's a double signature account, and you've got my signature there. You can draw it out of the Bank of North Dakota, which is right downtown. Not bad, considering you made some transfers to your grandmother. You oughta be able to pay some entry fees with that."

Cleve pocketed the passbook and lit a cigarette. "I'm out on bail. I can't leave the state. Besides, the season's about over."

"What are you going to do?"

"Try to find some kind of a job, I guess."

"You've earned some college credit here."

"Nine hours."

"It's a start." Steiner folded his hands on the desk and beamed as though the accomplishment were his own. To some extent, Cleve admitted to himself, maybe it was. "You could continue over at Bismarck State—or, you know, they've got a community college down at Fort Yates. You ought to be working with young people, Cleve. They look up to you. They listen to you."

"You're just talking about one guy who decided to be my tail because he's scared shitless of getting the crap beat out of him." He spat a stream of smoke and resisted the urge to feel good about Steiner's assessment. "Anyway, I haven't been acquitted, and some people think I have an alcohol problem."

"Well, that's up to you. With or without treatment, if it's a problem, it's up to you."

"I want to be acquitted. My lawyer says they can retry me if they think they have a good enough case."

"They can also appeal this last judge's decision. That's why you're out on bail. If their appeals fail, they can take you back to court." Steiner noticed the ashtray had been moved, and he slid it across the desk toward Cleve. "I'm sure you're not anxious to go through all that again."

"No. I want them to find the guy who killed Bertram."

"You really didn't do it, did you." It was not a question, but a conclusion.

"I really didn't do it." Cleve planted his elbows on the arms of the chair, balanced his ankle on his knee and studied the ash at the end of his cigarette for a moment. "There were times when I wondered if maybe I missed something. Maybe I was too—" He gestured, drawing circles in the air next to his head. "Too drunk to remember. You get to doubting your own . . . your own memory, I guess."

"Pretty scary place to be."

"My lawyer says there were unidentified fingerprints and that Felch handled the whole thing like a load of infested garbage that he wanted to dump as quickly as possible. And the police just figured they had their man."

"We get a lot of Indians in here, Cleve." Steiner tapped the end of his pen against one of the papers he was supposed to be signing. "When you think real hard about why that is—Well, the reasons add up to some indictments against my race. But I don't know what the answer is."

"Neither do I."

"I don't want you back here."

Cleve straightened, lowering his booted foot to the floor. "Yeah, well, nothing against you personally, but the hospitality hasn't been all that great, so I'd just as soon avoid another stay." He slid forward in his chair and flicked some ash into the glass ashtray. "Listen, about Jimmy Dawson."

"The kid's got problems."

"Don't we all? One of his problems is Dietz. Is there some way you could keep them apart?"

"Pretty hard as long as they're both part of the population. Dietz is gonna think he's back on top once you're gone."

"I know. Jimmy's gotta look out for himself, but just so you know—"

"We know. We'd like to see Jimmy start the paperwork toward getting into South Unit."

"I've talked to him about that."

"Good." Steiner went back to his row of papers, affixing his initials as he perused them. "Looks like the state's property is all checked in, and you're all checked out."

"All checked out," Cleve assured him. "They said I've got the purest piss in North Dakota."

"Well, that's fine. It's all for your own protection." He gathered up a ream of papers and offered a smile. "But I guess you've heard enough of that."

"It's etched on my brain." *Come on, come on.*

"And you've arranged for housing."

"Right. A guy I used to rodeo with has a gas station in Fort Yates. He's got a couple of houses chopped up into apartments, and he's holding one for me."

"Good." The wheels on Steiner's chair squeaked as both men stood. "You can't even come back to visit, you know, being your case is still pending and you're under supervision."

"This place can get along without me."

"Yes, it can." Steiner offered his hand, and Cleve leaped at the chance to shake it and take his leave. "Good luck, Cleve. I hope they don't have to send you back here. I mean that."

The warden saw Cleve through a series of heavy gates. Rows of bars were rolled back into place and locks slammed shut behind him. His footsteps echoed along the linoleum corridor. Through the last gate he could see windows, the front door, the brightness of the sun—and Susan. She saw him, too. She smiled. The late morning air was already heavy with September heat, but Susan looked cool in her pale blue cotton dress. Her hair was caught up off the back of her neck, and she wore gold hoop earrings. Cleve walked a little faster. The last door was open, and he felt as though he were treading on air.

"Hi."

Jesus, he wanted to grab her and just hold on. But he stood there, feeling like a kid who'd knocked on her door. "Hi. Where's Bernie?"

"He said he had to take care of some business. Then he's going to meet us for lunch." She took a single step toward him, and hesitated. "You're ready to go?" she asked shyly.

With a cocky smile, he clapped his old straw cowboy hat on his head, pulled the brim low over his eyes and gave the rider's signal to open the chute gate. "Outside."

Susan was relieved by the chance to laugh. She opened the front door and gestured with a flourish. "There it is. The outside."

He strode past her and bounded down the steps, into the tree-mottled sunlight. Susan closed the door and followed. He turned suddenly and grinned, squinting into the sun. "The three of us this time? We're having lunch?"

"If you'd rather see him privately—"

"I'd rather see you privately."

"Me?"

She looked serious as hell, and he burst out laughing. Spinning on his heel, he watched the treetops whirl above his head. His duffel bag hit the ground as he pounced on her, picked her up and spun around again, still laughing like a kid on a merry-go-round. Her shock turned to sparkle, and she gripped his shoulders, threw her head back and laughed with him.

"I'd rather see you and the old lady and someplace where there's not a fence in sight. Sweet, sweet Jesus, I'm free!"

"Yes, you are," she marveled. Her face loomed just above his, and her wildflower scent tickled his nose.

He laughed again. He couldn't hold it in. "Can you believe it?

"Can you?"

"Jesus, I don't know." He let her slide slowly through his arms and watched the warm sensation take effect in her eyes. He saw both pleasure and fear, and the combination sweetened the itch she'd planted under his skin. "It's been a long time. It'll take some getting used to."

Susan stepped back. "But you're out now, and Bernie's going to see that you're out for good. Do you—" She glanced at the canvas bag on the ground. "—have everything?"

"This is it." He swept up the duffel. "Cowboy Samsonite. You think you could stop at the bank before we meet Bernie? All I've got in my jeans is a book that *says* I've got some money coming."

"Bernie said to tell you he's buying. He's pretty pleased with the way things are turning out. I think it's quite a feather in his cap. That's my car." She pointed it out, but he was still waiting for an answer. "We can certainly stop at a bank, though. After lunch, we can go anywhere you like." She offered her keys. "Want to drive?"

The keys swung back and forth over her finger. He wanted to take them and slide under that steering wheel in the worst way, but he shook his head. "My license expired." He shrugged. "Guess I wasn't so sure I was going to need it again."

"I think you need to talk to Bernie."

They had lunch at the old train depot, an historic building with Old West styling that had fallen into disuse with the demise of passenger train service and been reclaimed as Fiesta Villa, a Mexican restaurant. Bernie had chosen it for its Indian tacos. "Almost as good as Mama used to make," he promised Cleve.

"My mother couldn't make a piece of frybread to save her life." The waitress set a glass of ice water in front of him. He downed it and held the glass up for more.

"How about Grandma?"

"Now you're talkin' good frybread." He glanced up and grinned boyishly. "Water's great here."

The waitress took the order for three Indian tacos. "We make the best Margueritas north of the Mexican border," she promised, raising her voice above the clangor of the train warning sounding just outside the windows. "Anyone want to try one?"

"No way," Bernie said. "They can keep their Margueritas. Right, Cleve?"

"Yeah." For the time being. He didn't know whether Bernie didn't drink, or whether he was just being nice. He did know he wasn't supposed to be drinking. But as the train rushed past the tall arched windows, he was thinking about Jace's two choices. He figured it would be nice to get laid first. "Coffee for me."

"I spent most of the morning over in Mandan, Cleve. The DA's appealing the judge's decision to the State Supreme Court. He reminded me that he still has the option to go to trial again, but he told the *Tribune* he probably wouldn't." Bernie chuckled and glanced across the table at Susan, who sat beside Cleve. "He knows damn well I'd rip him to shreds."

Right, lawyer, I'm sure she's impressed. "So now what happens?"

"We hope the supreme court upholds the appellate court's ruling. The trial was unfair; you were railroaded because you're an Indian. The jury convicted you because you're an Indian." Bernie glanced at Susan again. Cleve drank some more water. "They can try to go up the ladder, but I doubt the federal court will be willing to hear it. If all goes well, they'll have to try you again or drop the whole thing. Then you're home free."

"They'll give the bail money back and everything?" Bernie nodded. "What about the murder?"

"Probably show up on that TV program about unsolved mysteries."

"You mean they won't try to find out who did it?"

"Trail's pretty cold now."

Cleve scowled. "So people go on thinking I did it, and I got off on a technicality."

"People think what they want, and then they forget about it." Bernie took a chip from the basket in the middle of the table and dunked it in a bowl of salsa. "The point is, you're not sitting in the pen for something you didn't do."

"Right. That's the point."

The food was served: huge pieces of fried bread dough, topped with traditional meat sauce and salad. Cleve turned to Susan. "Ever had one of these before?"

"Not this size."

"Bet I could eat two of these." It took two hands to balance it for his first bite. "I'm not used to these late lunches, and I'm hungry enough to eat a horse and chase the rider."

After they'd eaten, Susan excused herself for a visit to the ladies' room, and Cleve remembered the issue that did demand a little privacy between him and Bernie. "What am I supposed to do about this kid? She hasn't brought it up for a while, but I know she will, sooner or later."

Bernie took a swipe at his mouth with his napkin and finished his coffee. "Do you really think he's yours?"

"He's not *mine*. I've never seen him."

"But you could very well be his father."

"Yeah, I suppose."

"What do you want to do about him? Do you want to claim paternity?"

"Jesus, I don't know. Seems like—" He picked up the knife he hadn't used, admired it and made it glint in the sun. "Like Susan ought to have him. She really wants him."

"Maybe you ought to have him."

Cleve laughed. "What would I do with a two-year-old kid?"

"Same thing I did with mine. Raise them. My youngest is ten now."

"Yeah, well, you've also got a wife and a job." Cleve set the knife down. "Probably a house, too. You got a house?"

"Complete with a mortgage."

"When you do what I do, you figure those things would slow you down."

"Maybe." With a gesture Bernie declined the waitress's proffered pot of coffee. "It's up to the judge, Cleve. You could claim this child and approve Susan's plans for adoption, and the judge might go along with you. Then again, he might turn you down. That kid's living on the reservation. The tribal court has the last word."

"Christ, I'm sick of courts."

"My advice to you is give yourself some time. As you said, you've never even seen this child. There are tissue tests they can do that would pretty much settle the question of paternity, one way or the other." He sat back in his chair and watched Cleve's face. "Of course, the mother's dead. You could decide to keep your mouth shut and let Susan fight it out with the court, Social Services, and all the rest. Might be interesting to watch, at least until they drop this case against you." He lifted one shoulder. "Then you can take off, go wherever you want, and forget about it. Ah, she's back."

Susan took her seat next to Cleve. "Yes, and my ears have been burning, but I don't think I care to know what was said about me."

He felt as though he'd been caught red-handed. "We were about to send the waitress in after you."

"I've got a plane to catch," Bernie said as he reached for the lunch bill. "Will you have a phone at your place, Cleve?"

"Not likely."

"I'll call Susan as soon as I hear anything new. Meanwhile, you don't travel outside a fifty mile radius without permission. No firearms. No alcohol or drugs." He smiled. "And if you need me for anything, you call me."

It was an hour and a half drive to Fort Yates. Cleve slid down in the passenger seat, pulled his hat down over his face and pretended to sleep most of the way. The straw hat permitted him to watch the grass wave in the breeze as the hills rolled past his window. The open weave also allowed the wind to keep his face cool and blocked the glare from the low afternoon sun. He could roll his head to the other side and watch Susan drive. Either she was concentrating very hard on the long, straight, empty highway, or she was thinking. Planning. Coming up with a strategy. He wondered what it would be.

Most of the women he'd known were easier to figure than she was, but she was still a woman. She knew her assets, and she knew they interested him. She liked his, too. She must have, or she wouldn't have kept coming back. But he had something else she wanted— at least, *she* seemed convinced he did—and that made him uneasy. He wasn't sure why. It was just a little extra leverage. He didn't have to use it. What was wrong with keeping an ace in the hole?

He liked being with her. She'd taken him to the bank and then to a couple of stores, where he'd bought some underwear. She'd pretended to be shopping for men's jeans while he grabbed a couple of packages off the shelves and tossed them on the counter. "Help me find a shirt," he'd said, and she'd come right over.

"What kind?"

"Striped, plaid, and flowered."

"One shirt?"

"We could only wear solid colors, but not red. Red print. That's what I want."

He remembered how seriously she'd taken her assignment. He studied her face, framed in straw. She was pretty. Those eyes, those lips, that long, slim neck. She lifted her chin, and he noticed the subtle, steady pulsation beneath her soft skin. There were other women, but he'd wanted this one for a long time and for a lot of reasons. When they got to Fort Yates, he had the feeling she was going to invite him over to her place. He dozed off thinking about the first thing he wanted to do.

When he awoke, they were pulling into Cody Primeaux's gas station on the east side of town. Cleve pushed his hat back and glanced out the window. A man in oil-stained coveralls approached the car.

He waved at Cleve. "Hey, cowboy, they sprung ya! Be right with you, soon as I ring up a sale."

A little groggy, a little puzzled, Cleve looked over at Susan.

"Is this okay?" she asked. "Cody Primeaux's, you said."

"Yeah." He glanced out the window. He'd said Cody's, but he'd had her place on his mind. "Yeah, this is fine."

"I was going to offer to let you take my car whenever you wanted to go down to Little Eagle and see your grandmother, but since you don't have a driver's license . . ." She turned toward him. "I could take you down on Sunday if you'd like. That's my next day off. I usually spend Sundays with Sam, but I'm sure—"

"Don't worry about it. I'll find somebody to catch a ride with."

"I'd love to see your grandmother again."

"She gets up this way once in a while. You'll see her." He reached over the seat, grabbed his duffel bag and let himself out. "See you around."

"Yes. I hope everything . . . turns out."

He shut the door soundly, but he didn't take his hand away. He wanted to be with her now, not just because it had been two and a half long, celibate years, but because she'd seen where he'd been. Cody was going to ask all kinds of questions he didn't feel like answering. If he went to the bar, there'd be questions there, too. He wanted some time to get his bearings. He wanted space, but maybe not too much all at once.

He tapped the car once, as though pushing off. "Thanks for the ride."

The hell with her.

Susan watched him disappear behind a blue Chevy sitting three feet above the garage floor on a hoist. She should have asked him to come over for supper. Supper, and then what? What would a man just out of prison have on his mind? She knew damn well she wanted it to be her, and that was stupid. That was very stupid, Susan. This relationship was sticky enough as it was. Cleve needed to be with his old friends, and she needed to be with Sam. Playing with fire was the surest way to get herself sizzled—and probably get Sam burned in the process.

She drove to Vera's. The kids were home from school, which meant sure chaos. Two of them were fighting over a plastic tricycle in the front yard. "Why don't you guys take turns?" Susan suggested as she dodged a dog that had just been shooed out the door. The boys ignored her.

Junior, the dog chaser, held the door open as Susan skipped up the front steps. "Sam's been whining," he reported.

"Something wrong?"

"No. He just whines over nothing."

It was Sam's way of entertaining himself, but the children didn't understand that. They only knew that it got on Vera's nerves and made her yell at them. Eight-year-old Bobbi appeared from the kitchen with her small arms full of Sam. When he saw Susan, he squealed and reached for her.

"Hi, sweetheart. Have you been singing songs for Junior? Hmm?" Susan automatically checked his diaper and pulled his T-shirt over his little belly as she took him in her arms.

"He's singing up a storm," Vera said from the kitchen. "Damn pow-wow season's over with, I said. But he never quits. You girls get that meat fried up, and I'll do the rest." She bustled into the living room, one hand on her hip and the other fussing with her hair. "What did he say?"

There was no mistaking Vera's meaning. They'd talked about it and talked about it until the whole issue had become a knot in Susan's stomach. "About what?" she asked sitting on the sofa.

"About letting you adopt Sam. What did he say?"

"Vera, the man is only out of prison on a kind of a technicality. The district attorney will probably go through all sorts of contortions to put him back there." Sam stuck his finger in her mouth. She removed it, kissed it, and smiled, then continued with Vera. "I really don't think he's going to be anxious to join me in a custody battle, at least not on his first day out."

Vera folded her arms and lifted her chin defiantly. "You like him, don't you? It isn't just that you want Sam. You really—"

"I can't help but like him after all the time I've spent with him lately. Besides, he's always been remarkably civil to me, considering what I did to him." Vera was the only person in Fort Yates with whom she'd discussed the trial, and she trusted Vera to keep the story to herself.

"He had it coming. And now that he's out, you just remember what he did to Darcy."

"Darcy was a grown woman."

"If she wasn't pregnant, she might have lived through that accident. And what did he care? Big rodeo cowboy."

She spat the words like cherry pits as she sank to the sofa beside Susan. "You'd better keep your legs locked together *really* tight whenever he comes around. That's all I'm saying."

Susan glanced across the room at Bobbi, who appeared to be engrossed in television cartoons. "He's just a friend."

"How can you have a man for a friend? Especially *that* man."

"The same way I have you for a friend," Susan said. Vera leaned back with an incredulous *moue*. "Well, maybe not exactly the same."

Vera came back with the local expression, "Not *even* the same. You live with a man, you have babies for him, and you put up with his bullshit. But you're a friend, and I don't have to put up with any bullshit from you. That's the difference."

"You don't have to put up with Tommy's, either. As far as Social Service is concerned, Tommy's deserted you." Susan grabbed the opportunity to put the shoe on the other foot. "Did you ever settle that business at the store?"

Vera shook her head. "Maxner says he's going to take it out of my next aid check if I don't pay what Tommy owes him."

"He can't do that. That's Aid to Dependent Children, not dependent husbands."

"I sure like it when you say they can't do that, like you really believe they can't. Maxner's been doing it for years. There's no bank here. He's *it*. He sells the groceries, cashes the checks, and loans people money."

"But Tommy borrowed the money, not you."

"Tommy doesn't have any checks coming. Anyway, he's my husband. You know, the fifty Tommy borrowed wouldn't be so bad, but I don't understand how Maxner figures all this interest. It's up to a hundred and ten dollars now."

"In a month? Maybe Tommy borrowed again."

"Maxner says it's on the fifty. I told him last time

I paid my bill at the store. 'If you loan Tommy any more money, I'm not paying,' I said. 'You'll have to get it from Tommy,' I said. Right there in the store." She grinned. "I really cussed that skinny thing out that time."

"I don't see how he can get away with loaning money like that, never mind charging interest. I'm sure there must be a law against doing business that way."

"This is the rez, girl." Vera gave Susan's arm a little shove, and they both laughed. Susan was learning to laugh at reservation *status quo*, which was often so infuriating, it had to be funny. The laughter always culminated in a sound that translated into resignation, "Ahhhhh, cheez," a shaking of heads and a drifting silence.

Vera touched the baby's hair. "You must listen, Susan, I don't want Sam to go to just anybody. Him being the way he is, somebody could be mean to him, you know? Some of these foster care people just want money."

"Tell that to Judge Dunn."

"Judge Dunn thinks I should raise him. That old fart. He cuts his eyes at me and tells me not to be in such a hurry, well—" Vera's lower lip trembled slightly. "He might as well just say what he thinks of me. It's my sister's baby."

"Sam won't ever be too far away from you. You know that."

"I can't keep him much longer. I'm . . . going to have another baby."

"Oh, Vera." Susan felt her friend's helplessness. At least a piece of it. The choices would not be the same for both of them, but they were women together, just the same. "What about school and everything you've—"

"I'll finish school. I'm not giving that up." The hand on Vera's thigh became a fist. "I'm gonna have my tubes tied this time. Tommy can't tell me what to do. He doesn't even need to know about it."

Sam started in with his toneless whine again, and Vera shook her head. "That baby needs a lot of attention. I wouldn't mind giving it to him, but every time he makes that sound, I hear his mother wailing from beyond the grave." She looked at Susan. "You don't believe in stuff like that, I bet."

"I believe your sister haunts you." Susan rubbed the baby's back. "And I believe you care about her child."

"Not the way I care about my own," Vera said honestly.

Susan kissed Sam's downy forehead and smiled. "That's my job."

Cleve hooked one arm beneath his head and stretched out on the creaky rollaway Cody had borrowed from the Warrior Motel. Cody had offered him a basement apartment. By the time Cleve had scrubbed the place out and Cody had rounded up a hot plate and a couple of pieces of furniture, all Cleve cared about was the bed and the six-pack Cody had brought down. They'd had a beer together, but Cody didn't seem to know what to talk about, and Cleve felt like someone who'd been off the planet for two years. Cody finally slapped his knee and announced that he had to get back to work.

Cleve nursed another beer and listened to Hank Williams, Jr. crooning through the floorboards about his family traditions. He half expected The Man to haul ass up there and tell some fish to turn it off or use his headphones. He was glad none of his buddies could see the way he was spending his first night on the outside. He knew how to get to the local bar. He knew where he could find a willing woman if he wanted one. And God knew he wanted one. But he was staying right where he was, safe in his hole, where he didn't have to face anybody.

The buddies he had in mind were all convicts. The people he didn't want to face *used* to be his buddies. People he'd known when he was growing up, gone to school with, run the rez with. Jesus, his life had gotten all turned around, and now he was thinking like his only friends were a bunch of cons. But he'd be damned if he was going to justify the last two years to every person he met, or keep telling them he was innocent, or talk about what it was like in the pen. And he damn sure wasn't about to put up with any stares and whisperings.

He was back on the rez. He remembered promising himself and more than a few others that once he left, he'd be *gone*. They'd read about him in *Rodeo News*. If you stayed on the rez, it was because you were afraid to try someplace else. If you came back, it was because you had no place else to go.

The beer tasted like piss. The bed was lumpier than a cellhouse bunk. He had a bad case of blue balls, and not even his train would be coming for him.

What's the first thing you're gonna do, Cleve?

Shit. Hide out.

Chapter 15

Susan opened the door and found Cleve standing on the front stoop with one foot a step below the other, poised to retreat. He looked surprised, as though he'd decided she wasn't home. His dark-eyed magnetism made her heartbeat shift into a higher gear. He was wearing his new red shirt, his straw cowboy hat, and well-worn black boots that were freshly polished.

"Maybe I should come back another time," he said. He nodded toward the third door along the long, gray facade of the four-plex. "One of your neighbors just stuck her head out and said you were probably sleeping."

"No, no, come in. We're all nurses here, working shifts, so we kind of look out for each other." She touched her damp, straight hair as she stepped back and held the door open for him. "I had the hair dryer going."

He went inside, and she closed the door. The shades were drawn, and the room was clean, dark, and cool. He'd caught her at her worst: bare feet, bare face, and dressed in the cutoff blue jeans and T-shirt that had been handy when she'd gotten out of the shower. He looked her up and down and smiled. So she wasn't wearing a bra—big deal. She wasn't expecting company.

"Your neighbor probably got tired of listening to me pound on the door. You go to work at three, right?"

She knew the time, but she checked the clock, anyway, and folded her arms loosely over her chest. "It's only 11:30. No problem. I was just going to have some lunch. Brunch, actually. Would you like some?"

"Sure." He set his hat on a blue arm chair. He seemed to fill the room, like a stallion in a stall.

"Have a seat while I inventory the brunch fixings. Are you all settled in?"

He followed her as far as the kitchen doorway, then leaned his shoulder against the jamb. "Got myself a bed and a hot plate. Next thing I need is a job, and we all know jobs are always in short supply on the rez. But then, so are white cops and redneck judges."

She wondered what he thought about the presence of white nurses. "What can you do, besides ride bulls?"

"Make license plates." She showed him half a pot of coffee, he nodded, and she took two cups from the cupboard. "I'm a pretty fair hand when I have to be. You know, like an honest-to-God working cowboy. But not too many ranchers around here can afford to hire winter help. Cody's got all the help he needs at the gas station, too."

"Why don't you enroll at the community college here in town? Transfer the credits you earned in Bismarck and—"

"You been talking to Steiner?" She handed him coffee, and he lifted the cup, as though he were toasting her. "You sound just like him. My schoolboy days are over. I just took those classes for something to do." His breath chased the steam across the rim of the cup as he took a cautious sip. "Not bad."

"You said they were pretty interesting."

"The classes? When you spend your day being hustled from one little pen to another like some kind of feeder steer, anything seems interesting. Now I'm out in the real world, and I need to find a way to earn a living." He smiled. "You do make good coffee."

"Thank you. I make a pretty good omelette, too. How does that sound?"

"Fine."

She assembled the ingredients next to the stove and started whipping up eggs and thinking up solutions while he sipped his coffee. "You were in the army, weren't you? Maybe you could qualify for veteran's benefits." It had been a while since she'd thought about Mel, but she remembered that he'd enrolled in some classes at the University of Minnesota and collected monthly checks from the VA for about a year. He'd quit school and continued to receive the money until the VA caught up with him. She'd refused to help him pay the money back, and she didn't know whether he ever did. It had added up to a sizable amount, intended for tuition and living expenses.

"You're even *worse* than Steiner. I didn't think anybody had more answers than that guy, but I think you've got him beat."

"It would be worth looking into," she said.

"Maybe." He walked around her and helped himself to a refill from the coffee pot. "I ought to be able to find some kind of work. Once Bernie gets this legal thing straightened around, I can pick up where I left off."

"In the rodeo?"

She wanted to bite her tongue. She hadn't meant to sound doubtful, but it had come out that way.

"You don't think I can make it? Hell, I'm in better shape now than I ever was. You saw me ride."

"You were wonderful. But I also saw the way you were kneading your arm and trying to rotate your shoulder afterward." Actually, she'd learned about his past injuries from his grandmother, but she wasn't going to tell on the old woman.

"Everybody does that. You try getting jerked around by a two-thousand-pound bull."

"No, thanks. I think I'd rather walk. But I guess you can keep on riding if you don't mind living with some aches and pains." She slid the first omelette onto a plate and poured the second one. "I'll bet you're used to a more substantial lunch than this. How about a sandwich, too?"

It was his turn to say, "No, thanks."

"I guess you're the best judge of how much abuse your body can take."

"You gonna abuse it with your cooking?"

She liked the cocky smile that went with his teasing. "You can be the judge of that, too. What I meant was that the decision to quit is bound to be difficult for any athlete—I mean, if you're thinking about quitting—especially when you've done well as a professional. As a nurse, I've seen many—" The toast was up. She went to the refrigerator for margarine and a carton of orange juice and wondered what else he might like. Milk? Orange marmalade? Raspberry jam? She could have made hash browns, but it was too late. She backed out of the refrigerator, turned and Cleve was there. "Oh!"

"What's the matter?"

She elbowed the door closed. "You crept up on me."

"Just wanted to see what was so interesting." He relieved her of one carton and two jars and set them on the counter. "Are you afraid of me, Susan?"

"Of course not. Why would I be?"

"I just got out of prison." He took the milk and the margarine, leaving her empty-handed. "You've never been alone with me, unless you want to count the ride back from Bismarck. But you were busy driving."

He stood so close, she could tell what brand of bar soap he'd used. "I'm not afraid to be alone with you."

"Have you thought about what a guy like me might have on his mind, first thing after he gets out of prison?"

It didn't take much to figure it out. She could see it in his eyes and wondered if it showed the same way in hers. "Yes. I've wondered how you must feel about . . ." *Wanting. Being wanted.*

He touched the hair that lay against her shoulder. "I didn't feel too great last night, but I feel pretty good now. How about you?"

She flipped her hair behind her ear, leaving his fingers empty. "I'm glad you're out of prison."

"Why?" Her gesture was feeble enough to draw his hands to her shoulders.

"Because I don't think you deserved—" Slowly kneading her shoulders, relaxing her, moving in close, he parted his lips. *Too soon. Too easy.* "Oh, Cleve, let's not make things—"

"Yeah, let's. Let's just see what it's like." She stepped back, and he followed, as though dancing with her. She felt the hard, cool refrigerator door against the back of her calf. He smiled. "All those times you visited me, didn't you ever wonder?"

"No, I didn't. I didn't want to."

"Yes, you did. I saw it in your eyes. What would happen if the bad guy kissed the good girl, you were thinking."

"Things were too tangled up and too tense. I never thought—"

"Yeah, you did. You're a real easy read, honey. You've got this sweet, natural face that lights up when you like what you see." He slid his hands over her back, rubbing between her shoulder blades where her bra should have been. "Sometimes that face gets all dewy with sympathy. Not that I was looking for sympathy, but there are times when a guy takes whatever he can get."

The hand at the base of her spine was warm. He drew her hips against his, and she felt a flash of heat deep in her belly. "There, you see?" he said, smiling. "Your face goes soft when you're looking at a man you want, and you're thinking: What would happen? Would sparks fly?" She braced her hands on his shoulders, but the last thing she wanted to do was push him away.

Careful. This guy's fuse must be shorter than your memory, Susan. He just told you he'll take what he can get.

"It's okay to be thinking." His voice soothed. He pressed moist open lips above her eyebrow. "Would one kiss set him off, or could he handle two? Would

he use his tongue?" She lifted her chin and saw the
heat in his eyes. "Put your arms around me," he whispered. "I've been thinking, too. About feeling your arms
around me."

He covered her mouth with his, and, although her
hands stayed where they were, she took his kiss eagerly, welcomed his sweeping tongue and the feel of his
strong body against hers. His hunger was deliciously
palpable. She had forbidden herself to wish for this,
but she had thought about it often, many times in the
cool darkness of her bedroom at night, many times in
the bright, blistering heat of day. She was alone. He was
locked away. What would it be like to fill his needs?

He lifted his head and looked down at her. "You know
how long I've been waiting to do that?"

"How long?"

"Since you were sitting on that jury. The only one who
really listened to me. I wanted to kiss you for that and
for the color of your eyes."

*Don't talk about that time. Don't remind me of all
that I took from you, and all that you think I owe.*

It was better when they avoided the whole subject,
pretended it hadn't happened. It was *he* who had preferred it that way; didn't he remember? She'd always
wished they could just be two people who'd met under
absolutely ordinary circumstances. Oh, Lord, the way
he touched her hair, brushed it back from her face and
studied her eyes made it hard for her to breathe.

"I knew what the verdict was, before they ever read
it. You know how I knew?" She shook her head. "You'd
been crying. Remember?"

"Yes."

"When they polled the jury, and you looked at me and
said *guilty*, I wanted to take you by the shoulders and
shake you like a rag doll." His hand slipped from her hair
to her neck. " 'You know that's a lie,' I wanted to say. I
wanted to put my hands around your neck like this . . ."
He could almost encircle it with one hand. He wasn't
squeezing, but she felt his power, and her sense of her

own suddenly vanished. "Are you afraid of me now?"

"Yes."

"Then it's for the wrong reason." He touched the back of her neck gently, sending a shiver through her as he kissed her again. His mouth had mellowed the flavors of coffee and tobacco, and she savored the taste of him. She still wanted more when he took it away and said, "I blamed you for it once. I don't anymore. I wouldn't hurt you."

He was in a position to hurt her badly. She suspected he knew that. "Why did you come here, Cleve?"

"To see you. After all the visits you paid me, I owed you at least one."

"You don't owe me anything. And I don't owe you. I owed you the truth, and I put it in that deposition. That was the best I could do."

He corraled her in his arms and smiled. "Oh, no. You can do better than that."

"What do you want?"

"You know the answer to that." He slipped one hand under the her T-shirt and rubbed her bare back.

"Please don't." *It's too soon. Too fragile. If we add sex to this crazy equation . . .*

"Why not? Because you're enjoying it? What do you think I'm going to do?"

"I don't know."

"No more than you'll let me do." His eyes were full of mischief. "You usually wear a bra."

"I just showered. I wasn't expecting . . . anyone."

"I'm not just anyone." His hand brushed against the side of her breast, and she felt her nipple tighten. "Am I?"

"No. But right now—"

"I can wait. This is as far as it goes for now, right?"

She closed her eyes and sighed. "I hope so."

"Liar."

"Cleve, I think it has to be."

"Maybe so." He laced his fingers together at the small of her back. "I feel like we've known each other for a long time. I've never gotten hooked up with a woman where I've had to spend so much time talking to her before I got her in the sack." Her admonishing expression made him laugh. "Okay, okay. Maybe it's time I learned how. You picked the right time to teach me, and the visiting room at the pen was a hell of a place."

"That's not why—" She glanced away. "I wasn't trying to get hooked up with you. I mean I wasn't—"

"You mean you weren't fantasizing about sleeping with me when I got out on parole at the age of, what? Maybe ninety-two?" He grinned at her. "And here I was working my ass off trying to keep it in shape for you." She rolled her eyes and tried to push away from him, but he held her hips where he wanted them just a little longer. "You've gotten to know a lot about me," he said. "I guess I don't know too much about you, except that you like kids."

"You haven't asked about me." She sidled out of his embrace, and he backed off.

"I don't figure it's polite to ask too many personal questions, like, 'Did you ever sleep with her? Were you using a rubber?' "

"I never asked you that!"

"The hell you didn't."

"You know, our food's getting cold." She snatched the plates off the counter, but he was blocking her way to the table.

"I've eaten a lot of cold food. And I've thought about you all kinds of ways I don't usually think about a woman. Like, 'Wonder what she's doing now. Is she hanging out with friends, or sitting home alone? What kind of furniture does she have, and what does she like to eat for supper?"

"You had a lot of time on your hands."

"Yeah." He stepped aside and watched her put the plates on the table. When she came back for the condiments, he caught her arm. "You said you didn't have a boyfriend."

"I don't."

"I came over because I wanted to see you. Is that okay?"

"Yes. I was . . . I wanted to see you, too."

"About the kid?" She started to assure him that there were other reasons, but he cut her off. "I'd like to see him."

"Now?"

Suddenly agitated, he released her and stepped aside again. He put his hand over the pack of cigarettes in his breast pocket, then changed his mind. "Is he still with Darcy's sister?"

"He's with Vera, yes. I went over there early this morning, and I thought I'd stop by—"

"Would she mind?"

"I don't—"

He turned to the window and shoved his hands in his back pockets as he looked out. "He's almost two now, right? Does he look anything like me?"

"I think so, but you might not see the resemblance right away." She poured orange juice and tried to remember what she'd already put out on the table. Finally she turned away from the chore and stared at his back. "Cleve, we haven't talked about him much, and I didn't want to push you. I've told you that he was premature, and that he had some problems right from the beginning."

"He was in a car accident, same as his mother was."

"That's right. And because of the circumstances of his birth, he's a special child. His development has continued to be slower than normal."

"What do you mean?" He faced her slowly. "I don't know much about babies. You mean, he hasn't started walking and talking, stuff like that?"

"No, he hasn't reached that point yet, but—"

"I think I'll know whether he's mine when I see him. It's hard to believe I've got a two-year-old kid I've never seen. I had this buddy when I was over in 'Nam, and his wife had a baby after he shipped out. She'd send pictures all the time. We kept teasing him about it, telling him it looked like the mailman's kid."

"That's cruel."

"Yeah, I know. But when you're stuck in a mudhole and your future's doubtful, you have to find ways to laugh about it so you can hang on for another day."

"I guess that's true."

"And the world is full of mudholes."

"I guess I don't have much wisdom to offer about being stuck in one," she admitted. They stood quietly for a moment before she asked, "Do you want to go over there now?"

He smiled slowly. "I really want to eat that omelette first."

"The cold one?"

"Bet it's good that way. Then I'd like to see the kid. You got some time?"

"Sure. Vera doesn't have any more classes today, so she'll be there, too. We've managed to work our schedules so that I'm there when she's gone. I might as well tell you, she doesn't think much of you."

"Hey, Darcy came on to me." He held up his hands in a gesture of pure innocence, and she filled them with glasses of juice. "I didn't force anything on her. Wasn't even that interested, to tell you the truth."

"I didn't ask for that information."

"Maybe not straight out. Like I said, you're an easy read."

Susan parked in front of Vera's house. She ignored the engine's dieseling after she shut off the ignition, while Cleve thought about carburetor or timing adjustments he might make to cure the trouble. He'd kept his share of junkers running past their prime in his early rodeo days. Not that her car was a junker, but it offered him a problem he thought he could handle, the kind he should try first if all he wanted was to cozy up to Susan. She'd looked damn sweet in those cutoffs, and when he'd kissed her, he'd felt her nipples tighten under that

T-shirt. In another few minutes, he could have had her on the sofa, and the neighbor would have heard some *real* pounding. Could have, but didn't. He was definitely slipping.

He surveyed the black scuff marks on the front door. What the hell did he think he was doing? He didn't need to get himself into any kid situation now. The woman he'd fooled around with *once* was dead, and there was no way anyone could pin this on him unless he stuck his damn fool neck out.

"Maybe I should go in first and tell Vera you're here," Susan said softly.

"Maybe this whole thing is a bad idea."

"Vera has to face you sooner or later. This is a small town. It's probably best if—"

"I don't mean about meeting up with Vera. I mean I don't think I'm so anxious to get involved with this kid. I'm living in a hole in the ground, got no job, might be out on borrowed time—hell, I can't be worrying about some kid. And he damn sure doesn't need a guy like me for a father."

"Sam won't understand anything but whether you're friendly to him. He warms up to people quite easily."

"Well, I don't."

"You warmed up to me. That's pretty amazing if you think about it, sort of like the lion and the mouse."

"More like the wolf and Little Red Riding Hood." He chuckled, thinking again that he should have devoured her when he had the chance. "Go check out the house, Red. See if ol' Granny wants to let me in."

He sat in the car and waited for her signal. He knew he ought to be taking cover, but instead he was playing it stupid and leaving himself wide open. When he saw her in the doorway, smiling and waving him in he dragged his butt out of the car and ambled up to the front door.

He took a deep breath, walked over to Vera first thing, and offered his hand. She shook it and mumbled an

unintelligible greeting, lifting her gaze no higher than
his knees. Susan, *the traitor*, disappeared down the hall.
He had to say something.

"I'm sorry about your sister's accident. She was a
nice girl." Vera nodded and backed away. The little boy
sitting on the sofa caught Cleve's eye. He was playing
with several brightly colored plastic cups. Was he the
one? He wasn't so small.

Vera scooped the child up in one arm and snatched a
cup off the cushion. "Come on, baby. I'll get you some
juice." She paused on her way to the kitchen and turned
her head for a parting shot, but she still couldn't bring
herself to look at Cleve. "Susan's bringing Sam. One
thing I've got to say to you, mister bigshot cowboy.
Don't try to call my sister a liar."

Cleve worked to shake off the primordial resentment
he always felt when a woman issued him an ultima-
tum. Any woman. He watched these two pass each
other, each one with a child on her hip. Vera's looked
like a regular kid—thumb in his mouth, thick black
hair encroaching on the bright brown eyes that peered
back at Cleve over the strong bulwark of his mother's
shoulder.

Susan's baby had a similar thatch of hair, the same
favorite place for his thumb, and he rode with the same
confidence in Susan's arms, but there the similarities
dropped out of sight for Cleve. If this were Sam, he
was too small to be two years old—even Cleve knew
that much about kids. He didn't like the way the boy
was drooling all over Susan's white top, and he didn't
like the look of his eyes. They were small, and his
eyelids looked as though they'd been stretched taut and
clipped off without leaving any slack for a crease. Susan
brought him too close, the baby looked up at him, and
Cleve felt as though he'd been punched square in the
gut.

"Sam had a good session with the therapist this morning, and we're going to show you how we do his exercises to make him stronger. Aren't we, Sam?"

"Therapist?" Cleve echoed.

"Physical therapist. Remember, I explained that Sam's development has been slower than normal because—"

Cleve continued to stare. "He can't be two years old."

"Almost." The baby wore red corduroy overalls and socks that could have been fingers in a pair of Cleve's gloves. Susan shifted him in her arms, trying to give Cleve a better look. "I wish you could have seen how small he was, Cleve. Then you could really appreciate how far he's come."

He glanced toward the kitchen, then spoke almost inaudibly. "Darcy was already, you know, gone when he was born?"

"That's right. He's a miracle, this little guy. It's been a struggle, but you'd have been proud of the way he's fought for his life at every turn."

"*He* can be proud. I can't say I feel any—"

"It's okay. You can't expect to, not right away. Maybe you'd like to . . ." She started to hold the boy out to him.

"No." *God, no*. She looked hurt, and he stuck his hands in his back pockets and shrugged. "I haven't been around any babies since I was a kid myself. You'd better hang on to him."

"May we show you what we can do?"

"I guess so."

Cleve sat on the sofa and watched Susan make a fuss over the way the strange little boy was able to lift his head and chest off the blanket she had spread on the floor, draw his knees up with her help and scoot ahead, maybe an inch or two. He didn't even sound like a baby. The noises he made sounded flat, toneless, almost not human. Cleve's stomach churned with distaste for what he was seeing, and his head pounded with feelings of guilt over everything else he felt. The resulting rage rendered him speechless.

"He's made so much progress," he heard Susan say. "A month ago, he couldn't lift himself up like this.

His right side is weaker than his left, which means the damage to his brain, probably caused by the trauma at birth—"

Cleve made it to his feet without lurching. "I'll wait for you in the car." He was a damned coward, but so be it. Susan gave him one of her sympathetic looks, which didn't help. It only proved he was a damned *pitiful* coward. He tried not to bolt for the door.

Once outside, he gulped air and fumbled for a cigarette. He managed to light a match with his thumbnail, but he had trouble holding it steady at the end of the cigarette. He felt as though he'd just missed being hooked in the ass by a bull's horn. The smoke shored him up some, and he walked down to the car, propped one foot on the bumper and braced his forearm over his knee. He needed that cigarette.

He didn't begrudge Susan the half hour she kept him waiting. He could have walked, but he wasn't about to stoop any lower than he already had, and he didn't have any pressing business that would excuse a quick exit. He had a crazy notion that he was serving some purpose, maybe watching the car while she spent time with the boy.

The first thing she said was, "I'm sorry I kept you waiting so long." Cleve waved her apology away and flicked the butt of his last cigarette into the street. He could tell she disapproved by the way she watched it land, so he went out of his way to grind it beneath his boot heel before he got into the car.

"I guess I didn't prepare you very well," she said.

"For what?" He closed his door harder than he'd intended. "And who said preparing me for anything was your job?"

She stuck the key into the ignition, then turned to him. "You weren't expecting him to be quite so far behind the normal rate of development for a healthy child."

"That sounds like something out of a book, but it must mean he's not normal, not healthy—" He looked out the side window, avoiding her eyes. "And he's probably not my kid."

"Why do you say that?"

"Because Darcy knew a lot of guys."

"Do you have the nerve to tell Vera that?"

"I don't have to. She knows."

"Darcy named you."

"Only to her sister. She never said anything to me about it."

"You were probably in jail by the time she knew she was pregnant." He had no comeback for that one. "You're not denying Darcy. You're denying Sam."

"I'm just saying—" He knew damn well he shouldn't be saying anything, but he didn't like the look Susan was giving him. "—probably a dozen other guys . . ."

"Okay. Maybe you're not his father. Maybe you don't deserve to be. And maybe I don't deserve to be his mother, but let me tell you this." She gripped the steering wheel for support, and her eyes were full of blue blazes. "You were in the right place at the right time when he was conceived, and when he was born, so was I. I'm not sure why we keep bumping into each other the way we do, but I think it's more than coincidence. I think—" Finally, she couldn't look at him anymore. She stared at the hood of the car. "It was your idea to come over here today, Cleve. I'm very sorry you don't like the way he looks. I'm sorry he's not up to the standards you've set for your offspring. I'm not asking you to give him a home or pay for his support or even give him your name." She started the car. "Just help me get custody of him, because I *want* to do all those things. He *belongs* with *me*."

She was steaming, and he'd been put in his place, so they both kept their eyes on the road. She was headed for the hospital. "Where do you want me to let you off? I have to go to work."

"At the Tribal Office. I want to check on a job." He turned toward her. "Look, you told me plenty of times that this kid had problems. I guess I just wasn't expecting . . ." He swallowed hard. "Is he retarded?"

"I don't use that word."

"Well, I don't know the right word to use since I don't know a goddam thing about any of this. Give me a better word."

"The word is *child*. He's a child, Cleve. I've always spoken of him the way I think of him—a special child. You're like most people. You looked at him and all you saw was a handicap."

"Pardon me for being like *most* people for once."

"He's not a handicap. He's a child."

"Okay." He raised his hands in surrender. "Okay, but will he ever walk like a child, or talk or—"

"I don't know. How do you know what any child will be able to do?"

"This is different."

"Yes!" She arced the wheel and hung a left with a vengeance. "Yes, there's a difference, and the difference is brain damage, through no fault of Sam's. Nobody knows how much progress he'll be able to make. Not too many people thought he'd ever get out of intensive care. But he did." She hit the brakes, and he rocked forward. "Here's your stop."

He glanced at the mural above the entrance to the building. Feathers and tipis, blue sky and white clouds. Reservation daydreams. "I don't know what to say."

"Nobody asked—"

"Just give me some time to think, okay?"

"Fine." The motor raced, and she pressed the accelerator to kick the idle down. "It should be a new and interesting experience for you."

It griped the hell out of him to let the insult go unanswered, even if a gesture was all he could come up with. It had been a long time since he'd actually flipped anybody off, but the urge was there. He congratulated himself for trapping the bird in a tight fist as he watched her drive away.

He stayed away from her for the next several days, telling himself he had better things to do than put up with her attitude. The tribe offered him a job tending their buffalo herd. He told the property manager he'd keep looking. He inquired at every office and business in town, but there was only one other offer. Since riding herd on buffalo was better than sweeping out Maxner's store, he went back to the Tribal Office, dragging his heels, and was told he could start anytime. Without a vehicle, he'd have to hitch rides to get out there, but he figured he'd manage. He had before. He promised to ride the pasture over the weekend and see what the conditions were.

Standing Rock Community College stood between the causeway and a housing project on the outskirts of town. In the course of that first week he had walked past the sprawling single-story building a dozen times before he finally stopped in. Not to sign up. Just to have a look around. He decided the place would probably not be too busy on a Friday afternoon. He wasn't anxious to be noticed.

People seemed to smell the presence of a good piece of news wherever he went. Some of the faces were friendly, and Cleve was better with faces than with names. One guy he knew from somewhere offered him a handshake in passing and welcomed him home. The word "home" sounded strangely good to him. As he stood near the entrance, pretending to read the notices on the bulletin board, he noticed that there were actually students his age and older. A class schedule caught his eye. They held some classes at night. There was a reminder for students to complete financial aid applications and a phone number for the Veterans Administration.

Cleve investigated one hallway, tested out the weight lifting equipment, and wandered into the library. He asked the librarian if she had any books on retarded kids, and she helped him find one about birth defects and another about special education for handicapped children. As a member of the community, he was permitted to check the books out, which pleased him. In the last two years, he'd learned to appreciate libraries.

He invested in a reading lamp and bought a paperback novel in case he couldn't get into the other books. Over a supper of canned beef stew, he paged through the library books, then turned to the novel for a while. Later, he was drawn back to the books full of statistics, definitions, and photographs. One question led to another, and he read to find answers. Before he knew it, he was making notes on the back of an envelope.

Cody was on his way to Bismarck on Saturday night, so Cleve caught a ride as far as the local bar, which was actually two and a half miles out of town. He ordered a beer and took it to a corner booth. The juke box played Conway Twitty, and an old white farmer was shooting bumper pool. He was missing the first two fingers on his right hand and most of his shots, but he had no opponent. Cleve soon realized he'd felt more comfortable in the college library. He tried to take the edge off with a second beer, but it wasn't working. He didn't recognize a soul in the place, but he had a feeling they knew him. Three or four Indians, all avoiding him. Half a dozen white guys, all peering bleary-eyed through a blue haze. Christ, who did they think they were?

He took his third beer with him and hiked the two and a half miles back to town. Except for the occasional pair of headlights, the highway was dark. When he hit the causeway, he took the path along the backwater, avoiding streetlights. A group of old men who were sharing a log and passing a bottle hailed to him to join them. He hoped he was lying when he called back, "Some other time." The same guys would be back in the same spot early the following morning, waiting for the off-sale liquor store to open. Maybe they wouldn't go home at all. Maybe they *were* home. Home was just a place to stay for a while, anyway.

Nights were cold this time of year, but the air was still and the sky was full of stars. Cleve passed his apartment, crossed the street and slowed his pace for a walk along the river. There was a stigma attached to walking, as in "being on foot," as in having no car. Worse yet, no pickup. But after dark it felt good to be out walking.

He lit a cigarette, watched the smoke dissipate in the dark, and recognized where he was headed. The hospital was only a block away, and beyond that, staff housing. Off to his right a nighthawk's wings whirred suddenly as the bird dove, then soared, shrieking, "Pee-ik!" Susan worked until eleven. Was she a night bird, too?

"I know it's late," he said quietly when she opened the door. "I won't stay long. I just want to talk."

"Okay." She tightened the sash on her long, wine-colored robe and pushed the latch on the outside door.

He knew she must have smelled the beer on his breath as soon as he stepped inside, but to her credit, she didn't mention the terms of his release. "Tonight was the first time I've been inside a bar since I got out." Not that he owed her an explanation, but maybe he was offering one because she hadn't asked.

"Did you have a good time?"

"No. Too many rednecks out there, so I left." She didn't seem ready to condemn or congratulate. Her face looked soft and dewy, and her eyes were sleepy blue. "Just wanted you to know that basically I'm sober."

"I think I could tell if you weren't."

"Yeah, well, me showing up here this time of night, you might think it was because I'd had a few too many." He smiled. "But I suppose you've got a nose on you, too, like most women. You can probably tell me exactly what my blood alcohol content is, right?"

"I'm not *that* experienced." The desk lamp in the corner was the only light on in the room. Susan pressed a button on the aquarium, which stood in the opposite corner. The fluorescent light flickered, then illuminated the tank. "But you are," she said. "You've probably charmed your way past many a porch late at night."

"Hell, I don't know what's a good time to come over. Your hours are a little screwy."

She laughed. "This is fine. Would you like some coffee?"

"If it's no trouble." He tossed his hat on the chair and sat on the sofa. The plump cushions enveloped him, and he thought it would be nice to sleep there. He felt tired. "I got a job."

"Terrific. Where?" she asked as she disappeared into the kitchen.

"Out by the Youth Ranch." He heard a cupboard door close, and he had half a mind to offer to help her. The other half was lulled by the way the fish slipped silently back and forth behind the glass, almost in time with the easy-listening music on the radio. It was like crashing in the lobby of a fancy hotel late at night. No, it was even more comfortable than that.

"The Youth Ranch," she repeated.

"You know, north of town. The tribe has that place where they send kids who keep getting into trouble."

"I know where the Youth Ranch is, but I've only seen it from the highway. What will you do there?"

"It's not with the youth program." He slouched down further, nesting in the blue and tan striped cushions and listening to her rattle around in the kitchen. "I'll be riding herd on the buffalo the tribe keeps out there. About forty head."

"That should be fun."

"Right. Buffalo are about the dumbest, orneriest creatures in God's creation. You can put up a six-strand fence on eight-foot posts, and they'll walk right through it. Last guy quit within a month, they said."

"He didn't have your experience in dealing with stubborn animals. Black, right?"

"Right." The coffee smelled like the best part of early morning. He had to keep talking so he wouldn't drift off on all the comforts. "More like he figured out there was a limited future in it. But it's something to do, and it gives me a chance to be around horses." She handed him a steaming mug. "Thanks. You heard anything from Bernie?"

"This is banana bread. Only two days old." She set the plate on the small table next to his elbow, and he tried to remember the last time somebody waited on him. "I would have gotten hold of you immediately if Bernie had called."

"I wasn't sure. You seemed pretty mad last time I saw you."

"That wouldn't matter." She sat beside him with her own cup in hand. "I have more class than that."

She knew it, too. He had to laugh. "Hanging out with class might be a new experience for me, but not thinking. Thinking is one of the few things I've done freely over the last couple of years."

"I shouldn't have said that."

"No, you were right. I sounded like a jerk. I really didn't know what to think when I saw . . . Sam." The name was hard to say. He didn't know why. "I picked up a couple of books at the library. Did a little reading about it. I never knew how many things could go wrong with having a baby."

"You read about—"

"Birth defects, handicaps, that kind of stuff. Fetal Alcohol Syndrome." It was a condition he'd heard about, but dismissed as having nothing to do with him, especially when he heard the term in connection with the long list of reservation problems. The plight of the Indian. Jesus, he hated that.

"We see some of those children at the clinic, but with Sam it's a different—"

It had been nagging at him, and he had to get it out. "They don't know whether a man's drinking can affect his—well, his sperm."

"His genes?"

He nodded. "Darcy used to party a lot, but so did I. Steiner tried to get me to go through the treatment program at the pen, since I was supposed to have committed murder while I was under the influence. Maybe passing out when somebody's getting murdered ought to be a crime. Maybe . . ." Cleve rested the coffee mug on his thigh and looked at her, hoping he wasn't still sounding like a jerk. "I guess just about everybody I know likes to get a buzz on once in a while, especially after a rodeo. That goes for *white* cowboys, too."

She looked up at him. "I don't know whether you have a problem, Cleve, but I think it's a pretty safe bet that Sam's nervous system was damaged in the accident. That and the fact that he wasn't full term added up to some serious medical problems. Pregnant women shouldn't drink. That much we know. As far as any genetic damage caused by a man's use of alcohol, I think the jury's still out on that."

"I don't have the best luck with juries."

"Sorry."

He sipped his coffee and watched the fish for a moment, remembering. "He has funny eyes."

"Sam?" Staring at the aquarium, Cleve nodded. "They're not like yours. And yours aren't like mine, but we can all see." She spoke like a teacher. In fact, she reminded him of Mrs. Taggert, ninth grade English. Nice lady, as he remembered, even though he'd raised hell in the back of the room whenever he'd had a chance. But she'd always been the soft voice of reason. Like Susan. "Because of the damage to Sam's brain, there are some connections that are either weak, or they just aren't there. So parts of his body, especially his muscles, aren't getting the message to function properly. Physical therapy has done wonders, and the doctors are hopeful."

"Hopeful of what?"

"Not that he'll be capable of doing everything a normal person might do, but that he'll continue to grow and develop. At first, we just hoped he'd survive."

She meant hang on, Cleve thought. Like Grandpa. "That's not enough. There has to be a reason to survive. You need something to live for."

"And who's to say what that should be? Maybe he lives to be part of our lives. Sam has things to teach me." She smiled. "Maybe even you. Nobody can promise he'll ever walk or talk or ride a horse. We just keep working, and he keeps surprising us."

"So you don't have any idea what he's going to be like."

"I know what he's like now. I'm willing to take him as he is."

Why? What's in it for you?

"I can see how he'd be a lot of trouble for someone like Vera, with six kids."

"And another one on the way."

"Geez, it's time to quit." He reached for a piece of the bread. "My grandma had nine kids. Three of them died before they got to be adults. One got killed in Korea. My mother took off and left Grandma with another kid, and then she died pretty young. Some people probably figure if they have a whole bunch, they might get one or two to grow up and turn out right."

"Sounds like disposable children. There's no such thing."

"Oh, yeah?" He finished the slice of bread. "What's the judge's name? The one you've been having trouble with over this?"

"Judge Dunn."

"I'll try to talk to him." Later he'd be kicking himself for getting too comfortable on her sofa and letting her music and her sweet banana bread soften his brain. "I'll tell him I think Sam's my kid."

"Do you?"

"Maybe. I don't know what kind of proof this judge might need."

"What kind do *you* need?" she asked quietly.

"Some kind of blood test, maybe. I'll talk to the judge, and I guess I'd better get hold of Bernie." When she didn't look at him or say anything for a while, he felt a little bristly. "What's the matter? Isn't that what you wanted?"

"This may be the only chance I'll have. I'm kind of scared."

"You?" He set his coffee aside. "I'm the one who's running back to the burning barn here." She watched the fish now, and he could see how it worried her to put all her eggs in his basket. That bothered him. "You still willing to give me a lift to Little Eagle tomorrow? They're having a jackpot rodeo down there. If they won't let me enter, at least we could watch."

Happily, she perked up. "Tomorrow's my day with Sam. I could bring him along."

"You sure he'll be okay?"

"I think it would be good for all of us."

Including who? "Don't say anything to Grandma, okay?"

"I won't lie to her."

"Just don't go volunteering anything. Not yet, anyway."

Chapter 16

Grace Black Horse sat behind her quilting frame taking tiny, perfectly uniform stitches in the star pattern she'd recreated so many times that her failing eyesight was no hindrance to her. This one would be raffled off to buy jackets for the children in the Head Start program. She had to be working on it every chance she got, she said. She had no interest in sitting out in the hot September sun to watch a rodeo, but she told her grandson to come back when he got hungry, and, as always, she would feed him.

"Frybread the way you like it," she promised without looking up from her work. Her hand seemed too withered and stiff to be able to maneuver the needle from sky blue into yellow calico with such precision, but Cleve watched the familiar silver thimble ram the stitches into another perfect lineup. "I'll put raisins in it," she said, as if that would be the deciding factor.

He felt cramped under the low ceiling. The kitchen was on the north side of the house, but the darkness wouldn't bother the old woman these days. He was amazed she had any eyesight left at all. The white walls hadn't been painted since the last time he'd done it. Must have been eight or ten years ago. Same kitchen. Same lingering frying lard odor. The rough shelves above the gas stove were covered with blue and white oilcloth and stacked with commodity staples. No well-advertised brand names. All U.S.D.A. inspected and approved for Indian consumption. She had once used government surplus food as a last resort, prefering dried vegetables, either from her garden or gathered wild, and meat that might have been domestic or wild, depending upon the calf crop. Now he supposed her soup would be made from canned meat.

"Susan's with me," he said. She was waiting in the car, as was proper until she was invited in. "We thought you might like to—"

"Bring her back with you. She can eat, too."

"She's got this little kid with her. A baby that was left at the hospital. She's been taking care of him off and on."

Grace wagged her gray head. "Why do those girls leave their babies at the hospital? That's no good."

"This one had a lot of problems. He's not . . . well, he's real small for his age."

"He can eat, too, then."

"Grandma, you don't have to cook. I could take you all to the cafe in McLaughlin after the rodeo."

"Eee, this one. Always wants to spend his money foolishly. I suppose you got used to eating fancy like that."

Cleve laughed. "Not lately, Grandma. I can always go for some of your frybread. I just don't want you working too hard on a hot day like this."

"Don't mind heat. Just can't take too much sun anymore." She tied off a short thread and pulled another piece off a spool. "Come back when you're ready to eat." He turned to leave, but she brought him up short. "Sonny," she said. "You really like this white woman?"

"She's a good woman, Grandma." He couldn't say *good friend*, because she wouldn't understand that. In the old way, women didn't have men friends. They had brothers, fathers, and husbands. Even now, people would soon begin to assume that they were sleeping together. Why else would a man be with a woman? "I don't have a pickup right now," he offered as a possibility. "She gave me a ride down here."

She parked her needle and squinted to bring him into focus across the room. "They don't like to wait much. You'd better go. Bring her back with you."

He wasn't sure he wanted to bring Susan inside. It was the house of his boyhood, the one he'd been anxious to put behind him. From where he stood in the kitchen doorway, which was pretty much the middle of the house, his earliest secret shames mocked him. It was a "six-fifty" house, built by government *per capita* payments of six hundred fifty dollars in return for Indian land left flooded by Missouri River dam projects. It was bottom land, the best they had, and the payment was an insult. Nothing to do but take the money, Grandpa had said.

The house had only one bedroom, and in its one bed he'd been expelled from the womb of a woman he hardly remembered. He wondered whether she'd ever been asked if she really liked that white man, and what her answer might have been. Maybe, "He gave me a ride."

"We might not have time," he said lamely.

"No time to eat?"

"You know how these things go, Grandma. Don't be cooking a bunch of stuff, okay? I can't say—"

"Is she too good to eat at my table?" He stiffened, ashamed to face her. "Or is it just you?"

"It's just me, goddam it." He had to get angry. It was his only defense when she started in on him. "Haven't I always been an arrogant sonuvabitch, Grandma?"

"If she would eat with you in that jail up there, she would eat with you here." He started to walk out, but he paused at the door to let her have her last say. "Come back when you've had enough of that crazy bucking. There will be food ready, whether you come to eat or not."

He ducked through the little shed he'd tacked around the door so many winters ago to block the wind, and he stepped out into the light. The buff-colored flats and the tabletop buttes were sun-washed and windswept, the way he remembered. The way those who'd been there a hundred or a thousand years before would remember. The old woman had not changed any more than the hills, and if she were to move, those hills would have to move first.

On the south side of the house was the shriveled garden. Dry corn stalks rustled in the breeze. Scruffy radishes had gone to seed, the remnants of an old woman's industry. When she was gone, the buffalo grass would reclaim her plot. In the spring there would be wild onions, regenerated by those she'd made him leave behind, every fourth one, when they'd gone digging together in the days before he was old enough to hunt with his grandfather.

Memories. Let one happen in a place like this, and, like a Roman candle, it burst open and made a thousand more, all flying around the yard, mocking him.

There was Susan, waiting in the car with the windows down to catch the breeze. She saw no fireworks, but she couldn't miss the signs of decay. She had to wonder why he would let the old woman stay in this place. She held the baby up to the window and spoke in his ear, probably something like, "There he is. You know the one."

He lit a cigarette and walked over to the driver's side. "I'll drive."

"Are you sure?"

"I haven't forgotten how." He opened the door, and she swung her feet to the ground, then hesitated. "It's just a few miles," he said impatiently, "and we're out in the middle of nowhere, for Chrissake. Nobody's gonna jerk your license or impound your precious car for giving me the keys." The look she gave him said that none of this impressed her. He glanced at the baby. "You need to look after him, and I need to do the driving just now."

Susan moved to the back seat and strapped Sam into his car seat. She waited until Cleve had gunned the motor and scattered a gravel wake on the rutted access road before she asked, "What happened?"

"Nothing happened." He gripped the steering wheel and told himself to keep the speed down. He didn't want to scare anybody. "Try to get the woman out of her little hole in the wall, just for an afternoon, she won't budge. She wants us to come back up here for supper."

"What time do you think that will be?"

"Whenever the rodeo's over."

"Oh. Well, that's fine. Sam's feeling pretty sociable, now that he's had a nap. Right, Sweetie?"

Sweetie. Look at all the worry that kid caused her, and he was still a "sweetie." While Cleve was an arrogant sonuvabitch, and had been ever since he'd decided to try to make something of himself. He was also trying to feel sorry for himself because the old lady had a way of hitting the nail right on the head. He relaxed his grip with one hand, rubbed the back of his neck with the other.

"You got a mother somewhere?" he asked.

"Yes. Minneapolis."

"What does she think of you coming out here to work on a godforsaken Indian reservation?"

"Truthfully, not much. But then we've never seen eye to eye on how I should live my life. She didn't want me to take the job in Bismarck, either."

"I suppose Bismarck started looking pretty good when you told her you were coming here." He glanced in the rearview mirror and saw that she was bumping along, so he slowed down.

"She's never been to Bismarck, and I haven't been back to Minneapolis in a long time, either."

"What does she think of your plan to adopt an Indian kid?"

"That I'm buying trouble because he's handicapped." Sam started in on his monotonous singing, and Cleve realized that the sound didn't bother him so much as it had at first. The kid was having his say, too. "I guess she's not exactly enthusiastic about the Indian part, either," Susan admitted. "She agrees with Judge Dunn, although from a different perspective. He doesn't think Sam needs a white mother, and she doesn't think I ought to have an Indian son." Her voice became soft and light. "It's all so silly, isn't it Sam? We know who belongs with whom, don't we?"

"Must be nice, having it all figured out."

He stuffed his cigarette into the ashtray. They'd climbed the last hill. Nestled in the valley below was the tiny town of Little Eagle, with its makeshift rodeo arena on the outskirts. Pickups and horse trailers encircled the fence, and kids on horseback gave kids on foot something to wish for. A gust of wind made a dust cloud in the midst of it all. "I don't suppose they've wet it down or even gotten a tractor in there to break up the ground," Cleve grumbled. "That hardpan looks like cement."

"You've probably gotten spoiled by the big indoor arenas," Susan said.

"Yeah, right. Spoiled as hell."

He parked the car near the fence so that Susan and the baby could see without getting out, and he went to look for the rodeo secretary, knowing full well he was going to have to humble himself and he wasn't going to like it. He remembered a time when he was everybody's favorite.

There were some handshakes and some greetings for him as he circled the arena in search of the people in charge. He was directed to Pete Tallman's red pickup. Pete was taking entries. They'd been buddies once. They'd gone to boot camp together, sneaked off the post and gotten drunk together, tried to punch each other out and gotten locked up separately. Pete grinned, and Cleve knew he was remembering, too.

"Heard your lawyer got you off," Pete said. He offered a handshake through the pickup's open window. "Nice going."

"He didn't exactly get me off. It's kind of complicated." He wasn't going to start telling people he was innocent. They could think what they wanted. "I want to enter up in the saddle bronc. You taking entries?"

Pete laughed and shook his head. "Nobody's gonna take yours, cowboy. We're just peons here. You're a pro."

"Not anymore. I haven't ridden—"

"Shee-it, man, I heard about that ride you made up at the Pen. We'll let you ride exhibition."

"Hell, I didn't come all this way to be riding exhibition. I had to get special permission just to cross the state line to come to this thing."

"That's 'cause you are one dangerous dude." Pete laughed again. "We don't mind if you show us all up, but you're not taking our money. If I let you enter, they'll all be wanting their entry fees back."

"It's a jackpot, isn't it? Open to anybody."

"Not Cleve Black Horse. I'll put you down for exhibition. You can ride a cow, too, if you want. We don't have no bulls in this string."

"Shit, I ain't ridin' no *cow*."

"Not your styyyle, huh?"

Cleve resented the mocking drawl and the gleam in Pete's eyes, but he wanted to ride. He needed the high it would bring him. While he was trying to decide whether to eat crow or walk away, he caught a glimpse of a man buying pop at Isaac Tiger's stand. Scrawny guy with scraggly yellow hair and a vest. Maybe a hunter's vest. From the back, he sure looked a lot like . . .

"Pete, who's that guy over there buying pop?"

"Huh?"

"That skinny guy. You know him?" Cleve's heart pounded in his ears while Pete squinted out the window. Christ, get some glasses, Cleve thought as he edged away from the pickup. The man had his change, and he was about to turn around. Twenty yards away. Thirty, max. He could tackle him before Smith knew what was . . .

"Oh, that's that college kid from Sioux Falls. Doing some kind of practice teaching this fall. He's been here all summer doing volunteer stuff like painting the school."

It was the wrong face. Cleve released his breath slowly and reached for a cigarette. His palms were sweating.

"Like I was saying, you ought to remember where you got your start," Pete instructed. Cleve was still watching the college boy, but he was listening. He thought about telling Pete to save it for for one of his kids. "On cows. Remember? Your grandpa's and my dad's."

Cleve took a long, slow pull on his cigarette and eyed Pete. A lot of water had flowed under the bridge since he'd ridden any cows. A whole damn lake had formed. "Do I have to pay an entry fee to show you guys how it's done?"

"Hell, no. If you're a 'skin on the rez, you get a free ride. Isn't that what they say about us up in Bismarck?"

"That's what some say. Some also confuse doing hard time with getting a free ride, and they'll never believe any different."

Pete grinned. "Me and you know the difference. Remember Fort Leonard Wood?"

"I remember a lot of things, Pete."

"Not all bad, right?" He scribbled Cleve's name in his notebook and wrote *exhibition* next to it. "If we let you enter, the rest of us Indian cowboys would just be donating our entry fees. But if you wanna buck one out, we'll run him in for you, free of charge."

Cleve went back to the car and found Susan cooing and clucking to a fussy baby. "He's never seen horses before, and I think he's a little scared," she told Cleve.

Without commenting, he took the boy from her arms. Sam was as surprised by Cleve's move as Susan was. Man and boy stared warily at each other for a moment. Sam wore little blue overalls and a striped T-shirt, and Cleve thought he looked like a miniature farmer. Kind of cute, but he still had funny eyes.

"You want to ride a horse, Sam? If I can find us one?" Cleve looked at Susan, expecting the answer to come from her. She said nothing, but she looked anxious. "I'll hold onto you real good, and we'll see how you like it up there."

Cleve borrowed Isaac Tiger's palomino after promising three of Isaac's children that he wouldn't keep the horse long. He loped him in a circle, found his gait to be smooth and easy, then trotted back to the car, where Susan waited with Sam. Cleve leaned down, and Susan kissed the top of the baby's head before she offered him up. He held Sam against his chest for a moment while the horse side stepped. Susan reached out, as though she fully expected one or the other to have a change of heart. Sam squealed.

"It's okay, buddy," Cleve quietly assured. "I've got you."

He settled the child behind the swells of the saddle and held him securely within the fork of his legs. Every ranch-raised kid started this way, this young or younger. Sam squealed again, but it didn't sound like a protest. "Kinda fun, huh?" Sam patted the saddle horn with a little hand. Cleve and Susan exchanged smiles. His was tentative, hers hopeful. He still didn't understand what exactly she was hoping for with a kid like this, but he admired the way she stuck by him. Maybe even envied Sam just a little.

Cleve walked the horse away from the arena and headed for an old hay rake that lay rusting in the tall, dry grass.

Sam kept patting the saddle and hollering like a drunk trying to sing Indian. The racket didn't seem to bother the palomino. "Think you'd like being a cowboy?" Cleve asked. "Ride around all day singing 'git alowng little dowggies.' Would you like that?"

It seemed that he might, the way he was hoo-hooing and pounding away. He wouldn't need a lot of smarts to be a cowboy. You have to be a little smarter than a cow, Grandpa would say. " 'Course, you'll have to get a lot stronger in the legs. Can't fork a horse when you've got bum legs, boy. That's why Susan . . . That's why your mom makes you do those exercises." It made sense when he actually put it into words. She treated him the way mothers were supposed to treat their babies. "You think she's your mom, don't you. Did she say anything about me being . . . maybe your dad?"

They took a turn around the hay rake and headed back. He should never have said that aloud, and he knew why now that they were homing in on Susan. She stood there in her yellow top and blue jeans, shading her eyes with one hand. She reminded him of a bird watching out for her fledgling, and, *damn*, she made his own heart flutter.

"I think he's getting the hang of it," Cleve called out. A quick gust blew a puff of dust into their faces, and Cleve took his hat off and held it in front of the baby. Sam sputtered but didn't cry. "She's still there," Cleve muttered. "You can't see her now, but she's still waiting there for you."

And she was beaming. He tried not to beam back. "He's saddle broke now, and he's not horse shy."

"Oh, he was having a grand time. You should have seen the look on his face. He—" Cleve handed Sam down to Susan, but the boy screwed his head around to get another look and flapped his arms happily. "He hasn't shown this much interest in anything lately, including the aquarium, which used to be his favorite. He really likes this." She jiggled him around and made him laugh. "Oh, yes, he does. He likes riding horses. We may have to put one in the back yard."

Cleve could see her doing it, too. Just to get that kid to respond.

And Cleve liked riding horses, even those that didn't like being ridden. Pete had picked out a jug-headed gray who looked as though he'd rather sleep than buck. Bets were laid behind the chutes while Cleve propped a boot up on the bottom rail of the holding pen and studied the horse. Big, barrel-chested bastard. If he did buck, he was big enough to rattle a rider's back teeth.

The home-rigged p. a. system crackled and hummed when they announced him as a champion. The gate swung open, and he could feel the gray collect himself before he leaped into the arena, suddenly full of steam. They were a match. The horse was every bit the pro that Cleve had been. He kicked high and gave his body a little twist, just to challenge Cleve's balance. His forefeet hit the hardpan like a pair of steel-driving mallets, and Cleve's ears were still ringing when the gray jerked him into another jump. The saddle swells jammed into his groin and the cantle slapped his butt, but he spurred high, daring the gray to pour it on. They were one *hell* of a match. Pickup horns went wild, and Cleve let it all go to his head. *Damn*, he was good.

The minute the pickup man had him, he knew he was in trouble. He'd thrown his back out again, and he wasn't sure he could stand until the rider stopped near the fence to let him down. He walked stiffly, not daring to lean down and unbuckle his chaps. The horns were still sounding approval, and Cleve waved as he walked through the gate.

"Helluva ride, cuz."

"Nice one, Cleve."

"Thanks." Anybody who slapped him on the back was asking for trouble. He headed for the car.

"Hey, you okay?" It was Pete's voice, behind him.

"Great." Cleve kept walking. "You got a good saddle bronc horse there, Pete."

"Think I could sell him to a stock contractor?"

"Maybe."

Susan knew he had pain. He could see the sympathy in her eyes even before he got close enough for her to say, "Something's wrong, isn't it?"

"Nothing new. Just a muscle." He turned his back to her while he flipped open the front buckle. He wanted to feel a little more of that sympathy. "Could you help me with the buckles?"

There were three at the back of each thigh. She balanced the baby on one hip and worked the buckles against his thigh with her free hand. For a moment the intimate contact made him forget the pain.

"Sam thought you were wonderful," Susan said.

"How about you?"

"I thought so, too, but you hurt your back, didn't you?"

"Old news."

"We should alternate hot and cold packs on it."

"I should find a tub of hot water someplace." *And you should keep your hand right where it is, maybe a little higher.*

"Where could we find some ice?"

The black-and-white chaps slipped to the ground, and she bent to pick them up. "Isaac's pop stand, over by the crow's nest. Here." She'd tossed the chaps in the back seat, and she was already on her way. He dug in his pocket and came up with some bills. "He'll probably make you pay for it."

"Not when I tell him what it's for."

"Hey, don't tell—"

"Don't worry. I'll be right back."

She trotted off with the baby on her hip, hair swinging against her shoulders, and he groaned. He didn't want anybody coming over to check out his injury so they'd have a story to tell. She came back shortly, carrying a plastic bag full of ice.

"So where're the curiosity seekers?"

Susan smiled. "Isaac is sworn to secrecy. Sit in the car and hold Sam while I wrap this in diapers."

Pain shot through his right leg as he lowered himself into the passenger's seat. The effort left him a little shaky, but he situated Sam on his lap, took the keys from the ignition and dangled them for the child's amusement. "He can't quite sit up by himself, can he?"

"He's getting there." Susan rummaged around in the diaper bag behind the seat.

"We're both in bad shape, kid." Sam grabbed for the keys. "Did he really watch me ride?"

"He sure did."

"Should he have these keys in his mouth?"

"No."

"You can't have my thumb, either, baby. It's dirty."

"Here." She took a pacifier from the bag, cleaned it in her own mouth and handed it to Cleve.

"I'd rather have a bullet. It's a little more *macho*."

She smiled and slid her makeshift ice pack behind the small of his back. "*You* can bite on your thumb, but be careful. That used to be like giving someone the finger."

"Really? Who told you that?"

"Shakespeare. High school English. You always remember the dirty stuff."

"You remember that, buddy. When she gets after you for cussing, you remind her about the bad stuff she read in high school." She gave him a funny look, and he glanced at Sam, who was reaching for a button on his shirt. "Maybe he won't cuss. But, then, maybe he will. Right?"

"Right," she said quietly. "How does that feel?"

"Like somebody put ice down my shirt on top of everything else. How's it supposed to feel?"

"In twenty minutes, we need to replace that with heat. Do you think your grandmother has a hot water bottle?"

"Probably. She's always complaining about cold feet." Obviously, she knew better than to expect a bathtub in a six-fifty house.

"Ready to go?"

"I guess I don't have much choice. But if you two gang up on me about how I should've learned my lesson by now, I'm walking back to Yates."

"Boy, that'd show us."

A white-faced calf was grazing near the fence behind the house. Cleve knew the old chicken coop had been empty for years. The calf surprised him. A dog that could have been mistaken for a coyote came out from under the old pickup and barked. Cleve hissed at it as he followed Susan to the door, and it slunk back into the shade with its tail tucked between its legs. Grace met them at the door.

"Eeee, Sonny, look at you. All messed up again."

"It's no big deal, Grandma. Got my nurse along."

Cleve closed the door behind them while Grace greeted Susan with, "Whose baby is this, now?"

"Darcy Walker was his mother," Susan explained. "I don't know if you knew her, but she was pregnant when she was killed in an accident two years ago. Sam is kind of a miracle baby."

Grace squinted at the baby in Susan's arms, touched his arm, wiggled his foot, and made no comment. Susan knew what she must be thinking, and she wanted to jump to his defense. He was going to get bigger and stronger. If she could have seen . . .

"Where'd you get the calf, Grandma?"

"I've got cows," she explained as her guests trailed her into the kitchen, following the aroma of boiling beef. "Two cows. Every spring they get over into George Crow Killer's pasture. Only had one calf this year, so I don't know. George Crow Killer should do something about that bull of his. If he can't do the job, he ought to get a different one."

Cleve chuckled as he provided Susan and Sam with a ladder-back chair from the kitchen table. "Maybe he's trying to cover too many cows."

"Ayyy, that's right! Maybe George needs two." She hobbled over to the stove and lifted the lid on a big speckled white pot. A puff of steam escaped as she stirred the simmering soup.

Cleve helped himself to a piece of frybread from the sideboard before he sat down. It was still warm and contained the promised raisins. He offered Susan a piece. She exchanged it for the bag of ice which she'd carried into the house in her diaper bag, despite his order to "just leave it." He sighed and tucked it between his back and the chair.

"I don't think you should stay out here this winter, Grandma. If you don't want to stay with Grandma Mary, maybe you should try the complex. It's close to the hospital, and, for now, it's close to where I'm staying."

"For *now*, you say. That complex was supposed to be for old Indians, but old Indians don't belong there. They belong where they've always been. I'm going to die in my own bed."

"You've been saying that for thirty years. Any day now—"

"Sure. Any day. And this is where I want to be. Right here in my own bed with my family watching over me." She took a big knife to a can of mixed vegetables and cut the circle of metal from the top.

"Yeah, well, you're working on outliving all of us, old woman. Besides, Grandpa said the same, and we found him out there in the hills."

"Exposure," she recited as she poured the vegetables into the pot.

He tore off a bite of frybread. Exposure was the easiest explanation. Nobody questioned it; nobody was too surprised. Another old Indian couldn't make it all the way home. Open-and-shut case, quick as an open-and-shut grave.

"At least he was on his own land," the old woman reflected.

That was the way she always ended the story, and Cleve understood that the small lie had become truth for her. The frybread felt dry in his mouth. Actually, the body had been found on George Crow Killer's land after a six-day search conducted by a volunteer army of Indians. Nobody knew how he'd gotten there. His pickup was parked on his own side of the fence line, four and a half miles away. Maybe he'd wandered after a stray calf, as the investigator from the FBI had conjectured. He'd also mentioned the nearly empty pint of peppermint schnapps found in the pickup. That explained everything.

That explained nothing, but it ended the investigation.

"You can put the baby on the bed in there," Grace said, and Cleve saw that Sam had fallen asleep in Susan's arms. Susan thanked her and left the kitchen.

She came back smiling. "I hope you don't mind, Grace. I put those two big bears on either side of him in case he rolls."

Cleve chewed slowly and looked at the old woman. "Bears?"

"I won them at bingo," she said.

"Oh, geez." He swallowed and gave her a teasing look. She was piling the frybread on a plastic platter. "Are you getting hooked on bingo, Grandma?"

"Not for money. For prizes. I don't think that's the same. Did you see my picture of Jesus on the wall in there?" she asked Susan as she set the platter on the table.

"It's a lovely velvet painting of The Last Supper."

"I won that at the church. And I won a turkey last year at Easter time, but I gave it to Jake's wife to cook. I can't eat no whole turkey."

"Sounds like you're a pretty good player," Susan said.

"I find a boy or girl—maybe ten, no younger—and I say, 'You sit with Grandma and help me see the numbers on the cards. I'll buy you one pop, one candy. No more, or your teeth will rot.' " She cackled. "Eee, I have my favorites. Sometimes I let them keep the prizes, but I liked those bears. Biiig ol' black bears. Long time ago, there used to be black bears here."

"Not that you can remember, Grandma." He copped another piece of frybread. Even warm, it went down better with humor than with sorrow.

"I remember because I listened to my grandmother, who listened to her grandmother. Young people don't listen, and look what happens." She wagged her head. "They have nothing."

"I listened to you a lot. I'm listening now." He stuck his hand behind his back and slanted a disgusted look at Susan. "What we've got here is a bag of cold water and a wet shirt."

"It's time to switch to hot packs. Grace, do you have a water bottle?"

"Under the sink." She pointed, and Susan found it. "There's hot water in the kettle."

"I'm listening, too, Grace," Susan said, and Cleve knew he was in for being told on. The old lady would come up with some damned embarrassing story.

"You remember when your grandpa gave you that bottle calf?"

Sure enough. "The one with the gimpy leg? Yeah, I remember. Damn nuisance to have to feed him, especially at five o'clock in the morning."

"Your grandpa didn't think that calf could live very long."

"He was still a pretty scrawny yearling."

"Grandpa said, 'That boy will make a good rancher. See what he made of that frostbitten bottle calf?' "

"*You* made *papa* out of him." His choice of the Indian word for jerked meat surprised him. The old woman giggled behind her hand, and he laughed with her. "Starting tomorrow, I'll be ranching buffalo. Wouldn't Grandpa get a charge out of that? Sure hope I don't have to be doing it too long." The women exchanged one of those knowing female looks, and Cleve wished for a male ally. "If Grandpa was still around, he'd tell me to hang in there and do what I do best. He used to like to watch me ride."

"Here's the hot water bottle," Susan said. She reached for the soggy cold pack. "Sit up a little." He groaned as he straightened his back. He looked at Susan, then Grace. Years apart, same damn look in their eyes. He had to laugh.

The sun had set, and the hills were bathed in purple shadows. Cleve had been dozing much of the way back to Fort Yates, but when Sam started making himself heard from the back seat, Cleve sat up, stretched and yawned. His range of movement told Susan her treatments must have helped him.

He looked back at Sam. "He doesn't like being in that seat. Why don't you let him out? I'll hold him."

"It's not safe for you to hold him in the car," she said. "Not legal, either. He's okay."

"No, he's not. He's all by himself back there, and he doesn't like it."

"He knows we're close by. He's not crying. He's trying out his voice." She glanced at Cleve, but his attention was on Sam. Sam redoubled his volume, and Cleve winced.

"Right. Sounds pretty pitiful to me." Gingerly, he turned to face forward again. "He liked riding horse, though. Think he might be able to do that on his own someday?"

"I hope so. I've read about horse camps that have

programs for handicapped children, and they say that the animal often brings something new out in the child." She smiled into the rearview mirror. Sam was waving his left hand. When he'd been on the horse, he'd had both arms going, even the weaker right one. "Well, you could see how excited he was."

"Maybe it wasn't *just* the animal."

"No, I'm sure . . ." She had to be cautious now. She was inviting someone into Sam's life. She had to remember who that someone was. "He hàsn't been around many men. I'm sure you could offer him . . . a whole new . . ."

"Hey, don't worry about me. I'm no competition for you. Kids are a lot of responsibility, and *this* one especially."

"If I were to have custody of him, you would be welcome to see him, to spend time with him, to be . . ."

For about half a second he seemed to be considering the idea. The he shook his head as if to chase the notion away. "Don't worry about me." He offered a disarming smile. "Just don't let your baby grow up to be a cowboy. He's liable to end up riding some throwback buffalo range."

He watched the road for a moment. "I thought I saw Ray Smith today."

"Where?"

"Down at the rodeo. Saw this scrawny guy wearing one of those hunting vests. Just saw him from the back at first. Sure looked like him." He was still staring vacantly at the road ahead. "I don't guess he'd still be wearing the same vest."

"Did you get a look at his face?"

"Yeah. Just some college kid. But for a minute there I was thinking, should I wait 'til he turns around, or should I try to jump him before he gets a good look at me and takes off? Damn near made a real ass of myself, jumping some college kid."

"But you didn't." She felt a little guilty about feeling relieved. The discovery of Ray Smith would start the whole thing all over again, and she'd still have a part in it, at least through Cleve's part. "Do you expect to run into Ray Smith someday?"

"Expect it?" He lifted one shoulder. "I've thought about it a lot. Willed it to happen. Acted it all out in my head. I've cleared my name a hundred times in my dreams, but it's probably too much to expect. Nobody's looking for him."

"How do you know?"

"Why should they? Far as most people are concerned, he's not the one that got away. I am." The vacant look had faded, and there was an uncharacteristic urgency in his voice. "You know what being a cowboy meant to me? It meant not being an Indian. I mean, when I was *winning*, you know? When I was the man to beat. I didn't have to be an Indian every time anybody looked at me. They wanted to know me. They treated me with respect."

"You're still a cowboy."

"Maybe. But I'm back on the rez. I could have stayed in Bismarck, but I didn't. I came running back here."

"Your roots are here. Family and friends. There's nothing wrong with coming back to regroup after what you've been through."

There was another silence. The sky glowed with streaks of pink and purple, and a car whizzed by with its headlights on. Susan turned the switch on the steering column, not so much to see, but to be visible in the half light of dusk.

"I don't understand why Judge Dunn cares whether this baby gets raised by an Indian woman or not," Cleve said. "I don't think Sam's ever going to care about being an Indian. Some handicaps are worse than others."

"Oh, for Pete's sake, is that all you see? I wonder why you didn't just curl up and die when you were in prison, what with the whole damn world against you."

"I'm not feeling sorry for myself. I just meant—"

"Maybe the whole world *was* against you, Cleve, but you got yourself out of solitary confinement, out of the kitchen and into a trade, into some college courses. Then you got yourself a good lawyer, you got out, got a job on the reservation where there *are* no jobs. You're a fighter, just like Sam is. That's what I see." She almost said, *like your son.* She couldn't comment about his identity as an Indian. She didn't share that. But since they were both there with her now, she knew one thing. "The obstacles haven't been insurmountable."

"Easy for you to say." She was formulating her next protest when she looked at him, but he caught her by surprise. He grinned. "No wonder you're trying to get to know me better."

They dropped Sam off at Vera's, then proceeded to the heart of town and the alley behind the main street. A dog stared into the headlights, then snatched up the small, dead animal he'd been chewing on and trotted off to a neighbor's yard.

"Is this it?"

He'd directed her to the entrance to his basement apartment, which was marked above ground by a piece of metal railing. "I'll get my stuff out of the trunk."

Susan put the car in park. "Are you sure you don't want to stop over at the clinic?"

"It's too late."

"Twenty-four hour emergency service," she reminded him. "You could probably use a muscle relaxant."

"I don't need any pills." She shut off the headlights and the motor, but he made no move to open the door. "Your treatments did wonders."

"I'm glad." He leaned closer. She heard it, felt it, but didn't look. He wanted more than a kiss goodnight, and she did, too. Before he even touched her, she started feeling anticipatory flutterings. It would be hard to get away without giving in to those feelings, and that she couldn't permit herself to do. Not with this man.

He touched her cheek. It wasn't the gesture she expected, and she closed her eyes. He took it for the sign of appreciation it was and took her chin in his hand. She felt his warm breath. His lips grazed hers as she managed small resistance.

"Don't turn away from me, Susan. Don't—"

He turned her face to his again and kissed her softly. His lips were moist, and his tongue teased, just a little. Just enough. He was testing, not pushing, saving the eagerness she knew he felt. His hand was hot and damp. She turned more, and he kissed more. Just this much, she thought as he took her shoulders in his hands. She felt the strength in them and remembered how surely they had handled Sam. He turned his head, and she parted her lips for another kiss. Oh, yes, and he made it a harder one this time, more persistent, more open. He stroked her tongue with his, stirring up those flutterings until she whimpered softly.

"Come inside with me," he whispered.

That would be it. They would turn the corner then. Her voice was smaller than she wanted it to be, but she got the right words out. "No, Cleve."

"Let's go to your place, then."

"No." She shook her head. "No, we can't."

"Why not?"

"It's not . . . not a very good idea."

"Don't tell me that." He nuzzled her hair, pressed his lips to her temple and spoke softly. "I've thought it over for months, and I know it's one hell of a good idea."

"It's too risky."

"I passed all the blood tests before they let me out, Susan. I'm pure and clean as the driven snow."

"That's not what I meant. There are so many reasons why—"

"There's only one. I want to make love to you. Just you." He traced her collar bone with his thumb and the curve of her ear with the tip of his tongue. His warm breath on her neck and the pretty words he spoke made her quiver inside. "You were the one I thought about for two long years. Christ, Susan, it's been more than two years."

"I know that. I understand." It had been a long time for her, too. It was all she could do to hold her fingers back from his hair. "And I know it's not fair for me to . . . even let you kiss me."

"Why not? You've thought about it, too. Kissing and what comes after."

"Yes, I have." She swallowed hard and shut her eyes. "I've wondered whether that would be your price."

He stiffened. "My price?"

"For Sam."

Neither of them moved. Breaths came unevenly, some shallow, some deep. It was a terrible thing to think aloud, even if it might be true, and she was afraid to look at him.

"Would you pay it?"

Through the dark silence, the question came low and ominously, but the answer she knew she should give wouldn't come. Instead, she said truthfully, "I don't know."

"You don't know?" He held her face between his hands and her eyes flew open. His face was dark, but bright anger burned in his eyes. "You want my kid, lady? I'll give you my kid." He cut off her feeble sound with a hard kiss, sucking her breath away. Her senses soared with excitement, and he must have known, for he made it better and worse by taking her in smaller bits: her lower lip, the corner of her mouth, her chin. He coaxed her mouth open and taunted her with his tongue until it was almost pointless to ask, "How far will you go for it, Susan? Will you take two for the price of one?"

Her head was light. "Don't do this, Cleve. Please."

"Do what?"

"Use me."

He pulled back. "Use *you!* You're willing to use me, aren't you? Spend time with me to get what you want? Why can't it work both ways?"

She tried to come up with a coherent answer, but good sense eluded her. "We have . . . so much at stake. If we could just keep our relationship . . . somehow separate from—"

"Lady, our relationship is the damnedest mess there is, and I think a little sex might straighten it out."

"I think you're wrong." She sat up and fumbled with her hair. "You've just gotten out of prison, and you're not sure what you want right now."

He laughed bitterly. "I don't think there's much question that what I want *right now* is to get laid."

"That's honest." She wasn't afraid he'd force her.

"Probably normal, too, right?"

"Probably." Oh, God, maybe she was afraid he wouldn't.

"Good. Lately I've started to wonder." He jerked the keys from the ignition. "So the thing to do when you're craving something sweet is to go to the candy store that's open."

"Probably." She glanced at his hand, feeling around for the door handle. In a small voice she asked, "Is there one?"

"Oh, yeah. Twenty-four hours, just like the emergency room." She knew she'd given him the opening his pride needed, and she hated herself for it. Hated the suggestion more. "Doesn't make much sense to stand outside like the winos at the liquor store, waiting for someone to come to the door."

"Not if your needs are as simple as you say."

"My needs are like yours. Don't kid yourself."

Tears burned in her throat while she suffered him to clear out the trunk. She heard the saddle hit the ground first, then the bag she knew held his chaps, gloves, rosin, cigarettes, probably other things. Things she wanted to know about because she wanted to know him, be with him. Why couldn't he just tell her, just *promise* her, just say something . . . anything . . . the *right* thing. Whatever that was. Oh, Lord, her throat, her face, her eyes were so full of burning, and she didn't want him to see her cry.

"Here's your keys, white lady." They chinked in her palm. "See you around."

Chapter 17

The sky was godawful blue, and the sun was too damn bright. Buffalo were scattered to hell and back, fence was down in at least three places, and the screeching meadowlarks were enough to make a man want to puke. It was a good day to die. Cleve figured the ramshackle barn at the Youth Ranch would be as good a place as any.

Get drunk or get laid. After two years in the pen, it shouldn't have been too tough to manage both. The woman he wanted wouldn't cooperate, but that hadn't killed all his appetites. It just made it harder to satisfy them. Fate was playing another joke on him, and where all this fatal humor was coming from, he wasn't sure. Susan's rejection had bludgeoned the better of the two choices, so he'd done his worst with the other one. He'd gotten drunk enough so he couldn't go crawling to her door.

He figured the only reason he wanted her so bad was because he couldn't have her, but that knowledge didn't ease the wanting one damn bit. She'd wanted the kid all along; she'd made no secret of that. And all he wanted was to get her clothes off her, get her into his bed or hers and screw her so royally she couldn't remember what day it was. Then he'd put his pants back on and quietly walk out of her life.

That was what he told himself. But what he imagined was holding her in his arms for a long, lazy, dimly lit time. He thought of having a cigarette and watching her sleep. Later she would reach for him while he slept and whisper that she wanted him again. The next morning they'd share coffee in bed, and he'd probably wonder what day it was.

It was a stupid fantasy, and he was out of his everlovin' mind.

But what could he expect? He'd just spent two years in the state pen. How could he not be a little crazy? Besides that, there was a bass drum pounding out a grass dance inside his skull, and he was riding an old kid-broke plug, headed back to the barn to try to find a wire stretcher to fix fence for God's least fence-able creatures.

He swung down from the saddle and tied the reins to a corral rail. If he kept this job, he was going to find himself a decent horse. The chestnut had finally shown a little life when Cleve had headed him back to the barn.

"What are you doing with my horse?"

If Cleve had been a gunfighter, the scowling, scrawny, rawboned kid who'd crept up behind him would have been dead.

"Where the hell did you come from?"

The boy took a step closer. "I live here."

"You one of the inmates?"

"Residents. Are you Cleve Black Horse, the bronc rider?"

"Yeah, that's me." A smile tugged at the corner of Cleve's mouth. He liked being recognized, and he had to work at taking it casually.

"Then why ain't you out ridin' broncs, 'stead of my horse?"

So much for hero worship. "Tell you what, kid, you find me a better one, I'll gladly trade. I just started working for the tribe, taking care of the buffalo pasture. They told me I could use a horse from the Youth Ranch."

"Well, you took mine, but I guess that's okay." The boy followed Cleve into the barn, keeping up the chatter while Cleve went back to the cluttered corner where he'd found saddles and gear earlier. "I heard about you. You're the one who killed that white guy out on the interstate. How come they gave you life, then let you go?"

"Because I didn't kill anybody." He opened the lid on a wooden box, but when something scurried around inside, he closed it quickly. "And because they didn't give me a fair trial. You oughta clean this place up a little."

"Next weekend for sure." The boy leaned against an empty saddle rack. "So you got off on a technicality."

"You make a habit of walking right up to a man and sticking your nose in his business? You haven't even told me your name."

"Charlie Buffalo Boy."

"Figures."

Charlie folded his arms across his chest. "You're hung over, ain't you?"

"Yeah. So don't press your luck."

"That's no way to start out your first day on the job. Big Indian like you should know better."

"What makes you think I'm such a *big Indian?*" A metal tool box turned out to be full of nails.

"You got the attitude."

"What I need is a wire stretcher. You guys got one around?"

"Think so." Charlie hopped up on the saddle rack and chinned himself on a high shelf. "Yep." He jumped down, brandishing the needed tool. "I could ride out in the pasture with you, kind of show you the ropes."

Cleve examined the wire stretcher. "This'll do it for now. If I need advice, I'll be sure and let you know."

"I've been keeping an eye on things since that last drunk they hired quit."

Cleve didn't know whether to take offense or laugh. "How old are you?"

"Fourteen. I look older, don't I?"

"No. You look fourteen, which is too young to be mouthin' off to somebody who's in no mood to put up with kids."

"Somebody who's hung over." Charlie took a bridle down from a wall peg. "You're right. When you're feeling sick like that, you'd just as soon hit a kid as look at him."

"I'd just as soon he'd get his butt to school."

"I've been suspended for three days. Got in a fight last Friday." The boy hooked his thumb in an empty belt loop and struck a cocky pose that reminded Cleve of himself, twenty years younger. "So how about it? Want me to ride along? Show you where old *tatanka* likes to hide?"

"*Tatanka?*" Cleve chuckled. "Now who's the big Indian?" On his way out he allowed, "Suit yourself, Charlie."

Charlie punched a fist in the air. "Yeah!"

"The other horse back there in the pen looks pluggier than this one."

"He is, but the only other ones we got are some mustangs they adopted." Charlie tossed a saddle next to the corral and scrambled over the rail to catch his mount. "Meaner'n hell. Nobody can break 'em."

"Don't say *nobody*." Cleve watched the boy hustle. Who'd have guessed it would be so easy to make somebody's day? "I might be tempted to prove you wrong."

"I said *nobody*, Mr. Bronc Buster."

"Shit."

Charlie peeked between corral rails and beamed at his newfound friend. "You should quit drinking, you know. I did."

Cleve was tying the wire stretcher to his saddle and taking the conversation pretty lightly. "You did? When? Last month?"

"No, it's been over a year. They sent me to treatment." He led a nondescript sorrel out of the pen and heaved the saddle onto his back.

Cleve frowned. "For alcoholism? At the ripe old age of, what—"

"Thirteen, yeah. I was pretty bad off. Started sniffing gas when I was about seven, and from there it was a straight shot to hell."

"Well, you got me beat. When I was that age my grandma would have *given* me hell if she'd caught me drinking."

"Nobody caught me." The horse folded his ears back and balked at taking the bit in his mouth, but Charlie persisted. "They was too busy getting high themselves. Then I got into a white foster home, and *they* caught me. Got my arm broke for trying to siphon gas out of their car."

"So what did that teach you?"

"That wine was safer." He mounted his horse and turned to face Cleve. He suddenly looked much older than fourteen. "You go to work hung over very often? If you do, you're probably in big trouble."

"It's been a long time since I've been hung over, and if you keep talking about it, *you're* going to be in big trouble." Cleve stepped into the stirrup and swung his leg over the saddle. "Let's get these nags moving. It's a good day to die."

"That bad?"

"Haven't you heard that?" He tapped the horse in the ribs with his boot heel. The animal responded with a disgusted snort. "Old Sioux war cry. My grandpa used to say it when we were getting into something risky."

"What's so risky?"

"You're taking a risk, kid. Can't you tell?" The boy grinned at him, and Cleve shook his head. "Or maybe I am. Either way—" He swatted the chestnut's rump with the ends of his reins and got a trot out of him. "we're burning daylight, here. I've got an appointment at 11:30."

"Gettin' started early?"

"The appointment's with the judge, smartass." The boy was still grinning, and Cleve realized that he was actually beginning to feel pretty good. He chuckled. "Nothing worse than a reformed fourteen-year-old."

* * *

Judge Dunn knew Cleve as "the bronc rider," too. He decided to make use of the judge's interest in rodeo by putting a few stories to work. He offered the old man a cigarette and told him about the difference between the National Finals and the penitentiary's J. C. Stevenson Rodeo. Money, mostly. For the second time in one day, Cleve declared himself no murderer, and Judge Dunn accepted his word with a nod.

Time to get to the point, Cleve decided. "While I was sitting in jail, there was a woman killed in an accident. Darcy Walker. I think you've been involved with the kid she left behind." The judge nodded again. Cleve continued. "I didn't hear about it right away, and I didn't know anything about the kid until—well, I guess she told her sister that I was the father."

"What do you say about that?"

"Darcy and me had something going at about the right time. If she says he's my kid . . ." Cleve shrugged as he tamped his cigarette out in an ashtray on the judge's desk. "Then I guess he must be my kid."

"Have you seen Sam Walker?"

"Yeah."

"Are you here to claim him?"

"I'm here to, uh . . ." He sat back in the chair, elbows planted on the arms. Holding his hat in one hand, he spread the other wide. "I want him taken care of. I want him in a good home."

Dunn's craggy face expressed nothing. He'd asked these questions countless times. "Are you willing to take responsibility for him?"

"I'm willing to do what's best for him."

"And what's that?"

"Let's not beat around the bush, okay? I know about Sam's situation. I think the best thing is to let the nurse raise him."

"The nurse." Dunn seemed to need to digest the word. "You mean Susan Ellison."

"Yeah. He's pretty attached to her."

"Susan Ellison is a white woman. The boy is one of ours. I might consider her for a foster parent, but she wants to adopt him. At this point, I can't go along with that."

"Why not?"

Cleve didn't know why he'd asked. He'd heard it all before, how it was when the children had been taken away and sent to boarding schools and the villages were left bleak and silent. All part of a strategy, the judge said. When the white man said "save the children," he meant "steal the children." Whole generations had been raised in boarding schools—hell, Cleve had been there. He knew. Then the do-gooders started adopting the babies. If it kept up, pretty soon there wouldn't be any Indians left, according to Judge Dunn. And on it went. Cleve was half listening, but fully respectful, with his hat off and his eyes downcast.

"Do you mind if I ask you a question, Cleve?" The judge said.

His turn again? He sat up and made ready. "Shoot."

"Why the Ellison woman?"

"The boy has problems. Serious physical problems, probably mental problems. The woman's been with him since he was born, and she's been good to him. She's been just like a mother, the way I see it. And she's a nurse."

"She's a damn good-looking nurse."

He lifted one shoulder. "I won't argue with that."

"Are you sleeping with her?"

"No."

"Trying to?" The judge stared a hole in him. "You're thinking with your *ce*, my boy."

Cleve glanced away. The man was old and respected, and he'd earned the right to ask these questions. It was unthinkable to argue with him. "She'd be good for the boy," he said quietly. "That's all I'm thinking."

"What about you?"

"What about me?"

Dunn leaned back and studied him for a moment. "Would you be good for the boy? You say you're his father."

"I'm a rodeo cowboy. I do a lot of traveling."

"Not now, you don't. You can't leave the state."

"My lawyer's going to have that straightened out soon enough."

"And then you'll be gone soon enough?"

"Right. Early spring, with any luck."

Dunn nodded, briefly considered his own leathery hands, then looked up. "If you came to me, and you said, 'Judge, I'm out of prison. I've got a job. Got a place to stay. I want my boy.' I'd say, fine. He's yours. But you come to me and say you want to give him to a white woman. Just give him away." He sighed wearily. "No."

"She cares about him." He didn't add his next thought because it hit too close to home. *Don't you know how important that is?*

"Yes, she does. I have seen that she does. But the minute she has the papers in hand, she will be gone from here. And that boy, someday he looks in the mirror, and he wonders, who's that brown-skinned man? Who was his father? Who are his people?"

"I hope you're right. I hope someday he's able to put thoughts like that together, but chances are—"

A judicial fist came down on the desk. "That boy stays. And if you think of taking him yourself, taking him off the reservation and then giving him to her, just remember—" Dunn wagged a finger. "I can go after him. The Tribal Court has that right. It's been tested, and even *their* courts will back me up."

"You want to tear that kid apart, don't you?"

"I want them to stop tearing us apart. Stop taking our children." He eyed Cleve ominously. "And I want you to think about what it means to be a father."

"I've never been one. Never *had* one."

"I knew your grandfather. I know what kind of a man raised you. I remember seeing your picture in the newspaper back when you were a rodeo champion. A little voice in my ear said, 'See there, old friend. My boy is a warrior.' "

Cleve's throat prickled. "Listen, Judge, I've got no way to do right by this kid, except—"

"You'll find a way." By way of dismissal, Dunn straightened a stack of folders and set them to one side. "The nurse spends a lot of time with the boy. I have no objection to that. But still he has his family."

"For the time being."

"I have to be careful what allowances I make in matters like this."

"I don't want him in foster care. I won't have him put in some kid mill, like—"

"Now you're talking like a father." He lifted one eyebrow and smiled. "Maybe a little like one. Maybe that's how it starts sometimes."

Cleve couldn't bring himself to see Susan after his meeting with Dunn. He had nothing to offer, and he didn't want to dash her hopes for a solution to her problem. More to the point, he didn't want to admit that he couldn't take care of the whole thing for her. And he didn't want to see Sam.

He started hanging out at the college so he could use their weight lifting equipment. That posed a hazard, because people he met at the college thought they could save the world by signing everybody up for classes. He checked the schedule and admitted that there were a couple that didn't sound too bad. He signed a few papers to satisfy the education fanatics so he could lift in peace.

Sometimes he'd meet Charlie in the weight room, and they'd spot each other. Didn't hurt to offer the kid a few pointers. It was hit and miss. They were both on foot or hitching rides. But if a guy was going to be lifting weights, he needed a spotter.

The letter from Jimmy Dawson took Cleve by surprise. It wasn't that he hadn't thought of Jimmy and

Jace, Grease and Whitey—thought about them often, in fact—but he hadn't expected any of them to write to him. It didn't make much sense, but he felt bad sometimes about leaving them behind. He figured they might even resent him for the way he'd gotten out.

Jimmy Dawson. The return address contained the requisite inmate number. He wasn't even sure he wanted to open the letter. But he did.

Hi Cleve.

Hope things are going well for you. Jace got out this week, and I started feeling a little lonesome. Thought I'd drop you a line. Everything's pretty much the same here. Let's see, they let a group of us put on a car wash so we could donate to one of the group homes for kids. I was glad to help because once I was placed in a home like that, temporarily. Most of the kids have been treated real bad, so when they go there, they need a lot of help. I've been working in the law library, and I've applied for South (You know, suck ass unit) but I guess they're pretty backed up on applications what with the overcrowding. Seems like everybody wants a room at the pen (ha ha). I really need to get out of the old cell house now. I really do.

I know how you told me I had to learn to stand up for myself and not let people push me around. You're right. The resident shithead (meaning you know who) has been after me lately, and once, before I got my transfer to the law library, I had a real close call in the john out at the shops. You don't want to know the details. I'm going to report it. I know you would have handled it different, but I can't be like you. I wish I could. Anyway, I wanted to tell you that I'm not taking any more shit, and I hope you approve.

Your friend,
Jim

In principle, Cleve approved. In practice, he should have kept his advice to himself. He was out now, and

Jimmy was still inside. With Dietz. Jimmy had no means of looking out for himself. If he'd already narked, he hoped Steiner had moved the kid into South fast. There was no sure way for The Man to protect a snitch. Especially not a snitch like Jimmy. Cleve tried to imagine all the perverted stuff Jimmy had probably done so he could tell himself that if Dietz got to him, he had it coming. It didn't work. All he could see were the eyes of a scared kid. Then came Charlie Buffalo Boy's face. Even Sam's. Whose sins were they paying for, these kids?

Not Cleve's. He was innocent.

Christ, he was becoming a basket case. Charlie kept nagging him about his drinking, but only once in three weeks had he really tied one on. Another night he'd had a little disagreement in the bar with some redneck, but he hadn't been drunk. Just testy. He had reason to be testy.

Like this note from Susan, now. He hadn't seen her in three weeks, and she'd left him a note to get in touch with Bernie. A damn *note*. Hell, he wasn't going to bite her, and he decided it was time to let her know that. The meeting with Dunn was eating at him anyway; probably wouldn't hurt to mention it. It was Sunday. She had the day off, and her car was parked behind her place.

Her eyes lit up when she opened the door, and he wondered if three weeks had been a long time for her, too. She looked pretty in her faded blue jeans and pink blouse.

"I wondered if I could use your phone."

"Of course. Come on in." She knelt beside a blue and yellow star quilt she'd spread on the floor. "Look who's here, Sam. Remember Cleve?"

"Hey, he's sitting up on his own." He was surrounded by plastic cars and wooden blocks, and he was greeting Cleve with his grinning squeal.

"Isn't it wonderful?" Susan scooped him up and showed him off proudly. "And he's grown since you've seen him. Almost half a pound."

"I should take him riding again."

"You should." They turned from the baby to one another, and the smiles slowly faded. "Bernie didn't tell me what it was about."

"Yeah, well, it's not too hard to guess."

"No." She was worried, too. He could see it in her soft blue eyes. "I hope it's good news, Cleve."

"Guess I'd better call and find out." He went to the phone, but he hesitated to pick it up, even though he knew the die had already been cast. "I'll help you pay your phone bill."

"Take a deep breath and dial. We're thinking positive thoughts."

"Right." He took Bernie's business card from his billfold and punched out the numbers. "Bernie? It's . . . it's Cleve Black Horse."

"Cleve!" The familiar voice represented an ally, Chippewa or not. An ally with power. "Good news. The decision stands. The Supreme Court refused to overturn. The impression I get from the DA's office is that they're not inclined to go back to court with what they've got."

Cleve felt numb. "What does that mean? Does that mean I'm—"

"I'll be in Bismarck to meet with them next week to tell them to shit or get off the pot."

"You mean—" God help him. "—maybe charge me again?"

"Or drop the whole thing, which is likely. They don't want to go up against your new lawyer with what's left of their case." Bernie laughed.

For the moment, Cleve didn't have a laugh in him. "So what happens now?"

"With any luck, you'll be a free man in a week or so."

"And people will still think I'm a murderer."

"What people? People forget fast, Cleve. And who knows? Maybe they'll pick up Ray Smith on another charge and get him for this, too. It happens that way sometimes. The important thing is, you're no longer a resident of the North Dakota State Pen."

"Yeah. Yeah, I guess that's the important thing." *What about his life?* He slipped the phone back into the hook and stared out the front window. *What about his goddam screwed-up life?*

Susan had gotten back down on the floor with Sam, but she'd listened, pulse pounding in her throat. She wasn't sure what to make of what she had heard of the conversation, but the vacant look she saw in Cleve's eyes made her afraid to ask. They stared at one another, both unsure. She rose slowly, leaving Sam sitting on the floor, content to play with blocks.

"You don't have to go back, do you?"

"Doesn't look like it."

"The Supreme Court—"

"Turned the State down. It's a mistrial. If they want me, they'll have to start all over." She bit her lip, and he added quickly, "Bernie doesn't think they will."

Don't count on it, she warned herself, but the dizzying flood of relief came anyway as she whispered, "Oh, God," and went to put her arms around him. They held each other in silence, clinging desperately to the unguarded moment. She wept against his neck, and he pressed his face into her hair, stemming unmanly tears. "I'm sorry, Cleve," she said at last, even though it hurt to use her voice. "It's been such an awful nightmare for you. So unfair . . . so unfair. I wish—"

"No wishing." He tightened his arms around her. "Let's just hope, okay?"

"Okay."

"The thing that bothers me—" She heard the tremor in the deep breath he drew, and she held him more tightly, too. "Susan, what if they don't ever—if *nobody* ever proves me innocent?"

"They never proved you guilty."

"But I went to prison. In orientation they tell you things have changed now. You've been found guilty, and you're guilty until *proven* innocent. If they just drop it, how can I prove I'm innocent?"

"Do you—Were you hoping for another trial?"

"I don't know. I guess . . ." He sighed and rested his chin on the top of her head. "God, no. It would just be the same thing all over again."

"Not with Bernie defending you."

"With the jury. They see what they want to see, hear what they want to hear."

"If I had it to do over again—"

He leaned back to look at her, holding her shoulders. "I didn't mean you."

"Yes, you did. Don't try to justify what I did, Cleve. I've tried that, and it doesn't work. No excuses will take away the resentment."

"I resented you for a long time, but I understand how it happened, and I don't—"

"No wishes, you said. And no excuses." She took a swipe at her tears with the back of her hand. "If you forgive me, though, maybe I can forgive myself."

"Forgive you?"

"Can you do that?"

"Sure. If you really believe I'm innocent, then I can forgive you."

"No 'ifs,' Cleve," she said. She definitely wanted dry eyes and a stronger voice. It was no time to blubber and look pathetic. "Forgiveness has no strings attached."

"Does that mean I can't kiss you?"

"No it doesn't," she said quietly. "Not if it's a kiss we both want."

"Do we?"

"We do."

He took her face in his hands and lowered his head slowly, touched his lips to hers tentatively at first. She welcomed him, touched his tongue with hers and invited him to deepen the celebration. He put his arms around her, and she heard Sam's soft babble and the clap of wooden blocks. Her heart raced as she inhaled his spicy scent and tasted the salty remnants of her own happy tears. When the kiss ended, she pressed her face against his shoulder and admitted to herself that she had longed to hold him this way many times in the last three weeks.

"Oh, Cleve, I believe you. You don't have to prove anything to me. You were convicted by prejudice and by people like me taking the easy way out."

"I don't think it's been so easy for you, either."

"Maybe some good has come of it all."

"Maybe it's too soon to tell. Maybe if we take it slow—"

Sam let out an angry holler, and they turned to find him lying on his back, waving arms and legs like a frustrated turtle.

"Whoa," Cleve said as he scooped the baby up in his arms. He bounced him a couple of times, and Sam interrupted his protest to get a look at the man holding him. "You hear that, buddy? Once they get their paperwork done, looks like I'm gonna be a free man." With a Hollywood Indian delivery, he elaborated. "Free to follow the buffalo in peace, in the way of our people." He laughed, half embarrassed by his own joke. "Damn shaggy beasts. I spend half my time fixing fence out there. Tribe oughta get with the times and use beef for their powwows." All of a sudden he was animated. The news was beginning to sink in. "But it's a job, right? Good through the end of the fiscal year. 'Course, by then—"

He glanced at Susan. *By then, he'd be back on the rodeo circuit.*

"I talked to Judge Dunn a couple of weeks back," he said.

"You did?"

"I told him I thought . . . well, I was pretty sure I was his father, and that I wanted you to have custody of him."

"What did he say?"

He handed Sam to her. "Pretty much what he told you. He doesn't let white people adopt *his* Indian kids."

"Oh. Is that all he said?"

"Yeah, pretty much." She could tell there was more, but he was saving it. "I figure, if we're going to try to take this any further, we'll have to get Bernie in on it. Once this other mess is settled."

She heard that *we*, loud and clear. "Cleve—" She waited until he looked her in the eye. "Are you Sam's father?"

"I guess we'd have to get those tests done to find out, wouldn't we?"

"I guess." She picked up a couple of blocks and sat on the sofa with Sam in her lap. "Vera's having some problems, and I'm afraid—"

"What kind of problems?"

"Her husband's a jerk. That's the main problem."

"He hasn't—done anything to Sam, has he?"

"No. He's mean to Vera, though. He comes and goes as he pleases. Mostly he goes when the social worker comes. Then he turns up again, and Vera puts up with him." Cleve sat down beside her, and it occurred to her that he was easy to talk to. He listened. "She's trying hard to stay in school, and with Sam, it's twice as hard. I have to get him out of there."

"We'll talk to Bernie when he comes, okay?" He touched her hand, and she looked up. His dark eyes urged her to take heart. "Okay?" She nodded. "I've missed seeing you. I'd . . . kinda gotten used to us . . . talking."

"I've missed you, too. I'm sorry I was so—"

"No, let's not talk about that. I shouldn't have tried to . . ." He dismissed the subject with a disgusted cluck of his tongue and squeezed Sam's foot as he settled back against the cushions. "I enrolled in a couple of night classes."

"At the college?"

His eyes danced. "At the college, yeah. I've *been* to high school."

"I know."

"You were right. I'm eligible for VA benefits."

"Terrific!"

"Well, it's something to do. Something to keep me out of trouble." He smiled, pleased with himself. "I got my driver's license, too. 'Course, I don't have anything to drive yet, but I've saved enough to buy myself an Indian pickup. I thought maybe we could go up to Bismarck sometime and you could help me pick one out."

She laughed. "I'm not sure how you choose an Indian pickup."

"Well, I might have to own it for a while before it takes on real character." He winked at Sam. "Right, buddy? You guys give me a ride up, and I'll take you out someplace nice. Both of you."

"I think that could be—"

The phone interrupted their planning.

Cleve took Sam and was bouncing him on his knee when he heard Susan say, "As a matter of fact, warden, he's right here."

Warden? After a month, had they all had the same, *Hey, what about ol' Cleve* idea on the same day? His hands suddenly felt clammy. Susan traded him the phone for Sam.

"What's up, Warden?"

"Jimmy Dawson asked me to call you, Cleve."

"Jimmy?"

"He's in the hospital. He's—well, he's got a lot of internal damage. It's touch and go, so I thought you might want to—"

Internal damage? "Jesus, I just got a letter from him. What happened?"

"He tried to commit suicide. Jumped off the fourth tier."

"Jumped off . . ." A mental film came with the news flash, and another face became part of the picture. "Dietz got him. You know damn well—"

"Dietz may have been part of what drove him to it, but when it happened, Dietz was in the hole. I tell you, Cleve, the boy really doesn't have anybody. We notified his father, and the old man said—well, he refuses to see the boy, and the only other person he's asked for is you."

"He's conscious?"

"In and out. In and out of surgery, too." There was a sigh, sounding as if it were rushing through a tunnel. "It doesn't look too good for him, Cleve."

"I'll be there." He lifted his chin away from the receiver. "I need a ride to Bismarck. It's—" Susan nodded, and he spoke into the phone again. "I'll be there soon."

Susan gave him her car keys as soon as he got off the phone. His mind was spinning throughout the long, solitary, seventy-mile drive. Kid drops himself the equivalent of four stories onto a concrete floor, and his father won't go to the hospital to see him? Kinda made you wonder what kind of a father this kid had. Sure, Jimmy was a convict, and among lowlifes, Jimmy was considered the lowest. There was the crime, and then there was the kid. Skinny, scared, freckled-faced boy, barely old enough to draw hard time, who'd done his damnedest to get Cleve to like him. He'd thought about Jimmy doing something perverted to some other kid. Somebody even younger. The thought made him sick. The crime. The kid.

You look at him, and all you see is a handicap. I see a child.

A boy eventually became a man, and then what? Cleve wondered what they'd done to Jimmy along the way. This father of his, maybe.

No excuses, Susan had said. No justification. Just check in on him. That's all he had to do.

Jimmy was in intensive care. When Cleve gave the nurse at the desk his name, she told him that he was expected, but to keep it short. The guard stationed at the door was also expecting him. Steiner had paved the way.

Jimmy had tubes in his nose and his arm, and machines monitored his vital signs. Cleve winced at the sight of the purple and white face and the thatch of red hair sticking up amid white bandages. He turned a chair and slid it close to the bed, straddled it and touched the boy's slight shoulder.

"Hey, Jim."

Eyelids fluttered. "Cleve? You came, huh?"

"Did you think I wouldn't? How're you doing?"

"Not too good." His eyes rolled, and he squeezed

them shut, then opened them again and sought Cleve's face. "There's a button somewhere . . . sit up, so I can see . . ."

"I was in here once, too," Cleve said. He found the control. "How's that? They take good care of you here."

"Yeah." Jim's smile was as thin as his voice. "Drugs legal here."

"Got you flyin', huh?" Had to be morphine, the way the kid was twitching. Cleve wanted to fly, too. Straight out the door.

"Pretty high." Like those of a comic drunk, his efforts to focus were exaggerated. "Hey, thanks for coming."

"No problem. Susan loaned me her car. Remember Susan?"

"Yeah. You and Susan . . ."

"You were right, Jim." Squeezing Jimmy's shoulder was somehow comforting to Cleve. It was real contact. "She makes good coffee."

"Figured she would." Jim turned his face away. A dry, reedy sigh tore at Cleve's heart. "My dad won't come. You know why. Says I'm a pervert . . . fag . . ."

Cleve snatched a glass of water from the bedside tray and held the straw to Jimmy's lips. "Here, take a little of this to wet your whistle." The look in the boy's glassy eyes said he'd try, but not for his own sake. "I got your letter, Jim. Did you tell Steiner about Dietz?"

The straw slipped from his lips, and he turned away again. "Too late. Dietz . . . got to me. Got what he was after." When he turned back, there were tears, and, remarkably, a spark of life glowed with them. "I went to the pen . . . guilty as hell, Cleve. I know that. But the thing was . . ." He closed his eyes. The tears escaped from the corners and tracked their way to the bandages that encircled his head. "I really ha-hated having that shithead—"

"Shut up, Jimmy. You don't want to think about that now."

"I had it coming. I deserved . . . because there was this ki-kid I used to babysit . . ."

Cleve gripped the back of his chair. "Save it for your counselor, okay? I just came to see you and . . ." And what, for God's sake? *What?* "And tell you it's gonna be okay."

"It wasn't like . . . what Dietz did. I swear. But it was—"

"Jesus, Jim. Right now, the important thing—"

"This is important. I need . . . to apologize."

"Not to me. You don't owe me any apologies." The need was there, in that fading spark of life. "Except maybe for taking a flying leap off the tier. You're my friend. Guys like us need all the friends we can get."

"I'm still a fish, huh?"

"Yeah." Cleve laid a hand on the boy's shoulder again and offered a smile. "You sure are that."

"Couldn't live with it, Cleve. I know what a chickenshit I am."

"You're okay, Jim. And you're—" God, what was he supposed to say? *What do you need? Strength? Take some of mine.* "—you're gonna get even better. And nobody's gonna hurt you anymore."

"I'm sorry for the stuff I did. I wish—"

"You're forgiven, Jim." He glanced over his shoulder to make sure nobody was going to call him on this. "I'm no priest or anything, but I used to go to church. The way I understand it, you're forgiven."

No strings attached, kid. It's a good day to die.

Chapter 18

It was after midnight when Cleve returned Susan's car to its parking spot. The waxing white moon was etched at the height of a black velvet night, and there was frost in the air. He would surely feel it through his denim jacket by the time he walked clear across town. The thought of his alley full of stray dogs and discarded Popsicle sticks was suitably depressing. He welcomed the cold night. He felt cold inside.

He'd thought of putting her keys under the door mat, but when he saw the kitchen light on, he knocked at the door. She answered immediately, as if she'd been waiting for him to come, but he knew she was dressed for bed underneath that deep red robe. The backlighting from the kitchen lent a coppery glow to her hair.

"Sorry I kept you up this late," he said. She held the door open, and he stepped inside. "I should have called. You probably wondered if I'd run your car into a ditch somewhere."

"No, I didn't. I wondered if you'd take time to get something to eat."

"Cookies and orange juice."

"You must have donated blood."

"Yeah. O positive. The universal donor, they said. Felt kind of funny watching my blood drain into a plastic bag."

"You need more than cookies and juice, then. I have—"

"I don't feel much like eating." He wanted to toss his hat on the chair, sink down on the sofa and just close his eyes. "I'd better not keep you up any longer."

"I don't work tomorrow." She turned on the aquarium light, which bathed the living room in a soft glow. It felt peaceful, and he imagined slipping into the still water. "How's your friend?"

"Still alive. Barely. Damn kid took a nose dive and broke every bone in his scrawny body." He wanted to be angry with Jimmy, and talking angry helped, but it had to be quiet anger. He glanced down the dark hallway. "Is Sam still here?"

She nodded. "He's asleep in his room. I don't know what the judge would say about our overnights, but we do it on weekends sometimes."

"What he doesn't know can't hurt anything. You got any coffee left?" He could smell it, and he pictured her drinking cup after cup and keeping a vigil for him. Or maybe just for her car.

"Fresh pot. I read your mind." She smiled and beckoned him to follow her to the kitchen. "You're an easy read."

He tossed his hat, and the green chair's arm made the catch. "Nice trick, considering my mind's totally blown right now."

"Coffee's an easy signal to pick up. So is 'I need to talk.' " She offered up the steaming mug with both hands.

"Yeah?" It felt good to hold something warm. "Thanks. Funny. I don't know what to say." But after a couple of sips of hot coffee, he came up with, "Jimmy's only nineteen, maybe twenty."

"Was he able to talk to you?"

"Yeah. Some."

"Why did he do it? Depression?"

"I guess you could say that. He's kind of a pretty kid, you know?" He leaned back against the counter, cradling the mug in both hands. "He got raped."

"Oh, no." As if to protect herself from the word, she pressed her forearms over her abdomen. "Is he—"

"I don't know if he's gay, and I don't think it matters. Rape is rape, right?" She opened her mouth to answer, but he didn't want to hear it. He knew what question she was bound to be biting back. "Unless you're thinking maybe I had something going with him. Then it matters." She stood quietly, letting him look into her eyes and find what he would. "That's not what you were thinking," he admitted quietly.

"No. I was wondering about the extent of his injuries."

"They wouldn't tell me much. I'm not a family member, but none of his relations would come. I guess they're ashamed of him." He glanced away from her because the shame was within him, too. "Which really sucks when the kid's lying there trying to die."

"Yes, it does. It was good that you went, Cleve, even though it must have been—"

"I'm no better. I'm worrying about how it looks. You don't know this kid, and I'm worried about you thinking I might be like him." His gaze moved restlessly from the teakettle on the stove to the magnet that held a shopping list to the refrigerator door. "I'm worried that I might be like him. Shit, I *am* like him. In a lot of ways, you know?" He looked to her to understand even as he denied her the right to do so. "No, you don't know. But I do. Whatever I did or didn't do before I went to prison, once they closed the doors on me, I was *there;* I was an inmate."

"I was there." Quickly she added, "As much as I could be, anyway."

"Because of Sam."

"Because you and I became friends. I didn't go to the rodeo because of Sam. I wouldn't want to live there, and I can't even say it's a nice place to visit. I didn't like being searched and being watched, but in order to see you I had to—" She turned away from him and took a plate from the cupboard. "I can only imagine what it was like for you. But I try not to wonder—"

"But you have to wonder, don't you? I've kissed you. I've tried to get you to go to bed with me. You have to wonder." She confirmed with a quick glance as she opened the refrigerator door. "A lot of stuff goes on up there, Susan. You try to protect yourself, and you try to keep your cool, you know? Get through it the best way you can, one day at a time. You can't think about spending the rest of your life without ever getting a chance to . . . make love to someone again."

"I know." She set a small jar of mayonnaise on the counter and studied it briefly. "I don't like to think about that, either."

"Yeah, but on the outside, that's your choice. On the inside, you don't have too many choices." He watched her face from the side. Fitting the corners of several slices of pressed ham to the bread seemed to demand great concentration. The sides of her hair were caught up at the back of her head with a beaded barrette, and there was a bit of white lace poking out from under the red robe just beneath the curve of her jaw. His mouth went dry. "There were times when I would have done almost anything for ten minutes alone with a woman."

"But you'd let her have some say about what went on during those ten minutes."

"If she'd said the wrong thing, I'd have told her to get the hell going." He laughed at himself. "At least, I think I would have. You get a little crazy when you're locked up. You think about doing crazy things like . . . jumping off the tier."

She looked up, wide-eyed. "Did you think about doing that?"

"I thought about all kinds of things. Thought too much. Thinking'll make you crazy, too."

Back to the sandwich and the careful spreading of the bread. "Did you think about having ten minutes alone with me?"

"You've got no business asking me that." *Or tipping your hand like that unless you want me to see what to play next.* "Besides, you know the answer."

"You weren't seeing many women then." She turned, plate in hand, and looked up at him artlessly. "Are you now?"

"Probably should be, but I haven't gotten around to it." If she wanted off the hook, there was her chance. He accepted the sandwich and dangled the empty mug by its handle. "Is there more coffee?"

"I've made mistakes, too, Cleve. People don't always end up in jail for making bad choices, but they usually end up getting hurt. And when you get hurt, you promise yourself you won't make that mistake again." She took the cup. "You try to protect yourself and keep your cool."

"Yeah, you do. You learn to watch your tail." She poured him more coffee, and he told himself to finish this up and get moving. He didn't want to hear about old boyfriends. On the other hand, she looked so damn clean-scrubbed and innocent, he couldn't resist trying to get a smile out of her. "Yours is kind of a pretty one to watch. You been keeping close guard on it?"

"Absolutely." She tended to lose her heart first.

"So you deserve a medal. But in Jimmy's case—Well, Jimmy's kind of a *winkte*." He shook his head, chuckling. "All my Indian words seem to be coming back to me lately. Means he's kind of womanish."

"Being womanish is terrible."

"It is for a man. Especially in the pen. If he hadn't been so damn young, I'd have said, tough luck. Some people are just naturally target material." He bit into the sandwich and took a moment to chew before he expanded his point. "You see it in the army. Some guys, if they don't get beat up by guys in their own outfit, they get their heads blown off on patrol. You know, they're just . . . losers, I guess."

"And you have to look out for them."

"No." He swallowed, shaking his head. "Hell, no. Think I wanna get my head blown off, too? They have to learn to take care of themselves."

"But it's hard to turn your back on them."

"Well, sometimes you have to help out a little." He wished she'd eat something, too, instead of just standing there watching, as if he were the blue ribbon calf. But it was late, and she was willing to listen. "I talked to the warden. Told him everything I knew about, uh . . . this guy who did it. Name is Dietz."

"I remember Mr. Dietz."

"Yeah. So do I. I told Steiner I'd testify if that's what it would take. Jimmy told me more than he told Steiner, and he wrote me this letter, so I think if they put it all together . . ." He shrugged. "Jimmy had decided to narc on Dietz, but I guess he waited too long."

"Narc? You mean report him?"

"Yeah. That's something you don't do in the pen. Somebody bothers you, you take care of it yourself."

"If you can."

"If you can't, you . . . do what Jim did, I guess. Aren't you going to have anything?"

"I've been drinking tea." She nodded toward the kettle on the stove. "I should have offered you a chair."

"I know where they are." He sipped his coffee, then went back to his sandwich. "I've had enough sitting tonight."

She'd had enough sitting, too. She'd spent the evening with Sam, doing his exercises, coaxing him to try a new food, rocking him and singing to him, and thinking of Cleve paying a visit to a desperate, dying young man. She knew he was not out of the woods himself, which could never be far from his mind. "If you testify against this Dietz—" The mention of the name brought a quick flash of anger to his eyes. "Cleve, what if something goes wrong, like they decide to prosecute you all over again, and you end up back there?"

"That'll be Dietz's problem. He doesn't worry me." He set the empty plate aside. "Anyway, I'm not going back, am I?"

"No." Not to prison, she thought. And not to his apartment. Not tonight.

"After all, I've got you thinking all those positive thoughts."

She smiled and nodded. He knew all about her positive thoughts tonight. While he was gone, she'd made up her mind. She wouldn't be able to tell herself that she'd lost her head in the heat of passion. She'd asked him questions she knew the answers to. Had he thought about her? He'd told her before that he had, but she wanted to hear it again. She wanted to believe that he needed *her*, and for that reason, there'd been no other women. He was a man, and he had his fantasies. As a woman, she had hers. Every time he looked at her, her pulse quickened with a ticklish blend of wild hope and fear that he would make love to her. It was a delicious feeling, like the thrill of edging beyond safety. He would be exciting, even if he weren't good for her.

"Positive thoughts have worked so far," she observed.

"Yours, maybe." He took a step closer, and she held her breath. "I've been thinking my own positive thoughts, but it's not working for me. Wanna let me in on your secret?"

"Patience. Persistence."

"Sounds like some kind of game to me." He was ready to reach for her, and she was ready to take a step closer to him, but it was a big step. "I don't feel much like playing games."

"I know. Just now you felt like talking."

"So I talked. I told you about this kid who doesn't want to live anymore." He reached, but it was to set his coffee mug down on the counter beside her. "You did your part. You listened. Look at me, Susan." She looked up. He stood within inches, but still he didn't touch her. Anticipation made her skin tingle beneath her velour robe. "What's on my mind now? You getting any signals?"

"Yes." She swallowed hard. "Clearly."

"Good. You take what I had in mind last time I saw you, and you add three weeks' worth of thinking about how close we came. Maybe it didn't seem that close to you, but it was closer than I've been in over two years." His eyes swept over her—hair, face, the hollow of her throat. "Right now, you tell me to go, and I will. You ask me to stay, and I will. But not to play games. And I want more than ten minutes of your time." His voice was honey smooth, and if he had told her that her clothes were on fire, she could not have moved. "The lady has the final say."

He stared at her dispassionately, waiting. If he but touched her shoulder or her hair, she would readily melt against him. She wanted to be an "easy read" just then so she wouldn't have to have that say aloud. But when he turned away, he left her no choice.

"Don't go." He hesitated, remembering the sting of her resistance and wanting to hear more. "Don't go, Cleve. I want you . . . to stay."

His smile may have been cocky, but it appeared only briefly, before the kiss. He took her mouth deeply, confidently, claiming the space within for his tongue. She slid her arms around his back and ironed his shirt with warm palms. It was a kiss that drove a hard bargain, and she knew there was no turning back. Whatever his needs, she would try to fulfill them. She lifted her chin, and he feathered kisses along her neck, down, then back to her ear. His voice was low and husky.

"Show me where you sleep."

It was the first time Cleve had been down that hallway. The short passage had become a focus of speculation, a close, dark anteroom to the special place where she kept her personal things. They slipped past Sam's door, and he glimpsed the crib by the light of a small Donald Duck face plugged into the wall. He heard the shallow flutterings of baby's breath. He'd never liked the idea of going to bed with a woman who had kids in the house, but this seemed different. Sam was supposed to be his kid—his and Susan's, in a way. Almost the way it was supposed to be.

There was a night-light in her room and a double bed with a thick blue coverlet and matching ruffled pillows.

He closed the door behind them. She moved to the other side of the bed to close a window. The fresh chill of early autumn's night air filled the room. She stood by the window with her back to him and began working on the knot in the sash around her waist. Her difficulty moved him. He stepped close behind her and laid his hands on her shoulders.

"I'll go before it gets light. No one will know I've been here." She turned to him slowly, and he eased her hands aside. "Now let me do that."

"I don't have anything to hide from the neighbors."

"Good." He untied the sash and drew the robe back. The bit of lace that had teased him was part of a crisp white bodice, adorned with tucks and buttons, delicate things that made him aware of the size of his hands. The robe fell to her feet as he polished her slight shoulders with his palms.

"You're beautiful. You can't hide that from me. I don't know about any neighbors." He kissed her gently. "You're also scared."

"A little." She touched his face, then trailed her hand along his neck, her cool fingers finding their way into the open neck of his shirt. The move startled him.

"And anxious?"

Her smile was pure seduction. "That, too."

She had flipped open two of his buttons before he caught her hand. "I'm not hiding anything, either." He undid the rest of his buttons himself, pulled the tails free of his pants and tossed the shirt aside. He kissed her again and told himself to stay cool, but his eyes suddenly burned with wonder at the sweet sight of her lips glistening from the moist touch of his. When her hand brushed over his chest and his belly and swept past his belt, his whole body stiffened. It unnerved him. "Take my word for it, okay?"

"For what?"

"I'm not . . . nothing's hidden. You don't need to search me." He guided her hands around his neck and ducked to taste the side of her neck. "Just let me—" She leaned into his embrace and tormented him with catlike affection. "God, I want you, Susan. I want you so bad I don't know if I can . . ."

He tried to slow down, but any part of her he touched electrified him. He was like a bird on a wire. He lifted her in his arms and laid her across the bed. The touch of her hand would surely set him off, he thought, so he pinned her wrists on either side of her head and kissed her until her soft moan demanded his response. He took a foil packet from his pocket, then shucked his jeans quickly. The bed dipped beneath his knee. She was veiled in a red mist that blurred her features, and he ached wildly for her. His pulse pounded so hard in his ears that he almost missed her message, expressed in the single syllable of his name.

"Don't worry about it, honey. I came prepared."

It sounded like his voice, but what a stupid thing to say. You didn't tell a woman like this that you'd been prepared for weeks. The curse he muttered into the packet as he tore into it with his teeth sounded like his, too. No finesse whatsoever. His head was spinning, and he hadn't even been drinking. He was too damn old to be on the verge of an explosion.

She touched his thigh with an unsteady hand, and he almost came apart. He bunched the long nightgown above her hips, traced the sharp angle of her pelvic bone with his forefinger, and sought forgiveness with a desperate look. She bent her knees, and her body formed a cradle for his hips. He nudged her gently with his rigid member, then urged, then slid one hand beneath her buttocks and positioned her for his spearing. Her quick gasp heralded his exultant entry into a deep, tight haven. He trembled with the overwhelming joy the discovery of this place brought him. She tilted her hips, inviting him deeper, and he dove for the chance.

"Ah, it's been so long," he said gruffly.

"For me, too."

After a few thrusts, he came effusively in shuddering waves. Wonder and relief washed over him, and for a moment there was only pleasure. All his. In the next moment, there was the feeling of failure, and that, too was all his. Susan lay beneath him, her hands pinned by his to the mattress and her need still fluttering like a flag in the face of erratic breaths. He muttered his apologies as he buried his wet face against her neck.

"It's all right." She touched his shoulder, then his thick, coarse hair. "Oh, Cleve, it's fine. It's fine."

It was another moment before he could brace himself up and look at the mess he'd made of her. "I may be a thickheaded cowboy, honey, but I know that wasn't fine."

"Cleve—"

"I could have been fifteen all over again just now, going off like a damn firecracker." He tipped his head back and spoke to the ceiling. "Jesus, it felt so good to be inside you. I couldn't hold back." He shook his head. "I'm sorry."

"Why wouldn't you let me touch you?"

"What do you mean?"

"You pushed my hands away. You wouldn't let me—"

"I said I was sorry. I'm a little out of practice."

"I only wanted to touch you, Cleve. Not search you."

With a sigh, he turned over on his back and lay beside her. "I said that, didn't I? I don't know what I was thinking about."

She touched his shoulder. "I do. They searched me, too. But they let me keep my clothes on."

He rolled to his feet and swept his jeans up off the floor. Abruptly abandoned, Susan lay there stiffly, her throat stinging. She heard him close the bathroom door. Then she heard Sam.

Cleve braced himself on the sink and dropped his chin to his chest, avoiding his reflection in the mirror. He'd cheated her, and he felt like a jerk. He'd dreamed of being touched by her, but when the chance came, he'd pushed her away. Hell, she knew all his worst secrets. It was a wonder she was willing to touch him, be with him, hold him, Christ! No matter how often he washed himself, the stink of men living in stacked cages clung to him, lingered in his nostrils.

She knew. She had been there. She had seen him there, wearing the uniform of a prisoner. She had eaten with him in the damn chow hall, and she'd smiled and stood beside him, as if they were lining up together in the school cafeteria.

He wanted to go back to her and hold her again, just *hold* her. He'd have to walk through that door with some explanation, and he wasn't sure what he should say. You shouldn't touch me because that place sticks to me like cowshit? But still I need to be inside you. God! how I need you to spread your legs for me the way you just did and tell me you want me. Sure, that would thrill her. He stepped into the tub, turned on the shower and let the warm water drench him.

After a time apart, they converged in the small hallway, forced into awkward proximity and surrounded by doors. Entrances and exits, like fun house options. Susan closed the door to Sam's room, and Cleve ran his fingers through towel-dried hair. He'd put his jeans back on. He filled the small, nearly dark space with the citrus-y scent of her bath soap and the breadth of his powerful upper body. She felt at once heady and dispirited. His expectations had not been met. Hers, enhanced in dreams, had been truncated by experience. Like a long awaited prom night, sex wasn't all they'd imagined it would be, and the shortfall became a tangible thing, standing with them like a third party in the hallway.

"Did I wake the baby up?" he whispered.

"No." She slipped past him and pushed on the door that stood ajar. "Let's talk in here."

He followed her into her bedroom, closed the door carefully and waited for her to set the tone.

"He awakens in the middle of the night sometimes, looking for a little extra attention. He's sleeping now."

They stood quietly, then, each hoping for a sign from the other.

"So, do I get a second chance?"

She smiled, relieved. "Do you always head right for the shower after the first one?"

"Not always. Sometimes I head for the back door."

"At first that's what I thought you were doing." She laughed a little. "Then I heard the water running, and I thought, hmm, this man is extremely fastidious."

"Whatever that means. Lately, whenever I see a shower, I like to take advantage of it just because nobody's stopping me." He was standing next to the dresser with those personal things, like her hairbrush and lipstick, close at hand. He picked up a bottle of lotion, then set it back, exactly where it had been. "I didn't know it was going be like that, Susan. I didn't mean to . . . do what I did."

"What did you mean to do?

"I meant to make it as good for you as it was for me."

"Let's not do the old was-it-good-for-you-too routine. It was fine, Cleve, let's not—"

"You said that already." He leaned on the dresser, gripping the protruding top. "You insult me with that word. I know damn well—" He sighed and tried again in a softer tone. "I have some recollection of what it's supposed to be like. That wasn't it."

"The big IT. Let's do IT. How was IT? A much over-rated IT, if you ask me."

"Why were you scared?"

"For the same reason you were." She moved closer. "Why were you scared?"

He chuckled. "I don't know. 'Fraid I might have lost my touch, I guess." They stood face to face, feelings churning. "I wanted to touch you. I still do." His hand was suspended in the air for a moment before he smoothed her hair back from her upturned face. "I went too fast, didn't I?"

"Nobody was timing us. I wanted to touch you, too." His cheek felt warm against her palm. "I'm not on any jury. You're not a suspect of any kind. You don't have to defend yourself against me, Cleve."

"I wasn't trying to." A teasing lift of her thin eyebrows got her half a smile and an admission. "Maybe I was. I don't want you to touch me and find something . . . you don't want."

"I asked you to stay. I knew what I wanted."

He lifted the lace from her shoulder and rubbed it between his thumb and forefinger. "You look so pretty in this."

"I like the feminine way it makes me feel after wearing a uniform."

"I like that too." He opened the top button on the bodice, then the second, and down the line. "I can make you feel feminine, too."

"Only if you let me . . ."

He opened her nightgown like the kind of gift wrap too pretty to throw away, and the cool air made her nipples contract. He was watching them, smiling as though the gift had surprised him by popping out of the box or playing music. "First, let me," he whispered as he took both breasts in his hands. He put his forehead against hers and feathered her with his thumbs. "See, this is what I was afraid of."

"What?"

"This softness. Oh, God, Susan, you don't know how wonderful these are." He knelt and buried his face between them.

"I know how wonderful you make them-mmmm . . ." He suckled her, drawing her deep into his mouth and caressing her with his tongue, and she reveled in his need for nourishment as thought gave way to her instinctive need to be needed. She raked her fingers through his hair and held him to her breast until he lifted her and carried her to the bed, nuzzling her and muttering her praises with every step.

She sat on the side of the bed, and he drew her night-gown over her head and tossed it aside. But when his hands moved to his own zipper, she pushed them aside. "I'm not searching you," she promised. "I'm seeking you."

A deep, masculine chuckle helped him relax. "Seek and you will find."

"Indeed." She pushed the slouching denim over lean hips and looked up at him as she touched tenderly. "Nothing dangerous here."

"Don't bet on it. I want to take it slow and easy, but that thing has a mind of its own." He knelt between her thighs and put his arms around her. "Sometimes I think . . . sometimes I don't feel good about . . ."

"I know you're not a bad man, Cleve. Believe me. I know that."

"I want to show you how good I can be."

His kiss took away any protest she might have made. They moved into the bed together, kissing one another with eagerly open mouths, savoring the taste of each other's flesh. He suffered her to touch him, and when she had made his male nipples come erect, made his thighs tingle, made his stomach quiver, he begged her to touch him. She opened herself to him and funneled his self-doubt away, so that he touched her freely, without fear of leaving a stain. His hand was sure, his fingers gentle, planting an urgent need deep within her, then spreading it from that touchstone to the extremities of her body.

When he rose above her, his face sweat-slick and full of desire, she thought he looked as desperate as she felt. But he was beautiful, and she smiled to tell him so as she lifted her hips. "Please," she whispered. "I'm hollow and aching inside, and I want you so bad."

He took pains to provide protection, and sweet pain it was to hold off for that moment. Then he bit his lip and touched her deeply with his middle finger, turning her to liquid. "Is this where you want me most?"

"Oh, God!"

"Tell me, Susan." She trembled sweetly for him. It had to be for him.

"Come inside me come insi—ii . . ."

"Just say my name, honey. Say my name, and I will."

"Cleve."

"This much?"

"More. Oh, yes, more . . . haaa!"

"Too much?"

"I want you too much . . . too much . . ."

"There's no such thing as . . . just tell me if it . . . hurts you I don't want to hurt you ever, ever . . . I want to hear you . . . say my name."

Over and over she said it within the pleasured song she sang to him, and together they hung the moon.

They lay in each other's arms like play-weary children, damp, drained, and thoroughly unself-conscious. He thought about a cigarette, but didn't want to move away from her to get one. She wanted a sip of water, but thirst didn't prompt her to untangle her limbs from his. They traded touches freely now, enjoying one another's uninhibited quest for undiscovered curves and hollows.

"How do you feel about sleeping with me?" he asked.

She turned to press a kiss against his chest. "Actually sleeping?"

"Mmm-hmm. I'm drifting nicely. I promise to clear out before—"

"I want you to stay. I want to make breakfast for you."

"What's on the menu?"

"Anything you want." She hooked her arm across his middle and confided, "It was much better than fine, Cleve."

He grinned at the shadows on the ceiling. "Yeah? Give me a better word, then."

"How about exquisite?"

"How about, the best you've ever had?"

"That's more than one word." She lifted her head so she could see his face. "Men are so competitive. Do you think we keep score on you?"

"You probably do, you know? Some kind of computer network, where you just punch in a guy's name, how long it takes him to get it up, how many inches he's got, how many times he can get you to—"

"As if we'd ever tell anybody. As if we even *notice*."

"Don't lie, now. You go to a singles bar, and you watch what happens. Nice-looking guy walks in, all the women either sit up, kinda square their shoulders and dangle one leg a little bit, or else they all turn away and giggle up their sleeves. You can't fool us about all this networking stuff."

"You men have to make a tournament out of everything."

He hooked his arm beneath his head and quirked a brow. "So, what kind of competition am I looking at?"

She knew she shouldn't offer anything close to a serious answer, even though her instinct was to reassure him. "You mean, right now?"

"Yeah, right now. Or last year. Or five years ago."

She smiled. "The only competitors you should worry about are the ones who ride bucking horses."

"You bucked. A little."

"So did you. A lot."

With a finger he drew lazy circles on her shoulder. "I want to be the best you've ever had, Susan. I want to make you forget whoever your mistakes were."

She settled back into the cove of his arm. "I lived with a man for a couple of years before I moved to Bismarck. I forgot him long before tonight. I don't want to get involved in that kind of situation again."

"Was he mean to you?"

"He was selfish. He didn't care about *us*. He cared about *him*. I kept trying to change him. It was like a sickness with me."

"So you don't want any more live-in boyfriends, huh?"

"But you weren't talking about moving in. You were just wanting to be the best I've ever had." She moved her hand over his powerhouse of a chest. "The best what? Lover?"

"I guess so."

"You're the only man I've been thinking about lately."

"Thinking what?" She giggled, and he squeezed her shoulders. "C'mon, tell me."

"Thinking about wide shoulders." And she anchored her hands on them and scooted up so she could see the items on her list. "Thinking about dark eyes that smile sometimes and lips that tease and a deep voice that sends little pricklies running through me."

"Pricklies?"

"Sort of like I'm an hourglass and there's this stream of warm sand sifting straight through me."

He held her at the waist. "Is this the narrow part?"

"Mmm-hmm."

"And it settles down here?" One hand slid low on her belly.

"And prickles me."

"Is that good?"

He stirred and stirred and brought the feeling back. "Oh . . . yes."

"You're the best I've ever had, Susan."

He hugged her close, her length to his, and she laid her cheek against his chest. "I'm just the first food after a long fast."

"Maybe." He smiled to think how well she satisfied him. "But there was other food around. I've been holding out for the blue plate special."

"Was that the worst part of being in prison? No women?"

"Not after you started coming around. The worst part was when I'd be looking forward to seeing you, and you didn't show."

"I tried not to let that happen, but sometimes you get—"

"The *worst* worst part was the boredom. Especially at first, when they had me in the hole all the time. That's 'disciplinary segregation.' "

"What was that like?"

"Aw, you don't want to hear about—"

"Yes, I do. I want to know what it was like for you. I helped put you there, and I'll never—"

"Shh." He reversed their positions, tucking her under him. Her hair ribboned across the pillow, and she looked up at him with apologetic eyes. "You don't say that anymore, okay? I'll tell you what you want to know, but you don't . . . you're not to blame."

"Okay."

"Okay. So the hole is pretty much what you'd think it would be. You're in a cell for maybe fifteen days. You get one hour a day for exercise, one cigarette a day, and you shower three times a week. They bring you food, and if you behave you get paper and pencil, maybe a book."

"What . . . why did they put you in there?"

"Fighting, mostly. I went after guards, other inmates, anybody got close enough for me to take a swing at." He was about to touch her face, but he drew back, remembering, and rolled to his back to give her some space. "There were other incidents. Throwing my food tray. Tearing my house up." He turned to look at her across the pillow. "My cell. Your house is a six-by-nine foot cell."

"I saw them. I took a tour."

"Once I realized I wasn't getting anywhere trying to tear the place apart, it got better. I started using my time instead of letting it use me. But you can't stop those doors from locking you in, and you can't let yourself get used to that."

"What did you do about, like . . . sex?"

"*Like* sex?" He grinned, teasing her. "I like handled it . . . myself."

They laughed together, shaking the bed with it until she sputtered, "Oh, Cleve, it isn't funny."

"Why not? If we're laughing, there must be something funny about it." He touched a tendril of hair that curled at her temple. Most of it had escaped the barrette. She was beautifully disheveled. "You take everything pretty seriously, don't you?"

"Yes, I guess so. I wish I'd handled that jury myself." He nearly choked on another laugh. "Not like *that*," she protested, giving him a shove in the ribs. "It's like with your friend, Jimmy. Sooner or later you have to stand up for yourself."

"So you tried, and it didn't work out. Maybe I was really doing time for something else, you know? Just on general principles. Just for being a no-good cowboy."

"They don't put you in jail for that."

"They do for getting wasted and busting up a bar in a fight. They can get you for not paying two hundred thirty-eight bucks' worth of traffic fines. Unlawful trespassing, breaking and entering—"

She scowled. "This is getting serious."

"What, breaking and entering? Happened a long time ago when I was pretty young and cocky. I went looking for this woman I was—looking for. Door was open. I went in, tripped over some damn statue and broke it. Turned out to be the wrong house." She found a way to grin and gasp at the same time. "I paid for the statue, but the judge thought I should have knocked."

"So that's what it means to be a no-good cowboy."

"I guess. Followed in the old man's footsteps, even though I never laid eyes on the sonuvabitch. Must be in the blood."

"I don't think so."

"Why not? It seemed like a charmed life for a while there. It wasn't that I could do no wrong. I did my share. But I was pretty good at landing on my feet until the night I ran out of lucky breaks."

"So now, here you are."

"Getting you on that jury was a lucky break." He shifted closer and squeezed her. "Getting you in bed with me was damn hard work."

"I'll let you rest now."

"Rest? Maybe in a minute—" They kissed, and the stirrings started yet again. "Maybe not."

Susan smelled bacon and coffee. Her awakening was aided by the sound of Cleve's voice, then Sam's. Bracing up on her elbows, she saw Cleve's well-worn black cowboy boots, standing tall near the bedroom door. She reached for her robe as she tried to put an image together—the bare feet, the bacon, and the baby—but it was hard to make it add up to Cleve until she actually saw him playing with Sam, who was sitting on the counter. Cleve wore nothing but the faded jeans that fit him so well, and she smiled at the sight of his bare feet on her clean white kitchen floor and the red toy hammer sticking out of his back pocket. He glanced over his shoulder and smiled back.

" 'Mornin'."

"Yes, it is. I should have realized it sooner, but neither one of you woke me up." She laid her hand on his warm back. "And I appreciate that. Good morning." He hooked his arm around her neck, kissed her and had her smiling like sunshine. "Good morning, Sam. Are you making friends with Cleve?"

"Just teaching him how to arm wrestle. He always wants to use his right hand, but if I don't let him use it—see?" He pinned Sam's right arm to his side and let him use his left to grapple with two of Cleve's fingers, which Sam wanted in his mouth. "He works his left side a little more."

"You sound like a therapist." She helped herself to the coffee he'd made. "And you even changed him."

"Well, sure. Cleaned him up and fed him, too. I used to have to watch kids a lot when people dropped them off at Grandma's." Sam lost interest in the fingers, and Cleve picked him up, bounced him a little. "Been a long time since I changed a kid's pants, but it comes back to you."

She surveyed the kitchen: the bacon draining on paper towels, the toys, the baby food. "I don't know how I slept through all this activity."

"You must have been up late."

"I wasn't the only one." Sam reached for her, and she took him, but her smile was for Cleve.

"I'm used to getting up early, but I'm not used to sleeping nearly as well as I did last night. You've got a real nice . . . bed."

"Glad you like it."

"Mmm, I do." He clapped and rubbed his hands together, ready to get to work. "What do you want for breakfast? Eggs? Pancakes? I've earned a pretty good reputation for my pancakes, and I think I've got it figured how to cut the recipe down for two people." Sam squealed. "Three? You still want pancakes after you ate all that baby mush?" Cleve pointed to a box of baby cereal. "I fed him that stuff since it had a picture of a baby on it, but it tastes pretty grim if you ask me."

"Sam likes it. We've had to introduce foods slowly because he's had a low tolerance for complex carbohydrates and fats. He gets diarrhea."

"Geez, kid, you've got all kinds of problems, haven't you?" He ruffled Sam's hair, but the baby ducked away. He took up the box of Bisquick he'd ferreted out earlier and turned it to the recipes on the back. "Actually, we were getting along pretty well until he saw you."

"He usually won't have much to do with men. You're doing very well."

Cleve looked up and smiled warmly, studying the child in Susan's arms. When he'd first awakened he'd thought he'd heard the soft coo of a mourning dove, but in the dim haze of half-sleep, he'd recognized Sam's call. Susan had burrowed in by his side, and he wanted to let her rest. It amazed him that Sam hadn't let out a holler when he'd tiptoed into the room. The boy's eyes had actually brightened, and he'd answered Cleve's tentative smile with one of his own.

"I think I could get custody of him," Cleve said. Susan looked at him as though he'd just pinched her. "I think Dunn's willing to turn him over to a relative." He lifted one shoulder. "Which could be me."

She grinned from ear to ear. "Oh, I've been hoping to hear you say that. And then do you think we could go through the State Court?"

"For what?"

"The adoption."

"Oh, yeah." What else? He didn't have any better ideas, but he didn't like the tight feeling he was getting in his gut all of a sudden.

"It's all so complicated with these different courts, but I would think that once you had custody, as his father you could approve the adoption, and we could just bypass this tribal issue."

Bypass the tribal issue? Cleve stared at her. It sounded as though she would all but bypass him as well. Of course, there had been one slight detour last night.

Susan went on. "I'm thinking that once the judge turns him over to you, he shouldn't have anything to say about his living with me, should he? I mean, even before the adoption goes through." She shifted Sam from one hip to the other. "Obviously, I have a place for him with his own—What's wrong?"

He'd set the box aside, forgotten what it was for. His eyes were blazing. "Was that what all this was about? 'I want you to stay, Cleve. Make love to me, Cleve.' You'd do anything to get this baby, wouldn't you?"

"You don't really believe—"

"I don't believe in much, but you know what? I was actually beginning to believe in—"

The phone rang. They stared hotly at one another through two more rings before Susan answered, then offered Cleve the call. "It's Warden Steiner."

He stared at her as he snatched the receiver, then turned his back on her and barked into it. "You're gonna tell me Jim didn't make it."

"He died early this morning," said the quiet, steady voice at the other end of the line.

"Shit." Cleve drew a long, deep breath and blew it out again. "Was anybody with him?"

"Just hospital staff and one of our officers."

"His father never—"

"No. He won't claim the body, either, so the state has to—"

"I'll claim the body." Cleve stared out the kitchen window at a cottonwood, bare but for a few tenacious brown leaves fluttering in the morning breeze. "I can do that, can't I? He's . . . he was just a kid. No worse than the rest of . . ." He turned and saw the anxious look in

Susan's eyes as she listened unabashedly. "You think I could do that?" he asked Steiner.

"I'll, uh . . . We'll work on it together, okay? I think there's enough money in his account to pay burial expenses. He's got a decent burial coming to him." There was a pause, then a gentler tone. "He left some things for you, Cleve. Personal things he wanted you to have. He thought a lot of you."

"Yeah, I know. I didn't want to have anything to do with him at first, to tell you the truth, but then . . . Hell, we were just two dumb bastards stuck in the same boat."

"Not exactly. You learned to make the best of a bad situation. It's too bad about Jim."

"Yeah. I'll find myself a ride, be up there soon as I can." He hung up the phone and headed for the bedroom.

With Sam still riding on her hip, Susan followed him. "You can take my car."

"I don't need your car."

"You need transportation, and I'm not using my car. And I'm really sorry about your friend." She watched him button his shirt, unbuckle his belt and shove the tails into his jeans. "Please talk to me, Cleve."

"I'm sorry about Jim, too, but it's not like we were brothers or anything, so don't go bleeding your little heart out for me." He had to get closer to her than he wanted to get his boots. He wouldn't look at her.

"Cleve, before the call came, you started to say you were beginning to believe in something. What was it?"

"Shit happens. That's what I believe. So you might as well just take whatever the hell you can get whenever you can get it and don't question the motives." He sat on the bed, still rumpled, still smelling of the sex they'd shared. He tried not to breathe too deeply as he pulled his boots on.

"I don't understand you, Cleve. You told me you went to see Judge Dunn, and you discussed . . . well, as Sam's father, your right to decide . . ." She bounced Sam on her hip and gestured urgently with her free hand. "You said you thought you could get custody of him; and I know you can't be thinking about keeping him yourself. So I thought you were trying to help me."

"You thought." He leaped to his feet. "You *knew*. You white people are all alike. You just *know* all this stuff." He glanced at the baby, who, with two fingers stuffed in his mouth, was all eyes, all ears. Cleve took a deep breath and lowered his voice as he slid his gaze back to Susan. "You think you know what I'm thinking, but you haven't got a clue. You're so damn smart, if you don't be careful, you're gonna outsmart yourself."

"I *thought* you were going to help because you wanted to, but if you don't—"

"I wanted . . ." He moved in closer, watching her like a predator and putting the child from his mind. "You really want to know what inmates do about sex? Huh? Besides jack themselves off, I mean. Sometimes they get other people—other *men*, yeah—and sometimes they get 'em bad, like they did Jimmy. You learn to be careful so you don't get used, because if somebody uses you, then you really feel like shit. So you don't trust anybody, because you can't tell who's a user and who's not just by looks."

"I wasn't using you," she said quietly, standing her ground.

"Oh, yeah? Sure feels like you were."

"It had nothing to do with Sam. Nothing! You've been wanting—" She glanced at the bed.

"Sure, I have. I know I have, and it's made me forget every damn lesson I ever learned."

"It was what I wanted, too, even though I knew it would make everything between us even more complicated. But I want custody of Sam, too, and you know that."

"So what happens after you get what you want? What if I'm still wanting?"

"You're talking about two separate things, Cleve."

"*We* are two separate people. You and me—I don't know how we ever managed to get ourselves wedged under each other's skin because we are two different . . . too different."

Finally Sam started bawling, and Susan held him close, patting his back and eyeing Cleve with a suggestion that he was to blame for this.

"Oh, Jesus, I'm getting out of here." He shook off the accusatory look and headed for the door.

"You still need a car, and you can take mine."

He turned on his heel in the bedroom doorway. "You're still trying to rack up the favors, aren't you? Listen, the judge doesn't want to give that kid to you; he wants *me* to take him. And I don't want him." He looked at the child. "You hear that? I don't—"

Cleve ground his back teeth. The kid had every right to wail; he was the son of a no-good cowboy. The curse he muttered as he walked out the door was aimed at his own heart.

The funeral was a quiet affair. Cleve and Warden Steiner stood beside the open grave and listened to the prayers of a local minister, who knew neither Jimmy Dawson nor his family, which was probably why he agreed to do the service. Steiner's promise that Dietz would likely be sent to another penitentiary, where he would do harder time, didn't matter much to Cleve. The boy was dead, and Dietz wasn't. Justice was a kid's fairy tale, dead in the hearts of men. Remembering the sign in the Mandan courthouse, he couldn't say for sure about liberty. For the moment he had his, and maybe for the first time Jim did, too.

Two days later, Cleve hitched a ride to Mandan with Cody, who dropped him off at a used car lot. In the old days he'd have based his choice on color and flash, but now he wanted something cheap and dependable. He drove three pickups before he heard a sound engine. Twelve-year-old red and white short box with a dent in the passenger's door, but hardly any rust. The dealer almost lost the sale when he quietly suggested that Cleve could pay partly in food stamps. He almost wished he had some. The practice was illegal as hell, and he would have been glad to swing the deal for some undercover agent just to show that the art of trading with the Indians hadn't changed much in a hundred years. But it wasn't worth it. Nobody cared. Neither was it worth it to shop around for an honest used car dealer. He'd found his cowboy Cadillac, and he paid for it in cash.

He met Bernie at the Mandan courthouse, where it took less than an hour to clear him of all liabilities and legal encumbrances. The bond posted in his behalf was returned, charges were dropped, and he was free to go anywhere he pleased. Just like that. He wanted to know what the catch was, and Bernie laughed and offered to buy him lunch. Bernie had never done time.

Cleve ordered pancakes and bacon. He'd been thinking about pancakes since the last time he'd been with Susan, and he'd had a craving. Pancakes weren't going to satiate it. He was going to have to swallow his pride and go knocking on her door again, but he needed an excuse. He needed to get off dead center.

Outside the big booth-level window, the wind was kicking up a dust storm. The sky suddenly darkened, not with clouds, but with North Dakota topsoil. Cleve sipped his coffee as he watched. "Sure you want to be flying home in this?"

"Looks like a nice tail wind to me."

Cleve set the cup down. He'd drunk so much coffee he was floating. "Listen, you've done a lot for me, Bernie, and it might be a while before I can pay you what I owe you."

"I'm getting some mileage out of this case, Cleve. I'm doing some civil rights work in Minnesota. Indian rights. Your case gives us some leverage, got us some publicity. I'm also planning to do some writing, so I need all the credibility I can get."

"There's one more thing, and it's not going to further anybody's cause, except maybe one little kid's."

Bernie leaned back in his chair. "Did you have any blood work done?"

"No. I don't have to. I know he's my kid. I want custody of him."

"Nobody on his mother's side is fighting you?"

"They won't. They've got enough problems."

"Have you talked with the social worker?"

"Not yet."

"You'll need to do that. Get her on your side."

"I talked to the judge. He said, if I had a job and a place to live, no problem. But if I try to give Sam up for adoption, let a white woman take him, then he'll take him back. Can he do that?"

"He sure can. The U.S. Supreme Court has already ruled in favor of tribal jurisdiction in cases like this one."

"Chalk one up for the Indians, right?" He remembered how strange it had felt to relieve the little boy of his wet diaper and actually see him, all of him, for the first time. His own son. Sam's left leg, thinner than the right, was curved like a wishbone. Don't worry, kid, we'll make some muscle, he'd promised. He'd made a similar promise to Jimmy once.

Bernie's chuckle rankled somehow. "Jesus, Bernie, she's his mother. In every way that counts, Susan *is* Sam's mother."

"And you say you're his father. You're of one blood. That counts, too." He laid his rumpled paper napkin beside his empty plate and studied his client. "What is it you want, Cleve? The woman?"

"I want what's best for the boy. How could I take care of a kid, especially—" What? A kid who looked a little different, maybe wasn't developing quite on schedule? Or especially a kid who might embarrass him? He shook his head. "Especially a kid like Sam. He's doing real good. Even I can see he's getting stronger, little by little. Susan says there's no telling how much progress he can make with therapy and special education."

"Do you want the woman, Cleve?"

"I—" Cleve eyed Bernie, the family man. He wasn't talking about getting laid. "I don't know what I want anymore."

"You going back into rodeo?"

"Yeah, probably."

"Not much enthusiasm there."

"Gettin' old." He'd been saying that since the first time he'd been laid up with back problems. He always said it with a smile, but it was no joke anymore.

"No older than I am. A woman and a son can make it worth going home at night."

"Look, right now I just want custody of that kid because his aunt isn't . . . that's not the best place for him."

"Then what?"

"Then he's mine. Then we go from there."

Bernie reached inside his tweed jacket and pulled out a credit card as he picked up the bill. "You talk to the social worker. See if you can get her approval. I'll petition the court for you. But Cleve, you have to understand this." He tapped the edges of the card and the bill on the table for added emphasis. "In principle I support the tribe's efforts to keep Indian children from being taken from the reservation and placed with non-Indians. In *principle*, now. That's important."

"I never worried too much about principles. Kids, either, I guess. But this little guy—" Cleve glanced away from Bernie's rapping credit card. "He really has a way about him."

"And the woman?"

"The woman's name is Susan. And it doesn't matter what color she is, Bernie, she's Sam's mother now. It's fine for you to stick to your principles, but what happens to Sam?"

Bernie smiled. "It looks as though that may be up to you."

Chapter 19

❧❧❧❧❧ ❧❧❧❧❧

With the petition in the works, Cleve had not once heard mention of the word *adoption* in the days since he'd told Susan that he'd enlisted Bernie's help in getting custody of Sam. He'd expected some show of excitement, but she had responded with such reserve that he wondered whether she'd changed her mind. She'd offered him no invitations, and he'd said he had work to do, which was true. Most of the equipment at the Youth Ranch was in lousy repair. If he couldn't fix the pump on the stock tank and get the tank heater running he'd be chopping ice out of the backwater from the river all winter. Damn buffalo were getting spoiled.

He parked his pickup as close as he could get to the post office. It was almost 10:30 on a bright blue Wednesday morning, and he'd forgotten it was the first of the month. Mama's Day. The post office was like a shrine, and most Fort Yates residents made it their daily pilgrimage. Ordinarily the office workers' noon hour was the busy time, but on the first of the month when the ADC checks arrived, women with babes in arms and toddlers at their heels waited around for the envelopes to be dropped into the slots between 10:00 and 10:30.

Cleve didn't get much mail, but he had his own reasons for paying the post office a daily visit. He was interested in the bulletin board, although he tried to be discreet in checking the posters on it. He'd rented a box so he wouldn't have to ask the clerk to sort through general delivery for him. He knew he was probably kidding himself about the posters, but that display was an irresistible lure for him. The ritual always culminated with a letdown, which had become part of what he looked for.

His mailbox was empty. He turned away from it just as Vera Bone Necklace pushed the front door open, and they stood face to face. Not as discomfiting a situation as it once was, but Cleve didn't expect any friendly greetings. Like many of the women who were there early on Mama's Day, she had to head her old man off at the pass. It was probably the only day he ever volunteered to pick up the mail.

Cleve gave a polite nod, and Vera acknowledged him the same way. She was in one of his classes at the college. The teacher had asked him to help her with a problem once, and since then Vera had asked him for help once or twice. He'd gladly obliged. Math came more easily than Vera's trust, but he was working on both. He wanted Vera's approval, and he knew that was a switch. If he'd been going with Darcy, he wouldn't have given a damn what Vera thought of him. But Vera had more say over Sam than she'd had over Darcy, and he knew that Melinda Jefferson, the same social worker he'd been talking to, was also talking to Vera.

"Susan must be at your place today, huh? With Sam?"

Vera nodded. "She's watching him until I'm through with class for the day."

"Would you mind if I stopped over?"

"She says you've been acting funny, and she thinks you're mad at her."

"She does, huh?" He laughed, knowing that "acting funny" was Vera's term, not Susan's.

"You shouldn't treat her like that. Getting mad over nothing."

"I'm not mad at her. Why should I be?" The truth was, he'd been mad for several days before he'd asked

himself that question. It was an old habit. Nothing else
bothered him when he was angry. He'd gone to bed with
a woman and gotten up the next morning feeling like
part of a family. Big mistake, but not hers. She'd been
telling him all along how much she wanted that kid. He'd
gone off saying he didn't, which was beginning to feel
like a lie.

"I'm trying to help her," he told Vera. She nodded, and he figured they were natural allies. They both
wanted Sam off their consciences and out of their hair.
"So you don't mind if I stop by?"

Vera shook her head. "Just don't be giving her a
bad time."

He waited until Vera got her mail and left before he
turned to the bulletin board. He knew most of the wanted
posters by heart. They'd been there forever. Nobody ever
caught these guys. He stepped closer. Two new ones.
Two he'd never seen before, but one pictured a face he
would never forget. Ray *Taggert?* No aliases were listed,
but it didn't matter. Cleve glanced up to assure himself
that the clerk was busy selling stamps, then snapped the
paper loose from its thumb tack, folded it and stuck it
under his denim jacket.

Susan stood at the front window watching Vera gather
her books out of the back of her old white Thunderbird.
She was juggling a bag of groceries, too, and if Susan
had felt more energetic, she might have gone outside
to help. She'd been keeping a tight schedule for years,
always trying to squeeze more in, so it wasn't the hours
that were sapping everything out of her. It was the
aggravation of being left on hold for so long. She knew
that the social worker had interviewed both Cleve and
Vera recently, and she'd been feeling left out. Worse,
she'd been feeling powerless. She'd thought his getting
custody would lead to her getting Sam, but now she
wasn't so sure.

Sex always made everything more complicated, at
least for Susan. She'd learned the hard way. It meant less

to a man than it did to a woman, at least in the long run. No more live-in boyfriends, she'd promised herself—but she'd let herself love this "no-good cowboy" against her better judgment, and what else could it lead to? Being foolish with her own heart was one thing, but Sam's welfare was at stake. She had no idea where she stood with Cleve, and her baby—*her* baby—could be removed from her reach any day. And she was tired of hanging out on a limb, even though she knew damn well it was she who had put herself there. Again.

Through the window she watched Vera shuffle through the first light dusting of snow that had blanketed the unplanted yard. The black mutt tagged behind her. Susan opened the door just as Vera hissed the dog back. She'd barely gotten out the words, "Need any help?" when Sam hollered from the bedroom.

Vera directed her answer with a lift of her chin. "Only with him."

Susan headed down the hallway, talking as she went. "I thought he'd sleep longer. The therapist gave him a real workout this morning."

"Typing teacher gave me one, too." Vera deposited her books on the sofa, and they conversed between rooms as they went about their business, Susan changing Sam and Vera unloading her groceries on the kitchen table. "Tommy hasn't been around, has he?"

"He never comes around when I'm here. I thought you said he'd found a job."

"He applied for bus driver at the school, but the bus foreman doesn't like him." As if she read Susan's mind, Vera added, "Tommy's only had a few citations. Nothing major. You want some coffee?"

The first of the month, Susan remembered. Vera had money. She carried Sam into the kitchen and put him in the baby walker. She looked up at Vera. "Do you want me to stay around for a while?"

"It's up to you." She was already measuring out the ground coffee. "Most of my check went for bills already, so he can be as sweet as he wants, he's not getting anything from me. But if Sam starts acting up, you might want to take him for a ride or something."

"It worries me when you say that."

"Tommy won't do anything but cuss. And that's only if he's been drinking." She fit the lid on the aluminum pot and studied it for a moment. "Cleve Black Horse was asking about you today. I saw him at the post office." Her expression brightened, but grudgingly. "He's one pretty smart cowboy, that one."

"How do you mean?" Susan sat on the floor next to the six-wheel walker and absently spun the beads that were strung across the front of the tray.

"Well, he's in my math class. I've been putting off taking that math requirement because I'm so dumb in math. But that Cleve, he knows all the answers." The pot went on the stove, and Vera continued as she searched a cabinet for cups. "I tried to get him to just give me the answer to this one problem, but he showed me how to work it out. He should be a teacher."

"He'd rather ride bulls until he can't walk anymore."

"Maybe *then* he'll be a teacher."

"I think he's going to school so he can use his VA benefits. Which is okay, I guess." She knew she had no business wishing burning ambition on Cleve Black Horse, but she'd imagined him suddenly seeing some kind of light and announcing a new professional calling. One that would settle him down. Dangerous thinking, she told herself. You ought to know that by now.

Vera shrugged. "He's got it coming to him." Clean cups were a lost cause. She decided to wash a couple that were in the sink. "Those white teachers are *really* no good sometimes. They talk so much, you don't know what they said by the time they get done."

"All of them?"

"No, but there's this one guy—supposed to be teaching Tribal Government—*really* no good. I want to tell him just give our ears a rest once. Thinks he knows it all."

"I was told recently that's one of our problems. White people think they know it all."

"Nurses aren't usually too bad." Vera dried her hands on a dishtowel and turned with her hands on her hips. With Susan on the floor, Vera could have been instructing a toddler. "He's not mad at you. And he's not going to try to keep Sam. Sam belongs with you." She shook her head and slapped her thigh. "I can't keep him, Susan. It's not that I don't want to."

"You know, Cleve's surprisingly good with Sam." Sam bounced in his seat and babbled, as if he agreed. "The few times he's been around him."

"How is he with you?" Susan glanced up, but she offered no answer. "For sure, he knows his math. I thought he was just another one of Darcy's big cowboys, but maybe—" There was a knock at the front door. "I think that's for you," Vera said, and she turned back to the stove.

Cleve looked cold, standing on the step wearing an old denim jacket and a new black cowboy hat. Susan held the door open, and the bitter wind whipped across the bare floor. It made Sam laugh. Cleve stepped in, rubbing his hands together.

They exchanged nods, like opposing quarterbacks deciding what to make of each other, but the real story was in their eyes. Remembered intimacy, questions neither would ask, defenses ready in case there were answers.

"Vera said you were here," he said. A noise from the floor relieved the tension. Cleve moved first. He smiled and went down on one knee beside the baby walker. "Hey, Sam. How's it going?"

Sam stretched out his arms, and Cleve took him out of the seat. He stood, bounced the baby in his arms and turned to Susan again. "Melinda Jefferson wants to see me this afternoon, so I thought you might want to be there, too."

"Why? Did she say I should be there?"

"No, but . . . Maybe she's already made a decision on what she's going to recommend to the judge, I'm not sure, but I do know she's going to ask me . . ." He was struggling, trying to word this right. "Because she's asked me before, you know, who'll be taking care of Sam when I'm working." Susan stared at him. He shifted Sam from one arm to the other. "So I figure I'll just tell them I've worked something out with you. They admit that you've been good for him. They just don't want you taking over on him."

He waited, but she wasn't going to object to his choice of words. They were right on target. The look in his eyes softened. "It's not just you, Susan. You know that."

"I know." But that didn't make it hurt any less.

"Well, I'd have to have a sitter lined up, and for now, why shouldn't it be you? I think they'd go for it."

Of course. Why shouldn't it be her? "And then what?"

"Then we work it out between us. I'm willing to claim this guy as my son, but I can't take care of him myself. We know that. Hell, *they* know that."

"So I'm to be the baby sitter."

"You got any better suggestions?" He waited until Susan shook her head, and then he turned to Vera, who'd put a hold on the coffee. "Have you?" Another negative. "I work days, and I take a class two evenings a week. Can you work nights?"

"I think I could trade for eleven to seven. It's not a popular shift."

"You'd be there when the therapist comes, and I'd get the easy part." He smiled at Sam, who was fascinated by his hat. "When he's sleeping."

Wait a minute. "You'd sleep at my house?"

"When you're not there. Unless the judge gets on his high horse over it, and then we'll have to come up with something else, like—well, I'll tell him I'm applying for housing."

"Are you?" That was another red flag.

"Jesus." He sighed and glanced out the front window, as if he were hoping for reinforcements. He tried again. "By spring I'll probably be riding again, and a house would just be something else to—" She was watching him, trying to figure out what he was up to, and it obviously irritated him. "I will if I have to, okay? Whatever makes the judge happy. With a child I might qualify, but the waiting list is a mile long. It might look good if I applied, but I'd never get in." He paused. "So what do you think? Should we try it?"

The floor seemed to crumble beneath her feet. Her plans were falling apart, with *his* plans taking their place. She gestured, floundering. "I was hoping we could just go to court—a *different* court—"

"You're in Indian country, Susan. This has to go through Tribal Court. You've gotta trust me, just like I'm trusting you. I'm taking legal responsibility for this kid, and I'm trusting you to stick with him."

"Stick with him!" Scowling at the face under the hat, she reached out to take Sam away.

Cleve hung on. "Yeah, I know. You've stuck with him. That's why you're here. But you never know. Some guy could come along, and maybe he's not the kind of guy who wants somebody else's kid around—"

"Some no-good cowboy?" She laughed dryly. "You're the only one I know, and one's enough."

"Oh, yeah?" They stared at each other until the corner of Cleve's mouth turned up in a smile. He liked being the one who was enough. Susan dropped her arms to her sides in defeat. "Look, we're burnin' a lotta daylight here, and we both have to get to work. You want to back me up on this, or not?"

"We'll have him at my house? Permanently?"

Finally he handed her the baby. "I sure as hell don't want to put him in that hole in the ground I'm staying in."

"I guess it would look funny if we took him with us." She smoothed Sam's hair and fussed with his coveralls, then looked up at Cleve. "Presumptuous, huh?"

"Yeah, I'd say so. Vera's still his guardian."

"Vera," Susan said, and her friend was there. Sam went to his aunt. "Your classes are over for the day, aren't they? I'll stop back afterwards and let you know what we find out."

She put on her down-filled parka and followed Cleve outside. His pickup was parked along the street in front of her car. She quickened her step and grabbed his arm, turning him on his heel. "What happened to the notion that I've been using you to get what I want?" she demanded.

"You're fighting hard for that kid, and he's not the kind of kid most people would fight for. Not unless he was their kid. And if he's *my* kid, maybe using me . . ." He glanced away, squinting into the glare for a moment while he snapped his jacket in a couple of places to ward off the wind. Then he shoved his hands into his jacket pockets and looked at her again. ". . . makes some kind of sense. Anyway, I guess I really can't see you running off and leaving him for some guy."

"Things have become very complicated, haven't they?"

"Between us? That's understating it pretty good."

"It's going to get worse if we—"

"We'll work it out." His hand emerged from his pocket with a folded paper, rediscovered. "I've got something to show you," he said, and he put his arm around her, blocking the wind with his body as he guided her toward the pickup. He opened the passenger side door, and they stood in its shelter. He opened the paper and handed it to her. "I took this off the bulletin board at the post office this morning."

"Is this—" She studied the photograph. The face was drawn, lips thin, eyes like a ferret's. It *had* to be, at last, "Ray Smith?"

He grinned as though he'd discovered gold. "Looks like his real name is Ray Taggert. I'm sure it's the same guy. Wanted for robbery and attempted murder in Montana."

"Have you told the police?"

"Haven't had time yet, but I'm going to. I want to tell Steiner, too. I want him to know—"

"And Bernie! You have to call Bernie."

He slapped the paper with the back of his hand. "This is the one who killed Arnie Bertram, Susan. Not me."

"I hope they catch him so you can put this behind you."

"I'd like to catch him myself. I'd like to go to a *different court* all right, and watch some fast-talking DA nail this sucker."

They laughed together, and she slid into the pickup, forgetting her intention to take her own car.

They sat in chairs arranged near the end of Melinda Jefferson's desk, which faced the wall in the tiny office cubical. The fat, bespectacled social worker propped her feet up on the bottom drawer, which she opened for that purpose. Susan noted the size of the woman's ankles and wanted to suggest that she cut down on the salt. But she kept quiet. She kept her hands folded in her lap and concentrated on blending in with the gray furniture and yellow walls. Like Susan, Melinda was a non-Indian professional working on the reservation, which was a tenuous situation at best. Unlike Susan, Melinda had learned to avoid bucking the bureaucratic system.

Susan understood that Melinda was ready to place Sam with strangers in a foster home if the judge so ordered. But since she did not doubt Susan's sincerity nor her ability to give Sam good care, Melinda was willing to recommend that Susan be allowed to continue to play a role in Sam's life. A year ago, Susan would not have been satisfied with such a small concession. Lately, she was taking what she could get. It was either that, or walk away.

She sat quietly and watched Cleve play the game. Work the system. Get what you can. In a way, it was hard to see him reduced to that. Hard to realize that for all the effort he'd made to get away from the reservation, he still knew the ropes. She was baffled, or maybe more bothered by the way he managed to charm the pants off

Melinda Jefferson. Figuratively, thank God. He'd met with the woman only once, but they were old buddies. *Susan* had met with her many times, and *they* were professional acquaintances.

"Your attorney says you're open to tissue testing at the court's request." Melinda bounced the eraser end of a pencil on her calendar desk pad. "No doubts yourself, Cleve?"

"He's my son."

The unequivocal statement jarred Susan. She gave herself away by glancing at him sharply, but he ignored her, and, fortunately, so did Melinda.

"Of course we have the mother's word, through her sister, and with your assent, I have to say, he belongs with you." She smiled. "I can count on one hand the number of men who have been willing to say that without somebody having to drag it out of them."

"I don't have any reason to doubt it. You've seen Sam. He kinda looks like me." Cleve folded his arms and leaned back, smiling, letting the woman have a good look. "Actually, he looks a lot like my Uncle Jake's kids."

Melinda shifted in her chair, dragging her attention from Cleve to Susan. "I can stress the idea of continuity of care with the judge, which I think will look good to him as long as Cleve is applying for actual custody. You're sure you can manage both Sam and your job at the hospital?"

"I have been all along."

"Unofficially," Melinda reminded her. "The judge still has it in his mind that Vera's been the care giver, and he's pretty old-fashioned about these things."

"Traditional," Cleve said. It was a correction that Melinda acknowledged but could not fully understand. Cleve smiled, charming her again. "I've got a grandma who thinks just like him."

She made a note on the file. "I'll find some way of mentioning that. It'll be worth some points."

"I think he knows."

Melinda smiled. "I'll get over there today and have a talk with the old gentleman. We should know something soon."

Cleve was full of surprises today. Susan dammed up her amazement until they got into the pickup, and then she let loose. "What was all that business about him looking like your Uncle Jake's kids?"

Cleve started the pickup, smiling when it turned over on the first try. He glanced at Susan as he put it in gear. "He does. Sort of. When they were babies."

"Do you really believe—"

"My own bullshit?" He laughed. "Basically, yeah. Enough to make it convincing." He checked the side mirror for traffic. "We're going to keep him out of a foster home, Susan. After he's with you a while, they're not going to try to uproot him."

"While we were talking, I was thinking about who I could get to come in at night whenever—" He turned, his face suddenly stony, and she knew she was on the verge of saying the wrong thing again. "When you're busy."

"When I'm busy at night? You mean like out partying?"

"I don't expect you to—"

"They're giving him to *me*, Susan." He slid the gear shift back into neutral, and the engine hummed. "Maybe."

"You said you didn't want him." Quietly she added, "Remember?"

"Yeah, I remember." He stared through the windshield for a long, reflective moment, then half smiled as a small dog darted across the street. "It's hard to decide which bullshit to believe sometimes, isn't it?" He glanced at her, but no answer was necessary. "They'll probably get in touch with me. I'll let you know as soon as I hear anything."

In silence he drove her back to Vera's.

He would let *her* know. He was talking as though Sam were really his, as though he had the right to call all the shots. Technically, maybe he did, but he knew as well as she did that he wasn't going to stick with it long. He had rodeo on the brain, right? Come spring, she and Sam would stand on the doorstep and wave bye-bye, if she'd managed to teach Sam that skill by then. The sitter was going to need a sitter by then, and there was no point in making any bones about it.

He's my son.

Did he believe that? Oh, Lord, did the man believe he was actually a father? If he did, she'd been angling for it, but what if it went too far now? She wanted Sam's father to accept him, yes, for Sam's sake. But not to take him from her. Sam needed a mother. Sam needed *her*, and she needed Sam. This was one time when nobody could replace her.

I have to say he belongs with you, the social worker had said. He had an apartment. She'd never seen it inside, but Cleve didn't seem to think it was a good place for Sam. He could try for tribal housing, which was assigned by committee and was in short supply. Otherwise there was BIA, Public Health and School District housing, but he qualified for none of those. There wasn't much private rental property in town.

It was all for show, wasn't it? The way he'd claimed the family resemblance and planned aloud to try for a house?

Susan remembered coming into her kitchen and finding Cleve playing with Sam. Not just playing. Trying to help him get stronger. And then turning, seeing her with flattened hair and sleepy eyes, and smiling. Sam belonged to her, and Cleve belonged to no one. She had to remember that for her own protection, because he would soon be spending his nights in her home.

Cleve made the mistake of going to the local sheriff with his information. He was told to call the Morton County sheriff.

"That's the guy who arrested me."

The white man smiled. "That's right. Why don't you give him a call?"

He went to the BIA Police next. Captain Wilbur Charging Eagle showed more interest. He put in a call to the FBI and handed over the phone. The agent listened, asked Cleve if he would be willing to sign a statement, then told him to put the captain back on. While Cleve sat there bursting with the significance of his discovery, Charging Eagle hashed over the details of some vandalism incident with the agent on the other end of the line. After he hung up, he told Cleve to put his statement in writing. Cleve poured it all out on paper, handed it in, and the policeman checked it over as though he might be giving it a grade.

"This is good. You've got everything here. Names, dates, places." He nodded, still perusing. "Yep. It's all here." He looked up. "People usually leave out the most important stuff the first time around."

Cleve pointed at the paper in the policeman's hand. "I spent two years behind bars over that incident. The important stuff is burned into my brain."

"Well, if they can catch up to this guy, he'll sure have a lot to answer for. But you're off the hook, right?"

"Yeah." Cleve offered a mirthless chuckle. "Technically." But he was still squirming, and he hated it. He hadn't expected the sheriff to get excited over the poster, but he would have thought the Indian Police might show some interest in the proof that there *was* a Ray Smith. Or Ray Taggert. It didn't matter what the name beneath that face was, *that* was the right man. Not Cleve.

Somebody sure as hell ought to be interested.

On the way to the Youth Ranch, Cleve stopped for a beer. He drank two. Fortified for the cold, he headed out to fix the broken pump.

It was the cusp of winter in North Dakota. Fall, like spring, was never much of a season. The wind pushed the November sky from west to east, sliding it over the tops of the brown hills. Cleve stood beside the stock tank and just watched it for a while. It was like standing under a highway and looking up at thousands of big gray tires rolling just overhead. The dun-colored grass rippled and bowed across the flat over scattered patches of snow. After he'd let Susan off, he'd put on a dark blue hooded sweatshirt under his unlined jacket. The combination bothered him less than it would have two years ago. He'd grown up wearing hood sweaters with overall jackets, and it meant that he couldn't afford anything warmer. So be it.

He heard a rider at his back, and he knew it would be Charlie Buffalo Boy. He unloaded a small tool box and pulled on a pair of work gloves. He realized how much he'd missed the sound of a rider approaching across the flat. Company. Maybe some news. A hand with the work. Something a little extra for supper. He laid out his tools while Charlie tied his old plug to the pickup box. Didn't look up until the boy, dressed in a red hood sweater and overall jacket, stood beside him.

"You gonna fix that old pump?"

He was already taking it apart. "Thought I would."

"There's no electricity out here."

"There's a pump handle and a hired man."

Charlie tied his hood down under his chin, stuck his hands in his jacket pockets and watched. Cleve pulled the pump mechanism off the well shaft and hunkered down behind the corrugated aluminum stock tank, out of the wind.

Charlie squatted next to him. "Geez. You smell like beer."

"You've got a nose like a wife, Buffalo Boy. I had another appointment in town, and on my way back—" Cleve looked up. "Hey, it was dinner time. I stopped for a beer. I don't know why I put up with you." He went back to work on the pump, examining the rusty bolts.

"Because I help you out. Make your job easier."

"Yeah, right. Hand me that vise grip. It's in the top—" He pointed to the little tool box, and Charlie snatched up the needed tool, handing it over with an I-told-you-so gleam in his eye. "Thanks. Okay, you're handy to have around sometimes, but you talk too much. There's an extra pair of work gloves in there, too. You oughta have some gloves on."

"You never said you was married." At Cleve's glance, the boy reached for the gloves. "You said I had a nose like a wife."

"Figure of speech. Can of lubricating oil under the tray." Charlie was quick to deliver. "I've got a kid, though," Cleve confided.

"Yeah? How old?"

"He's two. He's staying with his aunt right now. His mother's dead." He found a connection that had rusted out.

"Too bad. Was she your wife?"

"No. Never been married. Hand me that wrench." Charlie rattled in the box and held one up for Cleve's approval. "That's it."

"Think you ever will?" Charlie asked, laying the tool in Cleve's large gloved hand.

"If the right woman comes along, maybe."

"How do you know? What makes her the *right* woman?"

He wished he knew. "The way you feel about her, I guess. The way you get along together and the way—"

"The way you get it on together?"

"There's a whole lot more to it than that."

"It doesn't hurt to try 'em out, though, does it? I mean you did." Cleve looked up from his work. Charlie shrugged. "Obviously. I bet you've tried out a whole bunch of 'em. *Still* haven't found just the *right* one." Brimming with adolescent knowledge, the boy grinned at the man. "But you've got a kid."

"I'm not claiming to be the best example. The kid was an accident."

"Aren't we all. What's his name?"

"Sam. His name is—" The second time he said it gently. "Sam."

"Sam Black Horse?"

"Not yet. I'm trying to get custody of him." The rusty bolt claimed his attention again. The oil helped some. He applied extra muscle.

"You are?"

"Yeah," Cleve replied through the strain. The bolt finally gave. Once it was off, Cleve looked up again. "I am. Saw the social worker this morning, in fact."

"You got your dad's last name?"

"Nope."

"Neither do I."

"These days it doesn't matter." He discovered a rotten seal, which he thought he could replace. "Hand me that whole tray, would you?" He held out his hand and saw the way the boy moved eagerly to do his bidding. "You think I'm crazy, trying to get custody of a baby?"

"No. Not if you're gonna look after him." Handing over the tool box tray, Charlie beamed. He'd been asked for his opinion. "How're you gonna look after a little kid like that?"

"Well, that's just it. I've cooked up this scheme with this nurse who works nights, and with me working days . . ." He sorted through nuts and bolts as he spoke. Charlie hung on every word. "I'm a little worried. I could be getting myself into a hell of a mess."

"You never know until you try. What's this nurse like?"

"She's the kind of woman you wish . . ." He found the leather scrap he was looking for and smiled, not for the leather, but for Susan. "She's been with Sam off and on since he was born. She cares for him a lot."

"You tried her out yet?"

It was like laughing at a guy's joke and suddenly having him punch you in the gut. Cleve scowled. "If you were five years older, Charlie, you'd be picking yourself up off the ground. You ought to know better than to ask me that."

The color drained from Charlie's face, and his lip trembled. "You—you've answered all my other questions."

"That's one you got no right to ask." He raised one gloved finger to admonish the boy. "You remember. What's between a man and a woman is private. What's between you and a girl is private. You understand? You go around talking about it, you turn it into something shabby."

"Sounds like this nurse might be the right one," Charlie said in a small voice.

"Right or wrong, you don't ask, and you don't go around telling. You got that?"

"Yeah."

"Okay. So now you know." Charlie hung his head, and Cleve felt bad. "Right? It's a lesson." He laid a hand on the boy's slight shoulder. "You gonna tell on me for having a couple of beers on my way to work?"

"No." He looked up, his spunk reforming. "A couple? You said one. You keep it up, they'll find out, anyway. You ought to go to a meeting with me sometime."

"What meeting?"

"AA. I'm court-ordered to go every week."

"Well, I'm not." Cleve braced his back against the stock tank and set about rigging up a new leather seal.

"I'd go anyway. But if I don't go, they'll send me up to the State Industrial School, they said."

SIS, Cleve thought. The State Pen for minors. There were all kinds of treatments. He remembered Jimmy Dawson's. He didn't want to know what somebody else did or didn't do. You take one look, you put two and two together, and you mind your own business, he told himself. Guilty until proven innocent.

Some things you don't ask, and you don't go around telling.

But sometimes there was a need to tell.

"Come here." Cleve took the poster from his pocket. "I've got something to show you." Charlie edged closer while Cleve unfolded it. "This is the guy who killed Arnie Bertram. I hitched a ride with Arnie, but later we picked this guy up. Called himself Ray Smith. We made a pit stop at this one rest area. I fell asleep in the pickup, and when I woke up, Arnie was dead and this Smith had taken off. So that's how it happened."

"If they find this guy, are you gonna tell them he did it?"

"I already told them. I wanna see them nail his ass right up there." Charlie's eyes widened, and Cleve laughed. Truth between friends. You needed to be able to confess. To ask. To be forgiven and accepted and believed. He punched Charlie's shoulder and said with mock seriousness, "I want to see justice done."

Charlie considered. "So you were passed out when all this happened?"

"Jesus." So much for acceptance. "You don't quit, do you? I'm not court-ordered to do anything. I'm a free man, even if they never find this guy."

"I don't know much about women yet, but I got started boozin' early. I know a lot can happen when you're passed out." Charlie shrugged apologetically. "It was just an offer. Sometimes it's hard to go to your first meeting by yourself."

"I'll keep that in mind." If this was real concern, he didn't know how to deal with it. He worked on another bolt. "Don't they have meetings for teenagers?"

"I'm in with the big boys. Major league."

"Why the hell not?" He'd suspected this kid was a forty-year-old dwarf. "Look over there, Charlie!" Across the flat stood three mustangs, bushy manes fluttering in the wind. Charlie and Cleve watched quietly until the *gruello* stallion stiffed high in the air and raised his black tail. In a moment the three vanished.

"How many of those broom tails did the tribe adopt?" Cleve asked.

"I think there's five."

"How many guys have you got out here that might have the nerve to break one?"

"Nobody can break those suckers, Cleve. They're meaner 'n a drunk on Sunday."

"Ain't a bronc that can't be rode, kid."

"Or a cowboy that can't be throwed," Charlie enjoined. "But there's probably three or four of us would give it a try if you'd show us how."

Cleve nodded. He'd had his own horse when he was a kid. First there'd been the spotted Shetland that had bitten a chunk out of the seat of his pants, and then Grandpa had given him a green-broke bay mare. He'd named her Lady, and he'd taught her to behave like one. That mare and plenty more.

"It'll take a lot of time and patience to gentle a mustang. But once it's done, then you've really got something." He nodded, smiling. "Kinda like the right woman."

Chapter 20

❧❧❧❧   ❧❧❧❧

The worst thing about Cleve's apartment was the lack of windows. Fortunately, he wasn't spending much time "down under" since he'd been granted temporary custody of Sam. After work he would come back for a shower and a change of clothes, and if he didn't have a class, he would go to Susan's early.

Today the wind had been a mean-tempered bitch wielding an icy blade. He'd thawed out some in the pickup, but he was still shivering on the inside. He pulled the chain on the bare bulb above the mirror. Sure enough, his lips were blue. His shower consisted of some pipes, a plastic curtain and a drain in the basement floor, but the water was hot. He stood under it with his eyes closed. No class tonight. He could almost smell supper cooking over at Susan's. She'd been cooking for him, even though he hadn't asked and she hadn't invited. She always offered, and it always smelled so good. She cooked the way Indian women did, making sure there was plenty for whoever might be there. On school nights, she saved him a plate and heated it up when he came in just after 9:00. So he'd brought her some groceries a couple of times. She'd laughed and asked whether that was a hint. He'd said, no, it was the custom.

As soon as he stepped out of the water, he felt cold again. There was only one heat register in the whole damn apartment, and it didn't seem to put out much. He dressed hurriedly.

On his way out he left some dog food for the growing number of strays he'd been feeding. He watched the dogs jostle for position, and he thought about one for Sam— the small terrier, maybe. When he got a little older, if Susan didn't mind. Cleve would have to build a fence for it. He didn't hold with dogs in the house.

But it would be Susan's house. What he did or didn't hold with wouldn't much matter.

Maybe it wasn't a good idea to be going over there early whenever he had the chance. This wasn't like shacking up. This was more like his night job. He tried to think of it that way whenever he got those family feelings. Evenings when he watched TV while she dozed next to him on the sofa. Mornings when she came home from work and he had her breakfast ready. She had given him the combination to her post office box, and he'd been picking up her mail. He slept in her bed.

He lit a cigarette and then he drove around the block a couple of times thinking maybe he'd have himself a couple of beers, shoot some pool, then mosey on over to Susan's. Didn't want her taking him and his newfound dependability for granted. Of course, if he had more than a couple and then forgot to mosey, he'd be living up to her expectations.

And Charlie's. Charlie had persuaded him to go to an AA meeting with him, just for the hell of it. A dozen guys sitting on folding chairs in a little room at the community center, and Charlie acted as though they'd found Oz. He had to admit, Charlie had given a nice talk. Better than nice. It was a gut-squeezer, but Cleve hadn't said anything. He couldn't. He'd gotten a sandy feeling in his throat from listening to Charlie's confidences and remembering Jimmy's. Then he remembered some of his own. Things he'd told his grandpa, and then later, when grandpa was gone, things he needed to tell him. Hadn't told anybody else. After a while the need had gone away.

But he remembered waking up in a pickup and hearing the owl's call. Damn, that was a lonesome sound.

So he took the turn to Susan's because tonight he was hungry for whatever Susan was cooking, and he wanted to see Sam before he went to bed.

It was chicken cooked with pineapple and green peppers. She seemed to enjoy trying new recipes out on him, and he had to admit that even the strange ones tasted better than they sounded. She was feeding Sam real food now, chopped up in the blender, but he didn't get to try the fancy sauces. Just the chicken and rice, along with some carrots. He had a great time getting the carrots in his hair. He sent a cup of milk crashing and splashing on the floor, and they praised him for using his left arm to do it.

"He's a cowboy," Cleve said happily.

Susan cleaned Sam up while Cleve cleared the table and made coffee. Then Cleve held Sam and gave him his bottle while they lingered at the table to sip and talk, as had become their custom.

He brought up the subject that was never far from his mind. "I guess nobody's too interested in the fact that Ray Taggert, alias Ray Smith, was the guy who went into the john with Bertram. At least, nobody seems to be tearing up the territory looking for him."

Susan wondered whether he thought of the trial every time he looked at her. "How do you know?" she asked.

"Nobody got real excited when I told them. I called the sheriff's office up in Mandan today, asked them if they'd heard anything. He told me to watch the papers." He seemed almost amused by the man's insensitivity, which meant it was probably typical. "Like I'm butting into his business or something."

"Be patient, Cleve. You'll drive yourself crazy with this. I'm sure they're looking for him."

"For robbery and attempted murder in Montana."

"For whatever. When they find him, you'll have your chance to tell your story again."

"Bernie says if they catch him in Montana, they'll probably try him there. Then they might try him here if they think they have a case. We already know they screwed up on the investigation. They might not even use what I told them."

"But you told them. That's all you can do."

He chafed a little. "I didn't just pick a poster, you know. That's really him."

"I believe you." She looked at Sam, snuggled in the crook of Cleve's arm, eyes drooping as he nursed on the bottle Cleve held to his mouth. She smiled wistfully, then looked up at Cleve again. "I believed you before you found the poster. I believed you at the trial."

"I didn't know how guilty I looked until I got to court." With a shrug he glanced past her and sighed. "Because I *was* drinking that night. And my head was all messed up. Finding that face again, looking at it stone sober—it was kind of a relief."

"Hang onto that. Even if the law never catches up to him, you've identified him."

"Sometimes I think I ought to look for him myself."

"Where would you look for a drifter, Cleve? It sounds like that's what he is."

"I've been kind of a drifter myself."

"You had a purpose when you were traveling the rodeo circuit." The light from the kitchen spread a satiny sheen through his black hair. "Gypsy, maybe, but not a drifter."

"Nomad. Kinda like the old days, when the people used to move the camp, follow the game." He smiled and gave a sly wink. Curiously, he didn't mind claiming, "I was an Indian before I was a cowboy."

"Well, Ray Smith is a drifter. Besides that, he's a thief and a murderer. You have better things to do than to go out looking for him."

"You got a list?" She looked at him, puzzled. "Of things for me to do?"

"You said you promised those boys you'd help them break horses." She couldn't resist adding, "Which I hope doesn't break anyone's bones."

He was inclined to say something sarcastic, something that would make her back off, but the domesticity of the moment softened him. "You can come out and watch us. When I break a horse, I don't let him buck with me. I gentle him before I get on him. Takes a lot more time, but it's worth it. Those boys don't want to believe me. They want to rush everything." He'd been like that, too, and his grandfather'd had a hell of a time slowing him down, making him take the time to do things right. The threat of broken bones was no deterrent for a young man trying to make his mark.

"I suppose you have to gentle the boys, too, in a way."

"Yeah, it's kinda the same thing. Especially *those* boys." He set the bottle on the table. Sam was asleep. With his forefinger Cleve caught a dribble of milk at the corner of the baby's mouth. "So how about tomorrow afternoon?"

"If it's not too windy. Sam would love it." She smiled at the baby sleeping in the crook of Cleve's arm. "I saw your grandmother today when I took Sam to the clinic for a checkup. She's staying with her sister for a while. Might be a good chance for you to see her."

He smiled. "You sure are the little fixer."

"Just a thought."

"I guess I should tell her about Sam." He lifted one shoulder. "I know what she's going to say."

"What?"

"That she'll take him. Which is impossible, but she'll say that. She won't like the idea of me giving him to you.

"You haven't."

"I've put him in your house, haven't I? I've . . ." He looked down at the child sleeping in his arm and shook his head, reminding himself, "There's no way I can take care of him. No way."

Susan wanted to end his struggle by taking Sam into her own arms and letting Cleve see where the baby belonged. She resisted the urge. Instead, she rose to take their cups to the kitchen.

"I'll finish the dishes," he said. "You look tired. Why don't you go grab a couple hours of sleep?"

"With the clinic appointment, I didn't get much of a nap today." She stood in the kitchen doorway. "You want me to take him?"

"No, he's fine. I'm on duty now."

The hall light cast long shadows across the floor as Cleve opened the door to Susan's room. He moved quietly toward the bed. She was curled up on her side, sleeping as soundly as Sam was across the hall. He wished he didn't have to wake her. She'd been saying she got plenty of rest during the day when Sam napped and in the evenings after supper, but he knew that wasn't true. In the evening she usually hung around the living room with Sam and him. Whether to socialize or supervise, he wasn't sure, but it meant no more than catnapping. Now that she was really sleeping, he hated to wake her.

"Susan." He touched her bare shoulder, smoothed the hair back from her face. She stirred and made a soft, sleepy sound. "Susan, it's time to get up."

"Okay," she murmured. Without opening her eyes, she scooted toward the side of the bed where he sat and curled into a tighter ball near his hip. The covers slipped to her waist, and he saw that she wore bra and panties. Her back was long and lean, and her hair trailed behind her on the crisp white sheets.

He slid off the edge, knelt beside the bed, took her face in his hands and drew her out of sleep with a kiss.

"Can you call in sick?"

She sighed, eyes closed. "I'm not."

"You're going to be. Let me call in for you."

"No. There's no one to take my place. I've gotta get up."

But he hovered over her still. "You aren't the only nurse in the world, Susan. What happens when you get sick? They get along without you, right?"

"I don't get sick." She sat up and put one hand on his chest to push him out of her way. "This is my shift. Wait'll you see how I perk up after a shower."

He grinned, admiring the way her sheer bra molded itself to her. "I'm kind of interested in the way you're perking up right now."

"Hmm. You're imagining things." He laughed and moved aside while she headed for the shower.

"Damn right." He flopped back on the bed and spoke to the ceiling. "You were imagining. Dreaming. Willing. You can't fool me, lady."

Susan came out to the kitchen dressed in her white slacks and tunic. They had a cup of coffee together before she bundled up and they said goodnight, leaving him with an ache that was more than physical. He checked on Sam, then stripped off his clothes, crawled into bed and sought whatever vestige of heat and scent she might have left behind. The love they'd made in that bed weeks ago was such a sweet-hot memory that all he had to do was slide between the sheets and he was almost there.

Yeah, Charlie, he thought, that's part of what makes it feel right. When it stays with you like this, and you want to be with her and nobody else. When you want to be able to make her happy, and you're thinking, how can I? When you want her to be your kid's mother, then you know there's something right about her.

Of course, when you're wrong for her and she knows it, then you've got problems.

It was the first time Susan had ever fallen asleep in the staff room on her break. Darlene Spotted Elk found her dozing in the chair and let her sleep until she was needed to help take vitals. Susan was startled, then embarrassed. She sprang from the chair as though she'd felt an electrical shock. A diabetic amputee who was in with pneumonia needed help turning to his side. A child who'd fallen off a playground slide woke up crying. Otherwise it was an unusually quiet night, and Darlene told Susan not to worry about catching a little nap. But the embarrassment hung on. It wasn't like her to fall asleep like that.

An early winter hush enveloped the row of apartments in the gray light before sunrise. Susan let herself in quietly by the front door. The aquarium light was on, and there was a blanket on the floor along with some pudgy plastic farm animals in a corral made of her own shoes. Smiling, Susan stepped over the play field and turned off the light. She found Sam's bed empty. She pushed her bedroom door open and saw two large bare feet, heels up, extending off the end of her bed.

She tiptoed closer. Cleve's big body nearly filled the bed, but Sam's fluttery little sigh gave him away. They were asleep together, nearly nose to nose, both on their stomachs and each with an arm outstretched toward the other. Cleve's was curved beneath Sam's feet. Even in dim light she could see a resemblance in the shapes of their noses, their ears, their long fingers.

Her maneuvers were backfiring. She had thought it would just be a matter of signing a few papers. The laws had turned out to be more complicated than she could ever have imagined, but everything Cleve did redoubled those complications. He had never been one to play a simple part. He always surprised her. Just a matter of time, and he'd be off the hook, though.

Oh, but the hook was in her, deep. She never thought Cleve would get this close. Not to Sam, not to her. The stupidest thing she could do was to invite him to move in, but she kept finding herself thinking she might as well. That was what she'd decided with Mel. Why rent two apartments?

Mel was a leech, and Cleve was a gypsy cowboy. She sure could pick 'em.

This arrangement would drive her crazy. Always a dependable person, she wanted to be able to plan ahead. To count on something. To have something of her own, and to love and be loved *every* day. Sam would want those things, too.

Or would he want a father? For better or for worse, would he want this Indian, cowboy, vagabond . . . *rich man, poor man, beggar man, thief* . . . this *man* . . . who said, yes, Sam is my son.

She felt the way they tugged on her, both of them like magnets, and she sat down slowly beside them. Who was she to decide that she knew more than Judge Dunn or Grace or Vera or Cleve? A strange woman in a strange land. A woman long on nerve and short on peripheral vision. Why hadn't she learned? She was not the *only* nurse in the world. Not the *only* woman in Mel's life. What made her think she could be the only person Sam needed? And Cleve obviously didn't need anybody.

Just look at them, she thought. Cleve had asked little for proof, and had gone to great lengths for Sam, who was responding better than ever. The bond was self-evident.

But the hook was in *her*, deep. She loved them both.

She started to scoop Sam up, and Cleve stirred, turning to his side.

"No, don't get up." She laid a finger against her lips. "I'll put him in his bed."

Cleve blinked, glancing from Susan to Sam in sleepy confusion, then passed his hand over his face and groaned as he rolled to his back.

Susan picked the baby up without waking him. "He kept you up half the night, didn't he?" she whispered.

"Yeah. We made a ranch."

When she returned, he braced himself on his elbows and watched her take her robe from the closet.

"Go back to sleep, Cleve," she suggested softly. "I've got a few things to do, and then I'll just—"

"I'll clean up the mess we made later." For a moment they looked at one another. "Come here," he said.

She clutched her robe. He was wearing jeans. His hard-muscled chest was bare. He was big and beautiful, awakening slowly. "I'm afraid if I do . . ."

His voice was husky. "Don't be afraid of me now. How can you be afraid of me?"

"I'm not. I'm just—"

"You're tired."

"Not really." She laid her robe over the back of a chair. The tugging was hard to resist. "I fell asleep on my break," she confided.

"Come here, then. I want to hold you and maybe just talk." He smiled softly. "About Sam."

"If we're going to hold each other," she said as she sat on the bed, just out of his reach, "probably we ought to leave Sam out of it."

"Why?"

"Because . . . what's between us is . . ." He moved closer and reached for her. She went to him with a sigh, because it felt as though she were doing the right thing, and she knew she was doing it for all the wrong reasons. The story of her life. She knew only one thing for certain. "We can't let it hurt Sam."

He gathered her to himself, touching her cheek, her forehead, skimming lightly with his fingertips. "Have I hurt you?"

"No." Not unless the deep-seated ache could be considered hurting.

"I won't. I promise."

She'd heard that one before. "I'm not a schoolgirl anymore, Cleve."

"Let's get you comfortable," he said, and he began unbuttoning her white tunic.

"I hurt you once," she said.

"Is that why you're afraid of me?"

"It's just an example. You can't promise, because sometimes without meaning to—"

"You know what hurt me? That one time in the pen, when you didn't show up for a visit. Knocked me for a loop because I didn't know how bad I wanted to see you until that time when you didn't come." He chuckled as he parted her tunic like the leaves of a book. "But then, I *am* a schoolboy. All over again."

As though settling down to study, he propped his head on his left hand and kneaded her tightly wound neck and shoulder muscles with his right. "Does this feel good?"

"Mmmm."

"I could rub your back. Or your breast. Which would you like me to . . ." His hand followed the path of her bra strap, curved around the sheer cup. Her next breath got lodged in her throat. "I'll do your back later," he promised. Then he kissed her, pushed the strap over her shoulder and touched her and swore hotly, "I'll do anything you want, Susan."

"Don't say that. You know you don't mean it."

"I do now. Just say the word. Any way you want it. Any kind of . . ." So many buttons and hooks. He dispatched them impatiently. "I want to be able to see you. All of you."

"I want to see you, too. Where are you?" She ran her hand along his hip, feeling the seam in the denim, the frayed edge of his pocket, the hard bulge. "You're a beautiful no-good cowboy, I'm afraid."

"Stop saying that. I'll be good to you, I swear."

She turned her face away. "Don't, Cleve."

"Don't what?"

"Don't make me any promises. Just—"

"Just put up or shut up?"

"Yes," she said firmly as she looked into his eyes. "Just that."

He brought her along slowly, the way she needed him to, touching and tasting, prolonging every sensation until they were dizzy with it. There was no track nearby, but Cleve heard the sound of a train. She came to him as he eased into her, tunneling his way, making a warm, wonderful connection. She came to him softly at first, across the long, lonely time, through the tall grass, picking up speed, gaining power. He drove harder, and she moaned and shuddered and kept coming to him. She defied his oneness; she shattered his isolation. He fueled her, and she turned his energy into power.

Slick with sweat, arching, straining to meet all needs, he joined her in a soaring climax.

The morning became a lazy haze as they lay in a rumple of sheets and pillows and let their bodies be limp together. Sleep hovered close by, as did pleasure.

"Last time we made love, I had a hard time letting you touch me, and after that I thought, Jesus, what's happened to me? Am I that screwed up?" He reached up, dropped his hand over the top of the headboard for no particular reason, and smiled. "I didn't this time. It was nice."

"Yes, it was." She snuggled against his side. "It is."

"But you were holding out on me this time, weren't you? Just a little?" She looked up at him, questioning, but she knew what he meant. "I'm not moving in on you, Susan. I'm not taking over on you. I'm just taking my shift."

"This isn't part of it."

"No. This is just you and me." He touched the outside corner of her eye, then tenderly traced the dark circle beneath it. "But you're going to have to try to get more sleep when I'm here so you won't be falling asleep on the job."

"Sam's not sleeping during the day as much as he used to."

"He will this morning. Played us both out last night. 'Course, it was my fault. I got up during the night, tripped over my own boots, and woke him up. Then he didn't want to go back to sleep." He shifted closer. "You sure have a lot of shoes."

She remembered the collection on the living room floor and smiled as she imagined him playing with her shoes and Sam. "It's a quest for something wearable. They always seem to fit in the store."

"They make great corrals and stock tanks."

"I'm glad they're good for something. I guess I have weird feet."

"Let me see." He reached down, but she pulled away laughing.

"No!"

"What? I've seen everything else up close." He ran his hand down her leg again. Her second attempt to get away was only halfhearted, and he smiled. "Behave now and let me be the judge."

"They're flat and wide," she pouted as she raised one aloft.

He grabbed it, pulled it down and wiggled one toe at a time, still grinning. "Looks like a sound hoof to me. Lemme check your back teeth."

"Oh, you!"

He placed the sole of her foot against his hip and slid it up and down. God, it was nice to be this close. It felt as though they'd been together like this a long time. "You didn't tell me Sam had started crawling."

"He hasn't—" The news registered. *"Crawling?"*

"Well, scootin' along pretty good."

She braced herself on her elbow. "Scooting? You mean, actually covering ground?"

"Covering carpet, yeah." The expression in his eyes was soft and sheepish. "He kinda came to me."

"He hasn't done that before, not actually—"

He realized then that he'd been favored, and he squeezed her shoulder, easing her back down beside him. "He'll do it for you today."

She glanced away. She had missed a milestone, and she felt left out.

"Do you want me to go so you can get some rest?" he offered.

She looked up at him again. He made no move, and she knew he didn't want to. She didn't want him to. "No. Stay and rest with me. It's Saturday, isn't it?"

"Mmm-hmm. If the weather's good, we're going out to the ranch this afternoon, remember?" She nodded. "And maybe we'll let Grandma in on the news that I'm a father."

"She deserves that."

"Trouble is, Grandma Mary only lives a few streets away from me, and I haven't been to see her." He rolled Susan to her side and curled up behind her, enfolding her in his arms. "Been meaning to, but I've had a lot going on."

"So today you will."

"I guess it's about time. Old ladies can't wait forever." He laid his cheek against her hair. She made him feel so damned bighearted. "But we don't have to explain anything. We'll tell her I have temporary custody and that you're babysitting. Let it go at that."

"Temporary situations sometimes have a way of becoming permanent just because—" She stared at the clock beside the bed. Eight-fifteen. "Because time passes."

"Told you I wasn't moving in on you. I know that's what you're worried about."

"It isn't." She closed her eyes. "What I'm worried about is losing him, and I know it isn't right for me to try to take him away."

"You said you'd stick by him."

"I will, but—"

He tightened his hold on her, cupping his hand around her breast. "Then go to sleep. You don't have anything to worry about right now, okay? Nothing but the weather."

Cleve knocked on the door of the silver trailer on the "town side" of Fort Yates, where there were trailers, ramshackle shacks and manicured tract-style homes coexisting peacefully, side by side. On the "agency side" where Susan lived, streets and residences as well as agency buildings, be they frame or brick, smacked of government issue. Such was the nature of an Indian agency town.

Cleve's apartment was only four blocks away. From his pickup Susan watched him shift from one foot to the other. When the door opened, he dropped his cigarette in the snow, like a boy caught in the act. He was feeling guilty about neglecting his duty to the old women, and

Susan wondered about her role. Was she goad or buffer?

She knew she wasn't supposed to watch. This part was like calling ahead, making sure it was okay to bring a guest. She caught a glimpse of a thinner version of Grace Black Horse and wondered which sister was older, and whether it mattered. Cleve turned and nodded to her, and she flipped the corner of a blanket over Sam's face and slid out of the pickup while Cleve waited for her to join him.

Grace sat in the shadows watching a "Hee Haw" rerun on a flickering black-and-white TV. Mary offered coffee. Cleve asked Grace how she was, but he had to turn the volume down on the TV and ask again before she told him she was doing all right. Susan felt the old woman's eyes on her as she perched on the torn vinyl seat of a kitchen chair and unwrapped Sam.

"You still have that baby today?" Grace said.

"Yes." Susan slid Sam's snowsuit under her chair, next to her large purse. "He had a good checkup yesterday after I saw you. The doctor is amazed at his progress, and today—well, last night and today—he's actually scooting on his own. You know, after the accident—" The two leathery old faces, reminded her of Judge Dunn. Little expression. She didn't know whether she was getting through, so she kept talking. "His mother died in a car accident," she explained to Grandma Mary, "and Sam was really born after—"

Cleve laid a hand on her shoulder. She looked up at him.

"I've found out that this little guy is my son, Grandma."

Grace's eyes widened. "Ehhn' it?" From her chair she squinted at Sam for a moment, then signaled to Cleve to bring him to her. He put the boy on her lap, but he stayed close by. Sam stared at the woman while she looked him over, the matriarch ascertaining this kinship claim.

"I'm too old, Sonny," Grace said finally. "You'll have to watch out for him, unless you want that woman's ghost bothering around."

"I'm going to take care of him, with Susan's help."

"What?" Grace scowled at him and pinched her lips together. She jerked her chin toward Susan, but she spoke to her grandson. "You come to tell me you're marrying this one?"

"No. I—" He revised the claim with a gesture that linked him to Susan. "We came to tell you about Sam. The woman who was his mother never told me she was pregnant, but she told her sister."

"God looks after these special ones. Long time ago we said they were *wakan*. Sacred people."

"Susan's a nurse. She's been taking real good care of him, and he gets special therapy."

"He belongs here." She looked at Susan. "You staying here?"

"Yes."

"Your father was a white man," she reminded Cleve, as if some connection should be obvious to him.

"It didn't matter what he was. He wasn't around."

"Your grandfather raised you."

"He wasn't around that long either," Cleve said quietly.

"He died on his own land. He didn't run off from us." She raised a gnarled finger in his face. "You remember that. You remember who you are and who raised you."

"You both did."

She was quiet for several moments, she and Sam. She lifted his right arm, as if testing. He stuck his finger in her mouth. With a dry cackle, she handed Sam back to his father, but she spoke to Susan. "He's gotten a little fatter. You should feed him good, though. He's still too skinny."

Marvin Blue Mountain had his little gray mustang eating out of his hand. Marvin was the only one who wasn't anxious to ride. He just wanted a pet. He offered the horse a handful of cracked corn and flashed Cleve a gap-toothed grin. "It tickles," Marvin announced across the corral as the horse's lips scattered half the corn to the ground.

"Pretty soon he's gonna follow you to school," Cleve said. He stood outside the five-foot rail and woven wire fence, flanked by Susan and Charlie. Susan was trying to get a fussy Sam to "watch the horsey."

"Mine won't do that." Charlie's complaint became a white puff in the cold air. "I still can't get close to him with a halter."

"Did you sack him out?" Cleve had taught the boys to wave a gunny sack and toss it around the horse to "take the spook out of 'em."

"Lots of times."

"How long? How many times?"

Charlie shrugged. "Three or four. I got chores, y'know."

"Well, it'll take a while." Cleve propped his elbow on the top rail and watched Marvin lead the gray in a circle. "Does Marvin have chores?"

"He gets up at five in the morning to mess around out here."

"Is he getting his chores done?"

"I 'spose," Charlie admitted. Cleve knew he'd made his point, and he didn't belabor it. Charlie changed the subject. "Are you gonna ride at the Civic Center next week? Did you get your PRCA card renewed like you said?"

Without glancing her way Cleve could feel Susan listening for his answer. He knew she wanted him to give it up, which was why he hadn't told her anything about the card. "Yeah, I paid the dues. I can enter if I want."

Charlie's eyes lit up, as though his battery had just been charged. "Why don't you let me buck one of these broomtails out, Cleve? Just one."

"We want to make saddle horses out of them if we can. We don't want 'em to buck."

"The black one's gonna be mine, isn't it? Maybe I don't want a saddle horse."

"Then maybe you shoulda told me that in the first place. I'm not gonna let you ruin a good horse." He laid a gloved hand on Charlie's shoulder. "You sticking with the program, or not?"

"Yeah, I'm sticking." Charlie shoved his hands in his jacket pockets and turned a red ear toward Cleve. Marvin was turning the gray out, and Susan was getting into the pickup with Sam. Charlie knew he didn't have much time. "They might let you check me out and take me to the rodeo."

"We'll see."

Susan's challenge was coming. It was only a ten-mile drive back to town, but he knew she couldn't keep it until they got home. He could feel her bristling with it. Sam was waving his arms and singing, banging on the front of his car seat, so she turned the radio off to let Cleve know she wanted his attention just as they reached the end of the ranch's rutted access road.

She didn't beat around the bush. "Why didn't you tell me you renewed your PRCA card?"

He had to smile a little as he turned onto the blacktop. He was getting to know this woman pretty well. "You didn't ask. I didn't think it was any real news, anyway."

"Why now?"

"There's a sanctioned rodeo in Bismarck. It's as good a time as any." He gripped the steering wheel and watched the ice-ribboned road ahead, thinking he didn't have to explain anything to her. But he did, anyway. "The National Finals comes up in December, and obviously I won't be going to that. The season doesn't really heat up until early spring."

"You'd give up school?"

"That was just something to keep me busy," he claimed. But then he admitted, "At least, it started out that way. I'm doing pretty good."

"What if we lose Sam?" As if he understood the question, Sam switched from singing to a magpie chatter that drew Cleve's amused glance. Susan wasn't distracted. "What if they won't let me keep him while you're gone?"

"I'm not gonna stay away like I used to. I'll be back—" He looked at her briefly. "Real often."

"It won't work, Cleve."

"I think it'll work."

"What if you get hurt? What if you're laid up for months in a hospital in Texas somewhere?"

"Would that be an inconvenience for you?"

"No, it would be—" She turned away and stared out her side window, speaking to the brown hills. "It would be your own damn fault because you know you've put your body through enough of this foolishness, and it's time to quit."

"It's time to quit when *I* say it's time to quit."

No one spoke as he slowed the pickup, shifted gears and turned onto the causeway. They passed the college and the tract housing where Vera lived. The sun glinted on the frozen backwater. An old man was gathering a load of driftwood. They passed him, too.

Finally, before they reached Susan's apartment, Cleve asked quietly, "You wanna watch me ride in Bismarck?"

"Take Charlie."

He nodded solemnly. "Maybe I'll take all those boys. If the supervisor'll let me. They don't get to do enough."

There was little discussion of rodeo during the week. He was going. She was not. Susan thought about him a lot that next Saturday. She told herself this rodeo thing was in his blood. He rode because he had to ride. Even if he knew it was time to quit, he couldn't do it. And it was his problem, not hers. She'd already made arrangements to take Sam to Vera's that night before she went to work.

It surprised her when she heard the pickup outside. It also made her heart pound and sent her scurrying to the window. The headlights went off. The door slammed shut. Even in the dark, she could make out the outline of a cowboy hat. A cigarette glowed in the dark before it was dropped and extinguished beneath a boot. She opened the door before he knocked and regretted giving herself away when she heard his chuckle. But at least he was home.

"I—I thought I heard someone."

"Just the night shift." He tossed his hat on the blue chair and grinned at her as though he had good news.

He must have won, she thought.

"Surprised to see me?" he asked.

"Truthfully, a little."

"Why?" He grinned, unruffled. "Did you think I'd go on a party afterward?"

"No," she lied. "I just thought—".

"Bad news is, I didn't get my entry fee to the rodeo secretary on time." He draped his arm over her shoulders and thrilled her with a cocky smile. "Good news is, I'm not hurtin' anywhere."

"Were you late? I can't imagine you dragging your feet like that. You stayed for the rodeo anyway?"

Her rapid-fire questions made him laugh. He felt as though a ton of cement had been lifted from his shoulders, and anything would have made him laugh. "I had four boys with me. The ranch let me take their old Suburban so I could fit 'em all in."

"I'll bet they were disappointed that you weren't riding."

"Kind of. But they got to meet some cowboys, and we ate hot dogs and popcorn. I think they were glad to have me with them."

As was she. She smiled and slipped her arms around him, under his jacket. He kissed her. A man-coming-home-to-his-woman kiss, even though neither acknowledged it as such. He asked about Sam, who was reported sleeping, and she offered coffee, which he accepted gratefully. They sat together on the sofa, enjoying the peace between them. The fish swimming back and forth in the aquarium were all the entertainment they needed.

"I thought I saw Ray Smith again," Cleve told her. "It was just some redneck watching the rodeo. I keep thinking I'm gonna run into him. I keep seeing people who look like him. But they really don't look like him. I just think they do, at a glance, you know? Then when I get close . . ."

She covered his hand with hers. "Don't let it drive you crazy, Cleve. It's up to the police to find that man."

"What if they don't?"

"Have people been asking you about the murder lately?"

He thought about it. "I know they want to."

"You have to let it go. Your true freedom depends on that. People forget. They might have wondered, and some might still be wondering, but with time, they forget. Not every criminal gets caught."

"I know." He dropped his head back against the cushion and stared at the ceiling. "There's no way to put it right, is there? What's done is done."

"Yes."

"You told Grandma you were gonna stay here." Turning his head to one side, he looked at her, and she nodded. She would stay. By choice, not because this place was her last resort. What was it for him, now that he could leave again whenever he wanted? He'd made one choice that day, but there were others.

"You know that once I get permanent custody of Sam . . ." He sat up slowly, fumbling for words because he wasn't sure what kind of an offer he could make. "Well, you can't adopt him through this court. We'll have to—"

Get the hell off the rez. That's what I'm gonna do. Be a PRCA champion. Live like the king of the cowboys instead of some dirt-poor Tonto.

Cleve shook his head. The process of growing up was taking him one hell of a long time. "I guess we'll probably have to go somewhere else," he said.

She knew that wasn't what he wanted. "Things have changed, haven't they?"

"What do you mean?" he asked.

"You can't just give him away—" She remembered Grace's words. "Like a puppy."

"You had him first. I can't take care of him the way you can. Even if I don't go back on the circuit—" He saw the *if?* in her eyes. "I'm thinking maybe I should stick it out in school for a while. Maybe I could go in for something that won't make my teeth rattle so bad."

Oh, that sounded so promising. "You're good with the boys at the Youth Ranch. You're a good—" She caught herself. "You're good with Sam."

"Can't you say I'm a good father? Can't you—"

"You're a good father, Cleve." *And I'm nobody's savior.*

He smiled gently. "You're a good mother. I want to be able to see him, Susan. I want you to promise me that much."

"I can't take him." She pressed her fingers to her lips. What was she saying? But she closed her eyes and gave her head a quick shake. "I have no right. I'm going to take care of him, but I'm not going to try to bend the rules. I've said all along I'd stay if they'd let me have . . ." Her throat ached, and she didn't want to cry. She took two deep breaths. "You'll need a sitter, and I'm counting on getting the job."

He was astounded. "Without any legal claim to him?"

"He should have your name. He should have his great-grandmother and his cousins and his aunties. I can't improve on that." Smiling bravely, she laid her hand on his denim-clad thigh. "He should have you. I believe he'll come to know who he is and who raised him. He's been a miracle baby all along, and he's not going to stop here."

"What if *I* want to move away from here?" That thought scared her, he could tell. But he pressed with it. "Like, what if I finish school and find a job or something, and we leave? You gonna stick by him then?" He put his hand atop hers and closed it slowly, telling himself he was going to hold on tight because this was a hell of a woman. "Or will you stick by me? We're not just screwing around, Susan. You're not like that."

She was quiet for a moment. Then softly, "Are you?"

"I used to be. Like you said, things have changed. I said I'd never come back to the reservation, but here I am. I spent two years thinking it might be all over for me, but here I am. Starting over. Looking at things a little differently. Looking at you . . ."

"Differently?" Her eyes widened hopefully.

"Different from the way I looked at you two years ago." She glanced aside. "No, it's okay," he assured her. Then he chuckled. "It's not the best way to meet a woman, but it sure leaves an impression on you."

"You left an impression on me. I'm sure you've known that all along."

He could feel the trembling in her hand. "I also knew you were trying hard to shake it off. The way you felt about me. You didn't want to get mixed up with me, but you had no choice."

"There's always a choice," she said quietly.

"You chose Sam, I know. What about me?"

Her throat, her mind, her heart were full to the brim, and it was all about him. She could hardly take a breath for fear of spilling over everything she felt and scaring him away.

He reached for her, took her shoulders in his hands and looked deeply, through her eyes, into her soul.

"I want to be with you. Every day when I'm out there hauling bales or fixing fence—something else I swore I'd never go back to—I think about how warm it is here, you and Sam making it feel that way. I go back to my place and try to come up with a good excuse to come early."

"You don't need an excuse," she said softly.

"Yes, I do. No more live-in boyfriends. That's what you said. I don't want to be a live-in boyfriend. I want to do what's best for Sam, and I want what's best for me. And that's you." His smile was tentative. " 'Course I can't tell you that I'm what's best for you."

"You could try telling me how you feel about me."

"I've never been in love before."

She closed her eyes as she leaned toward him, and he took her in his arms and rejoiced. "Sweet Jesus, I think I am now. I wish I had half, even a tenth of the money I've played in over the years. Then I could promise you a nice house, and—"

Now the tears came. Warm, happy tears.

"Oh, Cleve, I love you, and I love Sam, and I just want you to promise me more children."

"What?"

"I want more children."

"Mine?"

"Yours and mine."

He laughed and hugged her close. "You have any problem with live-in husbands?"

"I've never had one." She looked up at him and smiled through her tears. "Sweet Jesus, I think I do now."

They held each other for a long, golden, sweet time, and then, without a word between them, they went to Sam's room and stood together in the doorway, Cleve's arm around Susan's shoulders, hers around his waist, and they listened to Sam's soft, shallow, sleeping breaths, every one a miracle.

And when Sam's father leaned down to kiss his mother and his mother lifted her hand to touch his father's face, it no longer mattered that the three of them had come together for all the wrong reasons.